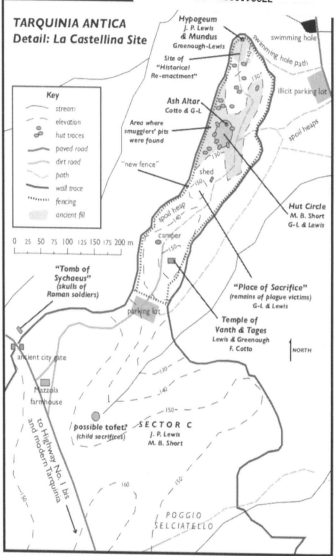

TARQUINIA ANTICA
Detail: La Castellina Site

Hypogeum
J. P. Lewis
& Mundus
Greenough-Lewis

swimming hole

Site of
"Historical
Re-enactment"

swimming hole path

illicit parking lot

Ash Altar
Cotto & G-L

spoil heaps

Area where
smugglers' pits
were found

"new fence"

shed

Hut Circle
M. B. Short
G-L & Lewis

spoil heap

camper

Key

	stream
	elevation
	hut traces
	paved road
	dirt road
	path
	wall trace
	fencing
	ancient fill

0 25 50 75 100 125 150 175 200 m

"Tomb of
Sychaeus"
(skulls of
Roman soldiers)

"Place of Sacrifice"
(remains of plague victims)
G-L & Lewis

parking lot

Temple of
Vanth & Tages
Lewis & Greenough
F. Cotto

NORTH

ancient city gate

Mazzola
farmhouse

to Highway No. 1 bis
and modern Tarquinia

possible tofet?
(child sacrifices)

SECTOR C
J. P. Lewis
M. B. Short

130

140

150

160

150

POGGIO
SELCIATELLO

THE CASTELLINA CURSE

BOOK I IN THE FINDS & KEEPERS ARCHAEOLOGICAL
ADVENTURE SERIES

CATE DELUCA

G Publishing Partners, LLC

BLURB: THE CASTELLINA CURSE

BOOK I IN THE FINDS & KEEPERS ARCHAEOLOGICAL ADVENTURE SERIES

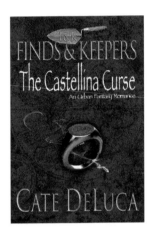

Meet Tanaquil Greenough, archaeology grad student with a sixth sense for danger.

Plucky archaeology grad student Tanaquil Greenough has a secret weapon she often uses to sniff out hidden features and finds, an instinct she calls her "Tanny sense." But her other super-power is less useful, and more likely to keep her from finishing her doctorate at all: her good looks and sweet nature, which have attracted the attention of not only the gorgeous and unscrupulous photographer Marc Short, but also Tanny's married academic advisor, James Pericles Lewis, himself under constant threat of seduction by adoring students of both sexes.

How will she work closely with Dr. Lewis without getting them both into hot water, or worse, into danger with ruthless antiquities smugglers, particularly once they open a pair of mysterious underground chambers, full of offerings of gold and blood, and release a pair of demons into the upper air of Italy? And what about Tanny's extremely unusual godfather, a shape-shifting warlock living in Florence who claims to be her great-grandfather and has a yen to be her partner for life?

Should he be trusted to help when the demons threaten to bring sickness and madness upon everyone at the site? It's a conundrum indeed, but nothing Tanny can't handle!

ALSO BY CATE DELUCA

The Castellina Curse

Deep Scansion

Place of Sacrifice

for Robin

CONTENTS

SNEAK PEEK: DEEP SCANSION

AN UNEXPECTED PHONE CALL

Call it my "Tanny-sense."

Mor says I've had it all my life. All afternoon I'd had a prickling sense of *something wrong* that I was pretty sure wasn't the New Jersey summer heat.

It was the second-to-last Sunday in August and Princeton's Opening Exercises were exactly a week away. My boss and academic advisor Dr. James Pericles Lewis was supposed to be on a flight from Rome arriving in Newark tonight.

Had it crashed? His kids were supposed to be at the Jersey shore. *Had they drowned?*

When my silenced phone started to dance on the surface of my desk, I jumped a mile. At an angry glare from my office-mate, I took my phone out into the hall, my heart racing.

The screen read "Dr. Lewis." It didn't take second sight to know something was wrong: he never bought in-flight phone service.

So where in the world was *he?*

Heading down the stairs and into the open air, I answered, "Dr. Lewis! Where are you?"

"Just leaving the site, Ms. G. Almost to Tarquinia. I know, I should be on the plane..."

"Are you hurt? Is anybody hurt?"

"I'm fine; we're all fine, but . . ."

There was a humming sound in the background, like a car changing gears.

"Listen," he said firmly, "I have to stay. I'll send an email with all the details of the plan once I'm back at my room in the Museum. Dr. Potts said it's all right."

"What's all right?" Dr. Potts was Department Head.

"For you to cover my classes this fall."

Oh, that was "something wrong" all right!

"All *four*?" I got into what *Mor* calls my "high voice." "But I've only ever done *one!*"

"It's only two isn't it? And you did great last time. Better evaluations than mine."

"Four. You moved two classes from last spring to this fall, remember, so you could spend all spring at the..."

"Four, that's right," he muttered. "Tanny, it's a huge ask. You'll have to dig out my notes for the other two classes – more on that later—but I've *got* to stay. Remember that flat patch you thought could be the entrance to the *hypogeum*?" He took a deep breath.

"It was."

He had my full attention. "You uncovered it?" I sat, plopping myself down on a bench in the shade.

"Late this afternoon: absolutely the last thing."

Today should have been devoted to clean-up and storage, but all the best archaeological discoveries seemed to happen on the last day at the dig. It is practically a rule.

"You inserted the camera?" I prompted eagerly. "And?"

His voice broke. "Unbelievable. It is unrobbed, completely unrobbed: the François Tomb all over again!"

"So, it's a tomb?" I gasped, leaping up and circling the bench. "Not an offering pit?"

"Yes to both. There's a human sacrifice covered with..."

"Male or female?"

"A girl in full Etruscan kit: boots, hat and everything. Throat cut, poor thing, and looks like her blood sloshed everywhere. Body perfectly preserved, covered with gold jewelry and flanked by Attic vases—the most beautiful vases you can imagine—full of *something*."

"Jim!" I used the boss' first name only in emergencies. "Who knows about the gold?"

"Only Angelo and I," he answered soberly. "Everyone else went home."

Dr. Angelo Cotto, distinguished professor of archaeology in the Department of Historical, Archaeological, and Anthropological Sciences of Antiquity of the University of Rome "La Sapienza," had been lead archaeologist at the ancient city site of Tarquinia—aka *Pian de Cività*—for thirty-odd years.

Universally loved at the site, he went by the nickname of *il babbo* ("Daddy").

"Where are you now? Can anyone hear you?"

"Nope. Angelo's driving me back to the Museum from their beach place in Lido di Tarquinia. Had to use the Museum scanner for my class notes. I'd written them all out by hand—for two classes anyway—all ready to send you. Promise me you'll teach?"

"Promise you'll make Angelo put a guard on the site?"

There was a pause and some rustling.

"*Ciao*, Tanaquil," Angelo's voice. "You wanted me?"

"*Ciao, Babbo!*" I replied, going on in Italian. "Make *il Prof* put a guard on the *hypogeum*, or thieves will cut his throat for that gold. Yours, too!"

"We are quite safe, *cara*," he assured me breezily.

I saw red.

"After that murder at the site in Val di Chiana where all the gold was taken? I mean it, *Babbo!* Tell *Il Prof:* you get security or Tanny doesn't teach!"

"You're right," he admitted. "In the morning I will call Tarquinia police."

Another rustle.

"How about," came the boss' voice slowly in a tone that made my heart leap, "after you do my classes this fall, you work at the site all next spring? Finish digging the Temple of Vanth and Tages 1 and add a chapter to your dissertation. We'll ask for an extension."

"A chapter . . . ?" I gasped. The working title of my doctoral dissertation was *Parsing the Iconography of the Vanth*, but I didn't mind adding a deity. "If you can get the Temple away from Franco I'll write a whole blessed new dissertation. But, won't he murder you? Or me?"

There was a murmur of talk; boss must have been on speaker-phone.

"His son has other fish to fry at the Museum, Angelo says. And there's always that tomb down by Mazzola's farmhouse."

Hadn't I always wanted full control of that temple? But, FOUR classes?

"The students will feel cheated!" I insisted. "This find will make you the most famous archaeologist since Howard Carter!"

"Moonshine," he chuckled, clearly tickled by the prospect. "Besides, no student has ever dozed off in *your* lectures, Ms. Greenough, whereas I have to post beadles to wake them up."

I had to laugh, but sobered fast. "And if I'm busy 24/7 what about the Riverbankers?"

As their chief babysitter I called his two children by the nickname—familiar to readers of *The Wind in the Willows* as what the Water-Rat called his fellow denizens of the River— that they earned one rainy night three years earlier during a semester in England.

They'd run away from the Lewis' apartment in the middle of Oxford to the house of retired archaeologist Fred Cole on the wooded outskirts of town.

Cloelia Agnes, then seven years old, and Larry Horatio, only three, had reminded Fred of the Mole and the Rat, escaping the terrors of the Wild Wood.

I should explain that both parents were spending a sabbatical year in Oxford at the time, taking turns working from home. Lavinia Bradley-Arnold, Dr. Lewis' wife and world-renowned expert on the Etruscan language *Rasenna,* had been on child-duty that day. She'd become so deeply involved in a verb sequence she ran out to check "for a moment" at the Bodleian Library, however, that she'd completely forgot the existence of her two children. Cold, hungry, and frightened, they'd set out for Saint Catherine College, where their father had his Thursday night seminar, but lost their way in the dark.

That disastrous sabbatical was part of why I ended up babysitting Moley and Ratty three nights a week. Their father, aka "The Badger," made their breakfasts and got them off to school, but had weekly choir practice and an evening seminar. Before Oxford, Lavinia had handled the children's bed-time, but never came home from her sabbatical year.

She eloped to Florence with her lover Caterina instead, to find true love and concentrate on finishing her huge Etruscan dictionary, *Lexicon Rasennese.* Since both parents had collaborated on making dinners, I—"the River"—also fed the three remaining Lewises for five weeknights by making extra-big babysitting-night dinners.

All the same, he and Lavinia were still formally married, and there were rumors of an air-tight pre-nuptial agreement. It was tricky working so closely with a still-married man so universally acknowledged to look like a nerdier version of another James, last name Garoppalo. True, the boss gets obstreperous after drinking even the tiniest amount of alcohol but he seldom drinks, his manners are pleasing, his laugh infectious, and his smile devastating. My high-school buddy John-Allen has been quoted as saying Dr.

Lewis could be "Mr. January" in the Hot Archaeologists Calendar.

As for me, I've been told by the same source I could be Ms. February, but he may be biased in my favor. True, I have been chased by amateur photographers wondering "how I got those eyes" and a clothing company once contacted me about modeling my favorite brand of site-jeans for their catalogue. Being Afro-Norwegian-American accounts for my looks and coloration. My cheekbones may be *Mor*'s, my nose Daddy Bill's, and my lips Grammy Jane's, but the combo of copper skin, loosely-curly bronze-toned hair, and pale-gold eyes is pure Tanny.

True, I sometimes dye my hair different colors or streak it with blonde. I also have a small tattoo in Greek along the inside of my left arm, though the boss says tattoos are barbarian. It can be transliterated as *Gnothi Sauton* and means "know thyself."

Ironic, because I didn't yet know the origin of my second sight. *Mor* said it was inherited from her *Sami* great-grandfather. Dad used to hint that there was something strange about Great-Grandma Susie. Who knew?

The boss was still talking.

"I've asked Alice and Delbert to keep them weekends, but please stay at our house all the time, if it saves you on rent. The kids will love to have you there."

Even without second sight, I could see pretty clearly how exhausted I would be by semester's end. True, I would know the material I taught inside and out, not a bad thing for someone needing to pass her prelims next summer. Getting rights to publish the Temple, most of which I had dug with my own hands, made the proposal sorely tempting.

I needed to consult with the father of Franco Cotto, current "owner" of the Temple.

"*Babbo*, can you hear me?" I said loudly, hoping we were still on speaker-phone.

"*Si, cara!*"

"You are certain, Angelo? About Franco giving up the Temple?"

His voice came loud and clear over the engine noise. "Franco must, *Tanina,* if it means keeping *Giacomo* here. *Il Prof* may be boring in lecture, but his excavation skills are 'tip-top.'"

So, I said "yes," *et ruat caelum* – "let the heavens fall."

1 See "Maps & Plans" for details of excavation areas in ancient Tarquinia.

2

NO GOOD DEED GOES UNPUNISHED

THE *CAELUM RUAT*-ED ABOUT THREE MONTHS LATER. IT WAS late one raw November afternoon, the Tuesday before Thanksgiving, and I was hurrying back to the Lewis house on Hawthorne Avenue. I had given two mid-terms that morning, and had been up late writing and printing them the night before. It takes a long time to construct a good exam, and they were very, very good.

Maybe too good! My T.A. and I had caught a student ogling the work of someone in the seat beside him. I had just left a meeting with the culprit in the presence of Dr. Potts.

Why anyone should cheat on an *Ancient Art History Survey* exam was the bitter question I was asking myself. *The whole discipline of ancient studies was just ridiculous, wasn't it?* I mean, I knew that *Environmental Stresses in Antiquity* was vital to modern understanding, but who else cared? As for *Ancient Drainage Systems,* I almost put myself to sleep teaching it!

It turns out that talking archaeology twelve hours a day— like saying the same word over and over—made it just seem like nonsense. And losing sleep over "nonsense" when all my friends seemed to be hoisting a beer without me was a hard thing, especially when I suspected that certain people in Italy were not keeping up their end of the bargain.

From what I heard through the grapevine, my former friend Franco Cotto was accepting his loss of the Temple of Vanth and Tages with a very bad grace, publicly ridiculing my inability to locate the temple's lost cult statues, for starters.

"And Lewis calls her a genius," he fumed to *Panorama*. "But he only keeps her around for her looks and her *spaghetti carbonara*."

He keeps her around. He keeps her around.

"Because he trusts me," I shouted into the wind, the only other presence in the street.

Sleet was predicted for Wednesday, but the wind whipping my cheeks already seemed to have picked up some precipitation. Everything hurt: my face, my joints, my heart. It figured. A student had come to office hours a few days back with what sounded horribly like the flu.

Now I had it, thanks.

One good thing: I'd made it through the interview with Dr. Potts and the student without being sick. But he dismissed the case as having too little evidence, though a comparison of answers clearly showed a one-for-one correspondence between the two sets of nearly-perfect answers, and though the cheater had been barely bumping along with a "D" before now.

Dr. Lewis would have believed me, I told myself as I toiled up the front steps of the big house, let myself in, and staggered down the hall to the bathroom to be sick.

Elementary school had been out since last Friday, so last Saturday Delbert and Alice Bradley-Arnold, Lavinia's Princeton-dwelling parents, had put the Riverbankers on the plane to see their Lewis grandparents in Tucson before getting onto their own flight to Miami.

I had the whole cavernous place to myself until Sunday afternoon. *Oh, joy!*

What does it matter if he trusts me, I mused, spitting miserably into the sink, *if he takes one of the zillion new job-offers, and I have to finish out with a new adviser and a new site?*

I'd been right about the boss' fame after that post of him opening the *hypogeum*. We'd watched it live ourselves in *Practical Archaeology* class—everyone's assignment being to write up pros and cons of the methods used—and now the whole world had seen it.

From the first gust of air exploding the dead girl's perfect little face into a cloud of ash and bone, to the last sickening crunch as the heavy golden pectoral ornament crushed her delicate sternum, it was an addictive loop shared an unthinkable number of times. But it was the part in the middle that put the name James Pericles Lewis on everyone's lips, making him the super-hero of archaeology.

It was seeing the boss catch a Berlin Painter lidded amphora full of ancient honey in his arms while holding back a whole rack of other vases with his knee that did it. Before then, he had been known by a small circle of experts for fine archaeological method.

I watched one particular interview with a CNN Science correspondent that filled me with deeply-nerdy joy.

"Tell me, Dr. Lewis," the woman had asked him, shortly after the clip went viral, "has there ever been such a sight, in the whole history of archaeology?"

"Actually, yes," he'd responded gleefully, his dark-lashed blue eyes sparkling behind their thick lenses. "In 1857, when Alessandro François and Adolphe Noël des Vergers excavated the famous François Tomb near Vulci—the François Vase at the Florence Archaeological Museum is practically the reason I became a classicist—they found everything perfectly preserved. Des Vergers describes the opening very poetically. Let me see . . ."

Staring into space he produced the reference in English, *"For some minutes, shapes, garments, cloth, and color were all very clearly distinguished: then, as the outside air came into the underground chamber where our flickering torches were almost blown out, everything disappeared.* Yes, it was very much like that in our case, too."

Yesterday, he'd been offered the Directorship of Etruscan Studies at Ca' Foscari in Venice and seemed hours away from accepting. A glorious coup for him but if he accepted his UNESCO-funded Tarquinia work would leave Princeton with him and he must hire Venetian staff, leaving all of us who had worked with him at *La Castellina* for decades out in the cold.

Speaking of cold, the house was like an ice-box. I would need to check the furnace. Down I went into the dank, dark basement, whimpering with misery.

"True, I did have a free Thanksgiving dinner lined up for me care of the boss, at the hottest new eatery in town with a "guest of my choice." I imagine he thought I would choose his gorgeous doctoral student Marc Short, rumored to be back in the States, but Marc and I were through.

How could I dine at all when I could barely sit upright, let alone keep anything down?

Staggering down to the basement, I lit the pilot light. The sound and smell of heat coming on was a comfort. While waiting for my drafty little bedroom to warm up I made some bouillon-cube chicken broth then, warmed through at last, I crawled into bed.

Mine had been the maid's room long ago, so one of the two landline phones sat on its bedside table. This now rang.

"Hey, Tanny-Sue," came the voice of my aforementioned buddy John-Allen Prester, aka Prester John, aka Father Allen, Assistant Vicar at All Saints Church in Rome.

"Prester John?" I whispered in disbelief.

"Are you there?" he asked a little anxiously. "Listen! You

know I've been corresponding with your dreamy professor friend?"

"Oh? He did ask me to recommend an expert in family law, and I mentioned you."

It felt good just to hear that familiar tenor voice. With his fair hair, dark brows, and sweet nature I'd had a crush on him when we were Koko and Katisha together at St. John's. He loved an acrobat named Gesualdo Verbicaro, but I was still as fond as anything of him.

"Well, turns out your Dr. Lewis had some business at *La Sapienza* a month or so ago, and dropped by here for church. Pretty broad-minded, for a Methodist. Anyhow, Waldo and I gave him lunch and he told us you were the best thing since sliced bread!"

"Very decent of him," I murmured, "considering."

"'Considering' what?"

I told him about Ca' Foscari.

"He didn't say anything about that to us, but he won't take it," he said emphatically, "not if it means betraying his friends."

"You think?" I answered, hope dawning.

"I do. Anyhow, I wanted to get his contact information in Tarquinia, so I just called your department secretary to get it. She told me you were sick, so I thought I'd give you call."

"Aww, Johnny, that's sweet of you! Well, I wish you were here, so you could use this dinner voucher the boss gave me. I can't even get out of bed, let alone eat anything!"

"Sounds like the least he could do, after all you've done for him. So, Tanny-Sue, why *do* you do all this for an old married guy, if you don't mind my asking?"

"He's not old," I snapped. I'm no fun when I'm miserable.

"Sorry! For this *not-old* married guy?"

"Well, he promised me the Temple of Vanth and Tages, for one thing..."

"And for another?"

"The kids would be up a creek if I didn't."

"And?"

"I'm his doctoral student!" I exploded. "He says 'jump' and I say 'how high!'"

"You're not in love with him?"

"Why," I flashed back, "did he say I was?"

"No, he said he had asked too much of you and that it was a bad habit of his. Let me get this straight. You kill yourself for him simply because you're a conscientious student?"

I paused, admitting, "I do love his children. They need a steady presence."

"And they love you back, from what I hear." He paused. "Everyone loves you, Tanny-Sue. Haven't you noticed? You have the Shaggy Man's Love Magnet!"

"So you say, Johnny," I laughed wearily, wanting very much to be alone. "Well, thanks for cheering me up!"

"My pleasure! Looking forward to having you over next semester. *Bacio-bacio!*"

"Same to you, ol' pal!"

"Listen, Tanny, about Dr. Lewis..."

"Oh, Johnny," I moaned, "don't ask me any more about Dr. Lewis!"

And I hung up.

What had he been driving at?

I stared at the ceiling of my little room.

Why did my heart ache so badly when he asked me how I felt about the boss? Why had I cut off my best friend in the world?

Repentant. I sent him a text: *Sorry to bite your head off, P.J.*

He answered at once: *Sorry I touched a sore spot. Call anytime!*

I stared at the phone, asking myself, *Did I kill myself for him because I loved him?*

My "tricky" cooking and babysitting job involved his driving me home from Hawthorne Avenue to my apartment on Witherspoon Street three nights a week if the weather was too harsh for me to ride my bike.

In the car there were strict "no touching" rules. At work or at home, he was likewise careful to call me "Ms. G." not "Tanny.

He was "Dr. Lewis" and never "Jim."

Advisors and grad students must take great care, working together so closely.

All the same, on the next night—Thanksgiving Eve, if you will—I got another call.

"*Ciao,* Greenough."

"Dr. Lewis?" I whispered, startled. "What time is it there?

"Middle of the night. A little bird told me you were sick so I thought I'd check in."

I frowned. "Little bird? What *little bird?*"

"Your friend Father Allen called me from Rome this morning. Told me the dinner voucher wasn't going to help at all," he went on in a rush, "so I pulled a few strings and parlayed it into food deliveries for the whole weekend, starting tomorrow. No turkey, I'm afraid. Italian and Vietnamese okay? Can you get it if they leave it on the front porch?"

"Sure," I answered faintly. "Be good exercise."

"He said, Father Allen said you were feeling pretty low." There was a long pause. I could imagine his mouth, right up against my ear. Made me shiver. "Are you still there?"

"Yeah, I'm here. Oh, I'm all right," I said, trying not to cry, "just got sick and had an argument with Potts about a cheating incident. Nothing a little hot *pho* won't fix, or a plate of *carbonara!*"

"Wish I could. I wish you were—I'm just so grateful, Tanny," he burst out. "If . . . if I were having Thanksgiving at home, I would say *I am thankful for Tanaquil Greenough.*"

"Thanks, boss," I said softly. "That means a lot."

"Well, I have to go," he said in a low voice. "Feel better soon, okay?"

"I will. Happy Thanksgiving."

"Yeah. Same to you," he whispered, and hung up.

By the time Prester John checked back in on me on Thanksgiving night, I had absorbed enough life-giving soup and slept enough to be almost human. When I told him that the boss had called and fixed everything up, he laughed at me.

"I know. I talked to him again and was he ever angry at himself! Are you sure that man has never tried any funny business, Tanny-Sue? He is super-fond of you."

"No way, José. It has always been strictly business between us. Except . . ." Then I stopped. I had remembered the *drachma.*

"Except . . . ?" he echoed. I could hear him smiling.

"There was a little clinch once," I admitted, "after he gave me a silver Attic *drachma* in thanks for my work on the Finds catalogue. He does get emotional sometimes."

"Hmm. Emotional about finds? And finds are what, now?"

"Finds are little bits of evidence of what happened at a site," I replied, "drawn, mapped and catalogued. Then the whole sequence is written up and the finds accounted for. If we don't do that, we're just treasure-hunters, not scientists."

"You don't get to *keep* any of the finds?" he asked. "You know, *finders, keepers?*"

"Not anymore. Not like the Elgin Marbles," I answered warmly. "The real *keepers* are the local experts who make sure the finds are conserved, displayed, and protected from theft."

"I heard your Dr. Lewis say something like that just yesterday on the news," remarked my friend slowly. Then he quoted, "*We are Keepers of the past, so that the future will know its roots.* Just before he said he'd turned down that offer from Venice."

That brought me upright in bed, headache and all.

"He turned down Ca' Foscari?" I squawked, clutching my suddenly-splitting head.

"Says he just likes living in the sticks, but I've got my own ideas. Tell you what," he added naughtily, "if he were free, *I'd* marry him."

"You go ahead," I countered angrily. "To be an academic, I have to publish, publish, publish, and teach, teach, teach. That will take all the time I have and all my energy. Marriage takes time and attention, *Mor* says, even without kids, and *with* kids, it would be murder."

"All marriage takes is the right partner," was the tart reply.

3

THE VIEW FROM TWIN RIVERS

I HAD MET J. P. LEWIS TEN YEARS EARLIER, WHEN I WAS A senior undergraduate fellow at the Rome Center for Ancient Studies and he was its Director. He and Lavinia still lived together then, and Clo was just a baby. After our field trip to Tarquinia, I was determined to go on to graduate school as an Etruscologist at Princeton, where I could study with both husband and wife: he an expert at Etruscan infrastructure, she at *Rasenna*.

At the University of Texas I had majored in Classics to honor my father. He had been an amateur classicist of illustrious line, great-grandson of the Great Classicist himself, William Sandhurst Greenough. Professionally, my Daddy Bill was a pilot and flight instructor, working first out of Ørland, Norway, where he'd met Aile ("Hailey") Niilasdatter, a base translator from Trondheim. When her parents teased her for marrying a "coffee-colored" man, *Mor* retorted that *Norwegians love their coffee*. It was a lame joke, but Dad went along with it.

They'd been transferred to Aviano Airforce Base in Italy near Pordenone, where I was born, and then to Lackland in San Antonio when I was four.

I knew he'd had a hard time at the base as their only Black flight instructor, but around us he was the sweetest, most easy-going man alive. I had never known why, one morning when I was fifteen years old, he took off from Lackland and crashed into a butte near San Jon, New Mexico.

The Air Force ruled it an accident, but it looked like suicide. *Mor* sued his doctors for missing all the signs. He'd trained two pilots court-martialed for causing a fatal gondola accident in Italy, and he took it very personally, she said. All I knew was that my world had fallen apart and my mother almost lost her mind, trying to find justice.

By the time I'd finished my Masters in Classical Archaeology at Princeton—working as Dr. Lewis' T.A. for a pittance —my mother had lost so much money to lawyers that my grocery money allowance dried up, and I had to find a second job in a hurry.

By then, Dr. Bradley-Arnold had moved to Florence and Dr. Lewis, at his wits' end trying to get tenure on top of being a single dad, hired me to come over on Mondays, Wednesdays and Thursdays to cook a big meal and put the kids to bed.

Meanwhile, *Mor* got an office job downtown and married Buster Sparks, a mechanic at the base. They lived on a ranch north of S.A. called Twin Rivers, where I went every Christmas, and where every New Year's Eve we had a big bonfire of tree-trash and ate home-made tamales.

My mother still insists on filling my worn-out knit Christmas stocking. That year I found in the bottom, next to the navel orange and the chocolate bar, a mysterious little package wrapped in white tissue paper. It felt like a soft-sided address book or planner.

"It's your Auntie Mary's diary, from when she was in Italy, *kyare.* Time you had it."

Tearing off the wrapping paper, I looked in wild surmise upon the neat black notebook, its pages corrugated with writing, edged in faded gold and fitted with a neat brass hasp, from which dangled on a worn, red silk cord, a miniature brass key.

"My *famous* Auntie Mary?" I whispered reverently.

I did have a humdrum Aunt Marie, on my mother's side.

"Oh, *Mor,* I thought you sent this to the San Antonio Museum of Art."

"I scanned a few pages for them," she said carelessly. "It was meant for you."

Mary Greenough Burnsey had been the official portrait painter of Congress, and hadn't done too poorly in the rest of the world either. She was famous for her striking portraits of eminent politicians and regular people alike and especially for her uncanny ability to reveal the inner woman or man, sometimes flattering, sometimes not. Whatever flair I had for sketch and design I traced to her, but my skills in metalworking were thanks to my step-Daddy Buster.

I had grown up on stories of Auntie Mary, but understood vaguely that she was also a direct ancestor of mine, since cousins still married cousins, back in the day. I knew that she had travelled to Italy soon after the American Civil War to find her muse, and stayed in Rome with her brother William "the great classicist" Greenough. I also knew that her death was nearly as dramatic as her life. After an extraordinary long, successful and prolific life as a professional artist, she died in a freak accident on her one hundredth birthday, when the balcony outside her studio gave way, pitching her fifty feet to the pavement.

"Oh, *Mor* image of a young priest of the era, posed for a formal photograph beside a tall Ionic column set off by a swag of heavy, Lizstian cut framing a long face full of character and charisma.

I'd seen him before, surely. But where?

Turning it over, I read the penciled name *Titono Empedicleo Benevento,* the date 1865, and the name of the photographer's studio: *Fratelli Alinari Fotografi Editori*. I knew for a fact that Alinari—famous for their architectural and folk-themed photographs—only took portraits of the rich and famous. *Hey, wait a second!*

"Isn't 'Titono' the first name of my godfather?" I frowned.

"Yes," smiled my mother. "Titono Empedicleo LoCieco. Named for this man Benevento, his great-grandson or something. Related to your Daddy Bill somehow. That second sight of yours is pretty much this Benevento's fault."

"But how so? Isn't this man a priest? I mean—"

Aren't priests supposed to be celibate?

"Read the diary," she said, and nothing more.

As always, it was wonderful to be at the ranch. The only trouble was that *Mor* and Buster spent the whole time trying to convince me to apply for an open teaching position in the Classical Studies Department here at Trinity University.

If I got it, I would still have to finish my dissertation, hoping the collection of ancient art at the San Antonio Museum of Art would be good enough. I'd have to give up the Temple of Vanth and Tages, and most of all give up Dr. Lewis, because, as Daddy Buster insisted, he "wasn't good for me."

That old chestnut.

"It's a dead-end, Tanny-Sue," Buster insisted while we worked together at the forge the day before Christmas, finishing up a set of fire-tongs as a present for *Mor*, "spending all your time raising someone else's children when you should be raising your own."

"I don't intend to raise *anybody's* children, Daddy Buster," I countered, giving the hot iron a vicious twist. "I'm a woman academic! We're not allowed to have children."

On New Year's Eve, after a couple of Shiners, *Mor* lit into me in turn.

"Who's going to watch these *Riverbankers* of his, if you're both in Tarquinia?" she asked, throwing a log into the heart of the fire. "Have you thought of that?"

I had indeed: had emailed him my concerns but had

Mor went right on. "He's using you, *kyare*. As a teacher and as a housekeeper, and first thing you know he'll use you as something else.

"Sure I have, *Mor,* and I promise I'll apply," I murmured, idly shelling peanuts and dropping them into my Dr. Pepper bottle, "as soon as I hear what the plan is for this spring. I mean, once I hear back from Dr. Lewis. If his plan looks impossible, I'll apply."

"What would make it impossible, Tanny-Sue?" asked Buster from his lawn chair.

"If I wind up having to take care of the Riverbankers *and* work at the site," I proposed, enjoying a salty swig of my sugar-sweetened beverage.

"And if you are under the same roof as that man," emended my mother.

"Yeah, I told him that in my email, *Mor.*"

"Deadline for application at Trinity was in October, but the secretary is a friend of mine, and she said they'd make an exception, since you're my girl," remarked *Mor.*

There was a long silence as we all stared at the fire and I finished my peanuts. Then the racket of fireworks—going constantly since well before dark—ramped up sharply to resemble nothing so much as an artillery barrage.

"Happy New Year, you two," I said, kissed them each on the cheek, and went off to bed.

Next morning, *Mor* threw me into the saddle of her Peruvian Paso mare Balada. She mounted Pablo, her favorite Paso gelding, and we went for a ride in the chilly sunshine, Texas sky spreading blue overhead.

We drew rein at the crest where you can see the Tower of the Americas. A small prop plane hummed slowly overhead. *Mor* said nothing, having said it all already and knowing I needed my space. I was mulling over the email I'd just received back from Dr. Lewis:

D ear Ms. G.,

Sorry to be so late in replying to your very cogent questions, but I have only just heard the answer I've been waiting for.

It is not ideal, but Anna-Maria Ficino, that's Dr. Cotto's wife, remember, the law professor, has agreed to let the Riverbankers live with her and Angelo at their place in Lido di Tarquinia for the semester, where they will attend the little local school, which has a surprisingly strong English program.

They have a nice upstairs single room with its own bath which you may have. Anna-Maria is home working on writing a textbook this semester, and says she is happy to cook.

As for me, I can live in my office in the basement of the Museum, as I often have before, and shower at the site.

Or if you prefer, I can move in with Angelo and the River-bankers. I have rented a scooter for getting around, which you could use. But there is no shower on the premises.

Your choice.

JPL

I thought it would be easier for Dr. L. if I stayed at Casa Cotto. I could help with the cooking, too, but it meant I would still be the children's first line of care. I also worried that, if their Italian proved not to be good enough, they might well lose half a year of education.

But why should any of this concern me when I had no legal right to them?

I might lose my heart to them, sacrifice my health and time to them, and still have their fates decided by a mother who had barely seen them in three years.

And, he still hadn't thanked me for my semester of toil. He hadn't even returned home for Christmas. I was to take them with me when I joined him there.

He keeps me around. I have no legal right to them. He trusts me. It's a dead-end, Tanny-Sue. If he were free, I'd marry him.

I felt an overwhelming sadness.

Balada shifted impatiently under me, tired of standing.

"*Mor,*" I asked suddenly. "What would Dad have said? Would he have wanted me to stay here and teach, even if it meant I would never have a site or grad students of my own?"

What a pointless question: she would surely tell me what she wanted me to hear.

She paused a moment to take

"Your father would not want you to give up your dream, *kyare*. He would want you to stay on in Italy, to be the best in your field, and become more famous even than Dr. Lewis."

I was stunned.

She looked me right in the eyes: pale grey to my golden brown. "He told me so, the morning he left us. I didn't know why at the time. He said . . ."

She looked upward to recall exactly.

"*'She's going places, Hailey. She has luck and heart as well as brain. We have to get her airborne, then trust her to fly.'* That's why," she gave a sudden sob and wiped her eye, "that's why Buster and I supported you for as long as we could."

Hearing Dad's voice again had filled me with sudden hope.

"Oh, *Mor,* you did great." I laughed, "and I've done all right."

"No, you haven't," she countered fiercely. "Because you took his money, you are so tangled up with that man and his children that you will never. . . never *get airborne.*"

I took her gloved hand in my bare one and squeezed it.

"Not 'never,' *Mor*. Dad also used to say, '*Hard isn't impossible, honey, it's just hard.*'"

❀

*E*xcerpt A from The DIARY of M. G. BURNSEY: Barnstable To Paris

[*D*rawn from the record my great-grandmother Mary Greenough Burnsey kept of her one and only – but life-altering – visit to Europe, made when she was thirty years old. All these excerpts serve to clarify the place in our family history of the mysterious T. E. Benevento.]

*D*edication page:
January 9, 1882

For my dearest Mary-Louise on the occasion of her twenty-fifth birthday.

Never forget that you are the seventh of the seventh, as I was myself.

Now do something about it.

All my love, Mama.

A rubber stamp at the bottom of the sheet:

Knowles General Store, Yarmouth Pt., MASS

JAN. 9, 1882

Dark day, very stormy: such snow. Lucky for me dear Cook ventured to Yarmouth last week. Result: presents and cake with Gussie and Mama and Papa. T, V & C sent cards & the Elders, letters. Today, I feel officially Elderly myself. Mean to "do something about it," as M. says.

FEB. 20, 82 - a fat graveyard.

"A green February makes a fat graveyard." My namesake Auntie Mary Baker Brown died yesterday, poor thing, or rather not at all poor. Mama very downcast: her last sister left, but this PM came running out to say Baker farm outside Cambridge is mine, and large bequest. Am stunned.

Again M. says I should "really do something now" and is in parlor with Mr. and Mrs. Burnsey planning something. A trip abroad with Bess? Heart racing! Must concentrate, hurry to finish portrait of Suzanne. S's. mother's birthday next week, and oils must dry in time.

FEB. 28, 82 - the death of a dear friend.

Another death. Suzanne Prentiss Smith, my dear, sweet Sue, is gone. I went down the lane with her poor mother's birthday gift when the girl came running: "Miss Mary, Miss Mary, the young lady has passed."

How could it be when I saw her well and hearty not two weeks ago? I went on into the house, gave the painting to Mrs. S., saw S. laid out in the parlor, more like a marble statue than anything else on earth. Dazed. Wonder if I could learn sculpture?

MAR. 5, 82 - in the snowy garden

Mrs. S. just left. Her praise for my portrait of S. was so great I had to leave the studio to cool myself in the snowy garden. But she followed me out and held my hands tight and blessed me and said I have a gift that will bring joy, not sorrow, that "I can see my Susie look right out of your picture at me and say, 'Don't you cry, Mama. See how happy I am?'" How we wept.

Later: I have to say, it made a difference to Mama, hearing her say that, for she was there with her, and she was very thoughtful this evening, talking quietly with Pop. "Come to my work-room in the morning, dear," she said just now, as we were leaving the table.

MAR. 6, 82 - in transport.

It is true and I am in transports. I am to travel to the continent with Bess and Stephen Burnsey in the summer, and may stay as long as I please in Rome, as I am to live with

William and Zeya! There! I have written it! Mama has convinced Pop that art may serve a useful purpose in preserving the likeness – in color and glance – of a dear one in ways a stiff tintype cannot.

I can hardly say what is more dazzling: the prospect of sketching from "life" the works of Raphael and Veronese or of being with my dearest friends for months on end! Even locked up in this diary, dare I say: my very dearest friend? St. is so much younger, and never shows me more but good fun and fellowship. Lizzie says men are revolting. I must be depraved. How will I bear it?

Ingrate! In a few months, if you are spared, you will see ROME.

APR. 13, 82 - on the SS. Servia.

So much is decided, but so much left to do. We are to sail May 12 on the SS. Servia, a very new, very fast ship, the "finest liner afloat" says St. I wanted to travel Steerage, to sketch the people there (and save a great deal of money so I can buy more paints in Paris) but Pop won't let me. I will find a way to see those people, and sketch them, I hope!

Burnseys' twin cousins coming with us, alas. a girl and boy, high school age, to go live in Rome a year with their father Uncle Joseph Readfield Peters. Bess says they are awful, St. says girl is nice. Names (I think): Thomas and Emmeline.

Pop has arranged for a friend of his, a Unitarian from Cambridge Fellowship, Minister Jasper J. Jarvey to be our chaperone as far as Rome. Pop says somebody from some city in Tuscany started Unitarianism, so he will go there, "and so will we," says St. (B & St. know Jarvey well, call him "Triple J" and say he's not strict.)

Mama and I fought about clothes. I said I will not wear the big bustles coming in style: in all that heavy cloth I will cook and also is a huge waste: could make three dresses of it. Threatened to wear Mama's old Bloomers, and nearly got a slap! Compromise was lighter fabrics and simpler design. Bess laughed and said the French ladies will "put us in the shade if we aren't smart."

MAY 13, 82 – at sea.

The Servia is the most wonderful ship in the world! Captain says we are to make the crossing in eight days, if winds stay fair. We use the most modern coal-fired engines AND sails to go faster than ever, and it is wonderfully built so that really nothing can sink her. Spent the AM with St.

Later: Boring man "V." at dinner spoke to neither Bess nor me, only talking with Jx3 and St. and flirting horribly with Evangeline (that is her name, not Emmeline) who is blonde & plump. Man talked on and on about "the destiny of young American ladies" traveling abroad, never once asking one of us "ladies" what we thought of our destinies. Maybe Lizzie right about men!

MAY 17, 82 – at sea, near Azores Is.

Clothes very heavy with salt spray after ten games of shuffleboard. Found St. kissing E. and told Jx3, who laughed at me and said "boys will be boys." I foresee there will be trouble!

Got revenge by sitting at the rail over the lower deck where the Steerage people take the air and sketched for an hour some of the interesting people. Steward told me many are failed immigrants going back "in disgrace" to home countries, but most look happy enough.

MAY 20, 82 – a day out of Portsmouth

Captain says will in port tomorrow, so must enjoy ship-board life all I can while I can. Sketched Steerage again today and the same man was there today as yesterday, staring boldly up at me, so much as if we were acquainted, that I tried to think: did he work in the linen shop in Boston? Was it he who fitted my new boots so nicely, the week we were in New York? I have to admit to sketching a good likeness of him, much from memory, and making St. jealous. So much the better, as he is flirting with E. again. And is it possible Bess likes the fat man from dinner?

Later: Had a long heart-to-heart with Bess, and we are re-pledged to be good friends to one another. She told me the chief reason for travel was as a rest-cure after the death of Freddie Blake last December. Never told me they were engaged, but this explains her moods. We made a pact not to let any man separate us, kissed on it.

JUNE 10, 82 – Paris, Victoria Palace Hotel

Just back from the Louvre: walking on air! Two whole hours sketching figures from "The Wedding of Cana" and many long stops at every Raphael I saw. Had to buy a new sketchbook – also many fat tubes of (expensive) paint – on the way back here, which I foresee will not last long!

Later: Evening at Brasserie Lipp. Could have stayed there forever sketching waiters and diners. Bess laughed at me, but St. was embarrassed, and Jx3 heard the two men next to us saying I was an artist's model they both knew, who sketches, "when she is not turning tricks." I was shocked by his language, but he assures me that is what they said. Bess agrees Jx3 is an odd man.

4

SAINT TANAQUIL

On the long flight from Philly to Paris, the Riverbankers were excited and talkative playing with their new games, drawing, anything but sleeping. The moment we took our seats for the short flight from Paris to Rome, they conked out. Clo was by the window and Ratty on the aisle, and both of them leaning on me, hot and heavy and fast asleep. I had no complaints. I didn't need the loo and didn't mind them leaning on me, not one bit.

I had a secret weapon that would keep me well-entertained for more than the mere two hours or so it took to cross France, the Alps, and the Tyrrhenian Sea, namely: the diary of my famous ancestress, sailing to Italy for the first and most momentous time in her long life. I've inserted above a few excerpts from the first part of her story, from before she reached Italy.

It made me think of my own first trip abroad, when I was wetter behind the ears than a trout, and had yet to be cheated by a taxi-driver or pinched by a man on a bus.

Great-Grandma's story turned out to be more of a roller-coaster than the heavy turbulence we hit over Corsica. As we followed the coast downward to Fiumicino,

I put the diary away and wakened the Riverbankers, pointing out landmarks. There was Elba, there was Cosa, there were Lago Trasimeno and Lago Bolsena. Here came the Port of Trajan, and the umbrella pines that led to Rome!

The moment the wheels of Alitalia flight 7615 touched the tarmac at Fiumicino on the first Friday in January, three days before their school started, the Riverbankers and I were filled with wild elation. *We had made it safely back to Italy!*

The word that Angelo had arranged for a ride-service to collect us, once we cleared Customs—a breeze. But, when we looked around for a dour man in a black suit, holding a sign labeled "Greenough and Lewis," we saw instead . . .

"Dr. Lewis." *Why did I sing it out as if he were the best present ever?*

Ten-year-old Moley danced around him like a mad rabbit, dark hair flying, crying, "Papa! Papa!" as the six-year-old Rat's hoarse tenor echoed her.

In an instant they were on the man's hips and around his neck like a pair of clinging vines, tilting the *occhiali* over his bright eyes.

Faced with the man himself I wondered if Buster was right.

Why else would I be feeling that pang of envy for Clo, kissing and kissing her Papa's face?

I gravitated closer.

Then the big SLR cameras started to go off with rich clicks and mechanical repeaters, and I heard my mother say, *with famous people, you will be the one who gets hurt, not him.* So, I put out a professional right hand. He took it in a warm grasp.

"Good to see you, Ms. Greenough," he said with the air of a condoling relation, though a smile was lurking. "May I help you with one of those carts?"

"And you," I replied soberly, then grinned in sheer relief. "You sure can! I think we brought everything they own."

"No, me, me. I'll push." cried the Rat. He slithered down and charged off blindly with one trolley while I gave chase.

Clo refused to dismount her Papa, who followed gamely with the other trolley.

The *paparazzi* were still clicking, all the way to the old blue Range-Rover standing at the curb. It was spattered in the white mud of *Pian del Città* and towed an open trailer.

I almost wept to see it, and when Angelo Cotto ran around from the driver's seat, I flung myself into his arms crying, "*Babbo.*"

Out from the clicking press stepped one young woman in a dark blue suit and red, French-tied scarf to hand me her card—*Françoise Pinard, Paris Match*—purring in my ear, "We would like to be your exclusive media outlet, *Mademoiselle.*" before vanishing with a smile.

As I tucked the card bemusedly into my wallet, the children threw themselves on Angelo. They were speaking in Italian and talked over each other eagerly.

"*Il rattuccio* is a wimp, *Babbo*. He threw up over Corsica."

"Did not. As usual, *la talpa* is fibbing."

"I thought you said they didn't know enough Italian for that school," laughed the boss, slinging bags into the trailer. Glancing at me, he lost his smile. "You're thinner," he said.

"And I have three strands of grey hair. Look," I boasted, pointing to one temple.

"Thank you, Saint Tanaquil Greenough," he said fervently, taking my head in his hands and kissing the place as if to *make it better.*

Wow. It didn't fill the empty "thanks" cistern, but it was a decent squall.

Then we all piled into the Range-Rover—Lewises in the backseat, and I in the front with Angelo. There was a greasy sack of *pizza rossa* for the kids and a *panino* for me. These we demolished in a heartbeat washed down with lemon Fanta. The Riverbankers promptly fell asleep again while the rest of us caught up.

The subject was the increasing role of science in archaeology and how much could be gleaned from even the smallest scrap of evidence. I shared learnings on the improvement of beef cattle under Roman rule from the fall seminar series on animal bone forensics.

Angelo linked that to a study at La Sapienza on the origins of Roman soldiers based in the DNA in their teeth. The boss followed up with what the pollen found in the *hypogeum*—in the vases full of honey and grain, the heaps of fruit and flowers—told us about the ancient landscapes of Tarquinia. Then we speculated on the meaning of the child sacrifice.

With every word, I was repaid more for every lecture I'd given and every grey hair on my head, repaid even for the flu and the loneliness. They had earned me *this*.

"We timed the opening of the jewelry exhibition for this Wednesday, so you could be here," Angelo said as we turned off the A12 for Lido.

"Just the jewelry?" I asked. "What about the vases?"

"Next month," spoke up the boss eagerly. "I'm waiting for confirmation to include the *hydria*. Wait until you see it: absolutely gorgeous."

"Tomorrow," added Angelo, glancing over with a smile, "*Giacomo* will take you and the *animali* to La Castellina for a sneaky preview,"

"Just wait 'til you see the *hypogeum* fresco," enthused *Il Prof*. "It'll add a whole new chapter to your knowledge on the worship of the Vanth."

"No doubt," I laughed gaily, wallowing in nerdiness.

I hadn't slept a wink on either flight, and as we rolled through the gate into the driveway of the Cotto's pleasant beach house in Lido di Tarquinia, well after midnight, weariness struck me like a physical force.

How I got my suitcase up the stairs to my little loft, showered and got into my nightie before falling asleep, I'll never know.

On that first Saturday morning in the Cotto's beach house on *Lungomare dei Tirreni* I lay a long time in bed, simply reveling at being in Italy again. Down the walls crept the sunbeams until they shone into my eyes but still, I hated to move.

Soon, however, I could smell *pancetta* frying.

I dressed in a rush, too famished to shower again. On went my flattering-but-tough site-jeans, my favorite soft, rose-flannel shirt with a new grey wool pullover, and my new yellow-silk Christmas scarf. Jamming my crazy curls into place with a long faux-tortoiseshell comb, I grabbed my site socks and boots before galloping down the spiral stair barefoot, cracking my head painfully on the low entry to the kitchen.

As the Riverbankers waved their forks, the cook turned from the stove, tucking a loose tendril of silky white hair back into its chignon.

"Watch out for the doorway," she said archly.

"Anna-Maria," I cried, rushing forward to kiss her cheeks. "Bless you, bless you." Then I sat down happily to a fry-up of *pancetta* and gorgeously orange eggs.

"How are things in the Wild West, *Tanina*?" She sat down a basket of good Lazio *pan integrale*, whole-wheat bread, and site-made apricot jam. "Were you riding horses?"

"At Buster's place? Did you, did you?" Clo demanded through toast.

"Yes, swallow that, please. But was so out of practice, I had to ride Balada," I admitted. "Even people who can't ride, can ride Balada. All Pasos are easy, but she's a rocking chair."

Clo accurately passed on to Anna-Maria all I'd ever told

her about *Mor*'s Pasos, finishing with, "Now I'm big enough to ride one, aren't I, Tanny?"

"Sure. I expect your ballet classes have strengthened up those long legs of yours."

Hunger assuaged, I noticed there were no menfolk around, if you didn't count the Rat.

"Where are the guys?" I asked Anna-Maria, busing my dishes.

"I need a smoke," she answered obliquely. "The *animali* can play in the yard." They rushed out of doors cheering. In a trice they were kicking their heels up on the swings. We followed more slowly, carrying their coats.

I don't smoke, but Anna-Maria has a sunny spot where she likes to.

"They are with Franco," she said, "trying to make him see sense. Let me ask you: is there *no* other part of the site you could take, beside the Temple of Vanth and Tages?"

Ouch. Tanny thrown under bus.

"Franco has worked for years cataloguing that part of the site," she went on sternly. "He is building a career on it. Why not take the Hut Circle? It needs expert attention." Squinting, she tapped off ash. "Marc Short lost his excavation-assistant position. Did you know?"

I shook my head in wonder. "He finally pushed the boss too far?"

This astounding news was such a distraction that I had to hand it to the professor of jurisprudence: she had my cross-examination well in hand!

She stubbed out her cigarette. "Yes, a month ago they had a major disagreement over techniques. Marc works for *Panorama* now, but still does museum photography for Giulia."

Giulia Pantano was the Director of the Museum.

I took a deep breath, trying to focus on the suddenly

fresher air, and the happy children. "I didn't know that," I answered faintly. "Marc's Hut Circle. Hmmm."

She waited.

What else was there? I ran the whole site over in my mind's eye, from the turning at the Mazzola farm all the way to the *hypogeum.*

There was an un-dug tomb far from the rest of the rest of the site that we called *The Tomb of Sychaeus*, a very lonely spot. Or the huge mound we called *the Place of Sacrifice,* but Dr. Lewis and I disagreed violently as to what might be under it. Then there was the Hut Circle, in a leafy dell not far from the *hypogeum.*

True, it had interesting traces of huts! At its northern end there was also a mysterious little mound, with a fine ilex tree growing out of it.

But, how could I bid farewell to my beloved Temple? It had been the focus of so many fond dreams over these last grim months.

Yet I doubted I could work comfortably at the site without Franco's friendship.

Little archaeologists in their nests must agree, Dr. Lewis used to joke.

Before I could change my mind, I put a hand on Franco's fond mother's arm. "I'll take Marc Short's area, Anna-Maria. I've always been curious about that mound with the ilex."

She was already on her feet pressing my face to her bosom, kissing the top of my head and weeping, "God bless you for this, Tanaquil Greenough. You are truly a saint."

Like anything dramatic it sounded perfectly normal in Italian. All the same, the Riverbankers were off their swings in an instant, pelting towards us.

"Is Tanny all right, Anna-Maria?" asked Clo, eyes huge. "What's wrong?"

"Nothing. I'm fine." I smiled, wiping my eyes. "We've just buried the hatchet."

Clo nodded wisely, but the Rat asked, "Where?"

Anna-Maria was meantime sending a text and explaining to me, "They were over at Bar Corsaro. Should be back *prontissimo.*" A moment later, the missing menfolk were pouring out of the Range Rover and pelting across the grass towards us.

I stood my ground, arms folded.

Franco is a handsome man, but his face was transfigured to almost angelic beauty as he took me in his arms, kissing my cheeks again and again, finishing with a juicy buss on the lips.

I took it like a Trojan.

His mother beat him off, fussing, "Don't let Angelica see you carrying on like that."

Ah! A serious girlfriend at last! I reflected, un-mussing myself.

Franco dashed off to his car, shouting, "I'll call my crew and meet you there, *Giacomo!*"

Angelo took his turn more soberly, planting two solemn kisses that meant a lot to me.

Dr. Lewis stood watching, hands on hips, a half-smile on his face.

Angelo raised one bushy white eyebrow at him. "Eh, *Giacomo,* you stand there?"

So, the boss moved in shyly, pressing me close in a good old American hug while the others cheered. When he stepped back, there were tears in his big blue eyes.

"I already owe her more than I can repay," he told Angelo resonantly, mopping his face with one of the supply of clean white hankies without which he never ventures forth.

"You can take me and the Riverbankers to the site, for starters," I suggested, stung that he had not directed that touching speech to me.

"Here," said Angelo, dangling car-keys. "Let her drive the

Fiat, to get used the shift. I'll meet you there with the Rover. The back is full of tents and sleeping bags from the cleaners."

"I'll back-seat drive," put in the boss, "And remind her how to get to the site."

"Good! It's been a minute since I drove there." I agreed. "What about Clo and Ratty?"

"Angelo can come back for them a little later," declared Anna-Maria. "First, we will make lunches. Then I have some puppies for them to see. Canela had a litter last week."

Cheering, the Riverbankers ran for the kitchen.

"Don't promise them any," warned their Papa.

"It's Andrea's car," explained *il babbo* as we crossed the yard. "He is studying in Florence and is happy for you to use it." Andrea was the youngest of the Cotto boys. I could recall a time when he had been running around this yard as Clo did now.

"How is university treating him?" I asked, the boss stalking along at my elbow.

"Very well," Angelo smiled, explaining that Andrea had inherited his mother's razor-sharp legal mind and would be studying law. When we turned the corner, there stood a battered white *cinquecento,* slightly foxed at the vents. I loved it.

"Works better than it looks, I promise," said *il babbo* critically. "Take the last stretch of road as slow as you can and you should be all right."

When I managed to put an elbow into the boss' sweater-clad midsection, he apologized for "clogging up the car." He'd left his scooter at the site but would drive it back to the Museum that evening. Sitting so close certainly broke all his ground-rules on Tanny proximity!

After some fraught down-shifting at the roundabouts, the Fiat was buzzing peacefully inland on highway *quaranta-quattro.* I settled back with a sigh.

Dr. Lewis, smiling broadly, said nothing. I eyed him, nettled.

"What? Is my driving that bad?"

He gave a shout of laughter.

"On the contrary: I can barely negotiate that last circle, even on a scooter. No, I was thinking a diplomat you were, just now. More than that: a peacemaker."

I didn't feel like a peacemaker. I felt like a fool. Worse: a doormat.

"I couldn't bear to have Franco angry with me," I admitted with growing distress. "But *you* know how upset I was. I worked up such a fine plan for how to dig the Temple. It kept me going all fall. All I can say is, Franco had better not ask me to see it. Now, Anna-Maria tells me that I've been assigned Marc Short's leavings. I know the Hut Circle is a good challenge, but . . ."

I groped for words.

"I mean I *know* that in theory, but it still *hurts.* It hurts to lose my dream of making sense of the Temple complex, of reconstructing the pediment sculpture, most of which I dug with my own hands. After last fall, it's just so *hard.*" I sobbed, breaking down entirely.

You promised. You promised, wailed my inner child.

Shaking with grief, I pulled the car over, yanked on the brake, turned on my flashers, put my face in my hands and bawled 'til I thought I'd turn inside out. I couldn't see how the boss was reacting, but he handed me two clean hankies in quick succession. Once the worst was over, he applied a third to my face so tenderly as almost to make me cry all over again.

"If I so much as hint at sharing your plan with him," he declared stoutly, "may I be struck dumb. You have my full permission to smile in a superior way any time he goes wrong."

"Thanks," I sighed, readying the Fiat to merge with traffic.

"Can I get you anything on the way through town? Coffee?"

"A few beers at Il Falchetto?" I joked weakly. "No, I'll feel better, by and by. Speaking of Falchetto, what's up with Marc? Why *did* you sack him? You did, didn't you?"

"Quite right," he nodded grimly. "All fall he poked around, taking his assistant's pay without making any progress on the Hut Circle. I'm embarrassed for you to see how he left it, so after literally five warnings, I cut him off as of New Year's."

He went on more forcefully. "I'm also irritated with Franco, who *promised* he would take the Mazzola tomb. I think *Dottoressa* Pantano talked him into protesting as punishment for my showing Marc the door."

"Giulia always did like Marc," I said tartly. "Especially when Riccardo was in Sardinia."

He snorted with laughter then sighed, "Oh, Tanny, you keep me sane."

"The Riverbankers kept me sane," I mused. "When they weren't driving me nuts."

5

I VIEW MY DOMAIN

THE MALE COTTOS WERE BOTH THERE BEFORE US, TOO BUSY arguing with two guys in blue coveralls and mud-spattered boots to worry where we'd been. One guy was at least pretending to talk on the phone. The other listened patiently to Angelo's harangue, arms crossed. Franco was looking soulfully towards the site as if longing to see his temple.

This little drama, I should add, was taking place in front of a gate I had never before seen. Neither had the boss, judging by his reaction.

"About time that fence appeared," he laughed. "Your idea?"

He was out of the car and running to the gate almost before I'd fully pulled up beside Angelo's battered Range-Rover and Franco's Lancia.

"The Museum promised this security fence back in October, *Tanina*," Angelo explained as I joined them. "We'd had a couple of thefts and someone built a campfire out at the *hypogeum* site. Suddenly yesterday, while we were all busy offsite, *boom!* They finally get a big crew to put it up, sinking fence-posts into sensitive areas. Now, no-one can find the padlock keys."

"Helluva fence, though," whistled the boss.

The fence was indeed made of a superior sort of black rectangular mesh, with razor-wire at the top and anchoring at the bottom.

The cleared area that ran like a narrow path along the outside edge of it gave me an idea.

"Do you mind if I walk the fence-line?" I asked Dr. L. "I'm dying to see the site."

"Great idea," he exclaimed. "I'll come along. We can see if they've managed to avoid destroying any features."

"Mind if I join you?" asked Franco. For a heartbeat, I thought Dr. Lewis was going to object and wondered why. Then he said, "Sure. We'll leave *il babbo* to sort this out."

Dr. Cotto rolled his eyes, and said, "Once the idiot from their office gets here with the key I'll come find you."

"I hope those puppies keep the Riverbankers away for a good long time," I remarked. "This path is gnarly."

"Yes, a little narrow," agreed Franco.

"Gnarly," the boss corrected him, giving me a conspiratorial smile, "*gnarly.*"

"Oh, *Tanina*," gushed Franco, "my mother is so happy with you that she will have a little party this evening. Also, *il Prof* has news to share." He winked at the boss, who frowned and blushed, shaking his head. Clearly this was meant to stay a secret.

"Meanwhile, Ms. G.," added Dr. Lewis in a rush. "I'm supposed to tell you that Tony has invited you over for breakfast at his place tomorrow morning."

"Sweet. I'd be glad to. His scones are the stuff of legend."

"Be careful, *cara*," warned Franco, pretty obviously eager to be conciliatory, "*Marco* is staying there, and Tony is *come si dice?*"

"Tony's getting a bad reputation with the police," the boss sighed.

"What for?"

"Maybe antiquities smuggling? Keep your Tanny-senses about you."

"Will do, boss," I answered soberly.

Marc Short was staying at Tony's place? That gave me pause.

We were going single-file. Dr. L. was at the front, I was in the middle, and Franco at the rear. Where the fence skirted the absolute outside edge of the bluff, we had to cling to the mesh.

"So, what was stolen from the site, last fall?" I asked whomever would answer.

"A couple of shovels from the Finds Shed," said Franco. "Rope from the camper."

"Had someone stolen the camper keys or did they break in?"

Franco shook his head. "No break-in and all the keys were accounted for."

"Except for Marc's," the boss added bitterly, "which have never been returned. I've told *il babbo* we must re-key the locks on the camper, the shed, *and* the *hypogeum*."

"The fence will take care of all that," remarked Franco with a shrug.

"Marc still has keys to everything else?" I shivered. That felt like a very bad idea.

Dr. Lewis grimaced his agreement.

"He is not such a bad sort," began Franco but we had come to a slight widening of flat ground outside the fence. It was at the base of the knoll on which stood the proud foundations of the Temple of Vanth and Tages. A handy tree-stump presented itself.

Franco begged leave to sit and contemplate his hard-won fiefdom. We left him there sketching out his excavation campaign, his notebook on his knee.

As he led the way, Dr. Lewis was so entirely silent that finally I had to ask, "Penny for your thoughts?"

"I think you know," he laughed, shaking off his mood. He

turned to smile at me. "So, what will you want to see first when we finally get through this fence?"

"The *hypogeum*," I answered at once. "I want to take a hard look at that fresco. I suspect it will prove me right about the Place of Sacrifice being full of plague victims!"

"Ha. The Place of Sacrifice is full of decapitated Roman soldiers and nothing but decapitated Roman soldiers."

"So help you God?" I joked. "What would you like to bet?"

"Easy. A bottle of *Vino Nobile*."

Montepulciano's finest red was the standard site-prize.

"Done," I said, stopping to shake on it.

As he took my hand our eyes met. For a long moment he seemed about to say something. His chest was rising and falling in some agitation. His hand was still snugly in mine.

"Are you all right?" I asked, absurdly happy with his discomfiture.

He blinked his black-lashed eyes as if coming out of some deep thought.

"Sorry, just remembered something," he stammered and released my hand as if burnt.

Like another rule of engagement, i.e., "no touching?"

"You will lose that bottle, mark my words," I assured him smoothly.

"Bottle? Oh, no you don't," he rallied, holding aside a branch for me to precede him. "The minute we open that mound, you'll see."

"Shh." I indicated more than said.

He came up alongside, staring along my pointing finger to a car parked at the base of the cliff. It was a familiar car, parked where I hadn't even known there was a road.

"Marc's old Lotus," I murmured, close to his ear. "But how?"

"The old swimming-hole road I expect," he muttered back. "It branches off before the crossroads at Mazzola's place."

"Swimming hole?"

"Before your day. A deep place in the stream where we used to swim before Tony started letting us use his pool. Mazzola's cows liked it, too. Always had to watch out for cow-pies."

"I'll bet! Is there a path down to it from the site?"

"Sure." He gestured to a place on the opposite side of the ridge. "It starts over there and cuts across the face of the cliff. Very narrow. We used to joke you had to be pretty hot to use it."

Suddenly he frowned and pulled me out of sight of the car, his cheek so close that I could smell his after-shave. He seemed oddly younger, so close up.

"What is it?" I whispered.

"Didn't you see?"

I shook my head. I'd been too busy wondering how old he was.

"Marc's down there with some fishy-looking gent."

Then we could both hear talking: Marc was on the phone.

"It's just like you said," he said in very clear Italian. "The thing is a nightmare." A silence as the interlocutor spoke. "Sure, I do! They're right here. It's the gate key we need," answered Marc, jingling something—his keys? "Yes, yes." Another pause. "We'll get on it."

Then footsteps crunching, two doors slamming, a car gradually leaving, and silence.

A moment later a *ping* from my pocket made me jump.

Signal was usually terrible up here and the message made my skin crawl.

Hey, baby, coming to Tony's tomorrow? Hot for you, Marc.

When I showed it to the boss, he frowned uneasily.

"You think there's a connection?"

"Absolutely, I'm apparently part of the thing they will 'get on,' but why?"

"He misses you?"

"Unlikely," I sighed. "After five years ignoring each other, some of them spent in the same town, he suddenly wants to 'catch up?' I guess I'll find out."

I tapped out a quick reply, *Yes, I'll be there bright and early.*

"So, you two are through?"

"Oh, *so* through," I laughed impatiently. "Come on, I want to get down there and see what they were up to!"

Why did I feel so antsy?

The slope here was steep but not impossible. I started down it, sliding from tree to tree to keep from going head over heels. He was right behind me saying cheerfully,

"Clearly they have discovered we have a fence. But why is that a problem?"

"I'll find out tomorrow at Tony's, I guess."

"Wow," I gasped once we reached the bottom of the slope and a well-used, well-graveled road appeared. "No more cow-pies here!"

Dr. Lewis looked it up and down, hands on hips. "Something's very wrong here."

My Tanny-sense was telling me the same thing. I saw a distinct glow along a well-trodden path that led up from where the road ended in a turnaround. It ran westerly around the northern cliff face.

If I covered my right eye, the glow was gone. Definitely a warning from my sixth sense.

"Is that the scary path you were talking about?" I asked, pointing.

"Yes, and no. It was never that wide. Someone's improved it."

I caught sight of a couple of rusty shovels, leaning against the cliff-face. "Here's what they improved it with, maybe! Are these your stolen tools?"

"Looks like it. I'm heading up that path to see what's going on."

He was off without a backward look, but I was right

behind him. After an increasingly breath-taking traverse we reached a stretch of fence. We were now at the western edge of the Hut Circle facing south. I recognized the mound with the ilex growing in it off to our left, but otherwise everything was a shambles.

What had been a pretty wood with open patches full of wildflowers was now barren. Haphazard excavations and a hodgepodge of little spoil-heaps were everywhere. A tall stack of plastic buckets, their handles rusty, stood by the fence, filled with wind-blown trash.

My new domain. My eyes filled with tears.

"I meant to clean it for you, Tanny," the boss murmured, finding another hankie.

"Why did he keep coming up here and *messing* with it?" I cried, wiping my unruly eyes. "And why is he so bent out of shape about the fence? It's not like he *did* anything here."

"And who was he talking to?" added Dr. L., possibly trying to change the subject.

"Oh, let's go see where everyone is," I sighed angrily.

It is a mile at most around *La Castellina,* the northerly tip of what had been the ancient town of Tarquinia, and we were soon back outside of the now-open gate. Franco's Lancia had been parked by the camper, beside the boss' red Vespa, but the Range-Rover was gone. Angelo must have gone to collect lunch and the Riverbankers.

Turning to move the Fiat inside the gate, I collided with the boss.

"Tanny, I," he began awkwardly taking my hand, both my hands, "for a long time now, I've wanted to tell you."

Was he going to apologize again? If so, I couldn't bear it.

I reclaimed my hands and interrupted harshly, "Since you have the Vespa do you mind if I take the Fiat back to Lido now?"

"Sure, sure. But," he objected, as what I'd said sank in, "you'll miss lunch, and you haven't seen the *hypogeum* yet."

Not even the *hypogeum* could tempt me to risk another glance at the hideous wreck of the Hut Circle, not today. My anger at Marc, Franco, at *all* men, was rapidly rising.

Had to get away quick or lose my saintly reputation.

I gritted my teeth. "I'll save that for another day. Guess I'm super-tired."

"Right. It'll be good for me to have some alone-time with the Riverbankers," he said rapidly, nervously, "but tonight at dinner, remember, we're having a little party to welcome you back, and I'll have what I hope is good news for you. It's certainly good news for *me*, and I couldn't think of how to thank you, so Anna-Maria thought you might like to know."

"Listen," I cut in wearily, "I've got to work on my plan of attack for the Hut Circle."

And burn my plans for the Temple of Vanth and Tages.

"Please? It will just be us and the Cottos, I promise. If you won't have to do a single dish and I get the Riverbankers to bed?"

"Sure, sure," I muttered ungratefully. "Just shout when you want me." Then I ran for the shelter of the Fiat.

Starting it up with a roar like a hundred sewing-machines, I wrenched it around then raced up the rough track swearing like a boatload of sailors.

I had cooled off enough by the time I met the Range Rover at Mazzola's, that I could wave with apparent good cheer. It seemed to me I needed very badly to think. How long since I had been entirely alone for a good ponder without the children without Dr. Lewis?

So, I thought, what was this good news the boss could use to "thank" me, other than his giving me the Temple, because it sure in hell wasn't that, not with Franco there?

What else was different?

Well for one thing, nothing like this sudden kissing and hugging and taking of hands had ever happened before, other than that single clinch over the coin.

Maybe he'd won a big grant, and I would get a chunk of the research money?

No, that wouldn't change his whole demeanor, would it?

Then the idea dawned in my startled brain that *he was acting as if he were single.*

Ah! There came the tingle of rightness I felt when justice was done or when I'd found a feature I'd predicted or I'd published a really good monograph.

No, seriously, had he got a divorce at last?

Why not? What else would have sent him to my old pal Prester John—an expert in family law—at Thanksgiving, before the subject of food-orders came up?

That's when the real lightning bolt struck.

In its flash, I saw that self-same pal in Lavinia's pretty parlor in Florence, shaking hands with her lover Caterina Bonifazzi. I knew that Caterina wanted children, and hadn't John-Allen written me last spring to say that Gesualdo did, too?

If she could be their surrogate, they might share a child with Lavinia and Caterina!

What had John-Allen said about same-sex marriages being easy to get in Belgium?

But, to marry Caterina, Lavinia would have to divorce the boss, who would then be free to *give himself to me.*

Or tie me down for life.

How could I be so unromantic?

Easy. I'd inoculated myself against this man, like some kind of toxin,

I pulled over and took a deep, deep breath before rejoining traffic.

Got to think. Got to think.

I got back to an empty house, went down to the cold, windy January beach, and walked up and down for perhaps an hour, thinking, thinking.

If he's finally free, why should he be stuck with me, or I with him, for that matter?

Doesn't he deserve a chance to play the field?

Maybe I should go away for a while, away from the River-bankers and the Badger, someplace where I can think!

Maybe a year in Venice? Ca' Foscari isn't just hiring directors. I saw a research position there when I was snooping about the boss' job offer.

If I stayed in Etruscology, I would see him wherever I went and would likely have the same dull ache in my heart I was feeling now.

My work is here, I argued with myself, here in Tarquinia, not in Venice. It's as much mine as it is his.

Why should I let my feelings for him keep me from working here? What were my feelings for him?

That brought me back to the dull ache.

When I could think no longer, I walked back to the Cotto's empty house and let myself silently in. I took a pear and a tangerine from the bowl on the dining room table and retreated to my room to write out my thoughts on the Hut Circle and take a long shower. Then I heard sounds of returning folk downstairs.

Just this once I decided not to help with dinner. I would act the part of the hard-boiled professional archaeologist instead of Saint Tanaquil. I went to the closet. If they wanted to thank me, I would look worth the thanking!

I put on my gold-silk lecture suit and a dab of my mother's gift of *Ma Griffe*, swept up my wild hair with a silver clasp, put on earrings to match, glossy dark lipstick, all that, and went back to work, waiting for the shout up the stairs I was sure would come.

"Dinner, Tanny," called Miss Clo, instantly making me wish I had been downstairs to greet her, to ask her about the puppies. I came sheepishly into the dining room, taking stock.

The food was on the table, family-style, with empty plates and full chairs all around, everyone seated but me. Someone had already served the Riverbankers, who were talking a mile-a-minute, shouting to Franco over their distracted father. There was an empty spot for me by the Riverbankers, at the far end of the table.

A lovely sponge-cake, dusted with powdered sugar and drizzled lightly with chocolate stood before the boss with its own stack of smaller plates. There was a knife in his hand, which he was waving. Glasses of red wine had been poured for all the adults and Fanta for the kids.

All the Cottos were frowning so concentratedly over a big sheaf of A4 papers covered with small print that I was able to slip quietly into my seat.

"You look really pretty," whispered Clo.

"Thanks. What'd you think of the puppies?" I whispered back. "Any good ones?"

"Ratty liked the all-black one, but I liked the gold one with a white star *here*."

She pointed to the center of her forehead.

"Can you get Papa to let us have a dog, Tanny?" Ratty asked in a stage whisper.

"How long will these take to translate into Italian, did he say?" Angelo was asking the boss. I peered over his shoulder. Looks like I was right. The boss had got his divorce.

"About a month," he smiled contentedly. "The adoption papers, two months. Lavinia was in a hurry to get them done, so she and Caterina can be married in Belgium, later this month."

"Bravo, *Giacomo*," cried Anna-Maria, applauded.

I couldn't help but join in, blowing my cover.

All the others, seeing me for the first time, did a double-take. "A glass for Santa Tanaquil," cried Franco, jumping to his feet and raising his glass, colliding with his father, who was pouring some out for me. Red wine splashed the front of my suit like gouts of blood.

My first thought was, *there goes my only nice outfit.* My second thought was, *what an omen, eh?*

With a cry of mortification, Franco ran to the kitchen for a towel, and was soon giving me a nice rub-down that ended in embarrassed grins on both sides. The stains remained.

"I should have saved it to wear on Wednesday," I sighed, looking myself over, conscious of the gaze of the boss' mournful, bespectacled eyes.

"It will be ready," Anna-Maria assured me. "Franceschino will take it to the dry-cleaners. Come, we will change you." She led me upstairs, chatting comfortably as I changed to more reasonable clothing. "It was a nice gesture," she smiled, hanging it up for me.

A knock came at the door, and Dr. Lewis called out, "I'm putting the Riverbankers to bed, Ms. G. You're doing breakfast with Tony, correct?"

"Yup, that's the plan."

"Fine. I'll see you at the site, sometime after that. *Hypogeum* tomorrow."

"Can't wait."

Anna-Maria had been watching me, and said, "You two are good together."

"Are we?" I asked guardedly.

"Of course," she laughed. "He did it for you, you know: the divorce."

"But Lavinia wanted—"

"Lavinia was pushed. Why do you doubt it?"

I blinked. "I, I guess I didn't let myself think about it."

She rolled her eyes in disbelief. "You too and your *not thinking.*"

"What do you mean by that?" I demanded.

She laughed. "You know very well what I meant."

"Not thinking about each other sexually, do you mean?"

"*Precisamente.* I do not blame you, *cara.* You have so much more to lose. But if he cannot break himself of it, he will go on being a very lonely man, the rest of his life."

Suddenly it was all too much, and I yawned cavernously, only just covering my mouth.

"Forgive me, Anna-Maria," I sighed. "I guess I'm too tired for all this drama!"

"*Boh,*" she shrugged. "Pirandello tells us we can only take so much of the truth in this theater of ours. Won't you come down for some cake first, *Tanina?*"

"Another time. Tonight, I'm afraid I would be bad company. *Buona notte.*"

"*E sogni d'oro,*" said Anna-Maria, getting up and taking the dress out with her.

"Oh, thanks for that," I murmured. "You're too kind."

Golden dreams? I thought, undressing.

What were my golden dreams?

I had to think. I just had to think.

6

DR. LEWIS AND MR. SHORT

IT IS STRIKING HOW VERY DIFFERENT THE NAME *JAMES* LOOKS IN different languages. I mean, *George* is as easy to see in the original Greek as it is in any other language, but not *James.* It started out as Yakob, and has been Iago, Diego, Jacques, and Giacomo.

This last is the name of a little church dedicated to Saint James that stands at the top of the town of Tarquinia, looking out across bare, rolling hills and out to sea.

There is a whole series of little churches on the *Via di San Giacomo,* from S. Giacomo at its western end to the Annunciata at the east and Chiesa del Salvatore in the middle. In the shadow of San Salvatore is a cluster of three little houses, the chief of which was called by us excavators *Sant'Antonio* after its owner and in keeping with the street.

Not that Anthony Ellingham was a saint: far from it.

But during the six seasons I had so far spent at *La Castellina,* going to *Sant'Antonio* at the end of a long week of dusty digging meant being headed to where scratches and sunburns would be cooled, hungry insides filled, and thirst for local wine and good company quenched, at least temporarily.

The vine pergola by the road was perfect for an *al fresco* party in autumn, but the terrace behind Tony's was the coolest spot to be on hot summer evenings. It looked across the valley towards the ridge of the ancient city-site of Tarquinia from this, its ancient necropolis.

Tony was a British ex-pat dealing in antiques, who at some time in the misty past had bought the first of three little buildings on *Via San Giacomo*, and spent the remainder of his money and life redecorating and expanding until he and his fortunate friends could range over that whole end of the block, or into the vineyard and pool in the valley below.

Unlike Marc Short, Tony Ellingham was refreshingly uninterested in me as, to be frank, a sex partner, being strongly attracted either to other men or to *objects d'art*.

True, it tickled him that I hailed from a city with the same name as his, and he loved to tease me about my accent, but otherwise I had been just another young face in a sea of young faces. But, when he had smashed up his vintage Morris Minor one dark evening six years back, I had written to ask how he was. Touched, he'd written back, and we'd been corresponding ever since.

Outside the Cotto family, Tony represented to me all that was generous and hospitable about Italy. If I sensed that some of the art on the walls was more expensive than he should have been able to afford—I've never seen even a *small* Morris Louis in a private house before—I refused to believe he was capable of any wrongdoing.

What can I say except that I was naïve? Maybe that was exactly why Tony liked to have me over for a chat, whenever I was in town.

Sant'Antonio showed itself in an entirely new aspect on that cold morning in early January than it did in summer. The sun poured through the leafless trees to add its warmth to that of the big fireplace in the big kitchen-cum-sitting area. As I hurried to shut out the chilly morning, Tony's liver-and-white springer spaniel Tiro trotted over to greet and be greeted.

The dog always had the air of one who knows his worth, perhaps because he had discovered the *hypogeum*'s false entrance, three years back.

"*Tanina.* It's been donkey's years," Tony smiled with genuine affection. "Your cheek is freezing, darling! I've just made scones. Sit! Sit! I'll bring them to you."

"I've never been here in winter before," I remarked, stuffing my wool hat into my jacket and hanging it in the armoire. "So cozy!" I sat down and gently pulled Tiro's silky ears.

"I like to think so. So, where is your handsome employer this morning?" he went on, extracting a cookie sheet from his industrial-sized oven and setting it on the range to cool.

"Touring the *scuola elementare* in Lido with Cloelia and Horatio," I replied, adding impulsively, "but he's missing a treat. What a lovely fire."

"Nice, isn't it? The older I get the more I appreciate a good fire. You will find me here at any hour, feeding it your odd twig. Help yourself, by the way: basket is to the right there. All my own rubbish," he added with a laugh. "Was pruning my little vineyard just last week."

I obliged him then sat as, with a snort of contentment, the spaniel curled up at my feet.

Tony looked keenly at me from under untidy salt-and-pepper brows. "Tiro likes you."

"He likes everybody." I laughed.

"Not everybody. He and Marc do not see eye to eye."

"Well, that makes two of us."

"Hmm." As the kettle began whistling, he went to it. "Tea or coffee, my dear?"

"Tea, of course."

"Of course," he laughed. Pouring the boiling water into a

big brown-betty pot he set it on the tray with a basket of scones, a bowl of whipped cream, and a jar of marmalade.

"It's real *chianina* cream," he pointed out as I helped myself to a scone.

"And these are real currants," I enthused. "Can't get them in the 'States."

He looked more stooped than I remembered him, with deeper frown lines between his arched brows, and a persistent cough. He set his half-smoked cigarette on a cracked dish.

"Smoking's going to kill you, *Tonino*," I told him.

"I've made some dangerous mistakes in my life, dear girl," he grinned, taking the overstuffed chair opposite. "I am therefore hoping for something much more dramatic."

"Surely not," I objected, pouring tea into already-milk-splashed cups.

He stirred sugar into his slowly, and took a long sip before answering.

"What do you really know about me, Miss Greenough?"

"That you are Italy's most hospitable man, Mr. Ellingham," I answered at once.

He toasted me ironically with his tea-cup. "Thank you, my most-naïve friend! I was sorry to hear that you and Marc Short are no longer an item, by the way. He promised that if I gave him my new Cooper, he would take you for a drive in it." He sighed. "My protégé has been staying here lately, when he isn't with his friend Cecco Casti, who is frankly not my cup of tea."

I said nothing, thinking of the pale young man I'd seen with Marc at the site.

Taking a long drag on his cigarette and blowing the smoke ceilingward, he mused, "It's a shame about you and Marc. I'd hoped you would make something of the man."

"Honestly, Tony," I sighed, "we're just no good for each

other! He hates for me to be independent, and I hate his bossing me around. And he is utterly amoral!"

"Don't you mean *amorous?*" He smiled.

"Oh, he's plenty amorous, Tony," I laughed bitterly, "with every woman he meets!"

"Who, then?" He looked me over. "You're not built for solo living, my dear."

"I'd better live solo, to work in my field." I countered with some heat.

"You might plow a good furrow in your field, *Tanina,* if you pulled as a *team* with someone. What if his wife were to *unharness* your handsome employer?"

"I'd say, 'Good luck to Caterina!' because Lavinia hates to be distracted from her Lexicon by the needs of babies. Or of anyone else," I added cattily.

"Meow." he laughed.

"Besides," I confessed against my better judgment, "to Dr. Lewis I am nothing but a nanny and cook-amanuensis. Hardly the basis for a life-partnership."

"Ah, but there's more to your Dr. Lewis than meets the eye. You've heard, of course," Tony whispered conspiratorially, his dark eyes sparkling with mischief, "that your precious *San Giacomo* knocked up his lesbian wife on these very premises? It took two bottles of my best Orvieto, but he banged her good, by God. And she *liked* it, from what she said to me next day."

Laughing guiltily, I took a second scone and ventured something about "Ratty's conception not being as *immaculate* as the Mole's."

He smiled. "I suppose you know why *San Giacomo* married her?"

"Rumors, Tony, only rumors," I said, shaking my head with seeming unconcern.

"*Oh. My. Dear.* I must tell you at once, even if it costs me my place on your Most Hospitable pedestal."

Settling his bony frame deep in his chair, tea cup and saucer resting on his belly, he began, waving a cigarette for emphasis.

"The story goes as follows: some three years ago, when he and the good Doctor had been fighting like cats and dogs. You can't imagine that, can you? But the man has a temper like Jupiter himself, over sleeping quarters, the heat, or something, he sits down, right where you are sitting now and says to me, *'Tony,'* he says, *'one fine day, I'll wring that woman's neck!'*"

"Why'd you marry her in the first place, old chump?" I tease him. "Anyone could see it wasn't a marriage made in Heaven."

"And you know what he says . . . ?

"'Blackmail, Tony, simple blackmail. First week I was in Princeton, she came to my intro seminar and she and I got talking afterwards. Stayed up all night talking, and do you know what? Those moth-eaten progenitors of hers forced me to marry her or lose my position?' Her father is some sort of high priest of Princeton Law School."

"Public Law," I clarified, "in the Politics Department. Princeton is weird that way."

"You already know the story," he cried, disappointed.

"No, no, I just know the Bradley-Arnolds. I took the Riverbankers to their house every weekend this fall, while I was covering the boss' classes. We chatted about law."

His smile became faintly unpleasant, like food gone a little "off."

"I'm afraid you are what they call a *facilitator,* my dear."

"Tony." I set my teacup down with a snap, "If one more person *blames* me for killing myself over that man's children, I swear I will . . . I don't know . . ." he was laughing, so I couldn't stay self-righteous for long, "I will toss my tea in his face."

"*Touché,*" he laughed, then continued, "Long story short,

her parents realized a rich prize had fallen into their web: a nice heterosexual fly to mask Lavinia's preferences and give them lovely grandchildren. Lavvy's Poppa wrote her a very strong pre-nup: *mess around, and I get any children and divorce you, but you can't divorce me, old chap, whatever I may do.*"

"Thought as much," I nodded, feeding the fire from the basket of trimmings.

"More than I did," he reflected, staring at my handiwork. "Thought that they were *both* closeted, for the sake of their almighty academic positions. My mistake."

"Oh, Tony, you didn't?" I asked incredulously, then burst out laughing again as he turned and said with loud emphasis,

"How was I to know? Gave him a nice feel-up when he stepped out of that shower *right there*." He rolled his eyes theatrically. "Talk about the temper of Jupiter."

The image of the encounter was so vivid that I howled with laughter, and was still recovering my breath when the clock in the kitchen struck nine. I wasn't due back at the house until lunch, but had an uneasy feeling that I needed to leave *now*.

Tiro awakened, listened, and began to growl.

Too late.

"Marc," said Tony somberly. "I was supposed to wheedle you into letting him back onto the site, but let's leave the dirty work to him, shall we?"

With a quick nod I got to my feet, saying with a sigh, "Take care of yourself, *Tonino*. Thanks so much for the nice cream tea. It was a lovely to see you."

"You are always welcome here. Come, give us a kiss," he smiled, not moving from his chair, and putting out thin arms to hold my face for a moment against his. "Such a short visit, my dear, but your boy hates to be kept waiting."

I responded with a kiss and a hug, startled by how slight he had become.

"Goodbye," I faltered, unaccountably weepy.

"Farewell, darling," he replied.

The moment I had bundled up, kept Tiro from getting out the door, and had shut it again behind me, I saw Marc, leaning on the gate, smoking. He tossed away the butt, curled one shapely lip, and sneered, "Finally."

Marcus Boethius Short, I must explain, is like a living, breathing Greek bronze: deeply tanned, muscular, perfectly formed, neither tall nor short, his dark hair curly, his eyes a rich hazel, his features faultless.

He had been Dr. Lewis' grad student but never earned his doctorate, instead working as a hired excavator and photographic technician at the site, and as such, I had known him for nearly as long as I'd known the boss, and very much in the carnal sense.

In our good times, Marc and I had been mad for each other, not caring where or when we made love, as long I protected myself with both chemistry and condoms, because even mad, I am no fool. No longer on the pill, I still had a stash of prophylactics in my pack, thanks to Marc.

He gazed at me in frank assessment as I let myself out of the gate.

"Looking good, babe, real good," he smiled, slipping a strong arm around my waist and pulling me close for a deep, deep kiss.

For a moment, I leant into him, lost in pent-up desire to kiss *someone.*

"Mmm, where you been, baby?" he murmured. "Busy with *massa?*"

"Why not just call me the n-word and finish your thought?" I countered, pushing him roughly away, my voice shaking with anger. "But thanks for reminding me why we're through!"

Fishing for my car-keys, I would have shouldered by him to the Fiat, but he jerked me back and pressed me against the iron bars of the gate, pinning my body there with his own.

"Aww, Mr. Short," I teased, to mask my fear and discomfort. "Always so sentimental."

"I'm just crazy for you, baby," he groaned, one hand gripping my wrist and his free hand roaming under my coat. "Remember that night here at Tony's, down at the pool?"

My skin tingled with a rush of desire. *We'd gone skinny-dipping, Marc and I.*

But in my mind, I heard Tony's voice: *he banged her good, by God, and she liked it.* Suddenly I saw *him* in the water—*San Giacomo* with not a stitch on—and pulled Marc closer, kissing him like crazy, hardly noticing that odd sound like a camera.

"God, babe, you've got to get me on the site with you," he panted, getting both hands under my blouse and sweater, still pinning me with his hot pelvis, "and spend every *pausa* with me in the camper. What a team, baby. With your brain and my camera, we'd be *rich*. Listen, I have to go into Rome for a couple of days for a photo-shoot, but let's do breakfast in town later this week, and you can tell me what the boss said about our proposal."

Catching a furtive movement in the corner of my eye, I recalled the camera sound and thought *blackmail or insurance?* Marc's words sank in with a flash of understanding.

"Okay," I said, wriggling free, "but don't hold your breath! I'll take a good look at the Hut Circle, before I agree to anything. Who gets rich off archaeology, anyway? No-one."

Releasing me with a laugh, he took no further action as I got into the car, backed it, turned, and took off down the narrow, walled street. But, in my rear-view mirror I could see him standing in the middle of the road, still laughing.

He clearly thought he'd gotten what he wanted. Now what I wanted was to go to the site and look for evidence of something that would make a person rich.

By the time I reached the Cotto's beach house on Lungomare dei Tirreni again, I was starving. I was snooping in the fridge when the equally-hungry Lewises arrived back from visiting the school. The Cottos were at Franco's girlfriend Angelica Iacomini's house for lunch at the other side of Lido, so it was just us for now.

Finding the makings on hand I'd decided to make *spaghetti alla carbonara*. It suited my mood to be ironic, and to make the Riverbankers happy. When four pieces of sponge-cake appeared on the table, I looked up.

"You missed this last night," said *il Prof,* avoiding my eye.

I could tell he was burning to talk in private, and I had a couple of thoughts to run by him myself, but for a long time nothing happened but eating and happy talk about the friendly people they'd met at the surprisingly good little school, and about the children's Italian skills.

"How have they kept up their fluency?" wondered Dr. Lewis, carrying dishes to the sink. "They understood almost everything they heard."

"Well," I replied slowly, "I guess we've been sort of speaking it at home."

"Yup," asseverated the Mole. "Tanny talks it all the time."

"As we've told you before, Papa," added the scratchy-voiced Rat in Italian.

I frowned, and responded in the same tongue, "I'll thank you not to speak that way to your Papa, Ratty. It seems a bit rude."

"Mi 'spiace, Tanina. Mi 'spiace, Papà," apologized the Rat.

"Saint Tanaquil strikes again," smiled the boss from the sink, so warmly that the antsy feeling returned worse than ever.

"What happened to our soccer game?" I complained. "Can't we do dishes later?"

"Sure, if you rinse this batch," agreed the boss promptly, removing his hands from the suds and drying them on a towel. "I'll locate the soccer ball. Saw it somewhere around here."

The dishes were rapidly rinsed. The ball was located, filled with air from a pump in the umbrella stand, and dribbled between the two Riverbankers down the winter-quiet, pine-shaded street, all the way to the beach. The air was sweet with wood-smoke.

"How was breakfast with Tony, Ms. River? Was Mr. Toad there?" Badger jammed his hands deep into the pockets of his jeans.

"Scones and tea, with a side of rude reminiscence," I answered with a meaningful glance. "And yes, the Toad was there. He was feeling his oats, if Toads do that."

"Was he now?" he frowned, his hands coming out and rubbing nervously together.

It struck me that he wanted very badly either to hold my hand or to wring Marc's neck, or both together. It struck me that I wished to goodness he would do the former, and soon. I dared not make the first move. They were *his* rules to break, not mine.

"Marc wants the Hut Circle back," I told him frankly. "Promises me the world if I help him get it, or more specifically, he promises wealth and unlimited sex. I said no to both."

"Good for you! Wealth?" He snorted. "From archaeology?"

"From antiquities smuggling, I suspect," I told him, lowering my voice. "I went back to the site just now, and guess what I found?"

"Hurry *up*," cried Clo from far out on the beach, running backwards.

"Throw the ball, Mr. Badger," chimed in the Rat.

"Can't look at it today," called their Papa to me over his shoulder, taking off at a run, "but tomorrow, we'll have the site to ourselves."

Our informal game of *calcio* began as a contest of girls against boys. When Franco and Angelica turned up with Angelica's brother Guido, it became U.S.A. vs. Italy.

Stretching my long limbs felt good, but being on the same team as *il Prof* was better still. He was nimble and canny; slim, ruddy and graceful; tireless and fearless in the press, guarding the Mole but leaving me to shield the speeding Rat and help him sink the goal.

And he's single! I thought suddenly.

We bought some Fanta on the way home, then ducked into a small *Cartoleria* open for the back-to-school crowd. Riverbankers wanted to get supplies, but I had thinking to do.

"Can I head back now?" I asked. "I'm happy to get them to school tomorrow, but I've got tons of reading to do before we go to the site tomorrow!"

"You got it," said the boss unquestioningly. "Go on back and when we're done here, I'll pick up some *pizza rossa,* get them to bed and scoot back to town, if you do morning duty. School starts at 9:00, remember. Shall we meet at the site at, say, 9:30?"

"Deal!" I said, and loped off to the house. Hurrying up to my room, I got out the rough sketches I'd made that morning at the Hut Circle and compared them with the copy of site plans the boss had given me. There were those strange features I'd seen, maybe made by Marc?

Suddenly I fell into a deep reverie, feeling again Marc's mouth on mine, his hands all over me, again imagining in his place—what was I calling him, *San Giacomo*?

Roused by the sound of a retreating scooter, I went downstairs for company and left-over pizza. Anna-Maria was in her study with book proofs, but Angelo was still there, reading the paper. An open bottle of Orvieto and a clean glass stood on the table beside my clean plate.

"Ah. Join me?" he smiled as I took my seat. "There's pizza, and cake."

"Perfect." I said gamely, pouring out. "How was your day, *Babbo*?"

I helped myself to *pizza rossa* and more sponge-cake.

"Splendid," he grinned. "They set the date: June 15, our own wedding day."

"Franco is *actually getting married?*" I goggled. "I thought you told me no-one in Italy gets married anymore. Housing's too expensive? High taxation? All that?"

"Blame yourself, *Tanina*," he said, refreshing my glass. "Now he is digging the Temple again, he will be able to mount an exhibition at the Museum, for which Giulia has promised him a raise. He's spent months reconstructing what we already have of the pediment."

All dug out of the ground by me, I thought, jabbing a vicious fork into my pizza.

"Anger doesn't suit you, *Tanina*," he said gently, raising his glass. "*Salute!*"

I raised mine with a sigh. "*Salute.* Congratulations to the happy couple!"

He drank deeply, then smiled.

"*Giacomo* is single, *Tanina.* What do you think of that?"

"Kind of freaky," I admitted through pizza. "How old is he, *Babbo?*"

"*Il Prof?*" He did a calculation in his head. "Thirty-five."

I nearly choked. "But, I'm just turning thirty. When did he start college?"

That brought a wide smile. "Didn't you know? He started his doctorate at nineteen."

"*Doctorate?* But that means he must have been—"

"Fifteen. He started college at fifteen. You've never heard that before?"

I blinked. "Is that why he is so frightened of women? He was always beating them off?"

"He was frightened of *one* woman. She had power of life or death over him."

I made a face. "Oh, surely not, Angelo."

He waved his glass at me.

"Oh, surely yes, *Tanina*. Take away his *Riverbankers* and what happens?" He made a dramatic gesture, like a man shot through the heart.

I knew how I would feel, if I could never see those two small people again.

"Oh, *Babbo*, that pre-nup of Lavinia's: Tony told me. And they are all he has to love."

"Not quite all," he insisted pointedly.

Why did I feel cornered? What was wrong with me?

"Hasn't he got a girlfriend or anything?" I argued, grasping at straws. "Half the undergraduates in his classes had a crush on him, so the temptation must have been hard to resist. Not someone here in Italy? Marc hinted that he there was a mystery girl he gave gifts to."

"Marc is a fool, and *you* are a fool, and blind! Has *Giacomo* never given *you* a gift?"

My mouth opened and shut. Then I pulled out the light silver chain out from around my neck. Suspended on it was my silver *drachma*: the source of my single clinch.

"Why do you wear it, if you feel nothing for him?" he asked, touching the coin lightly.

Hurt, I responded hotly, "I don't *feel nothing*, Angelo! Dr. Lewis is the reason I became an archaeologist: his passion, his genius, his kindness." I could feel tears rising. "I couldn't let myself think about it. I mean, it's *wrong*, loving your advisor, especially your *married* advisor. And a woman academic has no time for family."

"Yet you have taken time for *his* family."

"It was my *job*, a way to make a living," I began miserably.

"Are you saying you *don't* love them?" he goaded me. "You did it only for *money?*"

"*Babbo*," I clasped his hand on the table. "It was *never for money*. I would have *paid* money to see those children happy, to see him," my tears spilled over, darn them.

"To see him happy," he finished eagerly. "I knew it."

"Why doesn't he *show* me," I wept in a fierce whisper, "if he cares so much? I don't want to risk making a fool of myself if he doesn't, to risk having him—having him *knock me up* then leave me in the lurch. That's why I say, *I couldn't let myself think about it.*"

"Thinking, thinking," he muttered in disgust. "He says the same thing about you."

7

A VERY LONELY MAN

IT WAS A RELIEF TO KNOW THAT MARC WAS FAR AWAY IN ROME. Perhaps he was imagining that today, Monday, I would beg the boss for him to return to the site. It was even more of a relief to know I had both the boss and the site to myself. Maybe we could work a few things out.

By the time I'd dressed the Riverbankers in their new school-clothes, packed them a protein to go with their lunches (hot pasta provided by the school), bundled them into coats, crammed both them and their packs-full of fresh school supplies into the Fiat and driven them the three blocks to their school, it was a little before 9:00.

I kissed them both and made them promise to "tell me all" that afternoon, then drove off for *Pian di Cività*, wondering drearily whether even in this day and age the world would say: Ha. She slept her way to the top of archaeology—even if I never touched the man?

I was almost to the gate, taking the bumpy road at a far more decorous pace than I had the day before, when I heard a cheery *beep-beep* behind me. There in my rear-view mirror was a tall fella on a red scooter, grinning from under his black helmet, and my heart lurched with desire.

Whoa, Nellie, as Buster would say.

I slowed to a careful stop and he pulled up alongside, putting out a gloved hand, breath steaming in the damp, chilly air.

"Let's try your key. Bound to be pretty stiff the first time."

So, I killed the engine and handed over the keys as he maneuvered up to the gate, got the padlock open, the gate open, and returned. Handing my keys back our hands touched.

"Can you wash the windows while you're at it?" I laughed giddily.

"You must think you're in Oregon," he retorted, scooting off.

By the time I had locked up and pulled up at the camper, he had his helmet off and was stowing it in the little trunk behind the seat of the scooter. I had my Hut Circle plans under my arm. I also had my sketches of the strange new features the boss should see.

"Kids all safely delivered?" he asked as I joined him. "Wish I could have been there."

"Yes indeed! Clo skipped off hand-in-hand with that girl she met yesterday."

"Chiara? Terrific," he beamed, unlocking the camper and rummaging among the plans, producing one and spreading it out on the picnic table. "How about the Rat?"

"He and the other boys were kicking the *calcio* ball before assembly: got in trouble."

"Ha. A bonding experience. Thank you, Ms. G. Thank you, thank you, thank you. You are trading an awful lot of time and responsibility for a room with a hot shower, but I am so grateful you're there. It's," he looked down as if embarrassed or ashamed, "it's going to take me awhile to get their affection back. Do you think it would be good if I rented a place, just for us Lewises, and let you have some peace? Something less thrown-together, more planned out?" He squinted up at me uncertainly. "To thank you for all you've done for us?"

I had forgotten how thirsty I still was for thanks. I knew at once this was a key thing that had troubled me, that had made me pause and *think, think, think* over whether he was just using me. He hadn't said a thing, just now, about not being able to afford to rent a place—though I knew he couldn't—nor had he left me, the children's chief caretaker, out of his plans. He hadn't talked about himself or justified what he'd done.

In short, he was *not* being a selfish bastard.

But there was more.

"As for your teaching"—he paused to sigh deeply—"I've just heard from Dr. Potts about that cheating incident and I am 100% behind your decision, and told him so. I also received a copy of your student evaluations." He looked up again, as guiltily as if he wouldn't blame me if I bopped him over the head with a blunt instrument. "Some people blow off those evaluations, but I sure don't. The comments were overwhelmingly good. Did you read the one that starts, *I never imagined that Ancient Drainage Systems could be so gripping*? Spelling "ancient" and "imagine" incorrectly, of course. You are simply a wonder. It's what I meant to say last night, Tanny. Thank you, dear Tanny, for taking on an impossible task and doing it better than I could."

He reached out both arms to me in a gesture of apology and invitation. I walked right into them, earning myself such a sweet hug, and giving back as warmly as I got. If we lingered there a long moment, I reasoned, it was because so very many thanks were due, but the truth was it was healing. Something inside me was mending.

Maybe inside him, too. Maybe he had never meant for me to suffer like that.

"Well, then," he rallied himself as we released one another, "let's see what you've got on the Hut Circle. Thought I'd go down and force myself to look at the wreckage."

Accordingly, I set my edited plan side-by-side with the official master of the current levels of the Hut Circle, last updated, according to the note on the margin of the plan, in October of the year before.

"What are these?" he scowled at once, pointing to a series of little burrows I'd found along or under the new fence line. "And why is there a bite taken out of the mound?"

"That's what I was hoping you could tell me," I sighed.

He tucked my plans under one pea-coated arm.

"I'll help you open the *hypogeum* then go look over the Hut Circle while you wallow in the fresco for as long as you like. Fair enough?"

"Sounds great, boss," I grinned as he returned the master to its shelf.

Coming out, he shot me an unreadable look. We strode off together down the track, hands in pockets. It was a cold day of dull overcast: a typical Italian early-January. I tightened my scarf and turned up the collar of my coat.

Il prof sighed gustily. "I'm embarrassed to admit how little time I've spent at that part of the site. I was always at the Museum with the finds or digging up references for the vase publication and exhibition. Oh, speaking of exhibitions, the media will be here in force at the *hypogeum* exhibition opening Wednesday, remember. Even Angelo is considering wearing a tie. I, I hope the wine stain comes off your suit," he stammered. "I made a complete hash of your celebration last night, trotting out all that paperwork to show Angelo. I'd hoped it, that the celebration would be about you, not me."

"No worries," I assured him hurriedly. "Angelo explained everything, and what he forgot to say, Anna-Maria told me, the night before. Pretty sure Franco didn't mean to cause all that havoc! Anyhow, I dropped the suit off this morning;

should be ready in time and they said it would come right out."

"We are in the land of wine-stains, I guess," he joked weakly.

I forced myself to ask, "So how does it feel to be single?"

That got me a long look, which I did not meet.

"Hard to believe, really. I've got custody of the children, thank goodness."

"Really? Chalk one up for Prester John."

"Yes, yes, he's good. It's provisional, of course."

I did not ask what the provisions were, I suspected I knew.

A few hardy birds swooped along above us, loudly praising the quality of last fall's berries on the bushes along the path.

"They'll be drunk by this afternoon," laughed the boss. "Happens every year."

"Is Antonia-the-Owl still around?" Antonia was the big barn owl that had lived at the end of the promontory for as long as I could remember, terrorizing us campers in the summer nights with her eerie screech, her silent wings and her white, intent face.

"I imagine so," he shrugged.

A long silence.

"My sixth year at the site," I marveled, shaking my head.

He glanced at me. "A long time or a short time?"

"My whole life seems like. All the best parts." But still I didn't meet his eyes.

I also averted my eyes as we passed the Hut Circle, hurrying around the last corner of the well-worn path, then caught my breath at the changes wrought upon the north-ernmost end of *La Castellina*, sloping towards the distant purple ridges of Bolsena.

Last I'd looked, it was covered in a layer of earth and grasses, stitched here and there with wildflowers and shrubs. It was now laid bare, all its secrets discovered, or soon to be.

Cut back into the hillside was a flagstone-paved terrace bounded by a stone retaining wall. In the center of the terrace was a stone hatch perhaps a meter square, fitted with a bar of stout bronze, large enough for four hands to grasp.

We grasped it now, leaning well back to lift and slide the hatch into the neat groove that held it upright, its opening facing the cliff to the north.

After helping me down—it was only waist-deep, but he is a gentleman, and yes, I was very conscious of the touch of every one of his fingers on my hand and elbow, and encouraging me to use my phone for a flashlight, having forgotten the big steel mirror we usually used to light up interior spaces, Dr. Lewis set off for the Hut Circle, promising to take his time, explaining, "You'll definitely want a minute to look around."

I sat down cross-legged on the dusty limestone bier, carved to rise an inch above the rest of the floor of the squat chamber, all my senses on alert. The first thing I noticed was blood, the smell of it and the sight of it splashed over the walls of golden stone and in dark runnels alongside the bier.

I fancied I could see the pale shadows of vases outlined in spatters on the wall.

The next thing I noticed was a pulsating sound, as if of a generator someplace near at hand. It ran from the earth straight into my bones, setting my teeth on edge.

Maybe an underground river? I wondered. Limestone is known for that sort of thing.

Dismissing the faintly nauseating effects of both smell and sound, I turned my flashlight and attention onto the fresco. Of course, I had seen it in color film and photographs, but it was utterly different in person. The texture of the wall was distinctly different in the middle of the north wall upon which the fresco had been painted. There was a smooth area shaped like an old-fashioned tombstone. Or indeed like a small, arched doorway.

Had anyone told me about that or was I the first to notice it?

Then I began to study the fresco proper, my eyes mere inches from the plaster.

Against a white-washed background stood a city of blue walls, its ashlar blocks outlined in black. On the top of the wall black stick figures stood, tearing out their hair in standardized grief. At the base of the wall were heaped larger, more fully-rendered human figures. There were naked, red-skinned young men, clothed, white-skinned women, children, and old men, all lying dead, all pecked by neatly-rendered crows. On either side of this scene stood two figures. On the left was a man in a long white tunic, a wreath of green leaves on his head and a *lituus* in one hand, clutching his head in grief. On the right was a woman with wavy tresses on her shoulders, wearing a red hat, red boots and red long-sleeved, form-fitting dress, both hands raised in prayer.

In the sky above the city hovered small, green-winged female creatures, naked from the waist up, the straps of their blue fluttery skirts crossed at their shameless, red-tipped breasts. On their legs were high red boots and in their hands were long yellow torches alight with red fire.

They were Vanths, spirits who bring death by fever, whose iconography was the focus of my dissertation. But why put that fresco *here*? The Temple of Vanth and Tages had a terracotta pediment sculpture showing the birth of the god Tages and roof antefixes in the shape of Vanths. Its interior had plenty of room for frescoes, but we'd found nothing there like this.

The whole question of the function of the *hypogeum* was still moot, though underground offering chambers dedicated to the infernal gods had been found before.

Why here? Why a dead girl? Why all that blood and all that gold, all those jars of honey and olive oil and perfume?

To satisfy the hunger of something, of course, came the logical answer. *Something that loves to eat children, blood, gold, honey, olive oil and unguent, but not wine.*

Vanths like things that burn! Even gold burns. Wine quenches fire.

One of the obscure sources I'd read last fall in my quest for Vanth lore had been translated into Italian a century ago. It was a series of Albanian. folk-tales dwelling obsessively on the exploits of the *vanthu-piros,* the spirit bringing "death by fire." They gradually turned their victims into gold, first draining them of blood, then burning up their bodies with fever.

A footnote said this looked like a description of "fulminant hepatitis," which causes internal bleeding and yellow coloration of the skin and the whites of the eyes.

Looking more closely at the fresco, I saw it: a pale-yellow wash gilding each dead body, clear to see in the bluish light of my phone. I also saw that the arch-shape had nothing to do with the picture that sealed it.

Sealed it.

With one knuckle I tapped very gently on the center of the flaking surface.

Yes, it was hollow here! There were salty deposits, as if it were damper than the walls.

What if this fresco were sealing a doorway to another chamber – perhaps an oracle, or a mundus-*pit, connecting to the Underworld? What if this had originally been an antechamber to the main event? If all the offerings* here *were to appease and contain something* there?

That thought brought me all upstanding, so that I crowned myself on the low ceiling. Wincing, I leant around the stone lid and hollered, "Jim, Jim. Come quick."

A moment later he raced up the path panting, "What is it, Tanny? Are you all right?"

I explained what I had just seen, my words tumbling out just anyhow.

"Show me, show me," he begged. So, I hunkered to one side of the chamber and he stepped neatly in beside me, kneeling hip to hip. As he did so the pulsing sound surged to such a pitch that I nearly passed out, saying faintly, "Gosh, it's loud in here."

"What's loud?" he asked sharply. "Now, show me this arch of yours."

I showed him, and when he tapped where I had tapped, his eyes widened.

He whispered, "Pausanias describes an underground oracle in the wilds of Arcadia, where the consultant sleeps in the antechamber to commune with the hero-spirit of the pit beyond."

Then he turned the blue headlights on me.

"Tanny, you see what this means, don't you? It could be the epicenter of the whole sanctuary. Could the Hut Circle be like the village outside the *temenos* of Delphi, where consultants lived while they waited and where they made their offerings?"

"The ilex mound could be an ash altar," I cried, "like the great altar at Olympia."

"Yes. And the Temple held the images of the god, brought out for festivals."

"Consultants sought the power of the Vanth to curse their enemies, or to withdraw a plague—the great plague that filled the Place of Sacrifice with the dead we see here."

He raised an eyebrow at that old chestnut.

"Maybe! But one thing we can be certain of, Tanaquil Susannah Greenough," he declared resonantly, "is you are a blood genius without whom I would be utterly lost!"

And he pushed up his glasses and planted a celebratory kiss, right on my lips!

I have said he is an emotional man.

Maybe he had meant it for a fleeting congratulation, but I returned it so wholeheartedly, clutching him to my breast, and he came back at me with such a highly-focused blast of affection that it all quickly sloped past the ordinary boundaries of reason into the most intense sexual experience I'd yet had. Blooming coruscations of color shot through my being. He melted my bones, leaving me limp and breathless in his arms, like a dead thing myself.

"Why did you stop?" I murmured, my eyes blissfully shut.

"'Cos I thought you were dead," he whispered and set me carefully down. Stretching out beside me, he leaned on one elbow and stroked my wild hair.

"God, Pericles," I moaned, opening my eyes. "Where did you learn to kiss like that?"

"You inspire me," he smiled. "Pericles? Now, there's a name I never hear unless my mother is angry and uses the whole ensemble."

"Dr. Lavinia calls you James, and all your colleagues call you Jim. A kiss like that earns you special treatment," I remarked, tracing his fine profile with a finger-tip.

"Help yourself," he laughed, grabbing my hand to kiss it. "That name's been gathering dust, just like the rest of me."

"When is Franco due back, do you know?" I asked inconsequentially, rolling to face him.

"In a little bit," he smiled, going in for more. I gave him plenty. Pretty soon he was the one melting, all but one bit anyway. That was drilling into my thigh.

"You're not toying with me are you, Greenough?" he asked between drafts, drawing away with an effort. "Can I still call you that, by the way, or is it too *collegial?*"

"Call me whatever you like but don't call me late for breakfast," I whispered absurdly. "No, I'm not toying with you but I do have serious worries about love and work. As my friends and relations keep asking me: *what are your intentions?*"

"Why we aren't legally a team?" he cut in eagerly. "My question precisely. Tanny, will you do me the honor of marrying me and adopting the Riverbankers? I have a nice ring for you but I left it in my room. We could publish papers together, you could tell me where to dig, we could raise more babies. Please, Tanny, I'm such a lonely old geezer," he smiled wistfully.

"Geezer, ha," I whispered, pushing a strand of black hair away from his eyes. "You started college while still in nursery school! How did you fight off the cradle-robbers?"

He looked a little sheepish.

"I did have an older girlfriend in high school, an exchange student from Perugia: Luisa Bassi. She was sixteen, I was thirteen, not even entirely grown, and my mother kept a very strict eye on me. Lucky for Mom Luisa moved back to Italy at the end of the year, but not before teaching me a thing or two."

He smiled reminiscently.

I was seized with a sudden abhorrence for the name Luisa.

"In college I guess I was too obsessed with work to look at girl. Then Lavinia's parents blackmailed me into marrying her and I loved her the best I could. The thing is that I've always loved you Tanny, ever since Arca days," he sighed. "You were my pin-up girl. I kept your picture in my bedroom. I hope you don't mind!"

"That one of us together on the *Ara della Regina*? I saw that picture on your dresser one night last fall when I chased Tarquin-the-Cat into your bedroom. I noticed the look on my own face: so happy beside you, but you were so inaccessible! Marc maybe filled that empty place in my heart, but trying to love Marc is like, like throwing yourself into a briar-patch."

"Shall we get that image out of your head?" he laughed,

pulling me close. Then he broke away to ask sharply, "Wait, was that a 'yes?'"

"Mm-hm. A yes and a yes. And a yes," I replied, suiting actions to words. Then down we went into another tailspin, a free-fall of necking that somehow ended in him sitting cross-legged and me wrapped around him, sitting in his lap.

"Ooo-hoo," came a call from a little way off. "Where are you, *ragazzi?*" With a frantic effort I made myself decent and hopped onto the edge of the opening.

I called out, "Here, *Franceschino.*"

A moment later, Jim was standing in the hatch beside me running his fingers through his hair. "Tanny's found a second chamber," he panted.

Franco' eyebrows shot up as he looked from one of us to the other. "Truly? Well, there's pizza *per tutti,*" he grinned. "No rush!"

Off to the camper we went a moment later hand-in-hand, talking over our plans for what lay behind the blocked archway and for our future that now stretched ahead.

"Oh," exclaimed Jim. "I saw the 'odd thing' you found yesterday at the Hut Circle."

"Over by the swimming-hole path? A pit of about a cubic meter and some smaller ones?"

"Just so. Very suspicious. Much too square not to be man-made."

So, when we'd eaten, oblivious of the smiles and murmurings from Franco and his team before they went off to the Temple. Jim and I went down to the Hut Circle to give the bigger pit a look. Noticing a streak of yellow against a dark stone that formed part of the wall of the hollow, I borrowed Jim's wedding ring and scratched it against the selfsame rock. It left a nearly-identical streak, though the first was a richer yellow.

"Gold has been stowed in here, best beloved," I whispered.

He was too close to my ear. We had to take a break for a bit more smooching.

"Look," he whispered excitedly, reaching into the pit. "It still is."

On the worn tip of his Marshalltown trowel was a tiny circular cup of gold.

"Haven't I seen that on the pectoral?" I shivered. "Isn't is half a *crotalis*?" *Crotales* being the little jingle-bells decorating the edges of the *La Castellina* pectoral.

"I sure hope not. Let's give it a close look tomorrow when the exhibition opens. Gee," he sighed, "the kids get home from school in an hour. Any way I could run by my room in town for your ring, then meet you at Angelo's *asap*?"

"Sounds like a plan," I grinned. "And I think I have the needed things in my backpack."

"Oh, thank God," he said fervently. "I was going to beg a fistful off Franco."

Once we were back at the Cottos we took up where we left off by mutual unspoken agreement—me with a prophylactic from an ancient Marc-stash in my pack and Jim with more than enough wherewithal to fill it—but it was awkward at first. I'd be a liar if I said it wasn't.

We'd feverishly removed our clothes but then what? Oh, he looked good, there was no doubt he did: fit and comely. I'm pretty sure from the way he flushed up red all over that I looked good to him, too, but honestly, when you've taught yourself to think of a person as untouchable all of your life together, it's going to take more than comeliness to overcome it, if you know what I mean.

What did Jim say about the key? *Bound to be pretty stiff the first time?*

"Damn," I muttered, not touching him. "It's like making love to my father."

"I thought we'd agreed that I wasn't that old," he said diffidently, hanging his head.

"No-no-no," I burst out. "It's the whole advisor-student thing."

"I've asked Dr. Potts to take over as advisor," he explained, sitting cross-legged as before and inviting me down, "so there will be no conflict of interest and I will be working to get us a joint position so we can have more time with the kids."

"Mmmm," said I, then lowered myself until deliciously spindled, my arms and legs tucked snugly around him, adding significantly, "a joint position."

Then I kind of lost track of advisors, students, everything.

That night we treated everyone to *bistecca fiorentina* and Vino Nobile del Montepulciano at a favorite local restaurant and Jim gave me a lovely ring in rich yellow Etruscan gold. Its ruby signet was carved with a winged Psyche leaning, lamp in hand, over her Cupid. Once I gave him my Princeton Master's ring the betrothal was official, to be cemented on the first weekend Prester John and All Saints Rome had open after the paperwork was translated.

The Riverbankers approved, thank God, though Ratty looked a little thoughtful.

At the dinner Jim raised his latest glass of the garnet-red wine and gave the speech he'd planned for the night I ran off to my room.

"Last time I tried this," he began parenthetically, looking over his glasses at Angelo in mock sternness, "someone spilled the beans about my divorce papers and poured wine on the guest of honor. Please join me in thanking and honoring Tanaquil Susannah Greenough, whose right-hand man I aspire to be, and without whose goodwill and hard slogging my beloved children would have long since pined away (or run away), so that I could never have (nearly) completed my work on the Vases of the La Castellina *Hypogeum,* who moreover suggested we remove the over-burden of soil from La Castellina to expose the *hypogeum* entrance in the first place. I believe her exact words were, *'heck yes, boss, we can manage it.'*" Laughter sounded. "Who has now identified a second chamber off the original." Gasps rose. "Yes, it's quite true, and who has unselfishly agreed to supervise the Hut Circle, largest and messiest area of the site . . ." Prolonged cheers. "And who has now, thanks to the mysterious workings of God."

"And Venus," cried Franco to more cheers.

"Agreed to be my partner for life and foster-mother to my children."

"And mother to several more, most likely," inserted Franco, emboldened by past success, only to be raucously booed by his mother. I covered my face with my hands.

Jim raised a hand for silence and choked out, "To Tanny," as the others chimed in.

Jim sat, pushing up his glasses to wipe his streaming eyes. I leapt to my feet, raising my own glass in turn. "Though I suspect there is no precedent for a woman toasting her best beloved at a betrothal, hear me out: I will be brief."

"Hear, hear," grinned Franco. Jim smiled beatifically.

"I'd like first to honor one of the longest, most-correctly-used series of relative clauses in oratorical history." I joked to laughter, adding hastily, "I only want to say . . . oh my, this is difficult. I wish I'd written it out. That it has been my distinct honor to be of service to the finest man of my acquaintance, the best father and most considerate of employers, not to mention a dam-fine archaeologist, *whom* I love with all my heart and *with whom* I hope to continue to work, and play, for as long as I live."

"To Pericles." I finished, and we kissed on it.

"To Pericles." They all laughed, as the Riverbankers screamed and covered their eyes.

Reasoning that word would leak out in any case we took the *paparazzi* bull by the horns and sent a text that very night to Françoise Pinard at *Paris Match* with the basic facts: long-term "understanding," complex paperwork, imminent wedding, joint position sought once doctorate earned, ideally with Princeton University.

Mlle. Pinard begged for an exclusive photo-shoot at the site next day, promising to be discreet and not to interfere with our "important work." One of Angelo's specialists was hurrying up from Rome in the morning to work out how to take off the plague fresco. Other than that, we had no specific plans besides working out the Hut Circle debacle.

As for what happened in my little room after Mole and Ratty went to sleep that night, suffice it to say that the Badger rolled his scooter down the driveway not long before breakfast next morning, leaving behind a very sleepy River and not a single usable condom.

8

"THE LADY OF THE RINGS"

The second Tuesday in January dawned clear and cold in Lido di Tarquinia. The bare deciduous trees and graceful pines were etched black against the rich lavender sky. The children, alternately running and skipping down the leaf-strewn streets, were eager to get to school and I was eager to get to the site. I hoped to start organizing the wreckage of the Hut Circle.

Turned out that Jim was even more eager. He had arrived at the site well before dawn. Finding the padlock on the wrong side of the gate, I gave him a shout.

"Hey, sleepyhead," he called out, strolling up. "Where've you been?"

"Uh, getting your children to school?" I laughed as he opened the gate.

"Our children," he corrected, my arm around his waist and his around my shoulders. "Adoption papers coming soon," he added, pausing for a proper greeting.

"Get any sleep?" I asked.

He shook his head. "Had any coffee? Just made some."

"Nope," I admitted. "Barely got dressed in time!"

The good fragrance of fresh espresso met us at the camper. Boiling up a little off-the-shelf milk, he fixed me a *caffe latte* which I drank seated on his knee – or tried to. He rummaged in my clothes and we started in again like kids in a candy store.

Suddenly *Paris Match* was at the gate. Scrambling to tidy up, we were made to pose. Lewis and Greenough, frowning over the ilex mound, trowels in hand. Greenough and Lewis, spreading the site plan out on the picnic table by the camper. L. & G. pointing out key features to the press. G. and L. walking hand-in-hand down to the *hypogeum,* where G. consulted with the newly-arrived fresco team as L. explained to Françoise what might be behind it.

But the single photograph that gave us the most trouble was one of our two right hands side-by-side, showing off the very rings that in a month or so would be transferred permanently to the ring fingers on our left hands. Jim's would by then be expanded by a jeweler from pinkie-to normal-size, but its Princeton motto, Dei sub numine viget—Under God's power she flourishes—was already clearly legible, just as Cupid and Psyche were clearly visible on mine.

I only mention the details because later someone changed them.

Escorting Mlle. Pinard and her photographer back to town via Fiat, we treated them to lunch at Toscana, a favorite hang-out of the Museum crowd, famous for its *cacciucco* made with fish straight from the market at Lido and bread made on the premises. By the time we returned, the fresco guys had finished up and left the padlock on the outside of the gate.

We went home to do some work on the site plans but I'm embarrassed to say we accomplished absolutely nothing useful. When it was time to meet the children at school, it was clear the glad news had leaked out. Housewives were standing on front steps watching us go by, arms folded, talking about us with their neighbors, waving and kissing their hands to us, calling *"Auguri. Tanti auguri."*

That evening, by working with Angelo and Franco, we were at last able to work out a way forward at the site until the fresco was removed and could see what lay beyond the *hypogeum.* That evening I also called my mother, knowing that today's pictures would soon be leaking around the world. I didn't want her to hear the good news from some stranger.

But she knew all about it, and not from the news.

"It's been very hush-hush. Johnny told us just after you left that he's been working on those divorce papers, *kyare,* and you can bet we called your Pericles, right after *that!* Buster gave him a talking-to and warned him there would be hell to pay if he didn't treat you right."

I laughed, easily imagining that conversation.

"Did John-Allen tell you how he managed it, *Mor*? Kind of a surrogate-mother/sperm-donor mutual-aid project?"

"I don't like to talk about it on the phone. It's a little too up-to-date for me.

"But you're happy?"

"Ecstatic, so long as he lets you have children of your own."

"Let's me? The trick will be getting him to hold off until I defend my dissertation."

"So, when's the wedding? I need to buy a plane ticket. Buster won't come."

"Sometime in the third week in February. It's the "snow week" holiday but the translator is pretty confident she'll have the paperwork done by the end of this month."

"Valentine's Day would be nice, especially with that Cupid on your ring."

"I hear they have a big mass-wedding in Trani that day at Saint Valentine's tomb."

"If it isn't in Rome, I'm not coming! Where are you buying your dress?"

A long conversation followed, if you can call it that, me pushing for my gold suit and *Mor* insisting on an excuse lend me her mother's veil edged in *Hardangersøm* embroidery.

"I refuse to wear your regional costume if that what you're thinking," I said heatedly.

"Of course not. But my *solje* would look lovely on a simple white dress. They are wonderfully good luck, *solje*. Reflect away evil glances."

In the end I let her dress me however she liked, but my gold suit was beautifully clean by the next day, Wednesday, our big day with the media, thank goodness. Because far more hung on that exhibition opening than I could have possibly imagined.

We knew it would be a media zoo, what with the fame of "*La Castellina* Golden Boy J. P. Lewis" as *Panorama* called him, and the fact that our engagement news seemed to have lapped the earth's rotation four or five times. But not that today's zoo would breed so many more.

Since the world was seeing the jewelry collection for the first time since being unearthed the previous August, the Tarquinia National Museum intended also to teach the world a lesson on Etruscan culture. Museum Director Dr. Giulia Pantano set forth an itinerary that included all the museum's most prized possessions, from the Sarcophagus of the Spouses and the Apollo of Veii to the wonderful Winged Horses from the *Ara della Regina*.

And gold from the standing exhibition was also on display, alongside the *La Castellina* Treasure. Everyone likes gold. The more the merrier! Giulia certainly liked to wear it, from the rich studs in her ears down to a little Arezzo-gold chain on her ankle.

We certainly didn't expect any of the pieces to turn up missing.

I am something of a super-student, and insist on printing out useful materials when I go anywhere so it was natural that I had with me print-outs of the remarkably-good pictures taken of the jewelry *in situ,* before the *hypogeum* was emptied. I wanted to understand which item had been where and to compare it with how they were now displayed.

Honestly, I was so enthralled by the prospect of seeing them in person at last that I was entirely unconscious of the cloud of media witnesses observing in detail not just the objects, but also me and Jim.

There was a close-up in *Il Messaggero* of me frowning over the incised circles on the bone handle of the wicked iron blade found forced through the poor victim's windpipe and into the bier below. There was another of me smiling at a lovely oak wreath from an entirely different site. But there was also one of me pointing to my print-out and whispering to my best beloved,

"Pericles, where are the rings? Look at this photo from the opening. She was wearing a ring on every one of her fingers and I haven't seen a single one on display."

"Nowhere?"

We had been bitterly disappointed by the sight of a little cream-colored card where the great gold pectoral should have been, printed with the unedifying words, "Removed for further conservation." We had even argued over the appearance of one of the big granulated earrings, which seemed to me to be an entirely different color of gold than its twin.

"Dr. Pantano," I now asked innocently, "where are the girl's rings?" expecting to be told, *"You twit, they are right there in the case behind you,"* and *not* trying to make trouble.

"What rings, my dear?" she asked matronizingly, if a woman who looks regal enough to rule a small country can seem at all motherly.

"These," I said helpfully, holding up the print-out of the girl's skeletal hands.

The media crowded in to snap pictures of the picture. Some captured a shot of my own ring as well. To my absolute amazement Giulia said loftily, "I don't know what you mean. I have never seen those rings before in my life."

"But Dr. Pantano," I gasped ill-advisedly. "Aren't they in the vault? Or do you mean to say they never made it from the site to the Museum? Dr. Pantano." But she had turned on her heel and was stalking away, almost the whole media crowd snapping all around her, asking, "What is this about rings, *Dottoressa*? Do you admit they have gone astray?"

"Tanny, how could you?" cried Jim, grabbing my arm. "Giulia is our meal-ticket to continued work at the site. Even Angelo can't save us if she withdraws her support."

"But Pericles," I insisted, trying to wriggle free and wanting to weep, "where did they go? And where *is* the pectoral, really, and why *is* that earring a different color than the other?"

Out of the corner of my eye I saw the gleam of cameras, too late.

"Now look what you've done," growled Pericles in disgust, flinging me from him.

I burst into tears.

Our first fight right out here in the open with a growing circle of listeners. I ran like a coward for the stairs to the rear exit and darted into the ladies' restroom halfway there, leaving Jim to face the media alone.

I let myself weep freely for a moment before splashing cold water on my face and mopping it off with paper towels, accidentally knocking into the sink a bottle of hand-cream labelled *Egyptian Preservative Elixir*—a favorite brand of Giulia's.

It was made by a company called *Argo Omeopatica,* its logo a Greek warship known as a *penteconter.* On the sky-blue label was the very same picture of T. E. Benevento from Auntie Mary's diary staring back at me with the words *Our*

Founder in sweeping copperplate letters beneath it. Printed on the reverse I found *Via del Fico, 3, Firenze. IT.*

No wonder he had looked so familiar! I had seen this bottle a million times!

I had the uneasy sense this was no coincidence.

Darting out, I fled to Piazza Soderini where the Fiat was parked, ready to back to my room and starve myself to death rather than look Jim in the eye after embarrassing him publicly, but Mlle. Pinard caught up with me.

"Tanaquil," she called, rushing in front of the car. I braked and rolled down my window. I was relieved to see that she'd left her photographer behind.

"They tell me, *cherie*, that you the only member of the excavation team trained in metallurgy. Is that so?"

I shrugged. "I suppose so. Each of us brings special expertise."

"So, you would say that the earring made of paler gold seems out of place?"

"I would say that if it were tested for purity and trace elements it would prove not to be made of the same gold as true Etruscan work, most of which comes from a mine near Arezzo."

"How would you explain that?"

I looked around anxiously. *Why had no-one else yet come out? Where was Jim?*

"There was another ancient mine in Etruria?" I suggested feebly.

"But you don't think that is the reason. What do you think?"

"I think the original is missing, replaced with a replica made of some kind of alloy."

"What about the rings? Why haven't they also been replaced with replicas?"

"If Dr. Pantano is right, and they never made it to the

Museum, they must have been stolen from the site immediately after they were found, and never catalogued."

"Didn't Dr. Lewis remove the jewelry from the ashes of the girl with his own hands?"

"No, there were conservators, photographers," I began, then saw a vision of Marc Short glancing about furtively before sweeping the whole collection of rings into his camera bag. "They would be difficult to reproduce since each ring was set with a signet, like this."

I held out my hand with Jim's ring on it. She grabbed it for a close look.

"Etruscan is it not? Very beautiful," she murmured.

"Dr. Lewis bought this at the monthly Antiquarian Fair at Arezzo," I said. "It was found in a tomb nearly a century ago, then became part of a private collection."

"Is that so? Well, let me congratulate you on your engagement. Such a fine man!"

Turning hastily away, she was already unslinging her computer bag, no doubt rushing to write up a juicy article from my foolish confidences.

Starve myself? Why not just go hang myself? I reflected, realizing what I'd said about the jewelry possibly being faked and knowing our funding might well be sunk.

Driving off towards Lido, I wished with all my heart that it had been the Attic pottery and not the gold that had been put on display first. It is Jim's true passion, and there would have been no stealing and melting down, no argument with me about gold color, only the glorious collection he had worked so hard to conserve and present.

How wonderful were *those vases?*

Art historians prepare to drool—the announcement sounded in my head—as I list what he found: an Exekias black-figure bell krater (ca. 545 B.C.E.) full of wheat, on its obverse Eurykleia washing the foot of Odysseus as he clutches her throat, on its reverse Odysseus plowing with a donkey & an ox, watched by Palamedes, who holds baby Telemachus; an Exekias black-figure lidded amphora (ca. 545 B.C.E.) full of oil, on its obverse Diomedes bending over the sleeping King Rhesus with a sword, on its reverse Diomedes driven in Athena's chariot; a Euphronios red-figure calyx krater (ca. 510 B.C.E.) full of some cheese product, possibly yoghurt, on its obverse Nestor challenging Memnon, on its reverse Penthesilea challenging Achilles; a Berlin Painter lidded amphora (ca. 470 B.C.E.) full of honey, on its obverse a girl in a bear costume, holding a palm, on its reverse a poetess wreathed in asphodel, declaiming poetry; a Penthesilea Painter pyxis (ca. 460 B.C.E.), full of scented unguent, with a white-ground frieze depicting Baubo exposing herself (outside cave) before Demeter (in cave); and finally an Achilles Painter lekythos (ca. 445 B.C.E.), full of milk, with a white-ground frieze in which a living mother says farewell to her dead daughter.

It was easily the single most important trove in the history of Attic pottery. Men had sold whole collections of coins, and even murdered, for just one Euphronios vase.

But gold as we've seen is my *forte.* I did not think for a moment that Jim took the rings and I knew very well I was not wearing one of them. By Thursday morning, however, a strange image had appeared on the internet: the *Paris Match* photo of our two hands, but in place of our own rings, images of *two of the missing rings appeared on our fingers!*

Whoever had the rings must have faked this, it seemed to me, *to throw the authorities off their trail,* but I knew the results would still very bad.

I may be a cock-eyed optimist, but I had seen enough in the past six months to know how little the truth matters to tabloids.

But I get ahead of myself.

That awful Wednesday night I put myself to bed without any dinner. I peeped out early Thursday morning to find a horrible heap of papers on the breakfast table with headlines like *Prof Steals Gold to Impress Girlfriend* and *Girl Friday Shows a Taste for Stolen Gold* and even the loathsome *Side Benefits of Field Work Include Swag and Sex With Boss.*

Il Messaggero was now calling me *Signora Degli Anelli* ("The Lady of the Rings") and proposed a series of questions for me to answer. *How valuable are they? Who took them? Where are they? We think she knows but will she tell us?*

There was the whole exclusive *Paris Match* interview with me, "a brilliant quiet-spoken young woman of color," alongside a picture of the empty museum display case and its small card reading "Removed for further conservation," and underneath the screaming headline, "But Pericles, Where Did They Go?" with my observation that the rings had never been catalogued.

Hoping that the Riverbankers were getting what they needed, I remained on strike from the world, sipping water but eating nothing, continuing to wish I were dead.

Towards evening, the one voice I couldn't resist was heard outside my door, all the others having been ignored. Ratty whispered hoarsely, "*Mor,* please come out."

What had he just called me?

"*Mor,* Papa is sorry he got angry with you."

I had that door open faster than you could say, "Jack Robinson."

There stood the frowsy Rat, adorably ready for bed, his short, wet, red hair combed straight up into the air. "*Rattuccio,* what did you just call me?"

"Oh, that," he grinned proudly, coming in and sitting on the bed. "I figured that out. Can't call you 'Mamma.'"

"No," I agreed. "It's taken."

"And Caterina likes it if we call her *Zia.*"

"Oh, does she? So, what will you call my mother if you steal her name?"

"I don't know. What do you call *her* mother?"

"*Bestemor.*"

"That, then."

He grew sober, crawling onto my lap and into my arms.

"Papa is scaring us, *Mor*," he whispered. "He started to read to us, but now he won't say anything. Clo is crying."

Angelo, I suddenly saw, was right behind him. His eyes were full of worry.

"Please, *cara,*" he murmured.

A weepy Clo ran over to me the minute I appeared at the bottom of the stair. She was also damp and adorable and her Papa-eyes big with fear. There sat Jim at their bedside, staring into space like the lost soul in the Sistine Chapel.

Anna-Maria was watching him with concern. Angelo asked if I were hungry but I shook my head. I whispered to the Riverbankers, "Give me a minute with Mr. Badger, then I'll come read to you. Come on, Pericles," I said gently. "Let's go outside. I'll get our coats."

He got up. We got to the far part of the garden lit only by a faint starshine. No neighbors could hear us here. Their doors and windows were all shut against the chilly night. I pulled down two summer chairs from where they leaned against the wall and we sat down.

As if on cue, Jim put his head between his hands and began to sob full out: big Homeric sobs. If he'd broken my heart earlier, now he utterly wrung it.

"You're going to leave me," he choked out, "and I don't blame you a bit! Angelo says that the closer you get to someone the more you can hurt them."

I reached for his cold hands saying mournfully, "I'd give anything to go back and eat my words. You know I would, Pericles!"

He looked up, shaking his head.

"No, it was the truth. When I saw that I'd let those rings slip away without noticing, I was furious with myself, but lashed out at you. I killed the messenger!"

"Shall I give you something to be really angry with me about?" I offered. "Read this."

I showed him the message I'd received that afternoon from Marc: *Hey, baby just heard the news you and your massa are getting hitched. Tony says I'd better get used to it, but after Sunday, I was hoping for better. Meet me at Bar Impero. Marc.*

He raised one heavy eyebrow. "Sunday? *Massa?*"

My face went hot to the ears. "You know how I used to like calling you *the boss?* That's Marc's racist twist on it," I sighed. "Sunday he was at Tony's when I left and he tried to *convince* me into asking you to get him back onto the site," I looked down. "I remembered in time who I was kissing and told him to get lost."

"Kissing?" He was incredulous. "But that was *the day before yesterday.*"

"Meaning the *day before you and I finally straightened things out between us,*" I countered hotly. "We haven't dated since he left me for Karen Larsen five years ago."

"And by *dated* you mean 'had sex' I take it," he said in no little disgust.

"How dare you judge me," I raged. My eyes filled at once with tears. "You were *married,* remember? I knew the rules. No touching. No even *imagining* more than employer-employee relations. I was lonely as hell and you were always nearby setting off all my alarms."

"And Marc put out the fire. Is that it?"

I wiped my face without the benefit of one of his hankies.

"I guess. Oh, years ago, I thought I loved him but he was incapable of loving me back. Something's wrong with him. His parents were messed up. For a while I treated the relationship the way he did: as something fun to do when he was in town. Finally, he was so cruel that what love I had left just evaporated.

Call it a childish crush! *When I was a child, I talked as a child, I thought like a child..."*

"When I became a man, I put childish ways behind me. Are you saying you were a *child* on Sunday and here on Wednesday you are an adult?"

"I just kissed him, Pericles, and I have to say it felt good," I cried passionately. "I was single on Sunday, and looked to be single forever! I was half-planning to go work at Ca' Foscari just to get you out of my system. Otherwise I would be right up next to you non-stop all this spring without hope of any change. I was, oh I was horny as hell on Sunday! But believe me, the illusion didn't last long: I could feel him using me, so much so that you could argue I used *him."*

"Meaning . . . ?"

I groped for words.

"For an instant, for an instant I imagined it was *you* I was kissing," I burst out. "It's like what you just said about his putting out the fire. Maybe it's been *you* I've imagined I've been with the whole time I've been with him, *you* I've been 'dating!' But now I feel as if everything is, is finally true. Really *true* in the sense of being in alignment. Finally, the right thing is happening. I've finally joined the human race."

I paused to capture one of his hands in both of my own.

"I finally know what all those love songs are about, Pericles. I never mooned about Marc all night or missed him the minute he was gone." I pressed his hand to my cheek.

"And now you do?" He watched me with curious detachment.

"Cruel man, of course I do! Don't you miss me when I'm gone?"

"Is it kind of a dull ache around here?" he laughed shortly, putting his spare hand over his heart. "Yeah, I'm familiar with that feeling. Had it every night after driving you home."

"For years, maybe," I ventured, "you and I have hovered around the truth. We've been *thinking,* Angelo calls it, without daring to act on it. But the truth was there all the same. Yesterday," I looked up and caught his earnest glance, "I was the happiest human on earth. Now everything matters more, but everything hurts more, too. I think I got callous about hurting Marc every time he hurt me. I wanted to die for shaming you like that, Pericles. If Ratty hadn't come up to my room, I happily would have walled myself in there for good."

"Thank goodness for Ratty," he said soberly. "Yes, *everything matters more, hurts more.* It was as if you were an extension of myself, as if I owned you, as if what you said to those newspaper people were a personal offense. I never used to feel that way about you. You have always been an admirable, independent-minded colleague. Even when I was fantasizing about you in my spare time," he added with a wry smile. "Now, when I was angry at you it was because I was furious *with myself.* Do you understand?"

I nodded grudgingly. "I am never so angry as when I'm angry at myself. When I get distracted and break something or say something unspeakable."

He put a hand into his hair.

"It just boiled up in me! I swear I'll do better if you will forgive me this time. And promise me that you won't stop asking tough questions, just to spare me?"

I took his shoulders in my hands and looked him in the eye.

"How about I argue with you in private instead of right there in front of the cameras?"

He laughed. I could feel his tense frame relax.

"When I left the Museum on my scooter," he admitted, "I was in such a funk that I had a near-miss with a car at the roundabout. I kept wishing it hadn't missed."

I threw my arms around him, smelling the good wool smell of his coat.

"You are not allowed to be hit by a car or be hurt in any way, Pericles, do you hear me? Do, and I'll immolate myself!"

"That's settled," he sighed contentedly. "We can't live without each other."

9

SOMETHING WICKED

That night I sent a message: *Hey, Marc. Got to be at the site early. Can be at Bar Impero @ 7 AM. Tanny.*

Almost immediately I got back, *I'll be there. M.*

My Tanny-sense was bristling when I walked into Bar Impero Thursday morning. I was glad to see that at least there were no *paparazzi* hovering. I did see Marc a split-second before he saw me. He was talking with a large pale youngish man who sat by the front door. Looked like the "fishy-looking guy" Jim had spotted at the base of the cliff on Saturday.

Both of them wore black from head to toe, and hoodies. *Hiding from someone?*

I walked past them unconcernedly to the cashier. By the time I'd paid for my coffee and looked around again, Marc was sitting nearby. The other man was on the other side of the room reading his phone. I collected my *caffe latte* and joined Marc, kissing him on both cheeks and murmuring, "*Ciao Marco!*"

"Getting your 'Mrs.' at last, Greenough?" he sneered, smiling a fanged smile. He looked around theatrically. "Golden Boy still snoozing at your place?"

Stifling a strong desire to spit in his face I said coolly, "Pericles is at the Museum."

"*Peri-cleees,*" he parodied me in a sing-song voice. "So, are you sleeping with Franco, too, to collect the whole set? Angelo seems a little old for you but . . ."

I got up to leave. He grabbed my arm making a contrite face.

"Sorry babe, but Sunday I thought you were mine. You're *still* mine."

I sat down and peeled off his hand. I was tired of being grabbed by men.

"Sunday was farewell," I said. "*Thanks for the memories* sort of thing."

"So you *say.* Your body told me different."

"My body was lonely, Marc," I replied in a heated undertone. "Like yours is every time you meet an old flame."

"So, are you *lonely* for this Pericles of yours or is this just a little social climbing?"

I sighed. "Why are we meeting, Marc?"

"Like I said: I want back on the site."

"You seem to have forgotten, *caro,*" I informed him, slowly stirring my coffee, "that for better or worse the Hut Circle is *my* area now."

"You seem to have forgotten, *cara,*" he parroted, "that *I own you.* Would you like *Pericles* to see *this?*" And there on the screen of his phone was a picture of us, leaning up against Tony's gate in a passionate clench, my hand gripping his derriere.

I thanked a merciful Providence for the warning tingle of my Tanny-sense that had kept me from going any further that day.

"He already knows," I said, fighting down shame and fury and returning the phone. "If you show it to the media, I'll admit it. Besides, who has pictures taken of himself with girls?"

"Okay then," he went on seamlessly, "how about we get you the Temple back? I could fix it so Franco doesn't come into work some morning."

"The Temple is Franco's fair and square. I had no right to it."

"*Pericles* had no right *to fire me,*" he hissed.

A long pause as he stared at me. "So, you're not going to get me back in?"

"Nope."

Getting to his feet, he shook a finger under my nose and growled, "Oh, you'll be sorry. You will be *so* sorry." As he left, the other man fell into step behind him.

If I'd missed seeing the media at Bar Impero, the crowd when I got to the site gate should have cheered me. In the time it took to park the Fiat outside the gate and awkwardly reach through the gate for the padlock, fumbling with my keys, five correspondents rushed up.

Keep it simple, Jim had advised me. *Better still provide a written statement.*

No written statement. I would have to stick with *simple*.

"Signorina Greenough. Any developments on the missing rings?"

"Yes, last night Dr. Lewis began a thorough review of site records. He will be here later with a report on his findings."

"Do you think this theft is the work of the gang who attacked the site in Val di Chiana?"

"We are still hoping for a simpler explanation." I replied and got my key into the lock.

"Like carelessness among the Museum staff?"

"Not at all. The filing system is quite complex."

"We know you are engaged to marry Dr. Lewis. Is it true you are already pregnant?"

"No, but today I will start work on an area called the Hut Circle," I said as pedantically as possible, my heart racing with anger, "which we hope will tell us a great deal about daily life in the third century B.C.E."

I had the gate open by now and slipped through. Not daring to leave it open long enough to get the Fiat through, I left it to the mercy of the media. I noticed that the Range-Rover was safely inside, along with a battered white passenger van, but no red Vespa. Feeling a chill of worry, I set an alarm to call Jim in twenty minutes if he did not appear in the meantime.

The van had just discharged a crowd of ten to fifteen young people. They now milled around the camper, talking vigorously. The van had just discharged a crowd of ten to fifteen young people. They now milled around the camper, talking vigorously.

Angelo introduced them to me as his students, members of his field-work class from Rome, most of whom would be working at the Hut Circle with me on weekdays for the next month, camping at the site. It was a huge relief. So much needed doing. As we walked together down the track, I pointed out the supply shed, home of their site-issued tents and sleeping bags, assigned by numbers for the month and thoroughly cleaned between users.

Then we got down to archaeology.

"I am a great fan of your work, *Signorina* Greenough," said a serious, pale young woman with long, dark hair, dark-rimmed glasses and a round, piquant face. Her name was Silvia Girgenti. "Have there been any developments in your search for the Tages statue?"

"Actually, yes," I smiled, shaking her hand. "In November I heard from the daughter of an American soldier who passed away last summer. In his effects, she found the letter I had sent him five years ago, and, well, let's discuss this later."

We had reached the shambles of the Hut Circle. I gathered the group around me and—unrolling the plans we'd worked up with Angelo—showed them where we could begin clearing surface weeds and trash. After briefly reviewing our grid classification system, I opened the storage shed to issue finds-trays, and get them started.

Then my phone-alarm rang to remind me that *Jim was still not here.*

I tried calling him: *Call failed.*

Recalling suddenly his near-miss with a car at the round-about yesterday I knew for a certainty that something was wrong. I sent up a prayer like a command: *Lord! Send help!*

Then I found Silvia Girgenti and told her I needed to make a call from the camper. I gave her authority to give the students a break around 11:00 and told her to ask Angelo for guidance if I was late returning. Then I trotted back to the camper to try calling Jim from the land-line.

By the time I reached the camper, I had broken into a run.

Then I found Silvia Girgenti and told her I needed to make a call from the camper. I gave her authority to give the students a break around 11:00 and told her to ask Angelo for guidance if I was late returning. Then I trotted back to the camper to try calling Jim from the land-line.

By the time I reached the camper, I had broken into a run.

It connected, but his phone rang and rang, and then a strange voice answered, *"Pronto?"*

"*Dottore Lewis?*" I asked anxiously.

"*No:* wait a moment," said the voice in Italian.

"Hello?" came a faint but familiar voice.

"Pericles," I cried, shouting in relief. "What happened? Where are you?"

"Tarquinia General's *Pronto Soccorso.* Been better," he laughed weakly. "My poor scooter's had it."

"Didn't I tell you not to be *hit by a car or ever be hurt in any way?*"

"I know, I know," he muttered. "Don't go setting yourself on fire. Listen: my right shoulder's a wreck. They say I'll need surgery. Can you get here soon?"

"How fast does that Fiat go? Hang on, best beloved."

I ran to tell *il babbo*, asking him to keep an eye on my area while I high-tailed it into town. He sent me off with a concerned *bacio-bacio* and a promise that if I wasn't back by the end of school, he or Anna-Maria would collect the River-bankers.

I grabbed my pack and ran for the gate and I'm pretty sure I unlocked and relocked it, but I was halfway to town in the Fiat when the gears of my brain I grabbed my pack and ran for the gate and I'm pretty sure I unlocked and relocked it, but I was halfway to town in the Fiat when the gears of my brain sort of started to mesh.

"Right shoulder's a wreck."

Thank God he always wore a helmet. I wonder if the scooter's insured? Exactly what the hell had happened?

I took two turns around the roundabout. On the southern stretch I saw all that was left of the red scooter: just a rear-view mirror and a shattered plexiglass windscreen. There were black tire-marks on the outside edge of the circle just ahead of the wreckage.

I took two turns around the roundabout. On the southern stretch I saw all that was left of the red scooter: just a rear-view mirror and a shattered plexiglass windscreen. There were black tire-marks on the outside edge of the circle just ahead of the wreckage.

I could see the scene unfold: Jim is on the outer edge of the circle about to peel off for the site. A car brakes hard in front of him just before he reaches the turn. He's forced to veer onto the gravelly margins. His tires slip out from under him. He is thrown onto his right shoulder. Hard.

Wincing, I raced on to Tarquinia General, found a spot on a side-street, prayed I would not get a ticket, then ran all the way to the entrance marked *Pronto Soccorso*.

"He has just gone into surgery," the orderly at the desk

informed me. "You may go to the Recovery waiting area. You are his next of kin?"

I swallowed. *"La fidanzata."*

"Tanti auguri," he beamed. "You may take these and wait down the hall."

He handed me a big clear plastic bag. In it I glimpsed Jim's boots and clothing. Following his gesture, I came to a quiet, sunny waiting area where a young man sat. "Dad-To-Be" was written all over his haggard face.

Didn't they allow men into birthing rooms here? I wondered vaguely.

Then I unzipped the bag and found Jim's site boots wrapped in a bloody blue polo shirt and shredded black windbreaker.

Must've gone into surgery still wearing his jeans!

Inside his boots I found his valuables. I had just tucked these into my pack—putting his engagement ring above mine—when in strode Marc Short.

First thing I noticed was that he wore a nice white shirt and dark wool slacks. I caught a scent of cologne and his hair was still damp from a shower. He sat down beside me, concern written all over his face.

"So sorry, babe," he said soulfully, kissing my hand.

As if in the corner of my eye, *I saw him and his pale friend pull an unconscious Jim from the wreckage of the red Vespa.*

Jim was covered with blood and dust. The other two were laughing.

Startled, I pushed Marc away.

"How did you know about the accident? Was it already on the news?"

He didn't meet my eyes.

"No, I was at Tony's place, helping with a catalogue he's putting together. Tony saw it happen on his way home. Sounded pretty serious."

"Why didn't he call us at the site?" I asked sharply.

He shrugged. "No idea. How bad is he?" he added with genuine interest.

"Bad. He's in surgery, but I don't, they haven't said if..."

"Aww, cry on ol' Marco's shoulder," he crooned.

"No, thanks," I said, standing abruptly and wiping my tell-tale eyes.

"Can I get you a coffee? A *cornetto*? Anything?"

Suddenly I was ragingly hungry. "Anyplace around here have *panini*?"

"The usual *Caprese*?" he asked.

"Anything except tuna. Thanks."

"Anytime, babe." He stole a kiss and hurried off.

With a sigh, I rolled Jim's boots up in the ruined clothing and returned them to the bag. The Dad-To-Be smiled. "Your *fidanzato*? Who is ill, your father?"

"No," I said soberly, "my fiancé is ill. He was hurt in an accident. That was my ex-fiancé." I gestured after Marc. "You think he wants to be my *fidanzato* again?"

The man nodded emphatically. The man nodded emphatically.

I sat down with a sigh and asked, "You are waiting for a baby?"

"It's a Caesarian," he grimaced. "A little complicated."

We sat in companionable silence. Finally, I got out my laptop to update my site-log. I was still staring blindly at the screen twenty minutes later, when a nurse came looking for me.

"*Signorina* Greenough?" He led me into the surgery wing. Here I was made to put on a mask and paper clean-gown. Next, I was taken into a chilly surgical theater. A woman who seemed to be the lead surgeon came over to confer with me.

"Sorry for the low temperature," she apologized in slow but very good English. "It slows the heart. We wanted to warn you that there is internal bleeding. The clavicle—

collar-bone—snapped in two places. One piece has punctured a vein. Not the jugular, thank God! We are waiting for more blood to arrive from Viterbo before we proceed."

I blinked. "Would another pint help? I'm O positive."

"If you are willing, certainly," she replied at once. "I will call in the technician."

It was an hour later when I finally got back to the waiting room. A stained white paper It was an hour later when I finally got back to the waiting room. A stained white paper *panino* sack was waiting for me. On it was penciled the following message:

"Your ex left this for you and ran off. I think you made the right choice. Sciarra Paolo. Wife and baby girl both doing fine."

The *panino* was tuna.

I stared at it for a moment. I left it there and went to the Admissions desk.

"Do you know who brought Dr. Lewis in from the accident? An ambulance?"

"No, it was that same man I sent back just now with your lunch: "No, it was that same man I sent back just now with your lunch: Boetio Corto. He and his friend carried *Dottore* Lewis in between the two of them. Said the scooter cut in front of them and he couldn't stop in time. Traffic Officer," here he checked his registry, "Leonini Paola came in with them and made her report to our police office here. All part of procedure."

Why had Marc lied to me? The answer was obvious: *he'd cut Jim off himself.*

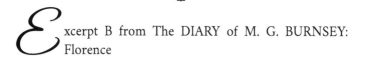

*E*xcerpt B from The DIARY of M. G. BURNSEY: Florence

. . .

[*They* make their way across France with plenty of complications in transport, weather, and lodging, but it is in Florence that things really start to happen . . .]

JUNE 21, 82 – Florence, Hotel Porta Rossa

Have only just reached our lovely room, but Bess says she is already bored, misses boat.

The ship from Marseille to Genoa was very noisy: not one of us slept and even Jx3 was out of sorts. Then it took forever to disembark. I never knew the hold of a ship could hold so much cargo and all of it had to be unloaded before we were let off—get enough cabs to get all our things to the railway terminal, make ourselves understood at the ticket counter and get to the proper binario, which is what they call a "platform" here.

Luckily for some of us Uncle Joseph met us at Customs and has taken over custody of the twins. They will catch a coastal steamer to Civitavecchia tonight. St. sad!

Once we did reach the correct railway compartment and St. had confirmed that all our luggage had made it onto the train with us, though he was wrong, Bess is now telling me: her vanity case is missing. She will have to make do with mine until we can buy a replacement.

I much enjoyed sketching the distant hill towns and picturesque wagons and people of all kinds.

St. says "Mary can't see a thing unless she draws it." Which I think is true.

JUNE 26, 82 – Florence, Hotel Porta Rossa

Early AM: Must tell at length of very strange encounter last night after dinner near Santa Croce. St. had just warned Bess about openly carrying her pocketbook, when a boy took it off her shoulder and ran around the corner.

We chased him, calling "Stop, thief!" but people just leaned out of their windows yelling something like "Zitta, zitta," and he got clean away down a very dark and frightening street. We tried to comfort Bess, but she was very angry with herself. Then we heard cries in Italian, "Help! Help!"

Turning a corner, we came upon a fight. Not a fight, really, more like a murder: four men beating up a priest with sticks! People here ordinarily take an active part in everything but no-one intervened or called out for the men to stop.

The sound was so horrible that Bess and I covered our ears, but St. keeps his revolver loaded with blanks. He shot it off twice in the air to frighten them.

The noise was like a thunderclap and suddenly everybody but us, and the victim, scattered. We ran to help the poor man to his feet. A cut over his eye was bleeding badly, so Bess sacrificed her handkerchief. St. asked in rather bad Italian if he lived nearby.

"In this building," the priest said in good English. "Bless you, bless you!" St. got him to his feet and helped him unlock his door and get inside. Bess and I ran around lighting lamps and opening doors.

The priest guided us out into a moonlit garden with little stone benches, where we sat him down. St. went to the fountain and rinsed out Bess' hankie while Bess pressed mine into action, sitting very close beside him on the bench.

I held the lamp, very envious of Bess. He is magnificent. Regret he's a priest.

I will attempt in words what I see in my mind's eye: a big head with dark hair worn long. Beautiful hands and a long, lean body. His face also long and lean, with a good jaw, pronounced nose, strong lines from eye-socket to jaw, firm lips. Eyes a clear, dark brown, large, long-lashed. What Mama would call "bedroom eyes."

"You are *dall' Inghilterra?*" he asked. I said that no, we were Americans.

"Ah, *Americani*," he laughed. "I have read of your Wild West and your six-shooters!"

We all introduced ourselves.

His name is Padre Titono Empedicleo Benevento.

"I must find a way to thank you," he said. We arranged to meet next day in front of our hotel at one o'clock, to lunch together. He will show us Florence.

Jx3 was angry with us at first for coming in so late, then glad about our rescue. Happy to let us lunch with Padre, as he is touring the Uffizi again with a college chum.

I am so eager for this luncheon today that I am almost shaking. I have just the sense to wonder if his attackers were the male relatives of some poor seduced girl.

JUNE 27, 82 – Florence, Hotel Porta Rossa

Early AM: I must write just one or two words about the extraordinary conversation we had with the Padre at luncheon yesterday. Somehow the talk came around to families, and how many aunts and uncles we had.

When I shared that I am the seventh daughter of a seventh daughter he took my hand, scanning my palm like a fortune-teller, as the most extraordinary feeling spread up my arm, like a drawn-out electric shock.

"It is quite true," he confirmed, adding in amazement, "But what is this? You will surpass all other women of your time in the skill of your hands."

Bess laughed, "In what, needlepoint?"

"By no means. First, in portraiture and then in the queen of the arts: in sculpture."

It was St.'s turn to laugh. "Did she pay you to say that, Padre?"

How dazzled I was. Yet in that moment I felt that it was true: that long years of struggle lie ahead of me, but I will fulfill my dream

When Bess asked angrily how a priest could be a fortune-teller, Titono—as I will call him—said that he, like Dr. J., has rejected the Trinity. He no longer serves the Roman Catholic Church.

He is not a priest after all.

"Tell my fortune, Titono," she said, pushed me aside. He looked then laughed. "You will marry a fat man and become very rich!" at which St. & I laughed and B. fussed.

St.'s was, "You will marry young and bring glory to your name," which he liked very much. Once I had wished to be the one he married. But now?

After lunch he showed us the Laurentian Library and the Bargello, walking with Bess, as I walked with St. I became sadly envious, but T. whispered to me at our parting, "Say you will sketch at Santa Croce tomorrow! Meet me at the memorial of Foscolo." *And so I will.*

JUNE 28, 82 – Florence, Hotel Porta Rossa

Late PM: Here I confess to myself that I "sketched tombs" at Santa Croce today while Bess and Stephen were at Fiesole and that I plan to "sketch" again tomorrow as much and for as long as possible, whatever their plans may be. T. assures me that there will be "no ill effects" from our encounter, that he can control certain things. My only fear is that I will have nothing to show St. & B., when we leave for Siena, two days from now, if I can bear to go. Now I know life.

JUNE 29, 82 – Florence, Hotel Porta Rossa

Late PM: spent long afternoon "sketching," after which T. presented me with three fine sketches to show very like my own work. Big farewell dinner with Jx3 and T. as well as St. & B. T. took me aside afterwards to say farewell. I wept. He said that Stephen would "protect me when my need came," but promised that he himself would stay by me always. How can that be? I had always laughed at drawings of a heart broken in half. No more.

JULY 1, 82 – Siena, Hotel S. Pietro

[They arrive in Siena on the day before the Palio of the Madonna of Provenzano. Only because they know Jx3 are they able to find lodging in the Lelio Sozzini house. The descriptions of the festivities are interesting but do not concern my family history. The very first part of their visit to Siena does.]

Leaving Florence yesterday a sad trial: no T. at the station and Bess making fun of my "long face over a certain long face." Jx3 regrets letting me go sketching alone. I have none! But T. left a gift for me at the hotel last night: a beautiful black cat in a birdcage! I wanted to call him "Empedicleo" or "Empy" for short but Bess thought I said "Impy" so we settled on that. He loves to lie in my arms.

I have tried all day on the train to sketch T's face, but instead my hand makes sketches of Bess or St. or the other people in the compartment, very fine sketches, better than I have ever made before. They are quick and sure, capturing the sitter's very essence. When I gave them away to fellow travelers, they made me sign them, telling me they would one day be valuable. I should have been happy.

Tonight, Impy cried until I let him out of his cage and now is purring in my lap. I have never seen a cat with such clear brown eyes. And such a dear white jabot.

10

A STRONG HYPOTHESIS

Reading about the uncanny shenanigans of my reprobate of an ancestor was an excellent distraction from two days of the horrendous fear concerning the survival of my best-beloved.

On the evening of the third Friday of January, a full day after being admitted, after two more surgeries, the intervention of a vein specialist, and three additional pints of blood, Jim was pronounced out of danger, having cheated death by literal inches. They estimated about a week before he could leave the hospital. He was not to climb stairs for a week after that.

One thing was clear: Jim would not be going back to his basement office at the Museum any time soon. I would need to retrieve any papers and books he might like to use at the hospital. I headed over to the Museum and parked the Fiat in the little piazza whence Jim had set forth so innocently on his scooter just the morning before.

I filled up the rear of the little car with a small suitcase of clothes and a box of books. On the seat beside me was the big desk-top computer that belonged to Princeton. I was on my last trip down the stairs to fetch his site notebooks when

Museum Director Giulia Pantano stopped me in the corridor. She was in thick leggings and a fluttery grey sweater, a file under her arm.

"*Tanina.* Allow me to express my horror at *Giacomo*'s terrible *incidente*," she began warmly, taking my hand. "I hope you bear me no ill-will for wishing Franco Cotto to continue at the Temple of Vanth and Tages. His work on the pediment has brought in thousands of new visitors to the museum every month. I felt I owed it to him to insist."

"You are very kind, *Dottore* Pantano," I replied with a smile, hoping to make peace with this powerful woman. "I have told Dr. Lewis he was wrong to ask for such a thing. I am quite content with the Hut Circle. There is so much more there than meets the eye."

"Whatever do you mean?" she asked sharply.

Confused by her reaction, I stammered, "Only that, that—once we clean and study the area—it will give us important clues to the meaning of the whole sanctuary."

"Ah, how interesting," she remarked in a calmer voice. "I understand you have spoken with Marcus Short about returning to work there?"

"About *his* returning to work there?" I frowned.

"Naturally," she smiled. "You will be short-handed with Dr. Lewis gone."

Gone. A lump rose in my throat.

"Jim will be back before you know it," I laughed forcedly. "With Angelo's students I have plenty of help. It was sweet of Marc to offer, but no, I won't be needing him this semester. I was glad to hear that his photographic work is bringing in plenty of income lately."

She gave me an odd look.

"Yes, I understand that it does." She gave herself a shake. "Let me know if I can help."

As I hurried off to the car her cruel shaft still quivered in my heart.

Gone.

I had not missed her references to Marc's return, nor her odd reactions. Suddenly I wondered what catalogue was keeping Marc busy at Tony's house when he wasn't trying to kill my best beloved? His admission had felt more like a half-truth than an outright lie.

Maybe the truth was something like this: Marc's photographic work on some sort of catalogue for Tony was bringing in plenty of income.

Tony sold art. He once told me he bought low from obscure antiquarians and sold high to finicky collectors. Marc was always hanging out at Tony's place. Tony very likely had catalogues of art for sale. Who better to take the studio photos for those catalogues than Marc?

Marc had been our site photographer for many years, getting vertical shots of newly-opened areas, time-lapse films of work in progress, and making a painstaking record of finds. Every object from the *hypogeum* had stood in front of Marc's camera before it went to the vault.

If he was doing well at Panorama and working for Tony, why go back to the site?

Every object stood in front of Marc's camera.

What if some objects never made it into the vault?

Buy low. Sell high.

Much more profitable to steal than to buy.

I visualized the path from the road to the Hut Circle, then the pits and the *crotalis* we'd found. Then I saw Marc sweeping the collection of rings into his camera bag, and photos of our real engagement rings replaced with crisp new images of the lost rings.

My hypothesis was complete.

Tony used Marc's pictures in a catalogue for illicit collectors. Once a buyer was found, Marc would take the originals from the vault, hide them at the Hut Circle, then move them to Tony's sometime later. Tony would cast fakes that came back to the Hut Circle and go back to the vault to mask the theft. The real pectoral was out there in limbo waiting for its cast to be made.

Then the corollary dropped into place:

Giulia allowed all this to happen for a cut of the profits. She could even have been the one moving the finds to the site.

But now that the site was fenced, they needed Marc, with his keys and a legitimate excuse for using them—back on the site. I must convince Jim to take Marc back or . . .

Or he would kill Jim and soften me up.

Holy crap.

I would share this hypothesis with my best beloved as soon as he was strong enough. They wanted to keep him sedated so I resolved to stay busy.

The Riverbankers and I accordingly spent the rest of that weekend looking for a long-term place to live. If Jim had to stay on their ground floor our informal living arrangement would soon become a serious strain on the Cottos, especially since we paid no rent.

After visiting what seemed like every place in Lido with an ad in the paper or a "for rent" sign in the window we found a little place on Via Pyrgi with no stairs. It was only four blocks from the school and one block from the beach and we could have it for six months starting February first. That would leave us at the Cotto's place around the corner on Lungomare dei Tirreni for little more than a week.

But the rent was astronomical and the owners would wait no later than the following Monday for me to locate a deposit.

A tearful phone-call to my mother made Sunday night solved everything except the burning question, *"Why didn't you call me yesterday?"* she scolded.

"I was on AirBnB just last night looking for a place to rent for a couple of weeks before the wedding. How about we just make it *your* place, and I could pay the rent for February, or maybe more than that? I'll see if I can change my ticket to fly out the first of the month."

"Could you?" I cried, hope dawning. "What about Buster? Won't he starve?"

"No, but he will eat all the wrong things. Hopefully they won't kill him right away."

That next morning, the third Monday in January, just a week since that monumental smooch in the *hypogeum* and after walking the Riverbankers to school, I went to visit my best beloved. The doctor had called to say he was awake and worried about something.

They showed me to a quiet single room with a view of the Castle.

He was awake and he knew me. With his right eye nearly swollen shut and his right arm lashed across his chest, I sat on his left, adjusting blankets and fighting down tears as I went.

"I expect I look awful," he whispered. "The doctor says my right lung is dicey and I'm still not out of the woods. I'm due another unit of blood." He caught his breath and went on. "I understand I got a pint of yours. No wonder I feel so perky!"

He so pale I could see the blue veins on his forehead. When he smiled his gums were almost white. I nursed his cold hand against my cheek. I couldn't speak.

"They tell me it's Monday," he remarked. "Riverbankers at school?"

"Yep," I blinked. I told him about the little rental house on Via Pyrgi.

"Brava, *Tanina,* I like the street name! About the rent: I don't think we should let your mom pay for more than her small share, if that. I have some grant money for housing socked away somewhere, but that may take a minute to get. Meantime call my parents. Ask my mother to sell some of the stock she holds for me and put the money into your bank-account."

"Okay," I said uneasily, wondering how I would summon the gall.

Painfully shifting his upper body, he turned to face me, gripping my hand.

"There's a lot of paperwork I was hoping you could help me with, sweetheart, if you can take a couple of days off from the site. First, we need to convince the UNESCO powers-that-be to subcontract their research grant to Angelo, at least while I'm incapacitated, so he can go ahead and schedule the removal of the fresco so we can open the chamber behind it. Next, I want to give you power of attorney, open a joint bank account, and write you into my will. But you're not next of kin. Not *yet*."

He paused to catch his breath. It took longer this time.

His eyes were a very vivid shade of blue as he said with solemn intensity, "Would you be willing to marry me this week, now, as soon as can be arranged?"

"But *Mor* can't come until next month," I blurted.

"We can still have the wedding ceremony as planned. I just don't." I could hear it in my mind, loud and clear: *I don't want to die and leave you and the kids stranded.*

"Of course, Pericles," I whispered, stunned.

He was so determined to speak his piece before collapsing that he pushed right on. "So, I called Princeton to ask Emmett—Dr. Potts—to take over as your academic advisor." His breath was coming with more difficulty. "He agreed to do it if," he sighed wearily, "if you put a colon in your dissertation title."

I was on the point of complaining, *"Parsing the Iconography of the Vanth" isn't stuffy enough for him?* But instead suggested gamely, "What do you say to 'The Meaning of *La Castellina*: Parsing the Iconography of the Vanth'?"

There came a faint shadow of his beautiful smile.

"That should work," he whispered. He closed his eyes.

"So how," I prompted gently, "can I help with this civil marriage business?"

He focused with an effort. "I think your friend Father Allen will know how to manage it if you could have him call me here. Oh, Tanny," he said faintly, "you can't think what a relief it will be to get you safely settled. If you hand me my phone, I'll get you Mom's number."

"So, Pericles," I asked shyly, "she knows, right?"

"Called her last week. She'd come to the wedding, but her school is in the middle of re-accreditation. We'll go visit next summer."

"And your father?"

"Dad?" his whispered tone became cold. "Doesn't travel if he can help it. So how did your student volunteers work out? I was so sorry to miss helping with orientation."

Wow. Quick change of subject. I made a mental note to find out more about his father.

I told him how that went and about my rising panic when he never showed up and my hypothesis about who did it and why.

"It fits all the facts," he agreed, "and I have a few more to add. There weren't any site and fence keys with my stuff when I woke up. They must have swiped them at the accident scene."

Rats! How had I missed that?

"Did you see Marc cut you off?"

"Yes. Listen, I don't want to scare you, but if that traffic officer hadn't come by . . ."

"There was a traffic officer? The orderly said you just came in with Marc and a friend."

"The officer must have left us at the door. She gave us a motorcycle escort to the hospital. Said it would be faster than waiting for an ambulance. She could see I was in a bad way. I had the strangest feeling even then."

He looked off towards the Castle.

"They didn't intent to take me to the hospital," he said quietly. "They were driving a van. Before the officer came up, they talked over how to 'get him and the scooter to Mazzola's.'"

"Mazzola's?" I echoed incredulously. "Isn't that the farm by the site?"

"That's what we've always called it. I believe," he paused a moment, "I believe they were going to throw me and the scooter into the ravine where the road turns, at Mazzola's place."

"Instead they were forced to drive you to the hospital," I laughed in horror.

"Do you know that Marc tried to get into the Recovery room after my surgery? You were home with the River-bankers. But there was a young father in there with his wife —she'd just had a Caesarian—and he said to the nurse, 'That's her ex! He's got no business with her *fidanzato*.' and they escorted him out of the room."

"Bless you, Paolo Sciarra," I breathed. "But won't they try again?"

"He has my keys," he sighed. "Whatever he needs to do at the site, he is doing it."

I tried to leave at once to put a stop to Marc's shenanigans, but his grip was strong.

"No. We have to pretend we missed all the clues and work with the authorities."

"What *authorities*? Aren't the local police in Giulia's pocket?"

"The chief of Tarquinia Municipal Police is a man of integrity, Angelo says. We talked about it, last night. His name is Colonel Pasquale Paolini, and Anna-Maria has worked with him on many cases in the past. She will call him, pretending she has questions for her book."

"Thank God for the Cottos," I sighed fervently. "But Giulia and Riccardo?"

"They mustn't know we know," he insisted. "And Marc mustn't know I overheard him and his pal. And Tony mustn't know we are onto him. We must play it cool, *Tanina mia.* Swear that you'll count to ten—to a hundred—rather than risk exposing yourself," he begged.

"Okay, I swear. But what if Marc threatens the River-bankers?"

That startled him. "In that case, run him off the road."

11

IN BOCCA AL LUPO

THAT SAME MONDAY NIGHT COL. PAOLINI, A COMPACT MAN IN his forties, well-built, handsome, and a full head shorter than either Jim or me, came over to the Cottos informally garbed in jeans and leather jacket. He looked he always did when consulting with Anna-Maria to add to his cover.

He liked the idea of getting Marc back on the site, the sooner the better.

"Let Ellington, Short, and his friend get comfortable," he told us, glancing around, leaning well into the table his hands folded as if in prayer, "but note down where they go, who they talk to, what they do, and when they do it, in this," he brought out a little black notebook, "to consult later for overlap with activities we're monitoring outside the site.

"We have your friend Tony's house on *Via San Giacomo* under surveillance, and will know when and if your *cattivi bimbi* come and go from there.

"It was brought to our attention by the regional postal inspector that Mr. Ellingham uses many different post offices to mail his art objects overseas, but *never the main post-office in Tarquinia*. This, of course, implies that he does not want any particular postal worker to notice outflows of boxes. And none of these couriers who deliver goods to him, I should mention, have license plates from outside the regions of Toscano or Lazio. None is a commercial courier such as DHL: they are all private, local vehicles."

"Because he specializes in stolen antiquities from this region, do you mean?"

The colonel turned his pale, intense eyes my way, as if noticing me for the first time.

"Yes, he seems to be a *specialist,* as you say. He is much wealthier than your average antiquarian. Dealers in legitimate antiques, such as those we find in Arezzo, where your *fidanzato* bought that lovely ring, *signorina*—he has showed me his receipt and its certificate of provenance—tend to keep as many of their treasures as they sell. *Signore* Ellingham, on the other hand, can afford to buy art objects at auction most museums couldn't imagine owning."

"The little Morris Louis," I whispered, remembering the gorgeous bouquet of color in Tony's living room. The colonel smiled.

"Precisely," he said.

"But Tony never kept his wealth a secret," Angelo objected. "He calls himself *the disreputable scion of millionaires.*"

"Ah," said Paolini, "not so, I'm afraid. *Illegitimate scion* would be more accurate. There were never millionaires in that family."

This was news to us all. There was much murmuring.

"His mother Margery Ellingham was an art student from Birmingham and his father, a Rumanian antique dealer by the name of Andrei Ardalean. They met in London at the British Museum. He was a gifted forger and she ran their little shop of 'antiquities' near Covent Garden until one night Ardalean was knifed to death in an alley. Tony has been wiser in his friends."

"So how," asked Angelo impatiently, "do we prevent these

furfanti from robbing the site of every object of importance the moment it appears?"

"We don't."

Our uproar was quelled by the colonel's shapely hand, upraised.

"Tell us what objects have vanished of course, and the whereabouts of our suspects."

Angelo shrugged. "I suppose we can use our *telefonini* to photograph any finds we come across and do detailed drawings when we can."

"And Marc will still be taking pictures for Tony's catalogue," I remarked.

Paolini again turned my way.

"Ah, this notion of a catalogue is very interesting, *signorina*."

"Colonel Paolini," pursued Angelo, "we suspect that objects already catalogued are disappearing from the Museum then being planted at the site for retrieval after dark."

"The last place we would look for them, if the alarm were raised," Paolini nodded. "Yes, while her husband Riccardo has had some run-ins with the law, both here and in Sardinia, until now, *Dottoressa* Pantano has kept her hands clean. I am hoping we can persuade her to cooperate with us in exchange for immunity. It would be a great scandal for Tarquinia if such an eminent local family were implicated in theft."

He got up to leave, apologizing for the necessity of allowing "the wolves to trap themselves," as he put it.

"May the wolf explode," joked Franco, quoting the old adage. We all laughed.

Very early Wednesday morning—or very late Tuesday night, Tucson time—after two days of chasing down paperwork and calling Prester John non-stop and likely more ahead, I finally took my own wolf by the ears as the Romans used to say. I sat in the quiet of the upstairs room the Cotto's place, set out my bank-book and credit card, and called Irene Morris Lewis, my mother the famous painter, is how Jim likes to introduce her.

"Hello?" Her voice was professionally calm and reassuring. "Tanaquil?"

"Hello, Mrs. Morris. Yes, it's Tanny."

"Please call me 'Irene.' I've heard so much about you, dear child, it's hard to realize we've never met. Last Christmas, Larry and Aggie talked about you non-stop."

"Ha," I laughed faintly, "I do apologize."

"Jimmy said you needed to talk with me about money. How can I help?"

In a rush I explained about the house rental, the accident, and her son's wish to cement things between him and me as soon as ever he was able.

"He's healing beautifully, Irene, and may be able to go home Friday."

"Home?" she sounded surprised, her voice suddenly like Jim's. "Back to the States?"

"No, no, sorry to be confusing," I stammered. "Home here in Tarquinia Lido."

"Home to *you*," she supplied quietly. "You have made my son very happy. Tell Jimmy I'm happy to sell that stock for him. Now, read me that bank information, slowly please?"

On the evening of that same long Wednesday January twentieth, a week since his "accident," in the presence of our children, the Cottos, Prester John and Gesualdo (and the completed paperwork), Pericles and I were married by civil license on the third floor of Tarquinia General, just as the lights were coming on at the Castle.

The legalities over, Angelo took all the others out for pizza at *Del Duchetto* before putting the Romans onto the train and the children to bed. Pericles and I shared a pretty good hospital meal then settled down for the night ourselves. They let me have a rollaway bed and permission to try whatever mischief Jim felt up for. I was content to lie next to his live self but he seemed think more was required.

Blood certainly seemed to be flowing to all the right places so we went for it. The delicate operation was made easier by our decision to dispense with prophylactics, reasoning, if you can call it that, that there is no convenient time to have children. Jim had worked out how I could finish my dissertation before any little stranger, tentatively named "Fred" after his Oxford friend, the late Fred Cole, chose to show up. I hoped for later rather than sooner.

The female philosopher Diotima says in Plato's *Symposium* that a married woman is pure immediately after sex. If so, I was purity itself!

Next morning, as Angelo got the children to school, I was walking from the hospital to the nearest Europcar. I had to rent a car big enough to get Jim from the hospital and my mother from Fiumicino. I was almost there when Marc hailed me from his vintage black Lotus Elan.

"Need a ride, babe? I'm going out to the site with my photo stuff: Cotto-the-Elder gave me the go-ahead to record progress at the Hut Circle."

I bent to reply and forced myself to smile.

"Congratulations! Thanks, but I'm doing errands. Gee, I also have to thank you for helping Jim after his accident," I went on blithely. On my side of the car I noticed the same large, pale young man who I'd been at Bar Impero. "Who's your friend?"

"Cecco Casti, from my days at U. of Florence. Pre-med."

I shook Cecco's hand through the open window but it felt dirty in more ways than one.

"*Ciao*, Cecco, I understand you also helped Dr. Lewis get to the hospital. Are you going to help out our photographic genius at the site?"

"I do whatever he needs doing," he smiled amiably, getting a big laugh from Marc.

A born minion! I thought bitterly.

I saw them off with a cheery wave and they moved off, never having asked after the health of the man they'd tried to kill.

The car rental agreement was reasonable. Soon I was in a Fiat Multipla, advertised as holding five people comfortably.

But would it hold my long-legged mother and what would surely be loads of extra baggage? In little more than a week, we would know for sure.

With a rush of pleasure, I thought of seeing her again. I was eager to see *"Bestemor"* amongst her Riverbankers, by whom she had provisionally been christened "the Gaoler's Daughter" as one of the very few female characters in *Wind in the Willows.* I had voted down another positive character— the Cart-Horse—suspecting that creature of being a gelding.

By the time I drove the Multipla to the site Angelo's students had already reported to the Hut Circle with the shed-key, helped themselves to the same equipment they'd been using since the Friday before—what an age ago that seemed—and continued with their work.

They clustered around sympathetically as I came up, asking after Jim and expressing horror and shock like the good people they were. Quashing a burning desire to tell them that *Reader, I married him,* I asked for general reactions to their work so far.

They reported being sore at first from all that stoop labor, but that this week was going better. The dark post-holes outlining one hut were already beautifully clear in the chalky soil. They were content to continue with their assignments. I took the opportunity of telling the women *sotto voce* to watch themselves around "the photographer." I told them he was something of a predator, and they were to report any bad behavior to me at once.

With that we went to work.

Seeing Marc skulking, honestly it is the only way to describe it, over by the ilex mound with his camera tripod while Cecco took a smoke, I took the official tomato-can ashtray over to Cecco and checked in with Marc.

"This is a great place to start, Marco," I smiled. "The arborist is coming tomorrow to see how to move the ilex without killing it. He says this kind of pine has a shallow root-system, so the center of the mound may be undisturbed."

"What happens to the tree?" Cecco wanted to know.

I laughed. "Angelo wants it next to the camper, for shade. Oh, Jim lost his keys in the accident. Did either of you find them? No? Oh well, someone may yet turn them in."

I left them to get on with it, whatever "it" really was, and wandered over to the fence. It didn't take long to find a disturbed place near where we had found the *crotalis*.

I dropped to my heels and parted the overhanging grass with my trowel.

"Anything interesting?" called Marc sharply.

He had been watching, of course.

I made a face. "An animal burrow, looks like. Hope I don't have to leave any traps and wind up with a dead bunny!"

Both men laughed and went back to work.

Truth was I had spotted an interesting pattern in the soft earth at the bottom of the little pit. It was something like the texture of burlap. I could swear there was at least one impression of a circular object. The minute the "photo crew" went home I'd melt a chunk of the wax we kept under the camper sink for preserving the pattern of a scatter of beads, and take an impression.

Meantime, I got up, brushing my hands.

The rest of the day I lost myself in work. It was the first of many good work days in what was to be the most productive area of the site. It was the foundation of all my future work, along with what lay behind that fresco. The last hour of the day I spent with the site notebook, entering fully and neatly the progress made. Then I snapped photos of the pages to share with Jim.

I also added a few notes to the spy-book I kept in my front jeans pocket.

It was nerve-racking to know that every bead and coin that appeared in the soil of the Hut Circle – of which there were many, along with spindle-whorls, dice, and game-pieces, all signs that people had waited here for a turn at the *mundus* oracle—would likely vanish at once.

Each weeknight he was in the hospital I had dinner with Jim and talked shop, then went back to the Cottos to tuck in the Riverbankers and spend the night. Friday, Anna-Maria took over so I could hang out at the site until late, then spend the night at the hospital with my *marito*.

The Friday tradition at *La Castellina* was to build a fire in the hollow south of the *hypogeum* before everyone settled down to sleep in our own "Hut Circle" of tents clustered around the amenities of the camper. "The Pit," as the hollow was known, was the top of an ancient well long since explored and refilled, its snow-white *vera,* the marble ring at the top, deeply grooved with centuries of rope-wear, a sharp contrast to the fresh black ash.

Guitars came out and people sang the sad *Lazio* tunes with their endless verses – the challenge being to see who could recall them all or make up new ones in time. Some-times, as tonight, a local talent brought out an authentic *Romagnolo* ballad.

The singer was a friend of Silvia's named Piero Pellico, who hailed from nearby Monte Romano. He said it was a song about *this very place.* He'd learned it from his mother's *nonno* not long before he'd passed from this life, when Piero was just five years old.

Silvia had just passed me the bottle, there was always a

bottle or six of home-made wine from the Mazzola farm to pass around on Friday nights, and whispered to me, "At first, Piero didn't want to work here because of this song. His girlfriend Sofia shamed him into it!"

I never forgot the song's title and refrain, *Sul Leccio,* Under the Ilex, but was in such a blend of despair and bliss over my two-day-old marriage that the words are lost.

The story went that a childhood friend of this *Nonno* of Piero's had come up to *La Castellina* when it was a place of uncut *macchia* of glossy-leaved ilexes and wild grape-vines tangled up together and he had found a golden thing under the ilex.

The golden thing made the child sicken and die, and his ghost was often to be found *sul leccio*, trying in vain to return the thing in the ground that had caused him a series of disasters, losing him parents, cattle, friends and finally his poor little self, *sul leccio*.

"And that was why," Piero said impressively into the silence at the end of the song, as we all sat spellbound and weepy, "this hill is called *La Storta Ammalata* and why no-one spends the night here, not if they can help it."

Of course, the students would all be spending the night here! The movement they made crossing themselves was like trees tossing in a high wind.

The following Monday, the twenty-fifth, Pericles was released, and for that last week of the month, while good work progressed at the Hut Circle, he stayed on the Cotto's sofa all day, dealing with wills and finalizing adoption papers long-distance, with help from Prester John.

On Sunday February first we moved into Via Pyrgi. On the second, *Bestemor* arrived.

BESTEMOR TO THE RESCUE

I'LL NEVER FORGET SEEING *MOR* STEP THROUGH THE EXIT FROM Fiumicino Customs. Her lean frame was resplendent in her best white-fringed-and-piped, turquoise-blue go-to-rodeo blouse, tucked into a concho belt and skin-tight, rhinestone-trimmed black jeans.

Her head was held high, white hair pulled back flamenco-style from her darkly-tanned, finely-boned face, steel-grey eyes glittering. As for the black-and-tan-with-red-roses Lucchese cut-work cowgirl boots that graced her long feet, they elicited gasps of admiration from those around me and murmurs of *"che bella Tessana."* People started clicking pictures on spec, hoping she was a movie diva.

She surely had enough suitcases and boxes for a diva: two carts full. One cart I now took over, risking my own discovery. I'd been hiding out behind a handy pillar but had to remove my sunglasses and lower the hood of my well-worn AIA-APA sweatshirt so she would know I hadn't forgotten to meet her plane.

"Sweetie," she cried, falling on my neck.

Sure enough, cries of *"La Signora degli Anelli,"* went up as I hustled her and her stuff to the curb where I'd left the Multi-pla, its lights flashing. A traffic officer was writing a ticket.

Numbly, I reached out to take it. Then the officer took a good long look at me and *Mor* and personally loaded the trunk and back seat with floor-to-ceiling "necessities," waving us off with smiles. Soon we reached the GRA and were speeding clockwise towards the A12.

"Well wasn't he sweet?" *Mor* marveled. "I just *love* Italians."

I looked at her sidelong.

"Buster'd better watch out. What possessed you to dress like a rodeo queen?"

She looked down at herself complacently. "I like to look my best when I travel."

"Did you wear that outfit last time you went to Norway?"

She considered a moment.

"No, I think I wore the black velvet top with the yellow fringe." Observing me keenly, she remarked, "Thank good-ness you've put on a little weight since I saw you last, *kyare,* but I don't like those circles under your eyes! How's poor Pericles?"

By the time I'd brought her up to date on absolutely everything and she'd asked all she needed to ask and told me all about things back home we were turning off for Tarquinia Lido.

Getting her things into the new house on Via Pyrgi (which hadn't taken long to move into the previous day, thank goodness, since we had so little stuff) and telling Jim—drowsing on the sofa in his robe—all about our adventures at Fiumicino took one hour.

When *Mor* walked in, she turned to Jim with hand outstretched, meeting him in person—I suddenly realized—for the first time, though they had spoken by phone quite recently, when he'd asked her and Buster if they minded him as a son-in-law.

"I warned you about the price of fame, James," she said,

kissing his cheek. "Remember what happened to John Lennon!"

"I'm a rock star, is that it?" he smiled. She fanned herself theatrically.

"With a smile like that, honey," she said, "you are a danger to society!"

"Quite true," I agreed soberly, kissing him properly.

Getting *Mor* showered and into more reasonable clothing and making a list of all the things she thought the rental house needed to make it "livable" took another hour. Buying all those things at the nearest shop, unpacking and situating them, then having lunch with Jim took another two hours— as she exclaimed over the neat design and functionality of everything we'd bought—and then it was time to walk down and collect the children from school.

We had almost reached the play-yard gate when I turned and impulsively kissed my mother. She was like a tsunami of affection washing over our sad world and I was over-whelmed with gratitude to have her capable presence beside me.

"Why, you're welcome, *kjare*," she laughed, just as the Riverbankers spotted her.

"*Bestemor!*" they hollered, throwing themselves upon her as if they'd known her all their lives instead of just twenty seconds. But she could handle them. Bracing herself against the onslaught, she kissed them loudly and hugged them hard.

"What a lucky grandma I am," she cried, stepping back and clasping her hands in admiration. "And wait 'til you see what I brought for you, back at the house."

It was good to know that some *of what was in all those suit-cases was not clothing.*

I relieved them of their packs and lunch-boxes. They skipped along beside her, each gripped firmly by the hand against the busy traffic nearby. By the time we'd reached home they'd told her of all the friends they were beginning to have, all the birthday parties they'd already been invited to, and all the projects that would be due at the end of the month. She nodded sagely all the while, commenting briefly here and there.

"Do you like Nutella, *Bestemor*?" asked the Rat during a lull.

"Like it?" she gasped. "I practically wear it as *eau de cologne!*"

That was it: they were hers.

"No, no, don't get up," she called to Jim on the sofa as we cascaded into the little living-room. He was now surrounded by area notebooks, laptop in place, arguing with Angelo—who had arrived moments earlier and sat in the armchair opposite—about where to place the command center for opening the *mundus.*

Dr. Cotto rose at once and went to greet my mother with hand extended. "*Signora* Sparks, so good to meet you," he exclaimed, doling out two quick air-kisses. "The *ragazzi* have been very excited about meeting you. *Giacomo,*" he turned to my best beloved, gathering up his jacket and notes, "I will leave all this with you and we will complete it another time."

And with a quick kiss for me and a ruffling-of-hair for the Riverbankers, he left.

"Papa," cried the Mole. "Did *Mor* tell you she got a ticket, but when the man saw *Bestemor...?*" But Rat talked over her, demanding bread-and-Nutella.

After their news and the bread had both been dispatched, Jim remarked,

"Talked with Prester John a minute ago. Our civil paperwork has been received in Rome as well as in Princeton, so it's official. And apparently Gesualdo's visit to Florence to see Caterina was successful," he added without thinking. "She's already missed her period!"

"Who's Gesualdo?" Frowned the Rat. "What period?"

"'Civil paperwork?'" Frowned my mother.

At which Jim conveniently blushed to the roots of his hair, a sign of healing so heartening that I started to cry, allowing my mother tactfully to remove the Riverbankers to be shown the house and grounds and to take a walk to the beach before we collaborated on a simple dinner.

"Oh, and this came for you by a local courier service," said my best-beloved as I mopped my face. "Return address is a Tarquinia post office box. Angelo is pretty sure it's not a bomb."

Inside the shipping bag was a small white gift-box marked in golden capitals with the words *Antiquità Colchis*. Its logo a stylized golden ram, its head curved back over its shoulder, its body outlined in granulation. The box was heavy for its size and jingled like keys.

Cutting the tape that held on the lid with one fingernail, I opened it to discover a bundle of keys. I knew those keys. At various points in the last semi-decade I'd been allowed to lock up, or open, *Sant'Antonio* before or after one of Tony's parties.

"Tony's keys," I whispered. "What in the world? Here's a note!"

Folded square to fit inside the bottom of the box was a note handwritten on A4 printer paper. I read it aloud with increasing disbelief:

Dear Tanaquil,

It has come to my ears that our mutual friend has come to harm through the agency of men we both know and that, motivated by the integrity which defines him, he has married you.

Please accept this wedding gift while I still have agency to make it, and take from the Cantina a bottle of wine in my memory when my time comes, a day I fear is not far away.

Legal documents follow, but meanwhile make yourself at home. If you choose to, you may yourself become the "most hospitable person" your friends have ever known.

And if Tiro needs a home, I hope you will give him one.

Affectionately,
A. A. Ardalean
known to you as Tony Ellingham
at Sant'Antonio, January 29, 20—

I sat silent with wonder. The gift and the letter lay loose in my lap along with my hands.

My best beloved stared at me in wild surmise. "He's giving you *his house*? I mean, *his houses*? The nicest property in Tarquinia? Damn, I've married an heiress!"

"The nicest property in the *world*," I insisted, then added with a fond smile, "outside of the Lewis house in Princeton, NJ, of course."

"Of course. What did you *say* to him at breakfast the other day?"

I fixed him with a keen look.

"You know what I think? He's trying to keep it away from Marc Short and Co., to whom he originally meant to give it. He called Marc his *protégé,* and said something about giving him the Mini Cooper. Dollars to donuts Tony was furious with him for trying to kill you!"

"*Nolo contendere*," he smiled. "And where can you get a good donut around here?"

But I was still filled with gratitude and disbelief.

"Probably there will be such a heap of red-tape," I murmured, "or a lien, or huge taxes, that the whole thing will be impossible."

"Probably," he chuckled, "but in the end we will get it for you."

"For us," I corrected him eagerly. "Imagine never having to worry about where to stay when we work at the site or how to keep the site records dry and safe. And holding parties!"

His fond look was worth more than any bijou property.

"Tony always has had an eye for quality, *Tanina mia,*" he said.

We told my mother of this unexpected windfall once the dishes were done, the small fry were asleep, and we all sat back in the living room with cups of mint tea.

"Goodness, Tanny-Sue," she gasped. "It's wonderful, but you're right, the legal red tape could be something tremendous. And speaking of legal," she went on seamlessly, "Does this 'civil paperwork' James mentioned earlier mean what I think it does?"

It was my turn to blush, though I don't do it as obviously as Jim does.

"Well, *Mor,* he was so sick, and I worried...he worried..."

Jim broke in manfully. "I'd waited long enough, Hailey."

"Ha!" she scoffed. "*You'd* waited long enough? But I didn't come all this way for a civil wedding, *kyare.* Half those suitcases are full of wedding gear."

"Oh, we'll have the ceremony at All Souls as planned, *Mor,* and our rooms are all reserved at the Hassler, thanks to a grant from Jim's parents. There's a suite for you, me, and the Riverbankers on the first night, and a single for Jim, then two nights for us newlyweds in a *matrimoniale,* while you hang out with the sprogs."

I beamed at her and Jim was nibbling on my ear.

"Hm," sniffed my mother. "Seems like you two are *already* on your honeymoon."

13

SEALED WITH A GOAT

THERE WAS WORK TO DO BEFORE WE WENT TO ROME, EVEN with Jim's right arm immobilized.

On the second Monday in February, three and a half weeks since Jim's smash-up and ten days before our wedding, we were ready to preside over the removal of the wall between the *hypogeum* and the chamber we were calling the *mundus.* The crew from *La Sapienza* had painstakingly removed the plague fresco to their laboratory in Rome for conservation and later mounting at the Museum. The air-testing equipment had arrived. The drill, fiber-optic camera and recording equipment were ready.

Under the later fresco an earlier one had appeared. Two grim figures faced each other across the still-sealed doorway, rendered in red, green, blue and black on smoke-stained white plaster. On the right stood a white-skinned Vanth, her green wings furled and smoking torch upraised. On the left was a green-skinned demon called Tuchulcha with a double-headed axe.

It was time to see what they guarded and remove it before someone else did.

On the night before the opening I had a dream.

I sat cross-legged in the hypogeum, *facing the blocked doorway, a pulsing hum loud in my ears. I watched horrified as the mortar in the arch began crumbling into dust and the stones shifted ominously and bulged outward more and more. The thrum of noise built and built.*

In a corner of the hypogeum, *as if a window had opened to another place, an ancient man suddenly appeared, hunched over an antique desk lit by a green-shaded kerosene lamp.*

He looked up sharply through smoked circular glasses and demanded, "Tanaquil Susannah Greenough-Lewis, stop at once!"

"But, Godpapa," I cried, "I have to know what's inside."

"Call me if you run into trouble," the blind man said and used the usual gesture.

The moment he vanished the wall burst like a huge pustule, releasing hundreds of flying creatures like wasps all glowing a sulfurous yellow. They spattered against my face and body and clustered around my nose and mouth as if fighting to invade my lungs.

"Godpapa, help," I shrieked. The creatures rose into the upper air and were melted by the downpour of rain that now fell in a sheer curtain from the sky.

My eyes flew open to the silence of our room and the echo of a cry.

"Good God, Tanny," Jim whispered. His eyes were big in the dark. "What a scream!"

I clung to him. "What if this opening is a bad idea? The Tarquinians must have had a good reason to bury that part of the site so deep."

"How can we *not?*" he argued. "Tomb-robbers will do with a sledge-hammer what we will do with fine tools. Besides aren't you dying to know?"

"Of course! But do we have any haz-mat suits? Or at least some masks and gloves?"

He considered a moment.

"Gloves, yes, a couple of flu masks, yes, but suits, no. Let me send Angelo a text in case there are any in Rome," and he suited deeds to words.

"You believe me," I smiled. I twined myself around him while he typed.

He took a moment out for a kiss.

"Your Tanny-sense hasn't been wrong yet. Listen: we still have some of those steel canisters from Alpha that I used last summer. It's a system lent to the Museum by a big air analytics company. It was a real coup for Giulia! If we do an air sample once we drill the first hole, we can get the all clear before continuing. Angelo set up something at the Museum last summer with Tina, one of his techs from La Sapienza. We could ask her back."

Message sent, we would have made another attempt at Fred, but it was that time of the month. I relieved my best-beloved's pent-up excitement then snuggled under his arm and slept peacefully until the alarm launched us into that fateful day. Leaving the Multipla in case my mother needed it, we took the Fiat. All the computers and books we needed were at the site.

There were an awful lot of people at the gate that morning. One was Marc, ready to record the whole event in still photography. Cecco Casti was absent.

I should have mentioned that another "animal-pit" had appeared at the Hut Circle during the last week. To keep up my appearance of trust in Marc, I'd set out a live-trap near the first pit to catch the "bunny" that made it. A day later the door was shut, but the hare inside it was anything but live. Poor thing had likely been killed by Tiro.

I didn't set it again, hoping to goodness Paolini soon had all he needed for an arrest.

I saw another familiar face at the gate: Françoise Pinard of *Paris Match*. She stepped directly into our path and demanded,

"Dr. Lewis, what you expect to find in this second

chamber you are calling the *'mundus?'* And congratulations on your recovery! How much longer do you wear the sling?"

"Until the Ides of March, Françoise," he smiled. "We suspect this doorway may hide a pit like a Roman *mundus,* an entry to the underworld open only on certain (unlucky) days of the year. As my wife Tanaquil made the actual discovery, she will be guiding operations today."

"Your *wife*? Wait, Dr. Lewis."

Turning gleefully on his heel, Jim allowed me to precede him through the gate before locking it in the media's stunned face and hustling me off to the *hypogeum*.

We have always made a good team. While Jim observed the camera feed via screen-sharing with my laptop a little distance away, I was in the *hypogeum* proper. I would drill a tiny hole between two of the stones that blocked the arched opening and insert first the air-sample tube and then the fiber-optic camera hooked up to my laptop on the limestone floor.

Tech expert Franco had fixed me up with a small mic and single ear-bud through which to communicate with a similarly-rigged Jim.

Two full haz-mat suits were still on their way from Rome. We had surgical gloves and masks and would rely on visuals and the air-sampling system to decide whether to use them.

Franco handed me the small-but-powerful battery-powered drill as I stepped down into the *hypogeum* and sat cross-legged on the floor.

I noticed it the moment my posterior hit the limestone floor: a buzzing hum that reached up into my flesh and bones and set my teeth on edge. It was like the hum I'd felt there before, but livelier, edgier, more disturbing and more disturbed, like a hive of angry wasps.

Oh hell, my dream.

"Anyone else hearing that buzzing sound? Pericles, can you hear it at your end?"

"No, nothing here. Franco?"

"No. No buzzing."

Odd. Sweat broke out on my upper lip.

After one false start the drill's sharp bit neatly punctured the mortar between two stones. I inserted the tube and its snugly-fitting fiber-optic camera and we went live.

A cry of disgust went up and I also shrank back once I realized what I was looking at. On top of a domed cover of some sort, covered in the ashy remains of flowers, lay a baby goat. Its delicate pasterns were hog-tied. Its eyes, nostrils, and mouth were *sewn shut.*

A sealing charm. I forced myself to send the camera up and around and under the sacrificial victim. Sure enough, the anus was sewn shut, too.

From its irregular shape it seemed that the little domed chamber—about the size of a large dog-house—seemed to have begun as a natural cave whose visible floor had been chiseled flat. A gleaming convex circular object now filled most of the space under the goat and flowers.

"It's a shield," I gasped. "Blue-green patina here and there so it's most likely bronze covered in gold leaf. I can see a hammered design of lions around the inner part of the rim. It is studded on the outside edge with rows of little circular bosses."

"Is it acting as a cover to something in the floor?" came Jim's voice in my ear.

I sent the camera snaking along to look. A bright rim of white mortar appeared.

"Yes. Are you seeing that, Jim? The shield is fastened in place with mortar."

"Let's take an air-sample, but I expect that anything interesting is under that shield."

If by "interesting" he meant "contagious," I hoped for "boring."

I extracted the Alpha canister with its air sample then

resealed the tube. There was nothing more to be done other than speculate until we'd heard back from the lab. Leaving speculation to Jim and the rest of the gang, I escorted the sample into town myself.

"Mrs. Lewis, Mrs. Lewis," came a couple of intelligible voices from the mob outside the gate as I shouldered past with the sample.

Once I realized they meant me, I thought, *Wow, news travels fast!*

I had an ulterior motive in going to the Museum. While waiting for the results I wanted to check the display of *hypogeum* jewelry—and the vault storage, too, if possible—for evidence that any more objects been spirited away. Seemed like a good opportunity.

When I parked the Fiat in the Museum lot, I noticed a blue Mini Cooper. Looked like Tony's new car. Borrowed by Marc? I hurried inside hoping not to meet either of them.

Tina the lab tech was primed and ready to test the sample.

"Give me a quarter of an hour," she said.

When I asked to go check on the collection, she said the Museum was closed on Mondays and I might do as I liked. I also told her about the likelihood of needing another sample the minute we lifted the shield off whatever lay below.

"I'll be here all day and all this week," she said with a shrug. "We're processing the last of the contents of the vases. Next week I'm back in Rome."

Off I trotted down the unlit corridors. Heeding my Tanny-sense, I left my site boots outside the entry to the exhibition hall and went on in socks.

In the central room behind the reclining *Sposi* was the case with the *hypogeum* jewelry, its security sensor glowing faintly in the dark. Shining my phone-light into it I saw at once that the pectoral was still missing along with one of the bracelets. Looking closely, I also saw that now both earrings were of the same color. Neither was as yellow as the bracelet on display.

From the far end of the hall came the sound of two voices speaking in Italian and brisk, heeled steps rapidly approaching. Cutting off my light, I took cover near the lab door and listened, my heart in my mouth. I silenced my phone.

"What about all the media? Won't it be risky?" asked Giulia Pantano.

"Marc says they can't focus on two things at once," softly sneered an unknown man's voice. "And I come and go so often now they won't notice when or if I do."

"You had better be right," muttered Giulia. Then came a *click* and a faint hum I hadn't noticed before ceased. *The case's security system being switched off?*

Sure enough, there came a small grunt as of someone lifting the case's heavy glass cover, and a metallic *thunk* as its props slid into place.

I peeked around the corner, pulse racing, and undertook to make a short video. In it we see Giulia lift with purple-gloved hands a heavy *something* the size of a bracelet and place it gingerly into a hard-sided camera bag held by Marc's minion, Cecco Casti. That was all I got before I sensed that Tina was looking for me and tiptoed for the lab-door as fast as I dared to go. I grabbed my boots on the way.

As I entered was Tina pulling a page from the printer. "All done," she said. "Goat hair, traces of mold, ashy organics, and gold, limestone and bronze signatures. There was also a rich collection of pollen that I will send on to Rome. No pathogens. Here's the report."

"Thanks a million," I smiled as I took it. Then I ran for the Fiat and gunned it for the Corso with a panicky certainty that Cecco Casti was close behind me. I had in fact just turned left onto it and was about even with Via Giordano Bruno when the Cooper pulled out behind me. But it turned right towards Tony's place.

The Range-Rover was in the lot inside the gate when I got back. Angelo was at the picnic table stirring grated cheese into a huge pot of red risotto. Beside it was a bowl of fresh *tarocchi*. A heart-warming sight. Hungry students were already moving in on it with plates.

"The air is negative for pathogens," I called out, waving the print-out. I was wary about sharing publicly what else I'd learned. "Glad you got here safely," I went on and kissed both his cheeks in greeting. "Did you get the haz-mat suits?"

"*Certo,*" he grinned. He wiped his hands on a towel and took the printout.

"No worries, *Tanina,* we will have the wall down before you can finish your risotto. Saw your *sposo* with Franco at the Temple just now. Tell my son I need him."

And he hurried off.

Filling two plates, I took them to where Jim and Franco sat talking on the stone foundations of Vanth and Tages.

"Risotto is ready but *il babbo* wants you down at the *mundus, Franceschino.*"

Franco hurried off with his food. Jim took his with a kiss.

"Wonderful work, sweetheart, though that goat almost put me off my feed. Franco was just telling me his team has uncovered a votive pit running along the whole north side of the foundations. It is full of gilded iron votive figurines!"

"Gilded iron?" I blinked.

Jim thereupon produced from his pea-jacket pocket something like an aggregation of Roman nails about three inches tall. Looking more closely I saw it had two little legs, two flattened wings, two sharp breasts, two upstretched arms, one spiky head and one torch, all coated with flakes of gold leaf.

"It's a Vanth in wrought iron," he said gleefully. "Right up your alley."

"Iron is the metal of the underworld," I mused as I took it carefully from him, "and easier wrought than cast. I suppose

145

the gold helped keep it from rusting away. How many in the pit?"

"Three hundred and sixty. One for every degree in the circle."

"Or every day in the solar year not counting the extras," I inserted.

"Or sixty from each of the sixty members of the college of *haruspices*," went on my best beloved gleefully, "or thirty for each of the twelve cities in the *dodecapolis*. They have identified twelve subtle variants, possibly made at twelve different smithies."

I handed it back to him with a whistle of amazement. "I'd be jealous," I laughed, "except that we have the world's biggest discovery awaiting us, yonder."

Did we ever.

14

ALL HELL BREAKS LOOSE

The buzzing was so strong this time—especially when combined with the smell of goat—that I nearly lost my nice risotto lunch. The little arch yawned open to reveal the now-crumbled remains of the little kid. A tiny spotlight had been set up by the camera team. It illuminated the rim of the shield and sent golden beams over the chamber's irregular walls.

The plan was to drill a viewing hole in the mortar under the shield and once again to ferry a sample of air down to the lab for Tina to analyze while we looked around inside. Based on what was, or wasn't, in that air we would make our plan for tomorrow.

Seemed simple but right from the get-go things went wrong.

First, the drill jumped out of my hand and took a gouge out of my left calf.

I gave a cry of pain and dropped the drill, shattering the bit. After clamping a hand over the welling blood and a quick bandaging job I was soon back in action. Adjusting my safety-glasses I held on like grim death and fired up the drill.

Though the smooth rim of mortar gave the lie to any

trouble, the drill jerked and juddered in my fist as if determined to go anywhere but straight ahead.

When at last I broke through all of *La Castellina* shuddered.

"Did you feel that?" cried someone from the surface.

"We don't *have* earthquakes here," complained someone else. "Not in Tarquinia."

"Tanny, get out of there," came Jim's digitized voice.

"Wait, wait," I pleaded. "Nearly done."

A moment later I had an air sample sealed in a fresh canister. Then I put the camera in. I was handing the sample up to the tech on the surface when I heard Jim's shout of horror. I looked up at my screen and screamed.

The camera was looking directly into the murdered face of a mummified man, a cord pulled tight under one ear. When I panned the camera back, we could see he was curled up on his side at the bottom of a well or cistern. He was wearing a withered wreath and priestly white garments stained black at his midsection. Scattered over all were hundreds of gilded iron Vanths like the one Jim had shown me. Everything was streaked with more ashy remains of flowers.

As I moved the camera something bright gleamed suddenly from between the dead priest's cord-bound hands. It was a sphere of gold the size of a softball.

I estimated that if it was solid, it might weigh up to thirty kilograms.

Millions of dollars of gold.

In that instant a flash of blinding light blazed from the heart of the ball. It came right up the fiber-optic cable and up my optic nerve, sending a dagger of pain flashing into my skull and down my spine. From there it branched through my body with a jolt that threw me backwards.

I was hovering above the site. Jim and I lay side by side, throats torn out, emptied of blood. Angelo lay sprawled on the ground in front of the camper, his back slashed as if with huge claws, and Franco was hung up on trees under the cliff, broken like a china doll. Marc's black Lotus was speeding away from the site, back along the road to town.

I awoke, my skin hurting and my mouth tasting of blood, and my head burned with pain. The little light left in the darkening sky was too brilliant for my eyes to bear, so I shut my them, trying not to lose my lunch from the exaggeration of every smell: the risotto on my lips; my own sweat mingled with a faint menstrual whiff; Jim's nearby sweat and aftershave...

"No, dammit." Jim barked somewhere so near to my ear and so loudly that I almost wept with pain. "We're not taking off that shield, Angelo, not until the sample comes back clean."

"We have the suits, *Giacomo*. We can't leave that gold here, not overnight."

"We have to go," I croaked as loudly as I dared. "Go. Now."

There was a beat of silence. Then I could feel someone kneel on the ground beside me. Jim asked urgently, "Good God, Tanny. What in the world happened? How do you feel?"

I conjured up a sickly smile. "Like some idiot drilled a hole in my leg and some other idiot bashed me on the head with a rock. And like a hot fork came out of that golden ball and stuck into my eye." I opened one eye a crack and asked, "Where is Marc?"

"Sent him to the lab with the sample," he muttered, "a little while ago."

"*What?*" I yelled, got up in haste and promptly lost my lunch into the bushes.

A bottle of drinking water appeared at my elbow. I swished and spat then drank, looking around uneasily. We seemed to be the only ones left at the site. It was almost night.

"He was the only one we could spare," muttered Angelo.

"He's going to fetch his minion Cecco," I groaned with absolute certainly, my skull nearly exploding with pain. "If we're still here when they get back, we're all dead, Pericles! Leave the gold, forget the haz-mat suits. We've got to get out of here quick! *Quick.*"

"Leave the gold?"

"It won't be safe in the Museum. We can't take it to the house. Even Paolini can't protect us from." At which point, I faded out. I had the oddest sensation of diminishing. It was if I were a ball of yarn unspooling. When I faded back in again, I was vaguely conscious they were arguing over the cultural value of the gold.

I clearly heard Jim say, "To have been collected and melted down, not worked at all."

"All right then, leave it. Leave everything. Let's get out of here." Snapped Angelo angrily as I stumbled up the slope supported by Jim's good left arm.

"No point in locking anything," remarked my best beloved. "They still have my keys."

"Should we call Paolini from the camper?" asked Franco, hastening along beside us. "Ask the police to come out and try to save something?"

"If it doesn't take too long," replied Jim dubiously.

But the line had been cut.

We raced for the Range-Rover, leaving the Fiat behind.

Or rather, Angelo and Franco raced and Jim helped me along, my eyes squeezed shut. "It's too bad about the gold," he said, half to himself. "Maybe we can call Paolini from town. How are you holding up, sweetheart? You're awfully hot to the touch."

"Oh, rotten," I laughed. "Pericles, what if they trash the site, starting with the Hut Circle. All my good work while you were out of commission, wasted."

"No worries," he said stoutly. "You kept great records and photos."

Then he and I tumbled into the back seat.

"Go, go, go," I cried. Angelo stomped on the gas and we were all flung back in our seats. Soon we were slewing from side to side and flying up towards the ceiling as he hit the ruts and potholes flying. We were fixing to pass the place at Mazzola's house where the track splits into two narrow lanes before joining the road to the highway when I got a clear message to stop.

"*Babbo, babbo*," I cried out. "Pull over and switch off the headlights! If they see us, they'll think we have it and will kill us all." Convinced, he pulled behind the farmhouse.

That very *minute and second*, best beloved, a blue Mini-Cooper jammed with three people—Tony, Marc and Cecco—shot by the other side of the farmhouse with headlights blazing, heading for the site. They nearly bottomed out on a pothole before gunning off again, skidding and slewing, just as we had.

"*Madre di Dio*," breathed Angelo into the stunned silence. He turned on the headlamps and high-tailed it for the highway. As I slumped against Jim's shoulder, I could hear the voice from my dream say clearly, *Call me if you run into trouble.*

"Pericles," I whispered, "Call my godfather! Call *Padre* LoCieco. *Mor* knows."

He repeated "Your godfather?" So, I knew he'd heard me, but I'd run out of time.

15

ON THE RIVERBANK

I woke with my head in Somebody's lap, the rest of me curled up on a high-backed wooden settle. The wood was dark, worn smooth and shining. A grand fire crackled in the stone fireplace off to my right, warming the top of my head and sending coruscations of light onto a strange creature that stood between me and the settle opposite. She was the living image of the Vanth upon the doorway to the *mundus*. She glared around hungrily, but I felt safe.

I knew this place and this beloved lap. How the Vanth came to be here I could only guess with horror and hope for a quick release.

In the wall beyond the far settle I noticed three shuttered windows. The Vanth now went to the first of these and listened intently. I could begin to hear familiar voices. Angelo was calling Paolini. We would soon be meeting *Mor* and the Riverbankers at home. I was helpless to do more than listen for as long as the Vanth stood there.

Suddenly the Vanth was joined by two more, then two more, until the creatures multiplied beyond reckoning, filling my hearth with their leering faces and the buzzing of their wings. I shrank back and back until I was a mere curl of blue light tucked under the heart of the One.

Yet even as I was aware of this constriction, the blue expanded outward into a cloudless, sunless sky that stretched above me. I walked barefoot across a lawn of tender grass that spread across gentle slopes to where far orchards of blossoming trees danced in a fragrant breeze, beyond a river where a skiff bobbed on the current. A sweet, piercing sorrow filled me.

Someone took my hand in a firm grip. A familiar presence was walking beside me. There was a scent like fresh-cut hay mixed with motor oil. I looked up and saw a broad, dark fighter-pilot, helmet under his arm. He looked down at me, a red light in his eyes.

"Dad," I cried out joyfully. "Daddy Bill."

"Tanny-Sue," he said sternly, "you should not be here. It is not your time."

"You left us before *your* time, Daddy," I cried, stung. "We needed you."

"That's why I'm here now, honey," he said in a gentler voice. "To warn you that this Godpapa of yours will send you back to the land of the living, and tell you that has a lot to teach you, but he has his own agenda. Whatever you do, *don't share his bed.*"

"All right, Daddy." I said uneasily.

Then he smiled at last and pinched my chin, looking into my face.

"You became a classicist just like your Great-Great-Grandpa. I'm proud of you, Tanny-Sue, and I'm going to be prouder still, but I'm out of time."

He kissed my cheek, leaving a mark I could feel for hours after I awoke.

"Wait here for your Godpapa, and kiss your *Mor* for me."

"I sure will!"

I wanted to add that I loved him but he had already

turned and walked off in the direction of the river. I sat down cross-legged on the soft turf and watched him sail back across the river and climb past the flowering trees and into the mountains until he vanished from sight.

I sat waiting for something to happen.

Gradually there came a troubling of the air like the first breath of a thunderstorm. A blue spark appeared perhaps a meter from my face. Sparkling now with many colors, it took the shape of a vertical eye and grew larger every moment. As it grew, I saw shapes moving in it as if it were a window to another place. Without any warning it opened out to swallow me, turning reality inside out, and there I was again at the hearth of my soul. A fresh breeze was blowing through the three windows, now flung wide to show the green world and an empty orchard.

Again I sat on the settle to the right of the hearth. I was clad in my nightgown and beside me I felt the One. On the settle opposite there was now a cube made of what looked like copper wire. In it fluttered a strange bird, white and green and blue, with red legs, yet not a bird. Staring out with green eyes, brandishing a tiny torch in one white fist, was the Vanth.

Half turned away from me, one arm along the mantle-piece of the merrily-burning hearth, stood a thin man dressed in clerical black, a shovel-hat on his big head, heavy shoes on his big feet, and a long cassock in between, over which, oddly, he wore a short sword.

Hooked over his big ears and resting on the bridge of his aquiline nose were silver glasses with the circular smoked lenses of a blind man. Even with them on, I reckoned I knew who he was. The resemblance to our mutual ancestor was uncanny.

"My godfather, Titono Empedicleo LoCieco?"

"The same. Pleased to know you."

He made two quaint bows, one to me and one to the One

beside me.

"Did you put the Vanth in that cage? Can . . . can't you . . . ?"

"Banish her entirely?" He shook his head. "No. You will do that yourself, when I have taught you. Until then, remember this: *she rejoices in having a living host, and will goad you into evil.* Especially do not fall into hate. Do you hear?"

"Yes, Godpapa," I murmured, inexplicably abashed. "Thank you!"

"Bless you, child!" Making the sign of the cross he vanished along with the hearth.

I sat up so suddenly that I dealt Jim—bending over me—a nasty blow.

"Sorry," I cried, rubbing my forehead.

"Hit me again," he laughed, rubbing his jaw. He turned eagerly to address persons unseen, "Hey, Riverbankers. The River's awake."

Clo and Ratty ran up from somewhere else but hung back in wonder and some fear.

"You've been saying weird things in your sleep," explained Clo anxiously.

"And I'm still not entirely cured," I sighed. "My Godpapa-the-warlock says he will teach me to cure myself the rest of the way." I looked around the echoing room. "Where are we?"

"Quarantine Wing of Tarquinia General," said Jim. "Dates from the 1919 epidemic. You do know you've been asleep for three whole days?"

"That's impossible," I gasped. "Gosh, when's the wedding?"

"In a week. Your mother and I have taken it in turns, staying with you. She is also the one who called *Padre* LoCieco. Or he called her, actually, the minute she picked up her phone."

"*Bestemor* is amazing," crowed the Mole irrelevantly. "She's teaching me to knit!"

Ratty made a face. "Is your Godpapa really a *witch?*"

"A warlock," I corrected. "*Mor* says it's a long story."

Suddenly I remembered another long story.

"The site. The gold. Is everybody safe?"

Jim's face darkened.

"Later," he said.

They got me back to Via Pyrgi and we ate a cheerful burrito dinner, thanks to the tortillas squirrelled away in my mother's suitcase. I can see her now, burrito in hand, about to tell Clo and Ratty the short version of how I happened to have a "fairy godfather."

"Your *Mor's* Papa was a fighter pilot when she was born," she began. "He was based in Aviano, which is up in northern Italy, not too far from Venice—you've been there? Good. it is less than an hour away from Venice. So, she was born in Italy, in Pordenone, near the base.

"When she was about a month old, we thought we'd have her baptized in the chapel on the base. Grandma Jane was still alive, and flew out for it, but we didn't have any friends yet at the base, so—who could be her godparents?"

"Why not Grandma Jane?" asked Clo.

Mor tilted her head to think. "Well, I guess it's better to have *extra* relatives. A week before Grandma Jane was set to arrive, we got a little note at the apartment we'd just moved into, addressed to *Tanaquil Susannah Greenough.*" The children both grinned at me. "We had just that day decided to use Great-Grandma Susie's name for her middle name, but there it was, mailed from Florence on her birthday. It had been sent to the first apartment we'd lived in, so it took awhile finding us.

"It read, *Dear Goddaughter, I am related to you by way of your great-great-grandfather Titono Benevento. I live in Florence, and I would like to be your godfather.* Just like that."

Clo made a face. "Does that mean his is your great-great cousin or something?"

Ratty blurted, "And I thought you said godparents shouldn't be relatives?"

Mor rolled her eyes. "Anyhow, we wrote back and he was at the christening."

"You said it was a baptism," objected the Rat.

"Same difference!"

"Ha," interrupted Jim. "You're where Tanny got that expression!"

Once the Riverbankers were asleep and *Bestemor* went off to the little guest room with a good book, Pericles filled me in on what happened after we left the site.

"Tony is dead, sweetheart," he said in a low voice. "We don't know whether they fought among themselves over the gold or—or exactly what happened. The police found him face up on the tarp beside the *hypogeum.* His throat was torn open as if by an animal, but there was just a drop of blood on the tarp, even though the doctor said he bled to death."

I frowned incredulously. "What are you saying?"

"I'm not sure." He put his hands into his hair. "There were deep gashes on his chest and shoulder like claw marks. And there were slashes down his back, Paolini said, when they turned him over. It was like whatever it was brought him down from behind then, well, then . . ."

"It drank his blood," I cried in horror. "What does that? A mountain lion? An eagle?"

"Some kind of bird—maybe an eagle. There were feathers between his fingers."

"Feathers?" The hair rose right up on the back of my neck but I forced myself to ask, "What color feathers?"

If he said "Vanth green," I was going to jump out the nearest window!

"Sort of a golden brown with spots."

I was madly Googling "barn owls" and showed him the Wikipedia entry: there was Antonia looking back at us with her moon-white face and golden-brown wings. With spots.

He stared at it incredulously. "Can owls get rabid?"

"Who knows? What about Marc and Cecco and the gold?"

He sighed. "Pretty sure your idea of leaving the gold behind may have not only saved our lives but also preserved the rest of the site. The remains of the priest-sacrifice were otherwise untouched and nothing else taken or destroyed. The Hut Circle is just as you left it. All the gilded votives were stolen, and the shield, and of course the gold mass is gone. Apparently, they brought a small crane to haul it out, which they left behind. Also, the Mini-Cooper has vanished from Tony's place, but Marc's Lotus is still outside the gate of the site.

"Once they left the site they just kept going."

We were both silent a moment, knowing why. *While the creature had feasted on Tony they had escaped it. But a sight like that would make them run as far and as fast as they could!*

A strange fury rose in me. "They left poor Tony to die," I growled. "I hope those votives are riddled with plague and that their precious gold mass is *cursed.*"

"May God avert," cried Jim urgently, and my mother came into the room, making angry hushing noises at us both, before going off to check on the children.

I repented at once, stammering mournfully, "Godpapa says I've got to, to watch my temper. I still have a Vanth. Maybe you should just lock me up."

"Maybe," countered Jim, "we need to tell you when your Vanth is flaring up. How about using a word like *Basingstoke?*"

He knows his Gilbert and Sullivan, does my best beloved!

"*Basingstoke* it is," I smiled, and kissed him for his wit. Then my silenced phone buzzed on the table. I stared at the screen: *Marcus B. Short.*

"Should I?" I whispered.

Jim put out his chin in the gesture for *dai.*

Go ahead!

"Marc?" Rather than put it on speaker phone, I sat close enough for Jim to hear.

"Listen, bitch, I blame *you* for what happened to Tony, and believe me, you'll pay."

And he hung up.

I methodically blocked his number before trusting myself to speak.

"Typical Marc thinking," I said at last. *"I steal the thing that is keeping the Vanth in check and now I'm blaming you for the consequences."*

"You think, you think that the *Vanth* did that to Tony?" wondered Jim. "But it's a spirit, isn't it? How does a spirit do that? I thought you said an owl."

I shook my head. "A spirit might take over a living creature?"

Then the phone buzzed in his sling and he dragged it out with his left hand.

"Paolini," he said, showing me the screen, then answered. "Yes, Lewis here! Yes, she is quite well. *Dimmi!* I think so." Checking his calendar, he responded, "Yes, the reception after Tony's memorial starts tomorrow *alle sette nel pomeriggio.* See you then."

He hung up and tucked way his phone left-handed.

"You're getting good at that," I laughed.

"Hm. I'm naturally left-handed. I had one of those teachers who make you change. So." He looked up with a smile. "Forgot to tell you that Tony's memorial is late tomorrow afternoon at the Tarquinia Cemetery with a wake/reception at the Museum to follow. Are you up for it?"

"Sure," I chirped gamely, my head beginning to ache. "How about I swing by his Cantina on the way to the Museum with my keys, to pick up a bottle of his own wine?"

A wave of tingling anxiety washed over me: a warning not to go there alone.

16

TONY'S WAKE

NOW THAT THE CORONER WAS SATISFIED WITH HIS CAUSE OF death—catastrophic loss of blood and a return of his lung cancer—Tony's remains had been cremated. They were to be placed a niche bought years before at the *Cimitero di Tarquinia,* appropriately nestled among the ancient tombs which had once covered the whole ridge.

It had sometimes given me pause to know that, after a final sacking by Saracen raiders in the 1300's the people of Tarquinia had moved from what was now called the *Pian di Cività* to found their new town of Corneto, so-called until Mussolini came along reviving ancient names, on a ridge which was riddled with ancient tombs.

Was it just that they wanted a fresh start, I'd sometimes wondered, *or had the magic lurking in the ancient city been worse than living among ghosts?*

It seemed fitting that the ex-pat Tony Ellingham, having put all he owned into his corner of Italian Heaven could leave his ashes there as well.

No-one could say that he was miserly in spending his ill-gotten gains here in his adopted country. He took, yes, but he also gave back more lavishly than any of us had imagined.

After a bout with prostate cancer ten years earlier—inspiring him to buy his niche and arrange for his cremation—he had paid for a new cancer suite at Tarquinia General.

Then there was the roast suckling pig toga feast he'd held in honor of Angelo's thirtieth year digging at *Pian di Città,* after which Lavinia's famous seduction had occurred.

I had been off doing field work and had missed that party. The skinny-dipping episode with Marc had occurred soon afterwards, at one of the picnics Tony held near the little river at the bottom of the hill, in which he chilled his wine.

Down the steep path we would troop from the main house like so many worker ants, each carrying some part of the feast in our arms or on our shoulders or heads, including the tables and chairs, though some preferred to recline on the grass.

Tony and Tiro had been Jim's companions five years ago when he hiked from the picnic site to swimming hole at the base of *La Castellina.* Tiro had flushed the black hare that led them up to the spirit door of the *hypogeum,* set into the middle of the cliff.

It had taken years of searching and the bodily removal of many tons of obliterating earth, but Tony had lived to see the discovery of the physical entry to the *hypogeum* at last, gleefully adding to add to his trade in antiquities. Just how widespread were his regional connections as a fence of stolen goods? Wide enough to spend lavishly on that cluster of three houses on *Via San Giacomo* overlooking the Tyrrhenian Sea.

Make that my *cluster of three houses.*

He had converted two of the simple, one-story houses into pleasant dwellings full of lovely works of art, their walls painted in vivid colors, their baths fitted with the best fixtures and tiles Italy had to offer. One, he lived in, the other he rented out to tourists, more often to visiting academics, but sometimes they were all open and the party ranged from building to building, terrace to terrace, room to room.

The third building remained rustic: the so-called *Cantina,* where Tony tinkered with making wine from his little vineyard in the valley, and blended olive oil from his own trees.

It was to this building that Jim and I repaired before the reception with my set of keys, to pick up some wine and explore the place, perhaps reliving some of its more interesting events.

My long-suffering mother agreed to take the Riverbankers home after the memorial, but warned Jim not to tire me, saying, "Remember where she was yesterday morning, *Jakob.*"

"We won't do anything strenuous," he promised, adding in a conspiratorial undertone as he got into the Fiat beside me, "Just a spot of polar-bear skinny-dipping."

"Easy-peasy," I laughed, elated to be alone with him. I was also filled with a recklessness that I would later blame on the Vanth.

We parked the Fiat at the end of the block then mooned our way, hand-in-hand down the street to the front gate, admiring the view of the sea. I hadn't been there since the chilly January morning when Cecco had taken Marc's blackmail photograph: the last time I'd seen Tony alive.

"Pericles", I asked on a sudden thought. "What happened to Tiro?"

"Nobody's seen him. I've put the word out that we will adopt him if he's found."

Borrowing my keys, he unlocked the gate. It swung silently open.

"That's new," frowned my best beloved. "The squeaking of Tony's gate was a warning to wayward couples to *straighten up and fly right,* as Grandpa Jim used to say."

"Get the wine first, then we mess around?" I suggested with a flutter of fear.

"His wine was never much good," said Jim as we reached the Cantina, "but I'm happy to drink some of it in his honor."

He set the key to the big padlock on the rolling door, pushed it back, but, *No wine.*

There was something I recognized as a metal-casting table, spattered with drops of yellow metal, and against one wall were about ten unopened boxes of a publication that looked from the sample on the side of each box to be a museum catalogue, labeled *Antiquità Colchis*, with the same logo that had been on my box of keys.

In one corner of the building was a little photographic studio, with a reflective umbrella, lights, and a velvet-covered tray. There was also a work table stacked with small white cardboard boxes like mine, and a roll of bubble wrap. A small refrigerator stood humming nearby, but all that was in it were two unlabeled phials of what looked like blood.

Beside the refrigerator was a medium-sized safe.

No wine, no olive oil, and no dust, either.

Recently used, and for purposes that seemed anything but legal.

"Call Paolini, Pericles, quick," I stammered. "We've got to get out of here!"

My sense of the impending arrival of *someone* was very strong.

"Right you are," he muttered and handed me the keys, phoning as he went. I locked up the Cantina in haste then guided Jim around to the terrace at the back of the house as he talked with the Colonel, my eyes everywhere at once.

"I agree," Jim was saying. "Okay, we'll do what we can," he promised, and hung up. "Paolini's guy just spotted Giulia and Riccardo racing off from the Museum in Giulia's Alfetta, right in the middle of their own party preparations."

"And he thinks they're headed this way?"

"Yeah. Giulia came out of her office saying something about *the Cantina.*"

"Rats! Did we say something about coming by here for a bottle of wine?"

"Maybe." He swallowed. "Maybe there's a silent alarm.

"Paolini's in Viterbo, but says he will meet some local men to meet him here as soon as he can. He said to delay them."

"We? Delay Riccardo and Giulia? How? Do you think they'll know we're here?"

"The Fiat is just down the street," he nodded grimly.

"Do you think Giulia suspects that we suspect them?"

He tilted his head speculatively. "No, but there's loads of incriminating stuff against them in the Cantina. If they find out we've been in there, we could be in some danger."

"So," I proposed eagerly, "we have to make them think we've been *here* the whole time, and haven't made it to the Cantina yet. That we *started here* and not at the Cantina."

We both heard a car-door slam, near at hand.

"Oh, hell!" I yelped as we dodged behind the outer wall of the kitchen.

Jim peeped out. "They're going straight for the Cantina."

"Quick," I muttered, dragging him down the path to the guest house and unlocking it with shaking hands. We stepped into the dark, cold, stuffy interior.

"Whew," said Jim, making a face. "Smells like a zoo! Marc and Cecco must not have been back since they took off with the gold."

"Or ever cleaned it when they were here," I agreed, tearing dirty sheets off one of the beds. "Open the windows! It'll smell better and they've got to hear us."

"Hear us doing what?" he asked suspiciously, throwing a casement open to let in the sweet February air. I had my coat off and was madly pulling my sweater over my head.

"What do you think? We have to convince them that we're clueless."

"I don't like the idea of facing those two unclothed, Greenough," he frowned, slowly removing his shoes.

"All the more reason for them to think we didn't expect company," I argued, peeling off the last of my clothes and crawling onto the bare mattress. "Hurry, up, it's cold over here!"

"Okay, okay! It's this wretched sling!" cried my best beloved as he struggled to get out of his t-shirt single-handedly and in a hurry.

"Happy to help, Pericles," I laughed, going to his rescue.

It took them a long time to sneak up on us. By the time the door of the guest-house swung slowly open, Jim's *delicto* was so very much *in flagrante* that it took the heavy click of a handgun near my head to bring us back to the present moment.

I squeaked. Jim dragged a stale sheet over us. We both looked out frowzily at two armed thugs in black balaclavas and jump-suits.

One thug was rather petite and wore a gold anklet chain above her sensible black flats. Jim, having lost his glasses, squinted up at them, asking in English,

"Sorry, but can we help you?"

"How did you get in here?" asked the small one gruffly in Italian as the larger one came menacingly over to our bedside.

"Might ask you the same thing," Jim replied saucily in the same tongue. He got the big thug's gun in his ear for his pains.

"I have keys from Tony," I pointed to the dresser. "You are trespassing on my property."

"Your property?" the smaller thug scoffed.

"He always did love her best," shrugged Jim, browsing on my cheek.

"What are you doing here?"

"Well, we *were* getting wine for the reception, but now..."

"He's demonstrating how he got Lavinia pregnant," I declared boldly. "It was too cold to go skinny-dipping."

"Yes," he asseverated solemnly. "An *historical re-enactment*, if you will. Not easy with this damned sling! What's your excuse? Are you stealing Tony's collection of bad wine?"

The thugs drew aside, whispering feverishly, perhaps believing us, perhaps suffering from a squeamish revulsion against shooting two naked people they both knew.

"We will take these," said the big thug at last, pocketing the keys. "Don't try anything."

Then they stalked out and locked us in but were too flustered to take our phones. Then they headed over to empty the Cantina.

Jim wanted to re-enact our re-enactment, arguing it would take them ages to carry off all that stuff, but I had no wish to appear to Paolini's subordinates in the altogether. Nor did I care to be shot by mistake, so I messaged Paolini with our, and the thugs', whereabouts.

As it happened, we were still barefoot when the police arrived to find Giulia and Riccardo dragging the safe down the hill to the vineyard on a tarp, her Alfetta long since filled.

"Your keys, *signorina*," the Colonel smiled, looking at our feet.

"That's *signora*," corrected Jim, tucking in his shirt. "Nothing to see here, pal."

*E*xcerpt C from The DIARY of M. G. BURNSEY: Bomarzo

*L*eaving their chaperone in Siena, the three friends choose the most pleasant transport back to the railway line that will take them on to Rome, namely a carriage driven by a certain Giovanuccio. Mary is inseparable from her cat Impy, with some curious results.]

JULY 7, 82 – Bomarzo

Late PM: Staying at the family home of our coachman, Giovanuccio Bezzecca. So many days have passed since I last wrote I hardly know where to start. Tomorrow we board the train at Attigliano—a mile or two away—for Rome at last. I must note down something of the dreamlike journey from Siena, since we have traveled through the most astonishing countryside, past crater lakes and through the most ancient and tenebrous (sp?) of forests, all the while singing or talking.

Again, I have not been sketching, being too busy with life.

The singing started on July 4th, the day we left Jx3 in Siena, when in a spirit of our Independence we began to sing "Columbia, the Gem of the Ocean," and went on to "My Country 'Tis of Thee" and "Yankee Doodle," which Giovanuccio made us teach him.

Then we made him teach us all the folk songs he knew, including a beautiful thing called "La Pesca dell'Anello," and something racy called "Leati Geppo." It was very jolly, and Bess began riding up in front with him, learning Italian and teaching him English. St. and I had a long talk about everything in the world, what he dreamed of doing and what I dreamed of doing. It was sweet.

I laughed at him, because he wants to make the best cookies in the world, and I want to make the best drawings in the world, but we agreed that we are both trying to make the world happier!

It was on the 6th, overlooking the strange Lago di Vico, that I kissed St., knowing I will never again see T. I am still very fond of St.—he is sweet and very good-looking in a mild way, and I think he now looks at me with new eyes, but he hasn't proposed, though we have taken to kissing whenever Bess looks away. He noticed I have stopped sketching, and says he is sad about it. I promised I would start again, when we get to Rome.

Poor Bess. Seeing us so debauched, she herself is determined to stay here with Giovanuccio! What of that fat, rich man she is to marry? And if St. won't marry me, what will I do, if T. is wrong? Margaret Fuller would tell me not to care. Mama already has six respectable daughters.

What is really on my mind is our strange visit today to the ruined Villa here, what they call the "Garden of Monsters." It is a valley full of huge, grotesque figures carved out of the living stone two centuries back and now overgrown with creepers and buried by drifts of leaves. Only the local people know of it, Giovanuccio says.

St. and Bess went with Giovanuccio, but I wanted to be alone, hungry again to sketch. We agreed to return to the secret entrance at the bottom of the hill no later than sundown. Bess and I were both tightly veiled and gloved against bad air. Impy cried until I let him go with me. He loved darting in and out of the carvings, peeping out from their tops and being good company.

I had just sat down on a stump to sketch the most amazing monster of all – a room in the hillside made to look like a hollowed-out head, its mouth the door and its eyes the windows – when I saw T. emerge from it in his black cassock and white collar, and beckon to me to join him. Our tryst was glorious, but when T. left me to adjust my veil and gloves, all I found on the "doorstep" was my cat. Now, Bess is asleep in our little room and Impy watches me with burning eyes.

17

MATRIMONIALE

THE FALLOUT FROM THE RAID ON TONY'S *CANTINA* CONTINUED for some time. The catalogues from *Antichità Colchis* proved to be full of glossy photos by "B. Corto" of Etruscan jewelry from *La Castellina* stretching back years. In the safe were many of the missing pieces themselves.

The bronze shield was found behind the safe, but there was no trace of the pectoral, nor of the golden ball. Since the scandal to the Pantano family was fairly complete, Angelo stepped in as Interim Director of the Museum.

A neighbor found Tiro wandering in the valley below Tony's house, half-starved, and offered to keep him temporarily, since our rental didn't allow pets.

We resolved to get him back to Princeton, somehow.

The mystery of the blood in the refrigerator had not been solved by the time our church wedding in Rome rolled around, less than a week later.

The wedding festivities would not be all that large so there was not too much to do, thank goodness. Not many folks could make it all the way from the States. We arranged a dinner-reception for twenty friends and relations at Ristorante Alla Rampa, conveniently halfway between the church and the Hassler. We still had cake, champagne and decor to deal with.

Mor would take care of the Riverbankers during our weekend honeymoon, then fly home at last to Buster, who'd had enough bachelor living. She was finding her long stint at babysitting her new grandchildren a little challenging. We wanted to let her have a bit of a treat before she went back to Texas.

Perhaps a couple of nights in Florence, instead of Via Pyrgi as usual?

I think I have quoted Clo as saying her brother was being "awful." The truth was that he took my illness very badly and everything else, besides. For some time, I'd had a strong sense that he needed to visit his Mamma Lavinia. Since she'd left them for Caterina, he periodically pined for her. This was definitely one of those periods. The difficulty was that Lavinia couldn't bear the noise of the children in the early mornings, the most fertile time for composing the great *Lexicon Rasennese,* her life's work, and requested not to have them stay the night.

Perhaps they could spend the nights with Bestemor?

After some heated back and forth, Jim booked her and the Riverbankers into a suite for two nights in the heart of Florence at the Hotel Porta Rossa.

They would spend their two days in Florence doing something fun with Lavinia and Caterina (and Siggie-the-dog), so their *Bestemor* could visit the Uffizi and the Opera del Duomo (and maybe squeeze in David). They would all meet for dinner and she would take the children back to the hotel to sleep. The third day, Jim and I would meet them at Lavinia's to see off my mother and collect Clo and Ratty for a leisurely train-trip back to Tarquinia by way of Siena.

Or that was the plan, anyway...

The day before the wedding, accordingly, we readied the

Greenough-Lewis/Sparks suitcases for their trips to Rome and/or Florence and/or San Antonio.

But I get ahead of myself.

Jim spent most of the brief time between our narrow miss with Giulia and Rodolfo—now glowering from their holding cell on the front page of *Il Messaggero*—and suitcase-packing day working with the authorities to sort and identify all the stolen antiquities found in and around Tony's place, while I alternated between napping and getting down to wedding business in earnest. A tough job, but someone had to do it!

Out of one large suitcase, *Mor* took my white linen, satin-lined, full-length, square-necked, Hardangersøm-trimmed wedding dress, along with my own *Bestemor*'s *solje* brooch, shining with its six silver-gilt "spoons." Clo had already inspected her matching Hardangersøm dress, fastened with its own little four-disk *solje*, and utterly loved it.

"Try yours on," she insisted, as I marveled over the intricate drawn-work squares that are the hallmark of such embroidery. Almost, I lost myself in them, feeling strangely attracted by the little rooms and hallways in the cloth, following them with rapt fascination. Then I recalled myself, recognizing the Vanth's lurking presence who, like the wiccas of old, were said to be entrapped by intricate knots and innumerable objects, obsessed with counting.

Knowing that she and I have nearly identical figures, mine being simply half a size larger, *Mor* had been able to fit the bodice exactly to my shape, and it fit like a glove. It was cut low across the bust and the long sleeves snug to the wrist while the skirt—its hem all trimmed with squares of lace—flared at the hips to make a rippling oval that brushed the tops of the white flats I'd found in Tarquinia.

Mor stood back to admire all that whiteness against the rich copper of my skin.

"Ah, there's my pretty girl," she sighed. With a look of

tender mischief, she handed me a circular hat-box covered in blue velvet, worn with long use. I shivered with anticipation.

I suddenly flashed on my parents' wedding picture. He, darkly ravishing in his blue Air Force Honor Guard tunic, striped trousers, peaked hat, trim white belt and aiguillette, she the picture of Norwegian beauty in her modern white dress, *solje,* and . . .

Her wedding crown.

At the press of a catch there it was, worth a fortune in hand-worked silver filigree, a cluster of three golden "spoons" shimmering at the base of each of the seven ball-tipped points. It was not "vulgar-big" nor too small, but a dainty crown worthy of a more royal head than mine. Under it, immaculately pressed, lay a veil of finest transparent linen, edged in Hardangersøm.

Without a word, my mother hat-pinned both into place, then turned me to see myself in the sliding-glass door: such a wonder of beauty that I stood amazed.

"Oh, *Mor,*" I breathed, turning my head to make the spoons dance and sobbing in a queer sort of painful joy. "I don't dare! I am so clumsy and it is so beautiful."

"Nonsense, *kjare,*" she said bracingly. "I will sew them onto your hair. Now let's get the dress off before you rip a seam. Later, you may rip it all you like, though I would save the veil, if I were you. So, you like it, all of it?"

I nodded, incapable of speech. What I thought was that *if there were anyone prettier in all of Rome on my wedding day, let them prove it.* Maybe that was just the Vanth talking.

While stowing the crown she remarked casually,

"You're not pregnant, are you? If you are, you shouldn't wear the crown."

"N-no, *Mor,* I don't think I am, that is, I had my period while I was..."

How could we be having this conversation?

Undoing the long line of hooks down the back of the

dress, she asked pensively, "Have you ever been—let's see, how to put it? Somehow *out of your body* while making love, as if you yourself hovered in spirit above the two of you?"

After a long moment of thought, I answered, "No, nothing like that."

"Then you can wear the crown. The rest doesn't really matter. It is just," she smiled slyly, "practice! But between now and your wedding day maybe hold off?"

"But *Mor,* we are already married! Poor Pericles."

"Poor Pericles can wait," she interrupted tartly. "Your father did. But, speaking of poor Pericles, I have something for him and for my new grandson: *trollkors.*"

From her suitcase she pulled out two small identical boxes of the sort that might hold a bracelet, and opened one up. In it was a hand-forged black iron loop about the size of a penny, crossed over itself and ending with two more loops, laced to a simple leather wristlet.

"These are very popular now in Norway, but I don't remember seeing them when I was a girl. They are supposed to be protection against trolls, but I thought that with the work you're doing with these death-spirits, the boys should have them. I hope you don't mind."

I assured her I didn't.

"Poor Pericles" waited as requested, claiming that the sofa in the living room of Via Pyrgi was comfier than the sagging *matrimoniale* in our bedroom anyway. With *Mor's* and the Riverbankers' rooms between the two sleeping quarters, we managed it, just.

"Hard to get that genie back in the bottle," muttered my best beloved.

The time finally came to pack those bags for Rome, Florence and beyond, and when Rat realized that he and Clo would soon be separated not only from his suddenly-indispensable *Bestemor* but also (briefly) from his Papa and me, he went into a tantrum the likes of which I hadn't seen since his third birthday, three years back. As *Mor* put it, he "wigged out," lying on the floor in a crying heap as we all worked around him.

The phone rang. It was Anna-Maria reminding us we were due over at the Cotto place for *arancini* and *branzino alla Ortygia* in half an hour.

Miraculously, Ratty recovered.

Next I knew, we were all surrounded by *paparazzi,* stepping off the train in Rome and into a pair of taxis. Then Jim was disappearing into his single room at the Hassler, and I was with *Mor* and the Riverbankers in a family suite down the hall.

Moments later, we were at the rehearsal at All Saints and moments after that were eating dinner at the restaurant across the street, calming ourselves enough to sleep.

Before waking to Friday, February 19, our wedding day, I had a brief but terrible dream.

I was standing outside the back entrance to the Museum, very early in the morning. A rumbling like an earthquake approached me from the direction of the site. Turning to look, I saw bearing down on me a huge snake, gilt-edged and black, that brushed my arm with cold scales before plunging into the ground, right where Jim's office was, as the whole world shook.

I awoke panting with fear in the darkened room. All the other inhabitants of the suite were still sleeping peacefully.

I thought they didn't have earthquakes in Tarquinia, I thought to myself. *Then again, according to Etruscan lore, snakes were signs of a prosperous sex life.*

This vision added to the fog of anxiety that hung over me all morning. When it cleared, I had been made up, coiffed and dressed and was about to leave for the church.

Clo, already in her Hardangersøm dress and *solje,* was coaxing her brother into a blue suit identical with his father's save for scale. I was looking eastward over the Trinità dei

Monti gardens as my mother sewed the veil and the crown firmly in place. Being February, there was the cold to consider, but *Mor* had brought white woolen shawls as big as togas for me and Clo, and for Ratty a down jacket, to wear over his suit.

What Jim did was a mystery. *Mor* had decreed we were not to meet until Angelo got me down the aisle. By mutual assent, the Greenough-Sparks-Riverbanker party had decided that taxis were a bother with the church being so close. We walked, with some skipping thrown in. I had to admire my crown in every window we passed, where all at once I noticed that my mother was lovely in pale blue, a simple wool ensemble that must have cost as much as my crown.

What chunk of real estate had she and Buster sold to make all this happen? I wondered with a pang. I was embarrassed not to have thought of it earlier, but unable ever to repay.

I believe there was a cloud of *paparazzi* buzzing around us all the way down the Trinità dei Monti Steps across Piazza di Spagna and up Via Babuino the four blocks to All Saints, but there was such a peal of bells ringing inside of me that I hardly noticed.

All at once, we were at All Saints, the organ was playing, Angelo had captured my arm, and there was Pericles awaiting us at the far end of the red-carpeted aisle, beside the altar: a slim, bespectacled beautiful tunnel-vision in blue. With the help of Franco, his best man, now beaming beside him in his own gorgeous suit of grey silk, my best beloved had wriggled into the slim jacket of a beautiful new suit— complete with vest; we archaeologists are an old-fashioned lot—dispensing with the sling for the first time since his, well, let's call it, his "accident."

When I got up close beside him, he looked to me like a cherry-limeade on a hot Texas afternoon: I just couldn't drink in enough of him. A weird desire literally to browse on his flesh arose in me and my face got hot. He caught my eye, whispering "Basingstoke, my dear."

"Basingstoke it is."

Father Allen got the proceedings underway.

We sang our favorite hymns, said what we needed to and heard a nice homily from the elder priest. Nothing much sank in until we had moved our rings from our right hands to left and the long kiss happened. Suddenly bells were ringing overhead instead of inside me, Jim was laughing, I was crying, and there was un-Anglican applause.

There were photographs, of course, and bird-seed at the church door, then those of us hale enough to do so set off on foot for our midday dinner at Ristorante della Rampa.

Once safely arrived, the toasts began. Angelo's tribute reduced me again to weeping helplessness. Franco's hints at a *large family of future archaeologists* got a shout of approval from my former boss. The feast was spread, the cake was cut, all that. There was even a tiny dance floor where Pericles and I were able to demonstrate proficiency at the basics of ball-room, each having suffered through cotillion, but Franco and Angelica put us to shame.

The guests were still chatting over their *grappa* and espresso and the Riverbankers were drooping against *Mor* when the five of us made our way the few steps uphill to the Hassler at last. Saying farewell to *Mor* and the children at the door to their suite until brunch at Prester John's place next day, Jim and I wended our way to the *matrimoniale*, hand in hand.

"Can you manage?" I asked dubiously as he undertook to haul me over the threshold.

"Pretty sure I can," was the game reply, "if you put your arms around my neck."

"Glad to," I laughed, and did. The threshold was crossed and so to bed. Our pretty clothes were thrown just anywhere. My dress suffered a slight tear in the underarm seam in the haste to unhook, but my crown and veil and chignon stayed in place until the second go-round, when Jim took a moment to reach for his pocket-knife and cut the threads.

Eventually we called up some cornflakes for a late supper, but even so late into the night, were hungrier for one another than food, I myself strangely so. I have said I wanted to drink Jim up. Well, the urge grew stronger, too strong for me to control.

As when I first been invaded by the Vanth, ordinary smells and tastes seemed magnified, now the scent of Jim's body and the salty tang of sweat on the tender skin of his throat drove me wild with a desire to eat him alive. I have given and received hickeys before, but this was something different. I honestly wanted to suck the life out of him.

"Basingstoke," he muttered, writhing in pain. I felt only a flash of anger, an urge to tear off the last bandage-tape and burrow into his wound, to taste the marrow of his bones.

"Tie me up, Pericles," I gasped, unlatching with a ferocious effort. "The damned Vanth wants your blood." With a nimble twist he was out from under and rummaging on the floor for his dress socks. "Glad to be of assistance, *signora*," said he, merrily knotting my wrists to the bedstead. There was a gibbous purple mark already visible just under his ear.

"Oh, *caro*, your poor neck," I mourned. "I'm so sorry."

"Badge of honor," he said stoutly. "Now let's give that Vanth something to remember."

It is a testament to the excellence of my best beloved that, though now more or less in complete control he did not stoop to domination nor to giving me pain for his pleasure. Instead, having been initiated into such mysteries by Lavinia, he proved himself expert not only in certain Roman maneuvers of which his Methodist ancestors would not have approved, but also in their more favored modes of sexual congress, delivering the goods in the clinch.

It was during this third bout of lovemaking that the strange visitation my mother had described took place. Some small person – who somehow was also me – was hovering in the room above us over the bandaged right shoulder of my own best-beloved. It was Fred!

"There's more than Vanth inside you, now, *Tanina*," Jim murmured as if in echo of my thoughts. He fumbled to release me from his socks before falling back exhausted, cradling his sore arm in his good one. I returned from a quick wash-up to find him like that, only fast asleep. All wildness gone, I covered him tenderly, spooned up against his long back, and slept.

I was walking beside my father in the Green Place. Bending forward, I saw beyond him a phalanx of people I knew from photographs and paintings to be my Greenough ancestors, starting with Grandpa Vincent and Grandma Jane, Great-Grandpa Gus and (scandalously) his first cousin Great-Grandma Susie, then Great-Great Grandpa "Great Classicist" William and his African wife Zeya. My Great-Great-Auntie Mary G. Burnsey the famous sculptress was there with them, but beyond her was not her husband Stephen Burnsey but...Padre Benevento!

18

UNEXPECTED GIFTS

I AWOKE TO THE SWEET SOUND OF RAIN PELTING AGAINST THE shutters of our window. I got up to open first the inner shutters, then the window. I pinned back the outer shutters and leaned out in my new lacy garnet-red nightgown and garnet-red robe—presents from Jim in my favorite color—to glory in the view. There lay all Rome, tinted pink in the dawn light and slashed with grey sheets of rain. Someone from inside the room padded over the thick carpet to join me. He was bare from the waist up, flannel below. Looking out at the view, he whistled.

"That's worth the cost of a suit."

I looked him up and down. "Your suit is just fine but don't your shoulders get cold?"

He shook his head, his hair a wonderful mess. "I sleep kind of hot. You, *mia moglie?*"

Yes, I really was his wife now, up and down and side to side.

"I like my nighties. Otherwise, uh, things stick together."

"You intrigue me," he said, pressing his bare self between said cloth-covered things, leaning me back against the tall, cool window. After some leisurely smooching, I asked,

"Did you like the wedding? I thought it was very pretty."

"I thought *you* were very pretty, *Ms. I-Have-Royal-Blood*. What's with the crown?"

"It's a Norwegian thing. Belonged to my *Bestemor*. So, my mother told you about King Ring? There's an African Queen back there, too, and I don't mean the old movie."

"Well, Your Majesty I just put it in the room safe."

"Good idea. What combination did you put in?"

"Combination? Oh, hell." His good hand went gloomily into his hair.

"Dammit, I'll have to call the Desk."

"The dinner was good, didn't you think?" I pointed out, determined to cheer him up.

"Your *carbonara* is better."

"Ha. Flattering my cooking will get you everywhere, *marito mio*," I laughed, hoicking up my nightie and robe the better to warm his chilly torso. He was cheered.

Speaking of cooking, it was suddenly time to dress for brunch. Rain had come and gone all morning, so we put on our site-tested waterproofs. With a wink, Jim knotted his red Christmas scarf over the purple mark on his throat.

"I hope there's plenty to eat. Got to keep you fed, you man-eater."

Squinting into the rain, we hurried down the Trinità dei Monti Steps.

Under our raingear, we had on the nicer-than-usual garb that *Mor* had urged us to buy, and that I always associate with that strange, strange day. It is pitiful in retrospect to think how much we looked forward to opening our presents.

Via Margutta was its usual quiet backwater self. There, waving madly from a gateway up ahead, were two children under one very large rainbow umbrella. Ratty ran impetuously forward, holding it tightly with both fists as his sister squealed and put up her hood.

"Finally," she complained. "Didn't you get *Bestemor*'s phone calls? We're *starving*."

"And the train is at two! And we want to open presents!" growled the Rat.

"Sorry, sorry, sorry," we answered variously, galloping up the stairs through the archway to the quaint upper apartment lent by All Saints to its Junior Vicar.

Out onto the little landing stepped the J.V. himself, his arms open wide.

"*Tantissimi auguri,*" he cried. "Waldo, they're here."

A shaggy, smiling head peeped out of the doorway behind him, and a big hand waved before ducking back in again. We toiled up the stairs.

"Do you have horse?" I panted. "We are hungry enough to eat one."

"Sorry, already ate it, waiting for you two to show up," he laughed, kissing us sequentially on both cheeks and drawing us in out of the rain.

Mor leapt up from a small formal sofa in the dark little living room, setting down a bowlful of half-shelled peas and running to peel off our waterproofs and hang them in the bath. I noticed with chagrin that Jim kept his scarf on.

My mother looked with great approval at our clothing and general appearance.

"Marriage suits you," she smiled, hugging first one then the other of us.

A loud *pop* was heard in the little kitchen, and Prester John appeared with two fistsful of Champagne flutes. Gesu-aldo was close beside him with the bottle. In a moment everyone had a glass of bubbly, even if only a splash.

"To the radiant bride and her worthy groom," cried my old friend, raising his glass. "Long life and happiness."

"Hear, hear," said *Mor,* and we all drank. Clo made a face at the taste, but Ratty asked scratchily, "More please, *Bestemor.* Get it? More/*Bestemor?*"

"Yes, yes," said my mother, rolling her eyes.

"*Mangiamo,*" declared Gesualdo, turning to fetch plates

already filled with every good thing and setting them down around the table with festive clanking. As we took our seats, I saw that the dining room's picture-window had a view nearly as sublime as the Hassler's.

"Oh, Johnny, what a place you have," I gasped.

"Nice, isn't it?" he smiled, glancing over at Gesualdo. "We're very happy here."

Once we were all well launched into our meal and seconds were circulating, it occurred to me to ask how they'd met.

"A rather dramatic story," said John-Allen, sitting back with a smile as Waldo grinned, "but I can keep it short to spare the sprogs. Before I went to theology school, I studied law, you see, Miss Cloelia," he began with an arch glance towards the child. She smiled radiantly, smitten. "Even studied Italian law, which told me that those people that we call *gypsies* have fewer rights than other people here. So, when Father Baker – he's the priest who gave the fine sermon yesterday – started a ministry to help those people, I was eager to volunteer.

He reached out for Gesualdo, who gave him his hand in a firm, smiling grasp.

"They call themselves *Rom* or *Dom* and live in camps all over Europe, trying to keep to their customs, often blamed for the crimes of others but falling into crime themselves. The Italian authorities—sorry, I will speed up, Horatio," he added hastily, as Ratty began to writhe, "had asked local churches to help with the children of the Rom, and I was the one chosen to go from All Saints. Long story short, Gesualdo saved me from being mobbed when the children loved me a little too much. He acted as interpreter and also taught them easy tumbling moves he'd learned at the circus, until first thing you know we had an exercise program both at the camp and at All Saints, both still very popular."

"I could teach *il rattuccio* to walk *la corda stretta,* 'tightrope'," Waldo smiled.

Jim blinked. Ratty fell with such regularity that his knees were a mess of scars.

"It will improve his balance," added the acrobat presciently.

"Can I, Papa? Oh, can I?" begged the Rat, his voice scratchier than ever with passion.

"Me, too," frowned Clo, who had already had several years of ballet.

Waldo touched the tip of her nose, saying, "This one already has beautiful balance. She we could start on the parallel bars."

"Oh, *could* I?" she breathed, her big blue eyes bigger and bluer. "Oh, please, Papa . . ."

"We," drawled her father, considering. "The people at the RCAS *have* been pestering me to be Director again. If I do, we would be in Rome all of next year, and you could."

"Living in Rome at the *Arca? Next* year?" I gasped. "With the Academy Library just around the corner? Oh, please, Papa."

"That's settled, then," laughed Prester John. "And you can have Sunday brunch with us every week after 9:00 AM service."

"And I can learn to walk the *corda stretta,*" exulted the Rat. And to celebrate he got up and ran three times around the table, cheering.

It was high time to get on with present-opening and take *Bestemor* and the Riverbankers to *Stazione Termini,* so we cleared away dishes, found a pad of paper and a pencil, and did so, seated around the dining table with its splendid view of the dome of Saint Peter's.

All of the gifts that Jim opened—a Deruta platter, a nice Moka *macchinetta,* a pasta-maker, a set of espresso cups, and so forth—had been brought to the church rather than mailed.

The cards attached to them made the work of the secretary—
me—relatively easy, especially when compared against the
guest book from the reception dinner.

But there was one last box with a postmark of *Tarquinia
Centrale* inside which were two identical silver-cardboard
gift boxes inside it labeled Agnese and Lorenzo. It had been
mailed to "The Lewis Family, c/o Father Allen Prester" but
without a sender's name. The assumption it had somehow
come from the Lavinia was based the fact that these were
names she and Caterina used for them.

"They're from Mamma and Caterina," cried Ratty happily,
reaching out for his.

"Why weren't they sent from Florence, then?" wondered
Jim and picked up Clo's box with a frown. *Were those embossed
on there?* I wondered, reaching out for it.

The chill of suspicion came a moment too late. Ratty had
already opened his box and was shoving one pink, freckled
hand into it.

"Ow!" he yelled, dropping the horrible thing onto the
table. It was a gilded iron Vanth votive like the ones from
Franco's temple pits—or the *mundus*—more like a bundle of
nails than anything. Ratty stared in awestruck horror as his
cupped hand filled with blood.

"Good God!" cried Jim, running after us as I bore off the
Rat to the kitchen sink. "Has he had a tetanus booster?"

"All up to date," I assured him over the rush of water as I
washed the cut clean.

"I'm going to have to open this for you, Clo," Jim told his
tearful daughter as he gingerly ran a butter-knife through the
tape holding the silver box shut, then dumped its contents
onto the table with a metallic *clank*.

Rat and I, his hand swathed in paper towels which I was
squeezing tightly to stop the bleeding, peered out of the
kitchen to see where a second gilded Vanth lay.

"Better get some tongs or something," I opined. "Here, put

them in my big purse, and we'll get them both to the Museum, for testing, once we get back."

"Definitely," frowned Jim.

"Read that," I whispered, pointing to the embossed letters: *Antiquità Colchis*. Just like the boxes we'd found at Tony's Cantina-cum-Bat-Cave.

"You should keep this mailing box, too, in case it's evidence or something," added *Mor*.

The Rat asked anxiously, "Can we still go to Mamma's? I want to see Siggie."

Siggie was Caterina's ancient Pekinese. He was a long white dust-mop of a dog originally named *Sigaretta*. Ratty was always lobbying to have a dog "just like Siggie."

Jim and I exchanged a long look. I shook my head stubbornly.

"He needs Lavinia," he wheedled, "and Florence isn't far."

"I'll be right there, if I'm needed," added my mother. "You take your little vacation."

"And Florence has a very fine hospital," added John-Allen quietly.

"It's probably nothing," I said at last. But my gut said otherwise.

Mor spoke up decisively, holding out her hands to the children.

"Who's for Florence?"

"I am," Clo sang out, taking one. Rat, nodding vigorously, took the other.

"Then what are we waiting for? Call us a taxi, somebody." The trusty Multipla been returned to the rental agency in Tarquinia.

"You're a taxi, *Mor*," I said dutifully. She rolled her eyes.

"You two want to go with me in the *cinquecento*?" offered John-Allen. "That way we will only need one taxi, and your grandma can have twenty minutes of peace."

"I guess I could go in the taxi with the baggage," allowed *Bestemor*.

I have forgotten to mention that much of her baggage was left behind in the form of clothing and gifts, leaving her much more portable.

Having worked out the timing so *Bestemor* would waiting at the station when the children arrived, the taxi was called. Gesualdo stacked *Mor's* two modest valises and the River-bankers' packs of clothing and toys beside the front gate, and soon we had all joined them.

"How can we thank you, Hailey?" Jim asked, wiping a teary eye.

"Visit us in San Antone this summer?" she suggested. "Bring your swimsuits!"

"Have fun in Florence," I said, kissing her soundly on the cheek. "Uffizi first?"

"No, the Davanzati Palace," she replied at once. "Studied it in Architecture class back in Norway." Then the taxi pulled up, was filled with *Mor* and bags and was waved out of sight.

John-Allen rolled the *cinquecento* out of its little shed off the courtyard, and the Riverbankers were many times kissed and piled in beside him.

"Give Siggie my love," I called out, "and your Mamma and Caterina, too."

"We will call tonight at bed-time," added their Papa. "See you in a couple of days!"

We waved until they reached the bend at the end of the street. I had a strong sense that there would be more to this business of Ratty's cut hand. There was a shoe, waiting to drop.

19

BLESSINGS AND CURSES

WHAT WOULD YOU ON A RAINY SATURDAY AFTERNOON IN Rome if you had plans for a cozy evening indoors and didn't mind getting wet before that? If you'd just heard you just might be spending the following school year, all expenses paid, at a beloved spot you hadn't seen in years?

Yes, we did that.

Catching the correct tram from Largo Argentina and the correct bus up the winding ways to Monteverde Vecchio, we descended outside the old walls and were soon standing with our backs to Fontana Paola, gazing at the handsome, wreath-bedecked iron gates of Villa Parrhasia, home of the Rome Center for Ancient Studies, aka the RCAS, aka the "Arca."

By then, the rain was coming down so hard we couldn't say which was wetter, the fountain behind us, or our legs. Our waterproofs were just that, but only came down so far and our rain-pants were back at the site.

For a moment we thought of calling on the Buoncompagni family, longtime Arca staff who lived nearby, but worried they might feel obliged to give us dry clothes. Taking a taxi seemed poor-spirited with all that Rome between us and our room at the Hassler. Besides, taxi-drivers hate wet passengers. Down the stairs beside the Arca we plunged, therefore, ogling the Villa and the Forge as we went by and talking non-stop about what we would do given the chance to live and work there again.

"What happened to the silver mesh thing you made for Arca Symposium?" Jim asked.

"The Council of Nine Chapel Grille, you mean?" I laughed. "It's gathering dust in my room back home. Buster shows it off to everyone who comes over, just to embarrass me."

"Why would it embarrass you? It is the prettiest piece of silver-smithery – or whatever you call it – I've ever seen. I've always said you know your metal, Greenough."

With a surge of pride, I nearly made some insufferable reply. I wanted to boast about my skills at gold-granulation but caught myself in time.

She will goad you into evil.

"Don't tempt me, *caro*, I'll get a fat head."

"Basingstoke?"

"Basingstoke, it is."

"I'd like a copy of that grille for Christmas, myself," he said wistfully.

"I'll give you the original. When's your birthday, Pericles?"

That won me a long smooch in the rainy middle of the Ponte Sisto.

Cutting in a zig-zag fashion across the medieval city, we made gradually for the Pincian ridge where the Hassler stood. Somewhere near the Pantheon we went wrong and wound up at the Trevi Fountain. In trying to go right again found ourselves on Via Dei Due Macelli at the foot of Via Rasella. This would not have been a problem except for what happened next.

We had decided to dash across Due Macelli together rather than wait for a light, so I had—forgive the details, they turned out to be important—held Jim's left elbow with my right hand and gripped the copper ring of my stout leather Florentine purse with my wet left palm when suddenly everything shifted. It was as if I'd removed a pair of sunglasses but infinitely stranger. Nearly all the shop signs changed and other people walking the street were superimposed on people around us, like overlapping film.

From Via Rasella there now came a terrific explosion that rocked the street beneath me so that I was thrown against Jim, who oddly did not seem to have been shaken at all. A billow of acrid smoke rolled towards us without being at all affected by the rain. There came a sound like hailstones on metal, the stench of charred flesh and bowels, groans and shrieks of agony.

"Basingstoke, Greenough," Jim cried, holding me by both arms sling or no. I was moaning and cowering in the middle of the busy street.

"Don't you hear them crying out, Pericles?" I shouted, covering my ears. "Or smell it, for God's sake? An explosion —just there—so many people, so many have been killed."

"In Via Rasella?" he asked sharply, looking that direction.

"Yes, yes!"

"Come on let's get you home." And he hurried me— blinded by a continuing fog of overlapping realities— through the lessening rain, up Via Francesco Crispi and left on Via Sistina to the Hassler. It is proof how shocked we looked, standing there, that one doorman helped us out of our dripping waterproofs and the other got us our key and guided us to the nearest elevator.

The moment and instant I rolled up my sodden leather purse and tucked it under my arm, I could think again. It was just as if someone had turned off a loud radio inside my head. The elevator felt like a sweet haven of peace. I leant against Jim, exhausted.

"What was that back there?" I asked him miserably. "What did I see?"

The elevator opened with a muted *ping*. He put a courtly hand behind my elbow and guided me to the door of our room "The Via Rasella massacre," he said quietly. "March 1944. It was a Resistance attack on a German column, a bomb crammed into a metal trash cart along with a bunch of nails. Killed about thirty soldiers, wounded about a hundred, but the Nazis rounded up well over three hundred victims in retaliation, took them to the Fosse Ardeatine—you've seen the memorial, near San Callisto? Shot them all, then blew up the caves on top of them."

"Sure, sure, I've seen the memorial," I frowned as we entered our serene, fresh room, bed made and everything in its place. Supremely comforting. "But why did I see it?"

"And I didn't," he pointed out, "even though I have read about the incident?"

"It wasn't just that. From that moment until we got here, I was seeing things, mostly violent things. At the intersection of Via del Tritone and Due Macelli, I saw a German officer shoot a man in the head and watched the man drop dead. Then on Via Francesco Crispi a man with a big mustache came up behind a woman in a costume with a big hoop-skirt and stabbed her in the neck." I sat at the desk and put my head in my hands and saw it still. "But the visions weren't quite *corporeal*. They were superimposed on real people, buses, cars."

I went to the window and looked out, relieved to see one layer of modern-day Rome.

He joined me "Have the visions stopped?"

"Yes," I said, realizing something else. "They stopped the minute I took off my purse. When I took my hand off the strap of my purse."

I unrolled the wet thing and laid it on the glass-covered surface of the desk. I looked at it hard. It has two decorative copper rings held the wide leather, cross-body straps.

"I got this from a shop behind the Uffizi three years ago,

after dropping off the Riverbankers to visit their mother. It was a new line, on sale for half the usual price. People didn't like that the copper showed finger marks and that it oxidized to green."

Jim frowned. "Is copper normal for purses?"

I shook my head, then remembered: *the Vanth was in a copper cage. Why was that important?* Then I poked the capacious body, which was unusually full: boxy.

"The votives are still in there," I exclaimed, reaching for the woven leather flap. But as I touched the copper snap, I felt a mild shock. Very deliberately I went to the sink, wet my hand, and held the ring again then walked to the window to look out.

Again came that sensation of wearing strange sunglasses. The rainy streets seemed twice as full as they were. A shadowy man in a neat grey suit and a grey homburg hat stumbled as he left the *Caffè delle Nazioni* opposite. He staggered straight through the bodies of several wet tourists and fell prone onto the street. He did not rise again.

Jim hovered at my side. "What do you see?"

I took my hand off the ring and the man vanished. The tourists returned.

"Another death. A heart-attack, I think."

"Try it without the boxes," he suggested excitedly.

I carefully set them on the sill, got my hand wet, and tried again.

"Ah, that did it." I turned triumphantly. "Nothing."

"Will it work for me do you think?" he asked hopefully. I hated to risk his touching so fell a thing, but since he insisted, I put the votives back in my purse. His hand wet and holding the copper ring, he looked out over the Trinità dei Monti steps.

"Anything?" I asked, smiling at the look of disappointment on his face.

He shook his head in regret. "I never did have your

Tanny-sense. Tell you what. Let's go to places where we *know* a death took place—like those markers you see on buildings, marking where a resistance fighter died—and check it out."

I made a face. "But I'm freezing and want that hot bath you keep talking about."

"Of course! No, I meant to try it tomorrow. We have the whole day at our disposal."

I wrinkled my nose. "Do you *really* want to spend one whole day of our honeymoon wandering around Rome looking for the sites of famous deaths?"

"Maybe not the *whole* day," he admitted, helping me out of my wet things.

We talked to the Riverbankers and my mother that evening. They had just eaten pizza with *Bestemor* at a place across the Arno. Before that, Caterina had taken them to a tiny shop full of Pinocchio things, and bought them each a miniature sailing ship, with a walnut for a hull. My mother reported that the Davanzati Palace did not fail to delight. On to the Uffizi tomorrow!

"How's your hand, Ho-*rat*-io?" his father asked.

"A little sore, but Siggie came and licked it."

"Did that help?" I asked. We were on speaker-phone.

"Mmm-hmm. See you tomorrow?"

"Supposed to be day after tomorrow," objected Jim.

"That's right, Mamma says we get to see Galileo's finger tomorrow," crowed the Rat.

"Ewww," opined Cloelia.

We ended up trying something else from Room Service that night, promising ourselves a real dinner out next night, at *Da Pancrazio*, the perfect ending for a death-filled afternoon.

What a blessing to awaken in my best beloved's arms, and see the sun streaming into the room! Rain was expected by afternoon, the front desk said, so we decided to carry out our experiment in time-travel earlier rather than later. A rainy afternoon in bed would be just fine.

Wetting one of Jim's handkerchiefs, accordingly, and wrapping it in a complimentary shower cap we tucked it beside the Vanths in my purse and set out to prove a point.

We would start with the site of one of the most infamous murders in Roman history: that of Servius Tullius, run down by his daughter Tullia not far from the Forum. The spot where Julius Caesar was assassinated was now buried at least ten meters under the Teatro Argentina, but the knife-shop where Verginia had met her death was somewhere on the floor of the Forum...

We took the Metro to Cavour station and walked down the Via Cavour, taking in the bustle of delivery vans, street cleaners, tourists and hawkers. At the crosswalk where the Borgia Stairway rises up through the Borgia Palace to the church of Saint Peter in Chains we stopped.

This steeply-sloping former street is also known as the *vicus sceleratus*—Latin for infamous alley—for the very reason we were visiting it today. For the past two thousand six hundred years, people have pointed it out as the place where Tullia Minor ran over the injured body of her father the king, Servius Tullius, so that her lover Tarquinius could be king instead.

Oh, and at least one member of the Borgia family was killed there, too.

We expected great things of our purse-shaped time-machine, but had only just reached the spot when Jim's phone rang, and the day took an entirely different turn.

THE OTHER SHOE DROPS

EVERY TIME A NEWS STORY OR DOCUMENTARY BEGINS WITH A specific date and time, you can bet that something bad is bound to follow. So, when I say that at 8:46 AM on Sunday, February twenty-first, the second full day after our wedding, Jim's phone rang, you know it was not someone from the AIA informing him he had just won the International Archaeology Day Grant.

In fact, it was Caterina, talking rapidly in Italian, almost incoherent with alarm. Fumbling for his ear-buds, Jim let me guide him to the *Rione Monti Bar*, where I went in to get us a couple of *cappuccini*. Then I helped myself to an ear-bud and heard her say, almost drowned out by persistent barking, "... so can you come by car right away, please?"

"We have train tickets for tomorrow at around 10:30 AM, Caterina," Jim responded in heavily-accented but competent Italian, "but I'll try to change the day. What's wrong, exactly?"

Ratty. I instantly blamed Lavinia for some kind of negligence, and had to bite back angry recriminations. *Whew! This Vanth-invasion was playing havoc with my blood-pressure.*

Basingstoke, Greenough-Lewis, Basingstoke.

In a voice unsteady with tears as she explained, "We were

coming back from breakfast this morning when he suddenly collapsed. Agnese and I were holding his hands and caught him, but, but he was limp, like a little dead thing, eyes shut, but hot, terribly hot. And he kept saying something. Lavinia says . . ."

"He spoke in *Rasenna*," came Dr. Lavinia's sharp voice, on speaker-phone at her end. "Roughly translated, it means *he, or she, is mine.*"

When she repeated the statement in Etruscan—or what Lavinia calls *Rasenna* from the name those people gave themselves – Jim exclaimed, "Tanny said that when *she* collapsed."

She went on briskly. "I want him out of here as quickly as possible. Caterina is very early in her pregnancy and mustn't catch anything. How soon can you get here?"

"By noon, if we can pack in time. What about Hailey— have you called her?"

"She is at the museum, she says, but will return to her hotel shortly."

"Well, keep him comfortable until we get there. I'll message you when we leave."

And he hung up.

"He as a fever, like yours. Maybe there was *fulminant hepatitis* on those votives in the *mundus,* after all. The air sample was negative, but maybe Marc somehow infected them."

"Damn him," I snarled. "Who does that to a child? To an innocent child? He *has* the gold for God's sake! He should pick on someone his own size."

"Basingstoke, my dear," he said, looking around uneasily. "He picked on me, remember? Can't blame him, not after I took you away like that."

With the kind assistance of the Hassler staff, our tickets for the next day were credited towards one for today and we were packed up and out of there in record time, sailing along in a taxi towards Stazione Termini.

After slipping into our seats on the 10:26 *Frecciarossa* 9310 from Stazione Termini, Rome to Stazione Santa Maria Novella Florence – and letting Caterina know we made it. We called my mother very quietly. Riders on Italian trains are not encouraged to use their phones.

"Have you talked to your Godfather yet?" she asked.

"Should I?"

"He called me a little while back. I told him to try you at around eleven."

"Can he help us?"

"He claims that there is more to this than just physical illness, but that he can help you cure Ratty, either way. Should I meet you at Dr. Bradley-Arnold's house? You'd better either take him to stay with Padre LoCieco or take him back to Tarquinia Lido. Either way I will get myself to the airport tomorrow, *kjare*, so don't worry about me."

"Oh, *Mor*, I'm so sorry that things have been so crazy."

"Nothing like a good adventure, I always say," she laughed, and hung up.

Lost in gloomy thoughts, I stared out the window until Jim felt I needed a comforting dose of honeymoon. Soon we were startled back to reality by the *ping* of my phone.

I frowned at the sender's name: *Titono Empedicleo LoCieco*.

When had I added him to my Contacts?

Jim and I read the message: *I am an expert on this hepatitis, Tanaquil, and can teach you to cure the coma, just as I cured you of yours. Bring your son to my clinic.*

Where are you, Godpapa? I wrote back.

Florence, Via del Fico. My assistant Massimo will collect you and the boy from the house on Lungarno Vespucci at 12:30. Your husband will not be needed.

That should have sent up a red flag, having read of the sexual proclivities of "T."

If his Papa gives permission, Ratty and I will go with Massimo, I typed back.

Convince him. came the message.

"No," said Jim. "Ratty needs to be at Tarquinia General."

"My godfather claims to be expert at this hepatitis," I pointed out. "Besides, if it's *just* hepatitis, why did he fall into a coma and say the same phrase in Etruscan that I did?"

I had him there.

We had just finished renting a car for Jim and Clo to drive home in when suddenly we were entering the main body of Firenze Santa Maria Novella terminal and had to grab out bags and get out. While I bought four *panini* in our favorite flavors – convinced that the children wouldn't have eaten lunch, and hoping against hope that the Rat was still hungry – Jim went to buy a paper and rushed back to show me the headline of the local Florentine daily, *La Repubblica*, translated roughly as:

Tarquinia Vecchia: Another man Mauled. "It was a gigantic bird. I'm lucky to be alive!" *Is La Castellina* **Curse to blame?**

He translated it rapidly aloud to me. My accent and off-the-cuff vocabulary in Italian may be better than his, but his reading skills are much better than mine.

"'In a shocking development of the *Lady of the Rings* scandal, another person has been attacked at the *La Castellina* area of Tarquinia Vecchia. It has been less than a month since the strange death there of art-collector and co-discoverer of the *La Castellina hypogeum*, Tony Ellingham and the disappearance of many valuable objects from the site.

"'Archaeologist Franco Cotto was working late at the part of the *La Castellina* site known as the Temple of Vanth and Tages when he reports having been attacked by an enormous bird. He barely made it to the shelter of a nearby camper with deep cuts to his back and arms.

"From there, he was able to call for assistance."

Jim broke off with the comment, "Must have fixed the phone line since the opening."

"Go on, go on," I urged anxiously. I felt something of a personal connection with that owl, knowing the kind of hunger a Vanth can generate.

"'Police armed with floodlights were able to drive away the creature. Cotto described it as being very much like the half-tame barn owl which has haunted the area for many years only "much larger." Soon afterwards he fell into a feverish coma from which he has not yet recovered. He remains under observation in the special quarantine ward of Tarquinia General Hospital.'"

Jim looked at me significantly. I nodded. *The Lewis Memorial Wing.*

"'Tarquinia Police Chief Col. Pasquale Paolini was asked to comment on the string of thefts and suspicious incidents connected with *La Castellina* that have occurred since last year's unforgettable opening of its so-called *hypogeum* exposed a vast collection of golden jewelry and valuable pottery, so desirable to looters. He said that two members of a theft ring had been captured in the act of stealing evidence from a safe at the home of the late Mr. Ellingham, and many, not all, of the lost items were retrieved. Items found in the safe including the ten rings that earned Tanaquil Greenough —the now-wife of archaeologist James P. Lewis—her nickname of *Lady of the Rings* when she discovered them missing from the Museum.

"Cotto's coma is indeed similar to that which Greenough-Lewis suffered upon opening a new chamber of this underground chamber and from which she has only recently emerged.'

"Doctors at Tarquinia General Hospital hope that Cotto will also soon recover but are at a loss to explain the behavior of the large owl. Avian experts from around the nation are meeting Tuesday at the Tarquinia Municipal Offices to discuss how to proceed. Archaeological student volunteers from La Sapienza have meanwhile been sent back to Rome. The site is closed to further excavation until working conditions can be certified as safe."

"'Is the site cursed? Updates will be posted as they become known.'"

In silence we wheeled our suitcases across the wide intersection to enter Via Santa Caterina da Siena. Finally, Jim remarked, "Maybe Antonia got rabid somehow, poor old bird!"

"Can birds *get* rabid? Don't you think they would have mentioned hydrophobia?"

"Oh hell, I don't know. What do *you* think got into the owl?"

"It's possessed by a Vanth! My research shows there is a close resemblance between Vanths and Vampires. In fact, *vanthu-pyra,* "Vanth of fire" is a manifestation of a Vanth as bringer-of-fever. Kind of a malarial goddess, really, if you think about it."

He shook his head gloomily, so deep in his musings that he nearly got himself run over by a three-wheeled *ape* full of firewood while crossing Via della Scala.

"Honestly, sweetheart," he complained as I pulled him to safety, "with the site closed and all this madness, how are we going to get *any* work done?"

"Well," I sighed, "My dissertation notes and my laptop are here in my pack. I can work on that while my godfather cures Ratty. What will you and Moley do?"

"She's got school projects and birthdays galore, apparently. Me, I have to finish proofing those book galleys and revise the site reports for publication."

"Boring," I teased him.

He flashed me a sly smile.

"They would be much more interesting with you gnawing on my throat!"

"Mmm. Tasty," I grinned, and I meant it.

We reached our destination at #28 Lungarno Vespucci

when my phone *pinged* again:

Titono Empedicleo LoCieco.

Your friend Franco will also need my help. We can discuss this after your arrival with the boy. Massimo is on his way. Watch for a black sedan with Benevento plates.

We rang the bell.

"God, I'll miss you, Pericles!" I cried. I pressed him against the door in a passionate clinch that he leaned into with a will. "At least we had the best wedding ever."

He broke away, glasses askew. "Agreed. What happened to the crown, by the way?"

It had taken a frantic effort to extract it from our room safe before we left for the station.

"It's taking up most of my suitcase, ready to hand off to *Mor*. She's saving it for Clo."

The door buzzed open. We stumbled into the inner yard. Clattering down the stairs was Clo herself. She leapt into her father's arms, or rather, arm, the moment she reached us.

"Whoa there, Moley old chap," he gasped. "Sling doesn't come off for a day or two!"

I rolled our suitcases out of the way. Seemed no point in taking them up.

"I've got ours all packed, *Mor*. I'll go get 'em!" said Clo, dashing back up the stairs.

"Think she's eager to go?" I whispered to Jim as we followed her more sedately.

"Apparently so," he whispered back.

Once we reached the landing, Caterina appeared in the doorway, wringing her hands,

"Thanks be to the good God. Come in, come in. It is terrible, just terrible."

Lavinia was beside her, hands on hips. "Well, *finally*."

As Jim hurried past her, his Ex hissed in my face, "*Now* I see how it was. You never actually *cared* for the children. You were too busy making love to my husband!"

To keep my own furiously-rising anger at bay, I forced myself to convert her caustic words to the truth. She was out of her mind with grief and possibly guilt that the only creature she had ever completely loved was now desperately ill.

I flung my arms around her.

"Forgive me, Lavinia, I'm so sorry he's sick."

Now Lavinia is a full head shorter than I am, with a cat-like grace that Clo has inherited. But it turns out she is very strong for her size. In a frenzy of grief, she twisted in my arms like Proteus and keened like Andromache for Astyanax, "Larry." Her whole body shook. "Larry."

"It's going to be all right, Dr. L," I murmured, praying hard I was telling the truth.

"*Mor?*" called Clo nervously from out on the landing, where she had assembled the suitcases and packs. "Someone's at the door!"

There stood a large young man in a trim black suit.

"*Signora* Tanaquil?" he said in a deep, resonant voice. "I am Massimo Benevento, from your godfather. Where is *il rattuccio?*"

I released Lavinia and waved him down the hall.

"What? Where are you taking Larry?" asked Lavinia in alarm, wiping her eyes.

"To my godfather's clinic here in Florence. He healed me, so..."

"You had *hepatitis?*"

"Yes, I think so," I stammered, knowing very well I hadn't, knowing that Ratty and Franco were afflicted with not one but two ailments: one physical, one metaphysical.

"Can LoCieco really cure *this?*" Jim asked in turn, leading a mournful procession down the hall. Massimo came next, bearing a little bundle of blankets out of which peeked out Ratty's unconscious face, an alarming shade of yellow under its freckles. Caterina brought up the rear, carrying his stuffed donkey and weeping loudly.

"*Si, certo*," answered Massimo calmly. "Ask anyone. *Signora*, where is your valise?"

Signora meaning me. Right. "Downstairs by the door."

Caterina handed me the donkey. I gave her a hug.

Massimo maneuvered past us with his burden and made his way down the stairs. I kissed Clo's cheek, Jim's lips, and followed. Jim put a restraining arm around her shoulders.

"*Mor!*" cried Clo. "Papa, where are *Mor* and Ratty going? Aren't we going, too?"

"To her godfather's house here in Florence, to get better. Someone has to stay here with him," her father replied as his voice faded behind me, "We need to get you back to school."

"Remember how fast I got better?" I added with a smile, halting at the landing.

She looked trustingly from one of us to the other. "Yes, *Mor*."

But then again, I thought ruefully, *I was never this sick.*

❦

*E*xcerpt D from The DIARY of M. G. BURNSEY: La Serpentara

[*T*he three friends arrive safely in Rome by rail. While the Burnseys take up residence on Monte Mario with Uncle Joseph – Evangeline now safely traveling with new friends to Sicily – Mary goes to live on the Janiculum Hill with her brother William "the Great Classicist" and his exotic wife Zeya, a Tutsi princess who saved his life in Zanzibar. Suspecting an African wife would not be welcome in the United States, he found work at the American Academy as its Chief Librarian and has begun his life's work on Latin Grammar and Usage.

. . .

*B*ess meets again the "fat" gentleman they had met on the crossing and – encouraged by her fortune as told by Padre Benevento – embarks upon a sedate flirtation with him as they see the sights. A stay in Giovanuccio's home in Bomarzo cured her romantic notions of settling there.

*S*tephen – heir to the Burnsey's Better Biscuits business, based in Boston, and having promised his father he would at some point visit some of the local biscuit-making factories, Italian biscuit tending to be of very fine quality – spends some weeks making good on his promise.

*M*ary is very happy to have a bedroom to herself – and her cat – and gets to work absorbing all she can of the art and atmosphere of Rome. She sketches furiously all day in the various museums and private collections and risks catching malaria during dangerous sojourns to Ostia Antica, Hadrian's Villa, and Palestrina. For the purposes of family history, we are interested only in her final, most fateful outing to the forest of La Serpentara, accompanied by Stephen...]

JULY 31, 82 – Rome, Janiculum Hill

I blame what has happened to me on a very fine show of engravings of Gustave Doré I attended at the French Academy five days ago, at which William introduced me to a man who had worked with the Master when Doré was gathering material for his illustrations of Dante, and had been with him at the forest of La Serpentara. He described it as being on an outcropping of the Appennine Mountains some miles southeast of Rome. He said it is very rugged and windswept, very atmospheric. I naturally had a strong desire to see-and-sketch it, as St. would say.

St. took me to the engravings show and very chivalrously suggested he accompany me to the forest while I sketched. It is a long day's carriage ride, with lodging only to be found in local peoples' houses, though there is a small colony of German painters who have taken over one house to themselves. Traveling as brother and sister, we put up in two rooms at a small house. I left Impy with dear Zeya, as I hated to risk any harm to him, also unsure if farm-folk would allow a pet on the premises.

The weather was fine the following morning, air was warm and fragrant, full of the scent of wood and leaf and wildflowers. We had a delightful picnic. I was able to do some striking sketches of the twisted oaks against the vast spaces of the valley beyond while St. caught up on letters home. That afternoon, we rode out together to explore the upper stretches of the forest. He was very dapper in his new brown Florentine riding suit and I weighed down by a black riding habit Mama made me buy in Paris, with more furbelows, ruffles, tucks and tassels than is strictly decent. We were far up the mountainside when dark clouds suddenly arose over the heights behind us. A cold blast of wind ran ahead of it, sending us racing down the mountainside to return our hired hacks and get into shelter.

We might have made it except that at a narrow place, where the road sinks between high walls and meets the road to town at right angles, a rough-looking man with a dark cloth over the lower part of his face leapt out, holding a long pistol. He told us to halt and hand over our valuables. St. started to pull out his gun loaded with blanks but two more men appeared from nowhere and dragged him from the saddle. Last I saw St. he was struggling manfully. I was violently wrenched from the saddle by the first bandit. I kicked and bit and screamed for help, but he was a giant of a man, far stronger than I. He dragged me through a gate in the wall into an overgrown field and over to a tumble-down cow-shed.

My attacker, pinning me against him with one mighty arm, took from the shed with the other what looked and felt like webbed saddle-girth. This he buckled tightly around my arms and upper body. Gripping the webbing to keep me from running off, which I sorely longed to do. He tore the black veil off my ridiculous top-hat, flung the hat into a filthy corner and knotted the veil around my head, forcing open my jaws with it like a horse taking a bit. I kicked him hard in the shin with my boots for that, but it was useless: he hung me on a stout hook in the wall of the shed by the webbing. My feet were just off the ground, arms pinned at my sides.

All this while I was screaming, "Help!" or "Aiuto!" but now there was a roll of thunder as the dark cloud rushed across the sun and the storm bore suddenly down on us. Then my attacker took off his mask, and I recognized T., though his physique seemed much augmented. With a glad cry, I stopped my painful struggling. But he did not remove my horrid gag, or unloose me from the hook! On the contrary!

He wrenched off my heavy over-skirt, and the linen bustle-skirt under that, leaving me in my flounced shift, and my boots, incongruously. I was screaming at him through my gag to "Let me go, let me go," which only made him smile, and here, really almost the strangest part, he snapped the fingers of his right hand and down fell the rain in a solid sheet, sounding, when the first phalanx of drops all hit the ground at the same moment, eerily like a shout of applause.

By a trick of the wind, the rain was full in my face, blinding and nearly drowning me, so that I didn't see what he did next, though I surely felt it. Mercifully I was not entirely new to the business, but I can only imagine that his —I hesitate to write it—member was, like the rest of him, far larger than ever before, as this time the pain was such that I gave a cry that must have been audible even above the rain. Yet dare I say that there was pleasure, too?

When at last he ceased and I hung there exhausted and slashed by the driving rain, he turned and cried out, in my own voice, "Stephen, Stephen, help!" From the lane, I heard an answering shout. In the brief time between that shout and Stephen's arrival, my attacker thrust a folded note into the collar of my dress, turned, altered in a way that will give me nightmares all my life, and flew off into the rain, perhaps all the way back to Florence, for when we returned to Rome late that night, shocked and sore and filthy, Impy was discovered to have escaped his cage. I have not seen him since.

That was all four days ago now, and I am safely married though quite ill with rough handling. I thought it wise to allow St. to consummate our marriage all the same, but finally have a moment to myself here in the cabin as he and Bess have gone up on deck with her fiancé Mr. Vanderbilt to say farewell to Italy for me, so have written all the above and read T.'s note at last. As I will allow no-one to read this until after my death, here is what it said before I destroyed it:

Dearest Mary,

I beg you to forgive the violence needed to force your slow-acting friend to marry you and support your art, giving you material things that I could not.

I hope you will believe me when I tell you no woman will ever measure up to you in my affections, though I live as long as Methuselah.

Burnsey is a good man and will get his heir in time, but call our girl Susannah. If she faces any cruelty, send her to your brother in Italy. I will watch out for her.

Until that day long distant when we meet again, I am honored to be your muse.

Tithonos

MORE FAMILY HISTORY

UNLIKE MY FAMOUS ARTIST FOREBEAR, I HAD NEVER (TO DATE) been ravished by a shape-shifting warlock when I went to Via del Fico, but like her I kept a journal. It was a good thing, too. Otherwise the next part of my adventures would have been impossible to reconstruct.

So many things happened during that week in Florence.

DAY ONE – SUNDAY

Massimo's black sedan's electric engine, its smooth suspension and its plush interior gave me the eerie sensation of being spirited away. Equally eerie was Ratty's utter stillness as he lay curled, heavy and hot and smelling strangely of illness, in my lap. He made no movement or sound besides his labored breathing. As I tucked his donkey against his cheek my rebellious stomach told me it was already well past lunchtime.

Not knowing what challenges awaited me at my godfather's house, I forced myself to eat half of my *panino,* though in my misery it seemed to have no flavor at all. I also tried to notice where we were going and how we reached it, rather like Hansel and Gretel and their crumbs.

We first went clockwise around the city walls then near

Santa Croce turned right into older, narrower streets, and made a couple of turns. Soon we were creeping past a line of respectable houses with trim green shutters along Via del Fico until we reached a sordid building more like a prison or repair shop than a house, its broad garage-shutter covered in graffiti. This door opened automatically as we approached, then rattled down behind us.

The generous, well-lit interior space could have indeed been a car-repair shop, but now combined the duties of garage with an apothecary. An electric charging station was built into the right-hand wall of the room, but shelves and shelves of beautiful old jars made of majolica or jewel-colored glass—each labeled in florid Latin lettering as to its contents—stood against every available meter of wall-space of the facing wall. Along this facing wall was a long white-enameled counter arrayed with an impressive set of vessels and burners and stills.

At the far left of the back wall was a door with a translucent panel that let in a green light suggesting a courtyard beyond. Herbs of all sorts and all conditions hung from beams overhead.

All along the wall to my left was a long wooden work-surface or counter on which were ranged mortars and pestles of varying size and material. Under the surface was an impressive array of storage drawers and on the wall above it hung a mouth-watering (for a metallurgist like me) array of highly-polished copper knives and choppers. In its far end was a steel sink and beside the sink, a solid wooden door set at right-angles to the translucent door.

The fragrance of the room was a remarkable combination of motor oil and fresh herbal scents of every possible variety. There was no smell of decay and every surface was spotless. Painted onto the upper registers of the back wall were the turquoise letters and stylized *penteconter* of Giulia Pantano's favorite line of cosmetics and nostrums: *Argo Omeopatica*.

Massimo bent to collect Ratty from the back seat.

"Please follow me," he said quietly and led the way through the solid wooden door at the end of the left-hand wall. Beyond it was a dim stairwell communicating with a front door and lit by a single barred window on the landing above. Up this stair Massimo carried Ratty and through the door at its top without knocking.

We stepped into a tall, saltbox-roofed chamber with whitewashed walls and a single window in the center of its outer, righthand wall. Loaded bookshelves lined the other three walls. In the wall opposite was a tall marble fireplace in which a clear fire burned briskly. To the left of the fireplace stood an antique tin tub rigged with modern plumbing and standing on a sloping drain of white tile. Beyond the tub a simple flush toilet such as might be found in a prison cell. An armoire and a dressing-screen took up the far left-hand corner.

In the center of the room was a cluster of furniture including a paper-strewn work table with a wooden library chair on each of three sides and a day-bed with a pillow and a neatly folded blanket. Between these and the far book-shelves was a fine, familiar-looking writing desk with a tall brass kerosene lamp, a bright flame glowing through its circular green shade.

From my dream-vision in the hypogeum—*of course.*

"Ah, here you are," came the now-familiar voice of *Padre* LoCieco from behind the dressing screen. "You have eaten? Good! Put Horatio on the bed, Massimo."

My heart leapt strangely to see my godfather roll briskly from behind the dressing-screen, wheeling himself over to Ratty and me in a wicker wheelchair of ancient make.

"Come in, come in, Tanaquil, my dear, and forgive my appearance. I believe I looked much younger in your dream."

It was quite true that his posture was sadly stooped and his hair was now silvery white. The length of his arms, legs and body also seemed to have shrunk in proportion to his big hands, feet, and head, making them even larger in contrast.

I thought of mythical Tithonos who was beloved of the Moon. Granted eternal life but not eternal youth, he shrank to the size of a cricket.

How curious that his name was Titono.

Though his eyes were obscured by glasses with smoked circular lenses, his long, clean-shaven face was still compelling.

How sad that he had lost his sight. LoCieco: "the blind one." Of course.

He took both my hands warmly in his.

"Brava, my dear," he laughed, kissing both my cheeks with whiskery red lips. "You have solved the riddles of both my first name and nickname."

"Didn't you have an ancestor named Benevento?" I asked.

He laughed heartily a moment, then stopped with a sudden frown.

Turning my hands over, he smelt my wrists as if I were wearing perfume. I was not.

"You are recently married," he asserted in an apparent *non sequitur.*

"Yes, that's right," I blushed and pulled my hands away, embarrassed. "By civil ceremony almost a month ago now. The church wedding was only last Friday."

"How sad for you to leave your honeymoon early, goddaughter," he exclaimed, then made his meaning clearer.

"My dear, along with scar and tattoo removal and of course the treatment of chronic hepatitis, I am a fertility expert. You are pregnant."

"Apparently *Mor* was right," I murmured with a shiver of elation.

He pushed the dark lenses onto his high forehead to reveal the bright, beautiful, clear-brown eyes of a much younger man. They were warm with sympathy and frank appraisal.

"And apparently you're not blind." I blinked in surprise.

"The spectacles have their uses," he remarked. "They mask my rather direct gaze. Also, they help me to concentrate my vision inward, to identify the pivots of several possible futures and see that a certain one falls into place. It is a bit like plotting a course for the future."

"Did you plot *this* future, Godpapa?" I asked on a sudden suspicion.

"No! No, of course I did not."

To my Tanny-senses, this sounded strangely like, *yes, yes, of course I did.*

"Heavens, my dear," he went on hastily. "Why would I hurt the ones you love?"

Why, indeed?

Wheeling himself alongside the day-bed, he decidedly changed the subject. "So, this is Horatio Lawrence Lewis?" I knelt on Ratty's further side, stroking the red hair off his hot brow.

"Yes," I said with a sad smile, kissing the hot forehead.

LoCieco felt his freckled wrist, peeked under his eyelids, pressed his skin, smelt his breath and then, extracting a stethoscope from the seat of his chair, he listened to Ratty's heart.

"Yes," he sighed, "it is hepatitis: dangerous, but only contracted through blood contact. We must begin with fluids at once, Massimo. When you reach the clinic, send Medea to me."

Massimo retrieved the Rat and gently bore him off, leaving me feeling bereft.

"With my treatment, the boy should heal within as little as five or six days," my godfather assured me, wheeling himself to a spot by the fireplace. "As for the other illness, we will count on your spirit to do its part."

"My *spirit*? Why, what must I do?" I asked uneasily.

He gestured to a wing-chair opposite.

"Sit, sit, *goddaughter!* I will explain."

I did as I was told. He leaned forward, looking deeply into my eyes. A sweet peace came over me, as if I had leaned against a fond shoulder.

"Do you remember the Green Lands of your own coma? Where you saw your father?"

"Yes. Was that my spirit, walking with him there?"

"Precisely. There is healing that must start there, in that liminal place. There are things that hold our spirits captive, that push our life forces deep within us."

"Like that cloud of Vanths that invaded me? You drove them all away but one. But why is that one still there?"

"She is the cloud, compressed into a single entity. I do not have the strength to banish her, only to contain her. Only another Vanth–or a higher deity—can destroy a Vanth."

"But then there's no hope for Ratty? He will be like me, liable to lash out at any time?"

"Not at all! Yours will annihilate his, and you will *both* be cured. I call it the Nemean method. To carry it out, you and I must enter the Green Lands together."

"But how? How did *you* appear in *my* spirit world?"

"The same way you will: by practice, and by channeling my *stregheria*—my 'witchcraft,' or what you call your 'Tanny-sense.' Oh, yes, it is witchcraft, my dear, and can be used for good or evil. You inherited yours at birth. How I came by mine, I will tell you shortly.

"*Stregheria* helps us to read minds and to travel in the spirit realm. It gives us the capacity to bless and to curse, to alter reality. It gives a certain charisma – what your friend John-Allen calls your 'Love Magnet.' Its chief gift is second sight, usually associated with one eye."

"My right eye," I murmured.

His voice fell to an avid whisper, his great eyes alight with something very like lust.

"No other of my descendants has more of this power than you do."

His descendants?

I had read the diary. I knew the violent secret of my Great-Grandma Susie's conception. I had seen Benevento among my ancestors at the moment of Fred's conception, and accepted that we were kin, that I had at least some of my *stregheria* from him.

But this man, my godfather, was his great-grandson. Right? *Mor* told me so!

My Tanny-sense told me something quite different.

"You are my great-great-grandfather Titono Empedicleo Benevento," I cried, aghast. "You are the man who raped my Auntie Mary."

He recoiled in disgust. "*Raped?* Oh no, my dear. That was all a show for Stephen. She enjoyed herself thoroughly."

"She was terrified and in pain. You gave her nightmares for years afterwards."

Then I felt all the blood drain from my face as the key fact struck me.

I whispered, "*How old are you?*"

His slow smile sent a chill right up my spine.

"When Mary conceived Susannah, I had been a *stregone* for as long as Mary had been alive. Before that I had been a priest for six years. I became a priest at the age of twenty-five."

"She was born in 1857," I murmured, doing the arithmetic. "She went to Italy in 1882, at the age of twenty-five. You became a *stregone* in 1857, a priest in 1851, and were born 25 years before that. You were born in *1826?* But that means you are now *one hundred ninety years old!*"

Oh, such a queasy feeling that fact gave me. *It was like meeting Count Dracula.*

"*Voilà*," he was sighing with mock regret. "Because of my *stregheria*, I cannot die."

"But Godpapa." I gasped. "Am I also cursed with eternal life?"

"Heavens, no." He laughed. "One is not born with such *stregheria*. It must be willed."

"Who willed you yours, then? And what sort of *stregheria* is it, anyhow?"

"Ah! Yes, now we come to it." he smiled, rubbing his gnarled hands together. "The story of how I 'got' my powers we will save for this evening, but as for what they can do...

"I have said I can control the flow of energy in living things. But there are four flows, four elements, in nature as well as in the human body: Earth, Air, Fire, and Water. Blood, for example, is a blend of them all. I can stop a wound from bleeding with a gesture or cause blood to flow to desired body parts. For that I have earned a great deal of money."

Frowning for a moment, I suddenly saw his point and hurried on to ask, "What about summoning rain? And how are you at lighting campfires?"

"Yes, those things I can do." He smiled slowly. "And summon spirits, and remove them, from you, or little Ratty."

"What about exorcising *La Castellina*? And what about Franco Cotto?"

"Let us ensure that you and the child are released from the bondage of the Vanth before risking our lives for a place."

"Risking our lives? But what about Franco?"

I suddenly wondered how the Cotto's were taking Franco's illness. There had been no time to think of it earlier. The prospect was ghastly. *He must be saved, somehow!*

My Godpapa shook his head sadly.

"The separation spell I would perform in order to exorcise that site is so powerful that the separator may well separate his soul from his body, or at least lose his *stregheria*."

"There is no hope for Franco, then, or for the site?" I

asked starkly, my easy tears rising. I stared at the fire, wishing I had never opened the *mundus.* "I am sorry I asked."

He reached over to lay a large, warm hand on my arm, murmuring, "If you wish it, dearest, I will save them. I have lived for a very long time."

From the doorway came a cold, feminine voice. "You called me, *Dottore?*"

The woman had a stunning–I might say bewitching–beauty, her green eyes tilting upwards at their outer edges, her features model-perfect, her skin nearly as dark as my own, her long, straight, dark hair, which reached well to her hips, curling slightly upwards at the ends. She wore black yoga gear that left nothing of her body to the imagination that was not covered by a long, blue-denim apron stained with chemical burns and potting soil.

The *Padre-stregone* roused himself. "I did. Tanaquil, allow me to present Medea Mariarosa. Medea, this is my goddaughter Tanaquil Susannah Greenough, or is it Lewis?"

I blushed as I took Medea's coolly-outstretched hand and said,

"Greenough-Lewis, according to the paperwork. Feels so odd, being someone new."

We exchanged air-kisses. Medea murmured that *it was a pleasure to meet me.* For an instant I had the sensation that she strongly disapproved of my presence on Via del Fico. It was quickly withdrawn, as if she had actively banished the thought from her mind.

LoCieco watched her keenly as he explained to me, "Medea is my chief chemist. She is an expert at making healing drafts of all kinds for *Argo Omeopatica.* She is also my chief nurse, seeing to my health and happiness," he added, reaching out a fond hand out to her.

This she hastened to take and kiss, looking hungrily into his magnificent eyes.

"Medea, my dear, do we have enough hepatitis serum for

the boy? And enough traveling oil for two people?"

She sized me up. "I believe so. I do have the makings for more of both, I believe, but I will check inventory. As for beds, if Tanaquil stays upstairs with Massimo and me, we can put the boy into the big room off the portico, once we finish his treatment."

"No," he replied sharply. "I would like my goddaughter to have the large portico room. It will be more convenient for," he seemed to catch himself, "for her to use the WC and shower."

He smiled at me. "The bath and toilet are across the garden. I hope you won't mind?"

I assured him it was fine, but Medea was clearly unhappy.

"But, *dottore*," she insisted with a flash of temper, "surely your goddaughter would be happier upstairs with Massimo and me? Besides, the boy will..."

"Do as I ask!" he snapped irritably. "And I would like you to show her around the clinic, and your laboratory, too." His voice softened as with an effort he added, "If you are willing."

It seemed to me that once again her face and mind had closed.

"Yes, *dottore*," she said. "When will you need the oil? I have set aside the pajamas the child was wearing as you requested. When will you carry out the procedure?"

"When the child is somewhat better, and," he added with a sudden smile in my direction, "when you have learned how to travel in the spirit realm, dearest Tanaquil."

"Until we meet again, this evening," he said, and kissed my hand.

Medea gave me a rather sickly smile.

"Come with me," she said, with a gesture for me to precede her down the stairs. "We will collect your bags and I will show you the laboratory."

And I will eviscerate you, I heard her think viciously, *the first chance I get.*

THE SORCERER'S APPRENTICES

DAY ONE – SUNDAY, CONTINUED.

"How long have you been here?" I asked as she turned on the lights in the lab.

She shrugged. "Ten years? Twelve? It is easy to lose count. We are always very busy. This week for example, due to this emergency, *il dottore* had to turn away two patients who had waited months for regenerative surgery."

"Impressive. Listen, I *have* to ask, being a metal-worker for fun, why are all those choppers and knives made of copper? Isn't it too soft for cutting?"

Now she really *did* smile. "Beautiful, aren't they? We are not allowed to use iron on any of our herbs. It literally takes the magic out of them. Of course, the copper wears out quickly with constant sharpening, but out local man is happy to make new ones for us, even with the price of copper so expensive. The company is doing so well, we can afford it."

"I've seen ads for Argo products in high-end magazines. Are they very expensive?"

"Very," she laughed with more than a touch of pride. "The

ingredients come from all over the world and must be absolutely fresh, so yes, they tend to be expensive. Our on-site spa treatments are yet moreso. You understand that *il dottore* is irreplaceable, a national treasure? His hands can truly work miracles on human tissue."

Judging from what I had read about his exploits with Auntie Mary, I could believe it.

She opened a cabinet to show one line of Argo creams guaranteed to erase age lines and age spots in as little as a week. I was no longer surprised to recognize a twin of the sea-blue bottle that Giulia Pantano kept for her use by the sink in the Museum's conservation lab.

When I said as much to Medea, she laughed musically.

"Dr. Pantano is one of our most loyal customers and has referred us to many others. She is a great friend of *il dottore*, and her friend Boetio does the photography for our catalogue."

The hair stood up on the back of my neck: a serious wave of Tanny-sense unease.

"In fact," she began, winced sharply, then stopped, her hand flying to her temple. "Ah, forgive me. We must let you unpack and rest a little." Not missing a beat, she went to a hook by the glass-paneled door, retrieved the car keys and popped open the trunk.

Glancing at her in some wonder, I got out the two suitcases and shouldered the two packs. I then followed her meekly through the glass-paneled door, trying to pretend all this mind control was quite normal. At the moment she'd winced, I'd heard in my mind's ear a faint echo of the word *"Silenzio"* for all the world like a guard at the Sistine Chapel.

I dared not wonder why. He might be listening.

Beyond the glazed door was a riot of light and color for which neither the building's grim exterior nor LoCieco's dark study had prepared me. It was four-sided portico, its smooth columns of dark red porphyry twined with an ancient grape vine festooned in new green buds.

Inside the little colonnade was a sunlit garden packed with all kinds of plants, some in pots of all sizes, some in the ground and pruned into tree-form. Small frames and trellises stood handy for use once the summer growing season arrived. I guessed that this was no pleasure-garden, but a pharmacopia of medicinals. The only unbusinesslike note was the simple fountain at its center, spouting a jet of sparkling water into the mild March sunlight.

This was where Stephen Burnsey washed out his bloody hand-kerchief.

I must have made a noise of amazement and praise, for Medea smiled in honest pride.

"You should see it in the height of the summer. I can hardly get through the grapevine to cut my materials, and the fragrance of the flowers is wonderful."

"And it all seems so Roman," I had to observe. "I feel as if I am visiting Pompeii."

She eyed me shrewdly. "This part of Florence has changed very little since Roman days. They say it was never destroyed, never rebuilt, only repaired."

Going clockwise, we came to three small doors on the western stretch of the portico.

"This is where our guests usually stay, and this first room is yours. We would have been happy to have you lodge with us upstairs, but feel free to use our common space. We have a little kitchen and a computer-printer work area I will show you. We also eat our meals there, Massimo and I, and you are welcome to contribute to our food-fund, and join us. Otherwise you must go out to eat." She smiled. "But that is lonely. Tonight, of course, *Il dottore* would like you to join him for a special welcome dinner in his own room at 20:00, that is, eight o'clock."

"I'll be ready, thank you."

I felt a flash of unease. *All this was for Ratty, wasn't it?*

Medea looked at me keenly. "You are fortunate. *Il dottore* will share secrets with you he has shared with no-one before. He has foreseen this illness."

That remark nagged at me for days.

She held out a set of keys, meanwhile, and spelled them for me.

"Here is the key to the front door by the garage. Here is the key to the smaller door to the North Wing if you would like to visit Horatio in the Clinic at any time. Our quarters are to the left of the surgery, up the long stairs. Here is the key to your room. With the open portico you may like to lock your door at night, but there is no real need. *Il dottore* owns the buildings on both sides as well. The big fire doors to the Clinic are locked at night, but can be opened from within by panic bars. Is all that clear?"

"Yes, except where to find the bathroom and the toilet? And is there a laundry room? I didn't bring many clothes with me."

"Of course." She turned and pointed directly across the garden.

"In the East Portico are three more doors like these: you will see they have signs. The center one is a WC and a sink. The room on the left is the Shower with a sink and another toilet. Just be sure to lock them from inside with the bolt when you are using them, since you will be sharing them with Massimo and me. On the right is the Laundry. We don't have a clothes-drier, but there are racks and plenty of clothes-pins. We set the racks in the portico to dry." She made a face. "Jeans take forever. It is one reason I wear yoga styles. They dry so fast."

All this was familiar from my days as a student in the Arca. I nodded cheerfully.

"Now," she sighed, "would you mind if I let Massimo show you the North Wing, after you have settled in, of course? I must start a distillation before *il dottore's* massage."

I agreed at once and thanked her profusely. Truth was I was relieved to be alone with my thoughts, if indeed I was alone? I seemed to hear faint laughter.

Seeing my little room with its narrow bed, narrow bookshelf, simple desk with wooden chair and study lamp, and its wardrobe, I was even more strongly reminded of my student days, ten years back at the RCAS. The room was cold, unsurprisingly. High in the outside wall was a narrow, unglazed window, fitted with bars against pigeons. The terrazzo floor also had no rug but there was a tiny electric oil radiator under the desk and I found blankets in the wardrobe.

With a sigh, I looked over my clothing.

I had three days' worth, all dirty and most too dressy. *Better start a load of laundry ASAP!* As I shook out my nice red cashmere sweater—stained with *carbonara,* alas—out came my *solje.* It flashed in a beam of afternoon light before rolling onto the floor with a musical jingle, quite unhurt. Seeing it gave me a sharp pang of longing for my best beloved, right at the heart. I pulled out my phone to check the time.

Nope, he and Moley would still be on the train. No coverage until Tarquinia Lido.

With another sigh, I took my washables off to the Laundry. After starting a load with soap that I found beside the little machine, I visited the neighboring WC I was ready for the rest of my tour and to visit poor Ratty at the Clinic.

The double fire-doors leading directly into the clinic from the portico were unlocked. I eased my way through one of them, careful to let it fall to with the gentlest of clicks. The big, low-ceilinged room was clean and orderly, well-lit both artificially and by windows high up in the wall opposite. Several enameled wardrobes and deep counters with plenty of storage under them stood along the left-hand wall. To the right, beyond a pleated-cloth screen, I glimpsed a surgical theater, a lab-office, and what looked like a pair of glass-fronted refrigerators.

In the middle of the Clinic proper, separated by a vital-signs monitor and an I.V. pole, were two raised hospital beds. One was empty but in the other lay the Rat, pitifully small, one little yellow arm fitted with an IV drip. I noticed that the pole was hung with two pouches, one large and clear, the other small and opaque, dripping a red-brown substance into the clear fluid before it went into Ratty's vein. Massimo, in a spotless lab-coat, was checking vital signs.

He looked up with a smile that had none of Medea's simmering envy in it.

"It will be a moment," he said. "Feel free to look around, but don't touch anything."

The surgery had caught my eye, so I started there. Once behind the screen, I made a bee-line for one of the refrigerators. Through the glass door I saw rows of vials of what looked like blood on the top shelf. Most of them were labeled 'hep ful' and all were marked with a person's name and a date, ranging from about four or five years ago until very recently.

"Helpful," I muttered, wondering where I had recently seen something.

"Changing the bed pan," called Massimo. "Back in a moment!"

At that, I looked around more generally. I covered my unmagical left eye and waited for something else to glow with Tanny-energy. At once I saw three "somethings."

The first was a slim black notebook on the desk labeled in white ink by a spidery hand *genealogia*. Into it was tucked a worn journal reprint. The second was a stack of identical, glossy-papered publications, the self-same catalogue for *Antiquità Colchis* that I had last seen in stacks in Tony's *Cantina*. The non-coincidence made me shudder.

But then I spotted a the third, much stranger glowing-thing. It was a spiky little paperweight holding down a small heap of receipts: a gilded iron Vanth.

Massimo returned just then, and on impulse, I called out, "Do you know Boetio Corto?"

"*Certo!*" he answered easily. "He was just here last mo—" but stopped on a gasp.

In a very different voice he said, "Come see how his color is already much better!"

Hurrying over I saw that it was true. The horrible banana-yellow I'd seen at Lavinia's had already faded to tan. Someone who didn't know Ratty might have thought he'd been out in the sun all week but his natural color is pink-with-freckles. His pinched face was still very hot where I caressed it. His breathing came ragged and quick from between his cracked lips.

Better, but still not great.

I pulled ubiquitous lip balm from the pocket of the corduroy tunic I'd put on in Rome that morning, a lifetime ago. "May I put this on him? He's not infectious by touch?"

He put up his head in the negative. "Still best to use your finger then wash your hands."

I did so, my eyes stinging with tears. Then I found a chair to pull up beside the Rat and held one of his soft hands, stroking the rough red hair off his dreaming forehead.

"Where did you get so good at curing hepatitis?" I asked Massimo.

He shrugged. "It is a recent area of specialization. When some of our patients come in wanting tattoo scars removed, we find they have chronic hepatitis from shared needles. About five years ago, *il dottore* read an article that convinced him to specialize."

He indicated the bag of dark fluid. "The serum has been very successful for us. Earlier, specialty was in other areas underserved by standard medicine."

"Yes, my mother told me he did the only safe abortions in Italy."

"We actually do very few surgical abortions, nowadays. Now, we give a series of two pills," he gestured vividly. "First one little pink one that kills the fetus, then a big white one given within twenty-four hours of the pink. Sloughs everything off: like a period, you know. Much safer for the mother than surgery. She feels fine in just a few days."

He had taken a seat nearby and we spoke easily.

"Godpapa has said he can heal with a touch," I asked. "Is that so?"

He nodded emphatically.

"I myself had a terrible scar left over from a scooter crash. It ran from *here*," he drew a finger from a spot in the thick hair above his broad forehead, across his eyelid to his cheekbone, "to *here*, but no more! Partly I was cured by Medea's healing cream—she also is a genius—but mostly by the touch of *il dottore*."

"He said something about fertility?"

"Ah, in fertility he is a national treasure! For women who cannot conceive, he calls down the egg!" Here he smiled conspiratorially, leaning a little closer, "And men come to him to become, you know, better able to please the ladies. You understand?"

"Understood," I said, blushing.

"I may tell you that the proof is in *il dottore* himself. He has amazing vitality at such a very great age." He pointed to himself. "I am myself proof."

The breathtaking epiphany struck me.

"*You're his son?*" I whispered.

"*Esattamente*," he smiled broadly. "My mother was housekeeper here." He sighed. "But I am a disappointment. I have no powers like his. He dreams of having a . . ." He winced, then stopped.

Had I faintly heard the words *Sta attento?*

I quickly changed the subject.

"So, you studied medicine, instead?"

"Yes." He seemed to breathe again. "Here at the university in Florence I trained to be a Nurse Practitioner. I was one of very few men in the program." He grinned. "It was great."

"You have a girlfriend?"

He nodded happily.

"She lives with my mother, in San Niccolò over yonder. I usually see her all day on . . ." This time the pain was obviously sharper but he pressed on. "Sundays, but will take Monday off instead, as this morning we had to get ready for you and the boy. Well, it's time for me to bathe your, you call him *Rattuccio*, now that he has stabilized."

He got up looking a little woozy. "I nearly forgot! *Il dottore* wants you to read his book on travel in the spirit world as soon as you can. It is on the surgery desk: a little book in Latin. Tonight, you are his guest, remember."

"*Sì.*" I smiled. "Dinner at eight."

With warm thanks, I apologized for keeping him from his mother today.

He laughed and got up. "One day will do no harm. Don't forget your book."

On the surgery desk I found a little antique book bound in white calfskin. Its title was stamped in gold on the narrow spine: *De Peregrinatione in Mundo Animarum*, meaning, Concerning Travel in the Spirit World. It was published in Rome in 1880.

On the title page I came face to face with an engraving of the author, *E. Benevento*, a young man in clerical garb, his lustrous eyes uncovered.

"There is my godfather when Mary knew him," I murmured aloud. "No specs."

As I turned to go, I caught sight of the Vanth and beside it the notebook and even moreso the journal article stuck into it. The Vanth I had no desire to touch. But, with a rush of dishonest energy, I scooped up not only my little primer but also the notebook, with inserted article, along with a copy of the catalogue of antiquities and walked calmly for the fire-doors.

If Massimo saw me take them, he did nothing to stop me.

I hurried across to my room and locked the door behind me. I needed to think and think hard over the many things I had just been told or had observed.

How long did I have, I wondered, sitting on my bed with my stolen goods, *before one of those mind-beams shot my way?*

There it was, a sense of beetling oversight. It was as if I were in a doll's house and someone had just lifted the roof, to see what I was doing!

Pushing back against the Observer, I opened my Godpa-pa's book. With a shiver I saw that it was about what I've heard elsewhere called "Lucid Dream Travel." People can apparently teach themselves to consciously direct their dreams. This must have been how he got into my hearth and how he'd caged my Vanths.

The sense of being observed only grew the further I read. Mercifully, it dispersed the moment a knock came at my door.

Hiding the other three bits of my reading material under my pillow, I answered.

"Yes?"

"Your wash is done," came Medea's voice. "Would you like me to hang it out? I have a load I need to start." I jumped up, unlocked the door and looked out.

There she was with a basket of damp sheets looking at me narrowly.

"No, no, I'll do it. Sorry." Almost shamelessly, I re-locked the door behind me. Almost.

"Have I not said that during daylight hours it is quite safe to leave your door unlocked?" she asked crisply as we walked around the quadrangle together.

"Sorry. At the Arca in Rome they taught us to lock our doors!"

I hurried to open the laundry-room door for her.

"Not in Florence," she smiled. "You can go out anytime and feel safe."

As we dealt with our laundry, I remarked, "Massimo says he has a girlfriend. What about you? Do you get out much?"

"Never," she said at once. "Everything I need is here."

Seeing my dubious look, she added, "I order all the raw materials we need online.

Massimo does the shopping or gets things I can't order. I don't have any family to visit. Something in the laboratory always needs my attention, or *il dottore*. It is my great honor to care for your godfather, Tanaquil," she finished simply.

I nodded, looking over the full clothes-rack. "So, I just leave the clothes out here?"

"A little to one side so *il dottore* can get past in in his scooter."

"Oh, he has a motorized chair?" *Why did this fact alarm me?*

"Yes, and if he must, he can get down the stairs on his own. If the night is beautiful, he likes to sit in the garden. When it gets warmer, of course!"

I recalled something he'd said about my room being *convenient*. It seemed to me at the time that he wanted to say *convenient to me*, but I had dismissed it as an impossibility.

Now, however . . .

Medea, watching me and said nothing.

"I should finish reading *il dottore's* text on Lucid Dream Travel," I said lamely. "I was hoping to ask him about it at dinner. At 20:00 hours, right?"

She nodded.

I regained my room and relocked it. I immediately felt that stifling weight of observation descend on me again. It was looking at my body and prodding at my mind.

I suddenly had to talk with Jim. I needed input from a

sane, outside mind to. I'd been here about four hours. He should have reached Tarquinia Lido by now.

I tried calling again and again. Nothing. Then I tried a text message.

"Hey, Pericles! Are you home yet?"

Almost immediately I got back, *"Just pulled into driveway. Call you in two minutes?"*

"Sure." So, I hung up and counted to sixty, about ten times.

Messaged him again. This time I got right through.

"Kept getting 'call failed' message." He wrote back. *"How are things?"*

"Ratty already a little better, but Godpapa says it will be a week before he can go. Meanwhile I am learning how to enter the spirit world."

"That is great news, but a week is a long time! And 'what' spirit world?"

"Tell you when I know! Things a little weird. Learned I am godpapa's great-great-granddaughter. But it wouldn't send. Just wouldn't.

All Jim got was a long, long silence, to which he responded,

"Can I call you tonight?"

"You can try. = -)" That message sent.

"Miss you like crazy."

"Same here. Hugs to Clo and everybody?"

"You bet. Same to you, darling sweetheart honey oh hell."

"Oh hell, is right. Dinner here is at 8. Should be in my room by 10."

"10 it is. Got to go."

Unable to formulate a reply I closed the screen. Then I started casting about for anything I owned that could ward off my godfather's interference.

That I had *something*, I had no doubt, just as I had a sense my time was limited. It was as if I had a grace period and it was nearly up.

Mor had provided me with something. *Quick, quick, what was it?*

Something shone into the corner of my eye: the *solje,* reflecting a stray beam of light.

What did *Mor* say? *People used to say they reflect away evil?*

Would it help, if I wore it at night? With no light to reflect?

Something dark and unreflective, then. The trollkors.

I hurried to Ratty's suitcase and rummaged. I'd have to wash *his* clothes, tomorrow. And there is it was in my hand: a small loop of wrought iron on a braided-leather band.

Iron. Medea had told me *it literally takes the magic out of the herbs!* What about *other* kinds of magic? Without more thought, I had it on.

The change was ludicrous: as if the roof had come off and the air was sweet and fresh.

I stood and stretched, laughing aloud.

Tucking the antiquities catalogue into a pocket of my suitcase, I took *Geneologia* to my desk, got my research note-book and pencil, and began taking notes on my godfather's family tree, setting aside the inserted article. It was a paper on the presence of *fulminant hepatitis* in bones found in the Place of Sacrifice at *La Castellina.*

I knew it very well. I had written it myself!

It was entirely dark outside the circle of my desk-lamp when the knock came at my door. "Time to eat, Tanaquil," came Massimo's voice.

I started guiltily. "Coming," I called. "I've been reading *il dottore's* book."

"He will be pleased when you tell him that." He smiled as I emerged.

Hopefully, I though with a pang of fear, *he didn't know what else I'd been reading.*

23

SHRIVING THE STREGA

STILL SUNDAY . . .

"*O*ne favor," Massimo said. "If you remove the dirty dishes to the common room when you come down after dinner— there is a large tray beside the table you will see. I will do them when I return from seeing Mother. That will make it simpler for Medea to ready *il dottore* for bed."

"Of course!" I agreed at once. I resolved also to do the dishes and save him the bother.

Wonderful fragrances awaited us as I was ushered to my place at what had earlier been the work table. Set out formally was a sumptuous dinner for two, brought in— Massimo said—from a nearby *trattoria*. The light of six tall candles in two silver candelabra shone on an array of silver utensils, crystal glasses and mellow, gold-rimmed china, set on a gleaming white linen cloth. My godfather had wheeled himself to the center of one long side of the table. A library chair waited opposite for me. Serving dishes were set out to either side.

Godpapa apologized that nothing would be as hot as it

should be if we were served in proper courses but this way we would not be disturbed.

"Medea is eating in the North Wing and our dear Massimo will dine with his mother and fiancée. I have kept him too long today, already! Farewell, *Massi!*"

He put out his hand to the young man who came swiftly over and kissed it, saying warmly, "I will not be late, *monsignore.*" Then I made a light-footed departure.

"May I ask you to serve us, my dear?" asked *il dottore,* so I gave us each a little *romanesco all'Albanese, spaghetti ai zucchini fritti* and *polenta alla baccalà,* that is to say, a delicious relative of broccoli sautéed in butter finished with wine and orange zest, fried zucchini tossed with spaghetti, and soft cornmeal-mush topped with fluffy morsels of reconstituted dried salt cod, much better than it sounds. For dessert there were three *tarocchi* in a silver bowl and a little sharp knife. A decanter of garnet-red wine stood at my elbow, and a bottle of Panna water.

"Only a tiny splash of wine for me, *goddaughter,*" he smiled. "It is a fine year of your favorite Vino Nobile!"

Though remarkably hungry, I forced myself not to drink off my wine too quickly, and it was truly prize-quality, not to devour my food in an unseemly fashion as my godfather ate and drank only the tiniest portions before pushing aside his plate and glass and answering the unspoken question.

How had he come by his stregheria and his astoundingly old age?

"When I was a still young priest serving here in the parish of Santa Croce, I was called to the bedside of a parishioner named Ottilia Prava. She was near death and sent word to us begging for the rite of Extreme Unction, or 'last rites.'"

"I was frankly surprised. Though she had never been formally excommunicated, Ottilia had more than once come under suspicion of practicing witchcraft. But, out of pity, I went.

"In those days the area around the Cloister of Santa Croce was a sordid, dangerous place. You may know that the Piazza Santa Croce was a place for public executions? Well, such things draw the *streghe* like a magnet, and priests were seldom to be seen there.

"The looks of the people I passed were anything but friendly and I was careful to hold my satchel with the blessed eucharist and consecrating oil close against me. Such things are of great use to *streghe*, as I knew even then.

"Her dwelling was over a stinking dye-shop. It was hot, airless. It was August, around noon, and her room was hung about and heaped up with bottles of withered animals, braided charms, bunches of herbs of all sorts, pestles, alembics, phials and jars. On a table by itself was a rotten pumpkin carved into a hideous face and decked with two horns made of bean-pods. It was quite sunken-in, and buzzing with flies. It was the sick-room of a *strega*.

"The woman herself lay on a verminous bed with sheets the color of *caffe latte.* She was skeletal with illness, filthy, and nearly naked in her rags. The smell was so unbearable that I opened the single window before coming to her. Forgive me, this is not a good story for mealtime." I had forgotten. "When I reached her bedside, her dull eyes brightened with a kind of unholy glee." I was suddenly on my guard, though not on guard enough.

"I brought her a glass of water from a pitcher on the dresser and held up her head. She drank greedily, gripping my wrist with one hand like a claw, then said with a strange energy,

"'*Padre Titono*, I suffer from torment, night and day, until I entrust my legacy to someone. Will you not take it from me so I can die in peace?'

"''I have no need for any legacy, *Signora* Ottilia,' I insisted, tired of the popular notion that priests were always after whatever they could get. 'Keep it for your own family to use and enjoy.' That made her laugh and then to cough. And when she coughed there was—excuse me for these distasteful details—a froth of blood on her lips.

"*You must take it,*' she said hoarsely. 'Who knows? With it you may do much good. I cannot die until you *swear to take what I give you.*'

"How could I refuse? If it were money, I knew many like herself who could use it.

"When I swore I would she released me and fell back, not quite dead.

"*On the table,*' she said faintly, '*the small box. It is yours.*' And on that instant, she exhaled her last breath on a harsh rattle such as I had heard at many other death-beds. Alas! she was dead, poor soul, and I was too late to bless her. Still, there was a look of great peace on her face and her soul, we could hope, was with God.

"I took my satchel and the wooden box and made my way to the district police. We were still under Austrian rule in those days to report the death. It seemed to me as I went, I took my satchel and the wooden box and made my way to the district police. And as I went, the people drew away from me in fear. I duly reported the death and location of the body, and filled out the death certificate. Returning to the Cloister I felt strangely tired, and worried that I had caught the typhus fever."

"On reaching my cell looked closely at the box. It was smooth to the touch and made of cunning joinery, with a close-fitting lid that I opened with some difficulty. The moment I did, however, I dropped the box with a cry of horror as out onto the floor leapt a *small grey mouse.*

"I was horrified. How could it have lived for two minutes in such an airtight thing, let alone two hours? But even as I stood wondering, the creature ran up the bare skin of my leg beneath my trousers and sank its sharp teeth into my thigh. But when I clutched at the place, I felt there only cloth. The mouse had vanished. Since that moment, I have had the gift of *stregheria*. She also willed me this house," he gestured at the room, "which has turned out to be a great blessing."

"She lived *here?*" I cried.

"Yes, but I do not bite. If you want my *stregheria*, my dear, you have only to ask!"

24

A PINCH OF BLUENESS

STILL DAY ONE – SUNDAY

After reading a good long while to the unconscious Rat, I went back to my room and called Jim, this time with no sense of oppression or interference. I kept my voice low, all the same, and jammed a towel along the base of my door.

After a quick check-in about Ratty's amazing progress, I told him about the *trollkors.* He laughed it off but supposed it couldn't do any harm. Then I shared all I could remember about the day and what I'd discovered in my reading, and in the lab.

It took a while.

I have to confess I left out the part about being pregnant. I suspected that would be the hardest part for him believe.

"A gilded votive?" he cried. "Not a copy?"

"Yes, and rusted like the ones from the *mundus,* not clean like Franco's. And he had a reprint of my paper on the Place of Sacrifice."

"The one from your Master's thesis or the one we did last year?"

"Master's thesis. Where I talk about *fulminant hepatitis.*"

HEP FUL. Hepatitis fulminans. The blood in those vials

in the surgery refrigerators had been culled from all the hepatitis cases my godfather had been treating since he read that article.

"Sweetheart?"

"I'm here, Pericles," I answered, going on in a rush, "Listen, did Marc take that last air sample to the lab from the *mundus*? Did Tina ever test it?"

"Yes, and it was clean. I figured that gave him the all-clear to loot the *mundus*. Angelo was peeved for going to all the trouble of using the haz-mat suits."

"Don't you think it's weird that the Vanth that infected Ratty didn't give off any traces of hepatitis into the air of the *mundus*? You'd think the air would be full of it! And Franco doesn't have hepatitis from that bird attack, does he?"

"No, just a coma like yours."

Again, I heard Massimo say, "il dottore *had read an article that convinced him to begin production on our serum.*"

"Pericles," I cried, "that article of mine had been read and re-read, and there were marginal notes all over it *in my godfather's handwriting.* It was just like the writing in the genealogy notebook and the inscription in my copy of his book."

I could feel him frowning over this piece of information.

"You say the article marked a page in his genealogy notebook?" he asked slowly, adding "And may I just say from those photos of it you sent me that the guy has been awfully busy over the past one hundred fifty years? What was on the page that was marked?"

"I am. Me. My branch, from Grandma Susie down. My name was circled in red pencil, with a star next to it. Lots of the pages had notes in red pencil, and some names were underlined, with question marks next to them. Some of these were crossed out, and three others were circled, with the word 'strong' next to them, but *mine was the only one circled and starred.*"

"Say that again!" I did, then he asked,

"Was there also a word next to your name?"

"Yes, 'strongest,' oh, and my birthdate."

That's when the big epiphany wave drew back, hit, and drew back again.

"Oh my God," I whispered.

He had provided the tainted blood for Marc to infect the Riverbankers.

To bring me here.

Hence the fancy dinner the night I arrived, the disappointment that I was pregnant, the lessons in Lucid Dream Travel, the healing we must do *together*.

"What is it?' he asked urgently. "What are you thinking?"

I told him, or most of it.

"Why would he do that?"

"Maybe he's tired of living, Pericles! Maybe he wants to pass on his *stregheria* to the strongest possible candidate?"

"Are you suggesting he plans some kind of *suicide* while you're there, so the damned mouse bites you? We've got to get you out of there the minute Ratty is well."

"The minute he is *physically* well, Godpapa and I are going into the spirit realm to cure his coma by flushing out the Vanth. Then we can take him home."

"Okay, but when you are about to do this metaphysical rescue session, tell me. I will beg, borrow or steal a car and get up there, to meet you the absolute minute it's over. Listen, sweetheart: Do you share food with the others or do they give you a tray or something?"

"We eat together," I answered, feeling a sudden chill of fear.

"Good, good. And don't take *any* medicine they give you, okay? Even if you get sick. Just stick with whatever you have in your emergency kit. If it's something major, give them any reason you like, but tell them you have go to Tarquinia General. Don't let them treat you in that clinic of theirs, or put you under sedation. And don't let that Godpapa of yours convince you to have a sleepover with him. Promise?"

"I promise," I assured him, recalling that Daddy Bill told me *not to share his bed*.

What I did right then, under cover of making a late visit to Ratty, was to return my godfather's genealogy book—with article—to the surgery desk. No-one was in the clinic, but I'd been shown the "baby monitor" in the Common Room, so I knew where the circle of vision ended. Racing along the southern wall, I dropped off the book. Then I raced back and walked slowly across the room to Ratty's bedside, where I stayed for maybe an hour, reading him more of *Voyage of the Dawn Treader*. His eyes were moving under their lids as I read and once he sighed, ever-so-faintly, when I called his name.

Finally, I kissed his hot forehead and went off to bed. It was a great comfort to know that Massimo would be in at midnight to check his vital signs, and that they were linked to the monitor. An alarm would sound if anything changed for the worse.

Crossing the shadowy quadrangle, I was trying to work out what Jim had not been willing to tell me when I heard a crisp *snip-snip, snip* from the garden and looked up sharply.

Medea was there in the chilly moonlight, copper shears in her hand, cutting fruits off a dead vine. She said nothing nor looked my way. I was silent likewise, uneasily wondering what ingredient to which potion must be harvested at night and in silence.

DAY TWO – MONDAY

Next morning it was just Medea and me at breakfast, but a basket of fresh *cornetti* stood on the mid-century formica-and-steel-tubing table. She set down her *La Stampa* with a smile.

"Massimo brought these up just now before going to San Niccolò. They're still hot!"

Massimo had today off, I remembered. *I could help Medea*

with Ratty-duty today, whenever she needed to go care for il dottore.

"Have you made coffee yet?" I asked.

"Yes, there's some left in the big pot. Help yourself."

I got myself a cup and plate and joined her at the table, breaking a *cornetto* in half, drinking in the blissful perfume of butter and wheat before eating it down to the last crunch of pearl sugar, some of which stuck in my tooth and was strangely bitter.

I had never had a *cornetto* quite like that before. Was it another strange thing about Tuscan bread, besides its being unsalted?

As Medea took her cup to the sink, I picked up her *La Stampa* and found the story of Franco's attack. It was covered in greater depth than in the *La Repubblica* Jim had bought at the station. Not only were there graphic photos of the ugly slashes on Franco's back but also a sidebar on Tony's death and the theft of items from the *mundus,* with details of the shield I had not yet seen. Its back was smooth, without any grip fittings: clearly made for ritual use only.

And what were those big letters scratched into the bronze?

The caption read: "A single word in the mysterious Etruscan language was inscribed on the underside of the shield, namely: *Flerkva*—meaning be purified. According to Dr. J. P. Lewis, this is a protective word used against the Vanth as a demon of fevers."

There was a photo of Jim, pointing to the shield. I stared at him for a long time.

"He is very good-looking, Dr. Lewis?" asked Medea, looking over my shoulder.

"I've always thought so," I smiled. "But that is not his most endearing—"

She cut me off. "Yet Boetio Corto was your boyfriend for some time, *vero?*"

I breathed in sharply. *That's right, she knew Marc.*

"Marc is even better-looking, you mean? Yes, but he is not as good."

"Not so good in bed?" she frowned.

My face grew hot. "Not as good a *person.*"

"Boetio has told me all about you," she went on angrily. "That you would not let him do archaeology, that he must now only do photographs." She shook the paper in my face. "And now he is treated like a criminal. Who knows where he is?"

She had used the singular *tu,* blaming me personally, not Jim and me together. I suddenly felt unsafe with her. I wished Massimo were there.

"But, Medea, we *did* let him back on the site. Besides," I cried, "he *is* a criminal! He took that gold and left poor Tony to die."

"There is no proof he was there," she said austerely. "Cecco Casti could . . ."

"Marc's car was found at Tony's place, and his fingerprints were all over the boxes they found in the garage. And I saw him with my own eyes in Tony's car, headed for the site."

"Bah. You were ill, the papers said so. Riccardo and Giulia Pantano were behind it all, they and also you. Boetio did nothing! *Nothing.*"

I opened my mouth to insist that *Marc had poisoned Ratty with an infected votive,* but realized in time where that poison may have originated.

"*You* released the Vanth," she panted. "You and that husband of yours uncovered what should have remained hidden, and now you are getting revenge on Franco Cotto."

"What?" I blinked. "Howso?"

"You wanted that temple of his, Boetio told me. And now he is struck down. Now, because of you, *il dottore* must take on a task that may kill him."

A wave of dizziness came over me. *Morning sickness? High blood pressure?*

"If you have finished eating," she snapped, taking my dishes to the sink, "please put away your dry laundry. I have my own wash to do."

Glad to be gone, I went downstairs, feeling distinctly odd. The steps seemed further off than they should be. The white-washed walls were glowing a sickly green and smelt strongly of bleach. The herbal tang of the garden rose up like a wall of choking fumes. When I reached the drying rack, my garnet-red cashmere sweater seemed to give off the acrid scent of blood. My hand froze in midair.

The sweater had been contaminated with hepatitis.

The flagstones rushed up at me.

*W*hen I awoke on the bed in my little room, Medea was just brushing off her hands.

"You fainted," she said matter-of-factly.

"My sweater was covered with blood," I cried, peering dizzily up at her.

Shrugging, she indicated a neat pile of clothing on my desk.

"There is a little *dust* on them, perhaps. You knocked over the rack, but I have folded them for you." The whole pile seemed to writhe unpleasantly.

"Thanks. How did you get me here?"

She laughed.

"Massimo is not the only strong one. I will get you something for dizziness."

The moment she was gone, I staggered over to the WC and I lost my breakfast.

After rinsing my mouth, I went back to my room feeling distinctly better. I was sitting up on my bed when Medea came in with a glass of water and a saucer upon which reposed two pills: one small and pink, the other large and white.

"You are sitting up. Good," she said brightly, though I sensed she was disappointed. "*Il dottore* is extremely worried you may have been exposed to the hepatitis. As a precaution, he wants you at once to take this pink pill and tomorrow morning to take this white one."

"At once?"

In early cases we give a series of two pills: one little pink one, given immediately, that kills the fetus, and a big white one that sloughs it off, like a period, you know; starts within twenty-four hours of taking the white one.

"Yes, yes. Or you will be as sick as Horatio, I promise."

Catching the horrid pink thing between thumb and forefinger, I made as if to set it well back on my tongue. Then I snatched up the water and gulped noisily, meanwhile dropping the pill under my desk. Later, I flushed it down the toilet and hoped no fish lost their young.

With a smile, Medea left me.

What to do? The white pill must disappear, tomorrow, and I must, within 24 hours or so, according to Wikipedia, develop severe cramping and bleeding.

How to do that, convincingly?

"No-one ever sees you bleed when you get your periods, do they?" came a small voice I had never heard before. "So, they won't know. Just act like you're in pain, ask Medea for tampons, and act sad. You have to act as if you've just lost *me*."

Damned drug, I thought, then heard a silvery laugh.

"It's me talking, *Mor*, not that crunch in your cornetto."

"Fred?" I gasped.

"Not Fred: Minnie. After Contessa Egidio-Doria."

"Erminia?"

"Yes. The twins will be Peter and Neely. No Fred."

"Twins?" I groaned aloud. "*Mamma mia!*"

How an unborn babe could be so wise puzzled me until a day or so later. Minnie explained she now had access to the wisdom of the One as well as free passage throughout the spirit realm. At the moment of birth, she would receive a kiss to make her forget all, or almost all of it. That early ability to swim, she told me, or to learn languages or other mysteries of early childhood are remnants of that tragic fading-from-memory.

At the time, however, I asked her the most important question on my heart.

"Tell me, where would you go if I did lose you, Minnie? Where do you come from?"

"You know the place, Mor. You were a pinch of blue yourself a little while ago and I was there with you. We all go back to it, sooner or later. Nothing is lost!"

"Nothing?" Tears sprang into my eyes as I thought of my Daddy Bill.

"Nothing at all."

25

SLEEPWALKING

DAY THREE – TUESDAY

Next morning, with another quick prayer it would do no harm downstream, I sent the white pill the way of the pink. Next, I set about counterfeiting a short, sharp miscarriage for the other inhabitants of Number Three. I hoped to God-slash-the-Oneness that the *trollkors* was still holding my thoughts in confidence.

Massimo was horrified, Medea solicitous, and my godfather apparently devastated to learn I had miscarried, advising me to rest and to distract myself by reading *De Peregrinatione* and attempting to reach the Green Lands. He was eager for us to enter them together the moment Ratty's physical health had improve. He encouraged me to ask any question I liked about what I found either in the book or in the Lands themselves.

Oh, I had questions, all right, but Minnie was my guide to new insights. She became the voice of my Tanny-sense, a feathered presence over my heart.

I worried she would be a visible presence when *Padre* LoCieco and I went to rescue Ratty from the Vanth, but she assured me that *by then, it won't matter.*

Setting aside my dissertation, I got to work on Lucid Dream Travel (LDT), and spent all day Wednesday on it, when I wasn't groaning or resting or running to the loo.

I practiced getting quickly to my hearth, where the copper cage still held the glowering Vanth secure on the settle opposite. Then guided by Minnie and the One, learnt to open the spark-portal wide enough to step through it into the Green Lands.

DAYS FOUR & FIVE – WEDNESDAY & THURSDAY

Point I.A of *De Peregrinatione* is translated roughly as *"Close your eyes and enter your own hearth. If the One is missing, call upon the One. Sit beside the One and visualize the blue spark in front of you"* a deceptively easy instruction.

At first, the spark would not allow itself to be visualized. Fumigation with appropriate herbs or smearing with something called "flying oil" made the process easier, said the text, but I reasoned that if my *stregheria* was so strong, I should be able to manage it unaided.

After three hours of solid concentration, I did it.

By Wednesday night, I was able to visualize the blue portal consistently and by Thursday lunchtime I could go out from my hearth into the Green Lands. I returned to my hearth by sitting cross-legged in the open emptiness and focusing on the air in front of my face. Once, I glimpsed Daddy Bill up among the trees on the mountainside beyond the river.

On Thursday afternoon, Minnie and I made a cautious exploration down the hallway that branches off to the right of my hearth. It stretches to an infinity of darkness lined with endless wooden doors. All but the first has a small brass plaque and doorknob. All were shut.

The unlabeled right-hand door led to recent memories. Others were attached to memories of certain people, Pericles being the first on the left. As I moved forward down the hall,

I found I could see in the gloom, though there was no light source I could identify.

Not far down, on the right was Marc. Opening it uneasily, I found myself looking at many more doors in a longish hall. I opened one labeled Bar Impero and there he was on the early morning of our last tryst, turning from Cecco and giving me that fanged smile.

I made a quick exit then I ran to open the Pericles door, finding another, longer hall. Down it we went almost to the very end to a door labeled *Ara Della Regina*. Opening it I saw a moment ten years earlier when I was a student at the Arca. I'd come to the dusty edge of the *Ara*, wanting to jump down but fearing it was too far. There he was, smiling, both his hands held up to take both mine. "I'll catch you, Greenough. Jump."

"The picture in his bedroom was taken next day," said Minnie. "He already knew."

Had I known, that soon?

DAY SIX – FRIDAY

The next morning, Friday was the third day since my "sad accident" and just a week since the wedding. Godpapa asked me to bring my breakfast to the garden and came there to see me in his motorized chair. He asked how I felt and how my training was progressing.

I told him I had found the hallway of doors.

Then I asked a question that had been puzzling me but that I must word carefully.

"Godpapa," I began, tearing off a morsel of plain *cornetto*. "I understand that Ratty caught hepatitis from being cut by the votive he handled. What caused the coma that Ratty and I had, and apparently Franco also had, and the infestation of Vanths?"

He stroked his chin, considering.

"I believe that there was a great burst of spiritual energy when the Vanth came out of that sphere, irradiating everything around it. I think that if you were to test the soil and objects for a certain distance thereabouts, you would find that they would show a lessening field of energy, the further from the *mundus* you go. It is possible, moreover, that the pet owl at site, you call her Antonia, I think, was lodged in the tree above the *hypogeum* and, somehow . . ." He shrugged.

"Maybe the burst ran right up the tree? It has its roots near the *hypogeum.* Or it traveled along a spring or up a well, that Jim thinks is hidden somewhere near the *mundus?*"

"Groundwater certainly increases the chance that the blast reached the owl."

Another thought occurred to me.

"Is the golden sphere dangerous to hold? If so, shouldn't we try to get word to the thieves? What if Marc or Cecco is in a coma like Ratty's?"

He looked up at me through those smoked lenses.

"I have heard no rumor of that, but it is a kind thought, my dear! It is to neutralize this *psychic irradiation* that I hope to perform a comprehensive exorcism at the burst-point. If we can place your friend Franco Cotto as close to that point as possible, I believe we can rid both him and the site of this Vanth infestation."

I frowned.

"You say 'rid.' Where would the Vanth or Vanths actually *go?*"

"It is best to send the exorcised spirit into some common object which can then be burnt: a broom, for example. There is a tree that overhangs the *hypogeum.* That might do."

"If you did not destroy it, would she still remain trapped there?"

"I believe so."

"Where will the Vanths inside me and Ratty go? There are no big trees in the garden."

"I told you that I plan to use the Nemean method," he said with a smile. "As Hercules was forced to use the Nemean

Lion's claw to pierce its own invulnerable skin, one Vanth will destroy the other! We cannot use this method with Franco Cotto since you will, God willing, be free of the Vanth after we cure Horatio."

"How soon can that be? I am anxious to get him back to school."

"Sunday looks auspicious. I must consult my charts for the correct hour. According to Massimo, the boy has nearly recovered from physical illness. How are *you* feeling, my dear?" He added gently. "Have you quite recovered from your sad accident?"

"Yes, Godpapa," I said soberly, remembering to look wistful.

"I am so glad. May I therefore suggest that you try a visit to your Pericles tonight?" he asked, rubbing his hands together. "It will be excellent practice for our venture, and will give you both a great deal of pleasure. And if tonight is not successful, you may try tomorrow."

I was incredulous.

"Are you saying I will go to him *in the flesh*?"

He spread his hands. "It can be done. Now," he went on, pushing back his chair, "I must go take my rest and let you get on with your studies. Let me know how you progress."

When he left me, I went to check on Ratty, deep in thought.

What was it about this suggestion to visit Pericles that made my skin crawl?

Almost, I knew.

Though Ratty was still lost in a coma, his color was entirely back to pink, white, and freckles, and all his other vital signs had returned to normal. He looked like a healthy little boy sadly lost in some internal land.

Massimo said that the fever might return in the afternoon, but hopefully not.

I hurried off to get our reading book and to give Jim an

update on Ratty and my psychic training. He warned me in no uncertain terms not to let my guard down.

"Listen, wife-of-mine, I've read M.G.B.'s diary," he said, heatedly, "and if he's as good at manipulating flesh and blood and eggs and whatnots as he seems to be, LoCieco'll conjure up an egg on you before you can say 'Jack Robinson,' and guess who'll want to fertilize it?"

I told him he was being disgusting.

"When is the Ratty-disenchantment set for?" he then asked.

"Fixed for this Sunday sometime."

"Right! I'll be outside your door early Monday morning with the motor running."

"I'll have *il rattuccio* and all our stuff ready to go."

"That's Saint David's Day," he laughed giddily. "I'll wear a leek."

I told him I was going to try to visit him tonight. He promised to hit the hay early. I promised to wedge my desk chair under the handle of my door as well as to lock it.

Meanwhile I read the next three chapters of *Voyage of the Dawn Treader* to Ratty, watching the small face relax and listen. After giving him a bed-bath as instructed by Massimo, who was cramming for pre-med exams and had gone off to the university library, I fed him soft foods to nudge him towards wakefulness. The custard vanished to the last scrape of the bowl.

When Massimo returned, I went out for a walk, past Santa Croce to the Ponte Vecchio, losing myself happily among the crowds of normal people shopping for wedding bands, eating fritters or gaping at the view. Afterwards I climbed the long stairs to windy Piazzale Michelangelo to view the stunning blend of natural and man-made beauty that is Florence.

Returning by way of the Ponte San Niccolò, I swung by the big Mercato di Sant'Ambrogio to get the makings for dinner. I had cooking duty that night and planned to try out my carbonara on Massimo and Medea, adding a trio of tiny lamb-chops and whatever greens looked good at the market. Then we would finish with an easy combo of pineapple and cocoa, tossed with the bourbon I'd found in the cupboard earlier that week: Marc's favorite brand.

It all went over well and I headed for bed in a good frame of mind.

To reach Jim's hearth I needed was something of his to touch. It had to be the *right* thing: clothing he'd had worn, nail clippings, hair: something with his DNA on it. I chose one of the area notebooks I'd borrowed for my chapter on the drainage systems of *La Castellina.*

Jim's handwritten notes from an exhaustive survey of the drainage systems and wells of *Pian di Civita* were a master-piece of careful site-keeping, as-yet-unmatched in neatness, thoroughness and accuracy, from the man who literally wrote the book on *Practical Archaeology.* They were written in flood-proof, soft, dark pencil: sharpened with a pen-knife and only rarely corrected. The pages were stained not only with the sweat of his brow and the grease of his fingers, though he prevents this by putting hankies under his hand. It is one reason he carries so many, but also occasional droplet of blood and maybe a tear or two.

The thing *was* Jim.

Accordingly, I clutched the grimy notebook to my bosom as I willed myself quickly to sleep that night. I was more than ready to see my best beloved in person.

There was my hearth with a roaring big fire, gleaming on the pair of tall settles of blackened oak that faced each other opposite it, the rest of the room quite dark. The copper cage was still in place on the left-hand settle. The Vanth seemed to be sleeping. I got up, child-sized, onto the well-worn seat beside the One.

With that Presence at my right, I focused on the air

between the settles, fitfully heated and brightened by the leaping flames, watching for the faintest shimmer of difference. I saw it, sparkling there sharp and clear, a weightless diamond of blue flame the size of a mustard seed.

In its burning heart I saw as through a pinhole camera my best beloved asleep in the little house on Via Pyrgi. I willed the diamond to open back and back until I was there in the room.

I hovered at the foot of the bed, filling my heart with the look of him.

He lay asleep on his back, the covers in disarray. He looked thinner and ill-cared-for. His jaw was rough with stubble, his dark hair all anyhow, and there were signs of restless sleep: his left arm was thrown over his head, the recovering right arm across his bare chest as if still in its sling. A frown creased his brow and he murmured in his sleep.

The curtain of the window onto the garden was open, flooding the room with pale moonlight that cast his long nose in sharp relief. People were partying, down at the beach. Sounds of guitar music wafted up to the house.

If he shut the curtains, he'd sleep better, I mused fondly.

Then I "went in" as we call it in LDT: leaning forward to fall into the region of his heart, entering his hearth and his dreams.

Jim's hearth is lovely: a leaping fire in a stone-built fireplace surrounded by a cabin built of mellow pine. A canoe hangs from distant rafters overhead. Crossed snowshoes hang over the mantlepiece. There is a big rag-rug on the floor. An old yellow dog is stretched out to the left of the hearth and an old man sits on the backless bench to the right. He whittles onto a shop-apron which he periodically empties into the fire. There is room in the center of the rug for a boy to flop on his tummy and stare into the flames, his chin propped on his hands: Jim.

The boy can't to see or hear me, but the old man pats the seat beside him invitingly.

"Tanny? Heard about you! I'm Grandpa Jim Morris, his mother Irene's Dad. This-here's our cabin in upstate New York. Like it?" "Oh, yes," I answer, admiring the gingham-curtained windows and the shelves piled with books and games.

"Lots of good memories here! Wish you could visit *out there*," he sighed, "but she burned down, twenty years back, just after *I did,* I like to say. But there's always a place for Jimmy here, and you, too, and little Minnie here, and the twins."

There stood Minnie at my knee, aged about three. She had pale-gold skin and wild hair and her Papa's blue eyes: so ridiculously adorable that I had to laugh.

Grandpa Jim took her onto his lap to kiss her soft cheek.

"The twins again?" I asked. "Tell me about them."

"Cornelia will be a dead ringer for Jimmie's Dad: a hard man with a hard death ahead. But Peter will be as like my Irene and your Jim as peas in a pod. You haven't met Irene?"

I shook my head.

"We're going next Christmas, Pericles says."

"Ha! Tickles me you call him that. Listen, sweet-pea," he added softly, "go sooner."

We watched Jim together, as Minnie leaned against her Great-Grandpa.

"Will he be happy, Grandpa Jim?" I whispered. "Will he live long?"

"He's happy already, sweet-pea," he smiled, gently pinching my cheek. "And he'll live longer than anyone thought he might, thanks to you."

I hoped he would die aged one hundred, all his faculties intact, asleep in my arms.

"Listen, sweet-pea, if you're going to visit, you'd better do it. Time's almost up."

"Will he feel it if I kiss him?"

"See for yourself."

Leaving Minnie with Grandpa Jim, I went down a hallway to the right of Jim's hearth and hurried through the unlabeled door.

I saw at once why he'd been tossing in his sleep. He was at *La Castellina,* wandering in a ruined landscape of cut trees and rummaged excavations, calling my name.

"Pericles. Over here," I called from the camper.

A little blue bird fluttered overhead.

Up the path he came on the run. When flung his arms around me like a drowning man grabbing a pier, I could honestly feel him up against me for an instant. For a flash I was beside him in bed, moonlight in my eyes, wishing I could close the curtain.

Next instant I was alone in my narrow bed on *Via del Fico.*

DAY SEVEN – SATURDAY

I phoned Jim first thing to ask how he'd slept and whether he'd seen me in his dreams.

"Yes," he exclaimed. "Yes, I was searching all over the site for you, a dream I have most nights, but for once you actually were *there.* Oh, I was never so relieved. When I woke up, I could have sworn you'd just left the bed to check on Ratty and would come back any moment. You didn't, worse luck."

"Did you close the curtains?"

"Did I what? Oh yes, I did. Can't think why I hadn't, before I went to bed."

When I asked him about Grandpa Jim's cabin, he was silent a long moment.

"It broke his heart, losing the cabin right after Grandma. Never went to the lake again."

"Do your sisters ever go there?"

"My sisters never leave Arizona. No, the cabin, or the land where the cabin *was*, is mine, but I've never had the money to rebuild."

"Maybe now you're rich and famous, you can." I laughed.

"Infamous and not rich." He corrected me and I could hear him blush.

"Tony was rich and infamous, poor guy," I mused. "Is it true he made a pass at you?"

"Yes, sweet pea, he did *feel out* my sexual preferences."

"Did you just call me 'sweet pea?'"

"That's right," he laughed. "I guess it was hearing you talk about Grandpa Jim. It's what he always called my Mom. Hope you don't mind."

"Are you kidding, *Jimmy*? Hope to see you again, tonight."

The day went quickly by in long stretches of writing and little errands of Ratty-care, laundry, and meals. That night, after another good dinner—Medea's spaghetti and *bolognese* —and again grabbing Jim's site notebook, I slept almost at once.

It was night. I was alone in a compartment of the little Siena-Tarquinia train. Its upper window was open, curtains curling and uncurling in the moonlight. At first the scenery flew by, fields and hills and little hamlets, a distant hill town, but then I was outside the train, flying on my own.

The landscape spread out under me like a map. The lights of cars indicated a road, the glow of streetlights and the sparks of light in bedrooms and kitchens showed a town. The sea shone far out yonder under the moon, and there glowed Tarquinia Lido.

I walked in dappled shadows down the long road from the station towards the beach. I was bound not to the little house on Via Pyrgi but to a light in my old room at the top of the Cotto's house. There I found Jim reading in bed, a blanket tucked under his arms and wearing a pajama top. When he saw me, he shucked the top off with one fluid gesture. I was admiring the unscarred beauty of his right shoulder when with a not-at-all-weakened right arm, he swept off the covers to reveal that he was ready for the strenuous making-of-love.

"Why do you hesitate?" he said in LoCieco's voice, and the whole charade dissolved.

I was standing, barefoot and in my nightie, at the foot of my godfather's day-bed. In the firelight I could see that he wore neither his glasses nor anything else, and, though I had glanced away at once, that his "whatnot"—as Jim had termed it—was awake and much augmented.

What had Massimo said? He made men *better able to please the ladies?*

His great eyes gleamed hungrily. He put out an imperious hand to draw me down.

"Sleepwalking," I squeaked, and ran for my room.

Before sleeping again, I tied my ankle to the bed-frame, hoping that any dream-untying would wake me.

Apparently, I can move chairs and unlock doors in my sleep.

FLYING OIL

DAY EIGHT – SUNDAY AGAIN

Ever since my run-in with the doctored *cornetto*, I had been careful to bring my own *cornetti* and *marmellata* up to the common room for breakfast I had made coffee, and was just sitting down to eat when Medea came up from the shower in her black yoga gear, her hair wet, her nightgown and robe over her arm. The hostility in her glance made me blink.

"Dinner was wonderful last night," I said brightly. "There's coffee."

"Thank you," she said with habitual good manners, her look softening slightly. "I understand that tonight you and *il dottore* will finally rid Horatio of the Vanth."

"We will certainly *try*," I sighed, sipping my *caffe latte*.

"Has he explained how you are to prepare for the ritual?"

I frowned at the term *ritual*, but shook my head. "Do you have any pointers?"

She laughed. "Don't bother showering until afterwards!"

"Is it a messy business?"

"Very. You must use flying oil."

I groaned, having read the description of this method in

De Pereginatione. The traveler must cover her or his whole body, arms, legs, even the soles of the feet with hallucinogenic oil: butter, laced with henbane and fly agaric.

She laughed bitterly. "You *will* wear a nightshirt, but will only have oil on, underneath."

I was silent, fearful that, while in the throes of Lucid Dreaming, my godfather, trying to breed a super-*strega,* would send Minnie back to the blueness and put a changeling in her place.

Medea, watching me closely, asked bluntly what I was thinking.

I wrote my thoughts on paper, but *not* that I was still pregnant, and showed it to her.

Her green eyes widened. "You know?"

Acting on impulse, I scribbled, *If I could arrange for you to take my place, I would! I do not want his child, nor his stregheria."*

"Would you swear to that?" she cried eagerly.

"To what?"

She wrote on the back of the piece of paper, *After you have released the boy and yourself from this curse, do you swear to let me make love to il dottore?*

Gladly, but how in the world could you pass for me?

"I know certain compounds," she said with a slow smile. "Find a reason to come downstairs, promising to return quickly—a visit to the *gabinetto*, perhaps, or to check whether *il rattuccio* has truly recovered, and . . ." She wrote the rest: *I will take your place.*

I do so swear, I wrote, filled with relief.

She ate the piece of paper.

Ratty was perfectly well in all but consciousness. For two days now he'd had no fever. But though he looked well, his brow was puckered and he tossed in his sleep.

Massimo murmured, "He needs to be freed. See how he struggles."

His words unleashed in me a terrible restlessness, as if the

Vanth inside me had broken out of its cage and ranged loose inside me. My hunger for Jim was terrible.

When I went to call him, my phone was dead. Thinking I had forgotten to plug it in I left it charging and went for a long walk, promising to buy myself a *panino* somewhere. But what I wanted was human flesh. Everyone looked good to me but the men were impossibly attractive. Catching my mood, groups of two or three would follow me at a distance. Diving into Orsanmichele, I lit a candle to the Virgin and prayed, shaking, for a quick end to this torture.

It was late afternoon when I got back to Via del Fico, 3, footsore and hungry.

A strange thing happened when I unlocked the door and stepped in. It slammed shut behind me, giving me so sharp a smack that I called out, "Hey, watch it." Then I grabbed the knob, ready to tear it open and give the person who'd closed it a piece of my mind.

But it wouldn't even turn, let alone open: solid as if the whole door was carved of stone.

I looked around and listened. No-one was to be seen or heard anywhere. Dead silent.

With a shudder of horror, I ran for my room. The phone was charged but still dead. There would be no comforting "Basingstoke" from my best beloved, no assurance that he would be there at dawn, ready to drive us hence.

There was, however, a tray with a light dinner on it, and a note that read,

Ciao, Tanaquil! When you see the first star appear over the garden, dress in your bath-robe and go to il dottore's room. There is a sealing spell upon the house, and on the house next door. Please read the reverse as to how to break it. Farewell and best of luck, Massimo.

I read the reverse, and hoped to goodness it would work.

While waiting, I forced myself to pack: my things, Ratty's things. I left nothing of his in the Clinic, nothing of mine in the WC, in the Laundry, nothing anywhere. All my notes and notebooks, my laptop and charger, were stowed in my pack. I checked under every piece of furniture, determined to forget nothing.

Setting out my nicest outfit, black sheath skirt and garnet sweater, for the morning escape, I went out into the garden and waited. When the star appeared, I went to my room, stripped, packed my clothes, put on my robe, and went to do battle with Vanths.

*H*e lay on his daybed in a greasy nightshirt. Medea, her face impassive, told me to go behind the screen and put on what I found there: a soon-to-be-as-greasy nightshirt and a jar of flying oil.

"Also rub it well into your scalp. And I must put it on the soles of your feet, once you lie down," she said apologetically, indicating a cot beside his.

The room was chilly but a hot flush came over me the minute I began to cream on the oil. Almost at once every smell, including the pungent brown oil, became almost overwhelming.

Dropping the nightshirt over my head, I came unsteadily out into the room. The cot shone like an open doorway at twilight. When I lay down upon it, I felt buoyed up on a mattress of liquid light. The ceiling soared high above. Were those stars painted on, or real?

Medea tied my godfather and me together at the wrist— my right, his left with a recently-worn pajama top of Ratty's. "This was so we wouldn't end up separated in the spirit world," she explained. But it seemed as if she were knotting a huge butterfly there.

Already, I was walking in the Green Lands, hand-in-hand with a very young LoCieco. We were in our white nightshirts but no longer sticky.

"That was quick," I remarked cheerfully as, with a simple forward-leaning movement, we began, gloriously, to fly, Minnie fluttering along somewhere behind us.

"Where are we going?" I called to him at length.

"You are taking us to Horatio's hearth."

Ahead on the rolling green horizon stood a familiar landmark: the big Lewis house at 175 Hawthorne Avenue, Princeton. Through the open front door we swept, up the stairs, bearing left and then right, into Ratty's little room at the back of the house, where he lay sweetly asleep under his mobile of flying birds. But, in the bent-wood rocker opposite, where a kindly Providence should have been, sat the Vanth.

With a hiss, she came at me, red claws out, white fangs bared, green wings spread.

Rising up on green wings of my own, I stretched out my dead-white arms, caught her in my long red talons, and then what mayhem ensued in Ratty's room.

The rending and tearing, biting and slashing were excruciating but liberating. With every cut I saw my own copper skin shine through, human and familiar.

When both Vanths had shredded themselves to bloody ribbons on the floor, I tossed them out the open window and into the yard below, simple as that.

Ratty sat up and looked around him in the morning sun, rubbing his eyes.

"Hi, Mor." he smiled sleepily.

"Brava!" smiled my Godpapa.

At which moment I awoke with a sense of elation, wild to go see if Ratty were awake and aware. But when I made as if to jump up, the knot at the wrist of my nightshirt stopped me cold. I was anchored me to a wide-awake godfather, as youthful in person as he had been in my dream. Under his nightshirt something monstrous had arisen and his luminous eyes said clearly how he meant to use it, upon whom, and when.

Suddenly, I recalled that Medea was waiting in the garden, eager to replace me.

With a quick twist I backed out of my nightshirt as well the knot that held us together, leaving him with my night-shirt but baring myself entirely.

For a moment I stood there, nude and greasy and panting with exertion, conscious of no Vanthian lust. I was just me again, and I was burning to be away.

His eyes flamed as he flung aside his own restraining nightshirt to show a physique so magnificent and a *membrum virile* so impossibly large that my gasps were entirely unfeigned.

"Together we will make the perfect *strega,* my dear," he declared.

"First, let me go to Ratty," I panted. "Let me see that he is truly free, and then you can make your perfect *strega.*"

"You swear? You know that there is no escape from here?"

"Yes, I know, and I swear . . ."

. . . that he would make his *strega. On someone else, of course.*

Snatching up my robe from behind the screen, I dashed for the top of the stairs, and *there I stood at the bottom of the stairs, bright-eyed and greasy-nightshirted.*

I froze, then he smiled up at me, whispering in Medea's voice, "It is not a mirror, Tanaquil."

"Medea?" I shivered. "How is Ratty? Have you seen him?"

She smiled my own bright smile. "Yes, he told me he is very hungry, and will be glad to see you again. The *dottore?*"

"Awaits you in all his youth and beauty, incredibly augmented. But lose the nightshirt."

Off it came with a cry as she ran up the stairs.

I hoped they would be quick about it. If Massimo was right, this fleshly improvement would end at dawn, along with the locking curse.

I had to quickly shower and dress before going to Ratty.

Maybe too quickly. He made a face when I walked in and squeezed him hard. "Oh, Mor, your hair smells really bad."

He was sitting up in the big hospital bed, talking a mile-a-minute with Massimo about Princeton. "Massimo," I begged, counting on *il dottore* being too busy to overhear us, "can you dress him while I get our bags? Are you certain about that spell? And is it as late as I think?"

"Yes, *signora,* the sun will rise in half an hour. Your *marito* will soon be here."

"Thank God, Massimo," I said fervently, running to my room. "Thank God."

When I returned, all my and Ratty's onsite possessions were either on my back or in the rollaboards by the front door. The gray sky above the garden was much lighter than it had been.

Ratty was dressed, shod and in his warm jacket, sitting beside Massimo on the marble bench, swinging his legs. An ungodly cry rang out from my godfather's room, like Sisyphus reaching the mountaintop with his stone intact. Then came small sounds of clicking locks and restarting electronics, all around us. Massimo smiled.

"I told you," he said.

At once, my phone buzzed in the back pocket of my jeans: James Pericles Lewis:

I'm at the front door. Can you let me in?

Sure can, I messaged back, *but we'd rather get out.*

Just as you please.

Taking Ratty by the hand, I turned to Massimo.

"Will I see you at the site for the exorcism?"

He shrugged. "I may have to leave. I have broken faith with *il dottore.*"

"Massimo," I cried. "How completely selfish of me."

"You had no choice," he smiled wryly, kissing our cheeks in farewell.

"Bless you," I choked out. "Let us know how you get on."

Ratty and I rushed into the front entry hall, dawn sunlight reflecting into the barred window above us. All upstairs was silent.

Rat yanked the door open and there stood best-looking archaeologist on earth.

"*Ciao, Rattuccio, come stai?*" he asked, scooping him onto his hip and kissing him.

"Starving," complained the Rat.

"Me, too," I agreed, as I rolled both suitcases free of that infernal house.

With a thoughtful look, my best-beloved threw open the trunk of a good-sized sedan.

"I seem to recall seeing a bakery near here. But first, would you do something for me, son?" he added, setting Ratty on his feet again. "Guard the bags a sec, and do not run in front of that garbage truck. Thanks."

Throwing his arms around me, heart-to-heart and cheek-to-cheek, he kissed me soundly. Then he observed us both.

"No creepy death spirits, no fevers, just my own sweet people."

"And you," was my glad reply. "No sling."

"Where's that bakery?" complained the Rat.

ETHICAL ISSUES

THAT NIGHT WHEN LAVINIA CALLED ABOUT HER ETHICAL issues, the Riverbankers were asleep and Pericles and I were blissfully *in coitu*, but it amused him to talk to her anyhow.

"Fire away," he said, putting her on speaker-phone and rolling onto his back. Since we otherwise kept doing what we had been doing, it was a good thing she did most of the talking.

"As you know, James, this LoCieco has asked me to turn this exorcism ritual. A very interesting survival, incidentally: a combination of bastardized *Rasenna* and Romagnolo, the dialect of Italian from just north of Rome, as I expect you know, into pure Rasenna. Now I need clarification on some ethical issues."

"E-thical issues?" gasped Pericles.

I paused for a moment, the better for him to concentrate.

"Yes. I asked him about it Saturday, after I asked him when he is planning to carry this thing out, but he was very coy. May I read it to you? I have it in English or *Rasenna*."

"English, please. Listen, Lavvy, I'm muting my phone for a minute, but you go ahead. There's a lot of background noise at our end."

Or there would be, shortly.

"All right then, but I'm sorry to say it not nearly as beautiful as the *Rasenna* and that the English won't rhyme. I've also had to alter the language to be specific to our situation, but here goes!" She cleared her throat and began, in a loud and sonorous sing-song:

"O Vanth the Beautiful,
We unworthy mortals call upon you in humble supplication!
O Vanth the Beautiful,
companion to Kairun, boatman of the Styx,
O Vanth the Beautiful,
Who lights the way for mortals to the halls of the dead,
O Vanth the Beautiful,
Winged emissary of the gods, comfort of the fallen,
O Vanth the Beautiful,
Who are the agent of fever and death, doing the bidding of the gods,
Hear the prayers of your humble supplicants!
O Vanth the Beautiful, we beseech you!
If ever you looked with pity upon the youth, fallen on a cruel spear,
Spare this pitiful victim, this young man brought under your
power,
and do not keep him any longer in your thrall,
O spare Francesco Cotto, here among us:
O Vanth the Beautiful we beseech you now to spare him!
Be satisfied with our thanks and praise,
Be satisfied and depart these lands and this sick one, O Vanth!
By the plenteous offerings once offered to you in this place,
Be satisfied and depart these lands and this sick one, O Vanth!
By the precious sacrifices, once laid in this place,
Be satisfied and depart these lands and this sick one, O Vanth!
By the shield and sealed goat, laid in this place,
Be satisfied and depart these lands and this sick one, O Vanth!
By the blood and gold and iron, once laid in this place,
Be satisfied and depart these lands and this sick one, O Vanth!

By the implements, fabrics and vessels, useful and beautiful, laid in
this place,
Be satisfied and depart these lands and this sick one, O Vanth!
By our own offerings of blood and gold and salt and incense,
Be satisfied and depart these lands and this sick one, O Vanth!
By the blood of these young goats and this young sheep,
We redeem from your power the soul of this young man!
And now, by the power of Begoia, Daughter of Flame,
of Nethuns, Son of Water,
and of Tages the Wise, Lord of Time Itself,
We send you from into this walnut tree, to be your abode forever!
Keep this place in peace and health and safety
Taking along with these our offerings <u>the life of the one who called
you forth,</u>
Be satisfied and begone, O Vanth!
Be satisfied and begone, O Vanth!
Be satisfied and begone, O Vanth!
Begone, O Vanth!

"And here is the modern part he wants put in, which will
be hard in Rasenna, so I may just put it into Aramaic, instead.
You said he was a priest, correct?"

"In the name of the Archangel Michael, foe of Lucifer,
and especially in the strong name of
Our Lord Jesus Christ of the Holy Trinity
Return to hell forever!
Begone!"

*W*e were unmuted by now, listening quietly to
all she said, my head in the hollow of Jim's left
shoulder and the rest of me lying alongside. I absently ran

my fingers along the worn strap of the sling that crossed his chest, thinking how well he managed with one hand.

"Where is the ethical issue, Lavvy?" Jim asked drowsily.

"Why, the verse to remove LoCieco from the face of the earth, of course. *'Taking with you the life of the one who called you forth.'* Didn't you and Tanny *'call it forth?'* Besides, I didn't sign up to lead a cursing, James. Taking life is not in my general line of work."

"Not mine either," he frowned, sitting up, as I, perforce, did too.

Jim looked at me. I took a deep breath.

"Let me ask Tanny," he said, handing me the phone, "she's right here."

"Hi, Dr. Lavinia," I said slowly. "We are pretty sure that my godfather called up the Vanth for reasons of his own. And he has been hinting that he intends to make this his last hurrah, but I don't know his exact plan."

"It seems to me," snapped Lavinia, "that in dealing with matters of life and death, we need to know *exactly,* and not just be *pretty sure* about it."

"I wish I could be clearer," I answered, "but I can't. My godfather has lived a very, very, *very* long time, and if he thinks this is the right thing to do, I'd say let him."

Before he fathers any more children, for one thing.

"Oh," she snorted. "Just let the man have his way, is that it? *Daddy Knows Best?*"

"Maybe if I had stayed with him longer, I would know better," I answered with just a little heat, glad to be Vanthless, "but I'm sorry to say that I didn't."

"I'm not." Jim couldn't help adding. "He's a horny old creep."

"Why, James," laughed Lavinia, "thanks for that deep insight. Very well, let me state here and now that I wash my hands categorically of any responsibility for what arises as a result of the reading of this incantation, either from its words or from any flaw in my translation."

"Duly noted," muttered my best beloved.

"Say, Dr. L.," I piped up, "did you say you asked him about the date?"

"Oh yes, I had to make hotel reservations. The answer is 14 March. Specifically"—she seemed to be checking her notes—*"between the hours of four and six in the evening, at the setting of the last waning crescent of March."*

"We will mark our calendars," said Jim promptly.

"To sum up, James," said Lavinia, "you *do* you approve of the incantation *as it stands?*"

"Certainly. I bow to your judgment in this matter."

"I'll remember that, when everything goes wrong," she said tartly, and hung up.

"To sum up, James. Such a pedant." Jim tossed his phone dismissively onto my cashmere sweater. "How did I stand life with that woman, Tanny-Sue?"

"You are an angel of patience?" I suggested suggestively.

"Bah! It was a rhetorical question, but I'll tell you: by having you to look at most days and to fantasize about most nights!"

"Naughty academic advisor," I said naughtily, browsing on his ear and being relieved that I no longer wanted to have it for supper. That night I slept dreamlessly beside my best beloved.

First thing in the morning, Angelo came over to fill up on my pancakes and to fill me in on the latest drama from the site and from the Museum.

"Giacomo knows already, *Tanina,"* he began, "but . . ."

Clo and Ratty raced by in a game of two-kid tag, laughing hysterically. They had already eaten their pancakes and way too much syrup, by the look of things.

"Outside, *ragazzi,"* I called, and they ran out into the yard. "Sorry, *Babbo."*

"No, no," he smiled, watching them go, "it is good to see them happy." Then he sighed. "My news will not make you so happy. The wedding is off."

"Franco and Angelica? Not because he is *ill,* I hope? She is too kind for that."

Angelo rolled his eyes at Jim, who answered hesitantly,

"No, Tanny, an old flame of Franco's from *La Sapienza* met him for drinks after our rehearsal dinner, and the flame, er, flared up again."

"That explains why I saw Angelica walk off in the middle of the reception. I remember now! Poor Franco! Poor Angelica."

"*Poor little man, poor little maid,*" murmured my best beloved.

Angelo clicked his tongue dismissively.

"More importantly," he added, "our friend Colonel Paolini is investigating your *Padre* LoCieco, very secretly, as his list of clients includes too many politicians. His telephone 'favorites' outside Florence include Tony, Marc, Cecco, Giulia, Rodolfo, someone called Guido from *Panificio Falchetto.*"

I opened my eyes wide. "*Mamma mia.*"

Jim nodded. "While you were there, we confirmed that LoCieco was the link between Tony and his clients. Medea Mariarosa is also involved but not Massimo Benevento."

"They would come in for a cosmetic treatment," Angelo continued, "or treatment for *disfunzione erettile* and there would be a catalogue from *Antichità Colchis* with pictures of authentic art objects and links to online bidding. They were still taking bids on the *Castellina* bracelets when you two flushed out Giulia and Riccardo."

"Catalogue," I squawked, slapping a palm against my forehead. "Wait here a minute." And I ran to dig out the forgotten brochure I'd swiped from my godfather. "I stole this."

Il babbo pounced on it and Jim hung over his shoulder to look.

"Damn, look at those," he exclaimed, pointing.

There they were, all ten of them: my infamous missing rings, along with plenty more rings, as well as coins, carved signet stones, and pairs of earrings we had never seen before, all described as being from *the same famous archaeological site*.

Jim sighed and straightened.

"Looks like Marc has been robbing the Ash Altar for some time. Yes, that's what we're calling it now, Tanny. You were quite right about making offerings there. It seems that visitors traditionally left behind gold rings among the burnt materials, perhaps when they asked the oracle their questions."

"Have we found blood chemicals beside the rings?"

"Blood, why?" asked Jim, startled. "No. We have barely begun to stabilize it."

"I suspect that the questioners cut their ring fingers to offer blood, once they made their gold offerings, then sprinkled salt, and maybe also burned some . . ."

"Incense!" exclaimed Angelo. "Brava! It is in the incantation of *Dttssa*. Lavinia! Ah, *Tanina*," he added, planting a quick kiss on my cheek, "we have missed you very badly."

"Thanks, Angelo." I blushed. "So, Guido from Falchetto is tangled up in this? Probably Marc and Cecco were there blabbing and had to let him buy in."

"*Esattamente*. He is cooperating with Paolini." He waved the brochure. "If anything has already been sold, at least here we have this evidence of what was found."

"Did they find the pectoral at Tony's?"

Groans from both my companions.

"No," cried Angelo in anguish. "We fear that they have melted it down for its gold."

"There is no photo of it in this brochure," sighed Jim.

"But it has great cultural value," I cried. "Its wearer was protected from evil."

"Very strong magic, Lavinia says," agreed the spouse, catching my eye.

"Magic?" I stared at him hard. The clear thought came into my head that LoCieco would want such a thing.

That whoever started this racket had kept the pectoral for himself.

Then I saw the vision: *a glow of gold, rising in the house east of Godpapa's.*

Angelo laughed. "What are you thinking?"

"I need to ask Paolini to search the house east my godfather's," I said. "They are adjoining, and he owns them both."

"They can't arrest him until he has exorcised the site," insisted Jim.

2 8

POISONED BY A WITCH

Turned out that while T. E. LoCieco's connection to the antiquities ring was not a surprise to Paolini, our plan to exorcise the site certainly was.

We were in his office in town, admiring its splendid view between the flags of Italy and the E.U. of the handsome Palazzo Communale across the way. I had always had a fondness for the Palazzo's medieval stairway, pierced by a vaulted passageway to the street beyond.

The day was overcast, the office chilly. Rain pattered against the windows.

"Let me see if I understand what is planned at *La Castellina*," he frowned, steepling his fingers. "You are *not* intending to fumigate the site against hepatitis, is that correct? Instead, you plan some kind of ritual to banish evil spirits from the site, and from *Dottore* Cotto's son?"

Jim looked at me with a *talk your way out of this one, Greenough.* challenge in his eye. But I had already spent some time concocting an answer.

"Yes, in part," I began slowly. "You see, that the votive that made our son Horatio sick was contaminated with *two* illnesses. One was the 'fulminant hepatitis' brought on by blood from LoCieco's lab. The other was the same kind of coma that affected me, Ratty, and Franco."

"Hmmm," Paolini allowed, still steepled. "What caused the coma?"

"Psychic irradiation from the *mundus,*" responded Jim. "I watched it happen on the live feed. It was like a blast of toxic energy."

Paolini frowned. "Why did you not catch it, if you were watching the same thing?"

"We now think," Jim went on, watching me, "that the force reached only a certain distance around it, and I was outside that distance. Tanny suspects that whoever sent those votives to our children may be out there in a coma, too. I say it serves them right!"

"Yet both your wife and your son have recovered. Why not use the same treatment on Franco Cotto? Why do an exorcism of the site?"

"We cannot use the same method that drove the Vanth from me and Ratty," I said. "For one thing, Franco's coma was caught a different way: from the owl we called Antonia."

"The owl that the experts say became rabid? There is a cure for that, surely?"

"Ornithologists say she is not rabid," Jim declared. "But they have found traces in her droppings of the same energy that remains in the soil around the *mundus* and in the tree. She has grown larger, they say, and has begun attacking hikers and dogs."

"Why not just shoot the owl, if it is sick?"

"It might not die," Jim said. "Or the Vanth might leave it and infect the closest human."

"Vanth, Vanth!" Paolini cried impatiently. "What is this Vanth?"

I took over. "We believe they are embodiments of viral

epidemic, but also oracular spirits that communicate with the dead. They serve Tages, the Etruscan god of magic, wisdom, and the underworld. Tarquinia was the religious center of the whole Etruscan Confederacy, and the center of that center, we believe we can prove, was the sanctuary dedicated to Tages and the Vanths that lay at the northernmost tip of Tarquinia at *La Castellina*."

"Tanny will tell you that in geomancy north is where evil resides," Jim went on. "And since 'offense is the best defense' the Etruscans enlisted the most powerful and dangerous magic they had—that is, death-demons to guard the northernmost part of Tarquinia. They started an oracle, enlisting the demons' help to answer questions only they and the dead can answer."

Feeling very much like a relay racer, I picked up the thread.

"We suspect that the *hypogeum* was originally a kind of dream chamber, like the hall at Epidauros where ill people dreamt of cures sent by the god Aesclepius. Only here the Vanth would answer questions, having first been given sacrifices at the Ash Altar. We believe that the *mundus* pit was the locus for the Vanth, the *path to and from the underworld of the Vanths*. I suspect it is a deep well, but we must first get back safely to the site, to find out."

"Fascinating," frowned Paolini, "but what about all the gold and the dead children?"

I went on. "At some point, the augurs lost control of the Vanths, who rampaged all over Tarquinia, killing at will. We know there was a plague of hepatitis around the year 358 B.C.E., soon after the sacrifice of 307 Roman captives on the Ara della Regina. I believe that the *Tarquinians* believed that the Vanths, mad with so much human blood, brought a plague to consume the whole town! I also believe there are plague victims under the mound at the site called The Place of Sacrifice. Jim thinks the soldiers are under there, but I believe the soldiers' bodies were burnt on the Ara della Regina, as depicted on in the Tomb of Orcus."

"Long story short," Jim burst out impatiently, "the augurs shut down the oracle. No more consulting of the Vanth, no more deals with the dead, no more cursing your enemies. They were *done*. They made a final human sacrifice—a princess and a priest loaded with gifts—then sealed up the dream-chamber-oracle forever."

"Then," I pointed out "they hid it under several meters of clean soil!"

"Yes, yes," nodded Paolini. "I have heard the story of the dog finding the entrance to your *hypogeum* chamber. But tell me, has anyone been sick, any year before this?"

We looked at each other, I thinking of the song "*Sul Leccio*."

"Possibly," answered Jim slowly. "Local stories tell of a curse."

"And the only way to dispel this curse is to have a witch-doctor do this ritual?"

"He claims it will work on the place and the owl and should also cure Franco Cotto."

Paolini looked at his watch.

"And if it does not?"

"Then Franco will die," Jim said bluntly, "and we will seal off the site permanently."

Paolini put his head in his hands, thinking hard while Jim and I sat silent, waiting.

In the long, peculiar silence that followed, I thought gloomily, *No more research into the meaning of the Hut Circle. No chance to find the lost cult statue of Tages.*

Suddenly the window blew open with a bang and the fragrance of wet streets.

Paolini looked up. "I give my permission. But how will you explain it to the media?"

"We could call it an 'historical re-enactment,'" I grinned, looking at Jim.

"Yes," cried Jim eagerly, "the *historical re-enactment* of an Etruscan purification ritual."

"To raise funds to repair the vandalism at *La Castellina?*" suggested Paolini.

I cheered and clapping my hands. "A fundraiser. We could surely use the money."

"I'll set up a GoFundMe site," offered Jim, "and invite the press to film the event."

What might they see? I wondered, thinking of poor Tony.

Paolini drummed his fingers on his desk, clearly having second thoughts. We held our breath until, with a sigh, he spoke. "It is possible that renewed publicity will bring renewed interest of the criminal element. Like the man from 'Star Wars,' *I have a bad feeling about this.* If the re-enactment is to be observed by the media, it is possible that imposters could infiltrate, and again try to kill you, *dottore.* I can put a guard at the site but you are safer at the Museum."

"Who's to say the *criminal element* will not take advantage of the brou-ha-ha at the site to loot the Museum and bump me off?"

Paolini shrugged. "An enclosed space like the Museum is much easier to protect with just a few officers. And I would be happy to arm you. Can you fire a pistol?"

"No, but my Grandpa Jim taught me how to shoot a rifle," Jim admitted.

"*Bene,*" was the prompt reply. "My brother-in-law has one that he uses to hunt birds. I will lend it to you."

"But I don't like Tanny being at the site without me. The phone signal isn't good."

"If I am at the site with my squad car and police radio, would you agree?"

Jim considered. "I guess."

"Aww, Pericles, you didn't really want to be part of all that mumbo-jumbo, did you?"

"No, but what if there is another explosion? Or your godfather tries some hanky-panky and I'm not there to beat him off?"

"We can pretend that you don't approve of your pushy young wife doing magic at the site, and that we had a big fight about it."

"Well, I don't, but we agreed."

Paolini cut in at last. "Perhaps there is a great deal of work left to do at the Museum, and you regretfully must continue with it, while monitoring the GoFundMe site for results? It will truly be a great simplification of security to keep you and the antiquities under observation," he went on, getting to his feet. "I'll also need to inspect the site in order to place my officers."

We agreed to consult with my godfather about where exactly the event would take place, promised to keep him in the loop. Then we cordially took our leave.

It was raining hard when Jim and I emerged into Piazza Trento e Trieste. He turned up the collar of his tweed lecture-jacket. I put up the hood of my waterproof.

"I'll buy you something hot at Tripoloni," he said, taking my hand as we dashed across the street.

"All right," I countered, "but let me buy you an umbrella at that *Tabaccheria*."

The only umbrella they had left was decorated with the leering *Tuchulcha* from the Anina Tomb, but was better than nothing. At Tripoloni we sat opposite each other, enjoying *macchiati,* a chocolate-drizzled meringue, and watching the world go by.

But then I got to thinking.

"Looks like my godfather really *is* a 'godfather,'" I sighed. "I'm sorry, Jimmy."

"No problem, sweet pea," he said, caressing my face.

"No problem that Godpapa set Marc and Cecco on you and risked our children's lives, all so he could screw his own flesh-and-blood?"

"Sssh, none of that, please."

Jim, a strict Methodist, hates swearing. Or I thought he did.

"It wasn't *just* to screw you," he went on reasonably. "I agree that he wants to die properly with his dynasty assured." Taking a bite of a meringue, he added thickly, "But I'm pretty sure the scooter business was Marc's idea to punish me for banishing him from the site and losing him big bucks. As for risking our children's lives, LoCieco knew very well that the hepatitis wouldn't kill them: he'd invented the cure for that strain himself. No," he said, finishing his coffee, "what beats me is just who gets this damned *stregheria* of his?"

I shrugged. "Not me, if I'm not establishing any dynasties. Medea wants it to round out her business at *Omeopatia Argo*. And if Massimo got it, he wouldn't be such a squib."

"Squib?"

"Weren't you listening last time I read *Sorcerer's Stone* to the Riverbankers?"

"I only listen when you read C.S. Lewis or Tolkein or Kipling. What's a squib?"

"Now who's the pedant?" I laughed. "Well, it's a half-magical wizard. Not muggle-born, you understand, just not very gifted."

"*It was Greek, to me.*" He quoted archly.

"Applesauce. You *know* Greek," I said archly back.

We kissed one another fondly for both being so insufferable.

"Ah, *i sposini cari!*" came a familiar but momentarily unplaceable voice from the doorway. "I *thought* I saw you two go in here. How's it going?"

Oh, hell! Françoise Pinard, Paris Match.

I jumped up to exchange air-kisses. "*Ciao, Françoise.* Your

Italian is too good for me to say *Bonjour.* Jim, remember Françoise Pinard, of *Paris Match?*"

He scowled. "I remember we had a howling big row after you talked to her."

"No, no, she was very kind," disagreed Mlle. Pinard with an eloquent moue, "and I have been given a promotion."

"Wonderful." I smiled. "Actually, there is something you can help with. A fundraiser." At a reluctant nod from Jim, I went on, "We're doing an historical reenactment at the site."

"*Meravigloso,*" she said at once, eyes gleaming. "Dates and details?"

"Fourteenth of March. Give me another one of your cards and we'll message you the rest."

With a smile of satisfaction, she handed it over and left us. Protected by Jim's grim *ombrellino,* the *sposino* and I went back to the Fiat by circuitous routes.

We'd hoped to lose her but only succeeded in giving her enough time to roust out her videographer. They would definitely get this clip on the Paris evening news.

Splashing across the cobbles in her heels, Françoise called out to us, leading with the microphone. After the preliminaries she asked me sternly,

"Will you not be reinfected if you go to the site, *signora?* Wasn't your son struck down by the same mysterious disease as yourself and Franco Cotto? Is the boy's health improving? Where did you take him for treatment? Is the disease contagious? Should the public be warned?"

"It is not contagious except through a cut, Françoise," I said patiently, climbing into the Fiat as Jim hovered chivalrously with the umbrella. "The public is quite safe."

Once we were both inside, she thrust her microphone through a gap in Jim's window, asking, "Your wife and son have both fallen ill since the *hypogeum* was opened, *Dottore* Lewis. Do you still deny that the *La Castellina* site is cursed?"

"Curse, nonsense," cried Jim. "They were just poisoned by a witch."

Which stunned her long enough for us to make our escape in a squeal of wet tires.

"Poisoned by a witch?" I echoed incredulously.

He winced, refusing to meet my eyes.

ELEMENTALS

The date of "historical reenactment" was the fag-end of winter: a good time to clear any stray demons, or *elementals* as my godfather called them, demons of earth, air, fire and water—off the site. It was also two weeks to the day from my escape from Via del Fico.

I'd heard not a peep from Godpapa LoCieco about the last-minute exchange of females on the night of Ratty's exorcism. In our phone consultations about the Big Event, however, butter would not have melted in Medea's mouth. Massimo was forgiven to the extent of acting as our chief intermediary.

I imagined that he was needed more than ever to keep *il dottore* alive. Or was Medea, blissfully alone with *il dottore*, busy working dangerous magic to keep him young and lusty? More likely he had been happy to find a willing receptacle for his last hopes and was at last releasing his long hold on life.

Franco was still deep in his Vanthian coma. No-one dared visit the site except during broad daylight, the students having long since gone home. Angelo, hoping to have his son and his site back, agreed with Paolini on staging the exorcism. He called them "an accurate copy of Etruscan expiatory rites, handed down by popular tradition."

Until such time as a completely new security system could be installed in the exhibition halls the golden objects found in the safe in Tony's Cantina had been returned to the locked vault in the basement of the National Museum of Tarquinia, close beside Jim's former office, The Museum was not only seeking bids for such a system, but also, in the wake of the arrests of Giulia and Rodolfo Pantano, a completely new Director, as well. Angelo had agreed to be Interim Director until fall, when he must return to his duties at La Sapienza.

The golden ball was still at large. So were the thieves who took it. Paolini was still casting about as to their where-abouts. No longer tormented by the Vanth, I sincerely hoped that Marc and Cecco had not been laid low like poor Franco. One comfort was that they no longer should have any interest in the site. There was therefore no real danger in our visiting the site, other than from an attack by a vicious owl.

In order to ready all things for its cleansing, visit the site we must.

As Ratty happily returned to the bosom of his school-pals and caught up with his lessons, Massimo came in person to Via Pyrgi as emissary of *il dottore,* to plan the ritual. He arrived late on the seventh of March and would spend the night on the couch at Via Pyrgi and visit the site with us, Angelo, and Paolini, early next morning. He must note the positions of trees and water, and the auspicious placement of the sacred fire. Then he would demarcate the sacred area.

That evening we gave him dinner at our favorite fish restaurant nearby and asked for news of Florence. He led off with news of Lavinia.

"*Il dottore* is delighted with the work done by *Dottoressa* Bradley-Arnold on the language of the exorcism ritual," he exclaimed. "He has asked her to recite it in person."

Jim nodded. "Her reading voice is very beautiful, if Tanny doesn't mind my saying so."

I smiled. "It is the truth, even if I do mind."

"*Mor* has a beautiful voice," spoke up the Mole loyally. "It's just lower than Mamma's! Remember that Christmas we went to hear her sing, Papa, how pretty it was?"

"Indeed, I do," was the prompt reply.

"I don't," said the Rat glumly. "I was asleep at Nonna Alice's."

"*In any case,*" went on Massimo firmly, "she asked me to tell you that she will be spending the night of the ritual at a little hotel in town, and that Caterina will join them."

"Which hotel is that?" asked Jim, gnawing on a lamb chop. He is not fond of fish.

"Hotel Palazzo Castelleschi."

"Heavens, that's expensive," I exclaimed.

Massimo smiled more broadly. "They will be sharing a suite with your friends Father John Prester and Gesualdo Verbicaro, thus (as she said) 'splitting the cost.'"

"John-Allen? But why?" I asked, bewildered. I also had an uneasy feeling about this sharing of rooms.

There was something going on between Caterina and Gesualdo.

"Waldo? Hooray," cheered the Rat. "Why can't he stay here, Papa?"

"Silly," the Mole reminded him. "'Cos he's staying at the Palazzo."

Jim wore his Cheshire Cat smile. "I've asked our friend Prester John to perform a prayer vigil for us in Tarquinia on the night of the 'historical reenactment.' The verger at old San Martino is letting him use the nave. I figure we'll need all the divine intervention we can get." He turned to Massimo to add, "I'm not fond of pagan worship, even if I do study it."

Massimo nodded. "I am myself a good son of the Church. I tell myself that it is to help suffering people that I work with *il dottore* and *gli elementali* but when he passes on at last,

I plan to start work at my father-in-law's pharmacy. Once he *is* my father-in-law."

"To that happy day, then," cried my best beloved, having had his limit in wine.

Once the children were safely at school next morning, Massimo, Paolini, Jim and I, with Angelo at the wheel, all piled into Range-Rover. The Colonel was in mufti the better to blend in with his surroundings. He had agreed to lend four of his men for the event: two to protect me from vengeful humans at the site and two for Jim and the treasure at the Museum. He himself would monitor things from his squad car near the gate.

I sat in front between Angelo and Jim. Massimo, Paolini, Massimo's equipment case and the irons stakes for marking out the delineated area were in the back.

"We will be calling upon two distinct Etruscan divinities," Massimo shouted to Paolini and us over the engine noise, "named Begoia and Nethuns. They control the elementals we call Vanth and Tuchulcha. Begoia, as I am sure you know, *Dottore* Lewis, rules lightning and wind—the elements of fire and air, if you will—while Nethuns rules water and earth."

"Originally, he ruled *wells*," Jim inserted. "There are sacred trees and birds associated with each of them, as well. Oak is for Begoia and Walnut for Nethuns."

"The walnut is better associated with the god Tages, *professore*," Massimo corrected him in some embarrassment. "Nethuns rules the willow, which likes its feet in water. The bird of Nethuns is the kingfisher, which eats fish and dwells by streams. That of Begoia is the white-faced owl, which strikes its prey like silent lightning."

"Does Begoia rule the Vanths, then?" I asked eagerly.

"You might say so, though Tages rules both Begoia and Nethuns."

"Nethuns therefore rules . . . uhm, *Tuchulcha*?" asked Paolini dispassionately.

"In fact he does. We invoke him against earthquake and to find springs."

I frowned.

How could we have forgotten the green-skinned, snake-haired, ass-eared bogeyman Tuchulcha, wielding a lethal, two-headed hammer? He stood opposite the Vanth on the doorway to the *mundus. What rituals controlled him? Had he also been loosed?*

Massimo glanced my way. "Tuchulcha does not possess. He fells and moves on."

"Was Tony *felled*," inserted Angelo from the driver's seat, "or did his heart fail?"

"Perhaps both," Massimo replied. "We think of Tuchulcha being like Apollo, the god of sudden death. He and the Vanth hunt together. Usually she sickens, and he kills."

"Why do we not exorcise Tuchulcha, then?" I asked anxiously.

Massimo shrugged. "Banish one and the other one goes."

He sounded so sure of himself that I yielded the question. If I had known just *how* that process would unfold it might have been otherwise.

We had reached the gate. Jim as outside man got down to deal with the padlock. Then he locked up behind the Range-Rover and got back in.

"Starting to rain," he remarked, as a gust of wind spattered drops across the windshield.

Once parked beside the camper we got out whatever rainproof gear any of us had thought to bring, and put it hastily on. Jim had forgotten his, but I had popped the *ombrellino* into my pack and now produced it. Regarding it with loathing, my best beloved tucked it under his arm, turned up his collar, and ran for the camper.

Massimo opened his case, very much like something for a trumpet, on the picnic table under cover of the awning. From its green baize-lined interior he removed an object made of dark, polished wood. It was about the size of a kitchen knife but shaped much like the fiddle-head of a fern, rounded and curling to a tight spiral. I recognized it as a *lituus,* used by the ancients to demark quadrants of the sky. With it, priests would make such mantic gestures as Massimo would need to make, to set a place aside as sacred.

In the case beside the *lituus* was slender copper knife rather like a very small scimitar, wrapped in a square of stained chamois leather.

With startling quickness, and murmuring inaudible words of power, Massimo drew the razor-edged knife lightly across the base of his left thumb, which I now saw was much scarred only to produce a dark line of veinous blood. With this, still murmuring, he smeared the *lituus* until no part of it was not damp. A little pressure from the chamois and the cut no longer bled. After a spit-and-polish of the knife he wrapped it in the chamois and the case was shut.

Lituus in hand and hooded against the rain, Massimo was ready to work.

"I must have my hands free, and cannot carry the posts and chain," he apologized.

Putting up my own hood, I grabbed one of two heavy canvas bags that held a dozen or so things like iron tent-pegs and a small hammer. Jim at once took that bag off my hands, exchanging it for the unused umbrella, blinking away the rain. I slung the other, equally-heavy bag on my shoulder with a jingling clank, as Massimo explained.

"First I must delimit the sacred area. Then we will install a series of iron posts linked with this iron chain. The posts will leave marks in the stone, *Dottore* Cotto, but it is important that we enclose the entire irradiated area and the tree, while the Vanth is still in it. Even a low enclosure of iron will hold her all the way to the zenith."

"Will birds and airplanes still be able to cross it?" I asked naïvely.

"Of course," he laughed. "It is not a barrier except to the

Vanth! A bird might fly in or out without noticing any change."

"So," I postulated, "if the owl flies out, we will know that the Vanth has left her?"

"Once the enclosure is in place and properly sealed, yes. Precisely."

Turning, he followed Angelo northwards, down the track. His hands were outstretched, and again he murmured under his breath. Paolini was close behind, writing notes on a pad.

Jim and I came last, clanking companionably. "You don't mind about my setting up the prayer-vigil?" my best beloved remarked a little sheepishly. "I kept meaning to tell you—"

"Not at all," I said, taking his free hand in mine. "I just feel uneasy about the four of them sharing that hotel. I've been wondering about Gesualdo." I frowned up at him from under my dripping hood, trying not to mind that he was soaked. "Do you think he might be bisexual?"

He considered a moment. "I do recall having a flash of jealousy at the rehearsal dinner, when he hugged you just a little longer than I thought he reasonably should."

"Yes, exactly. I hated to say anything to Prester John, but I wondered at the time."

"*Attenti, voi due,*" called Angelo from much further up the path than we expected him to be. We rushed to catch up, all thoughts of Gesualdo forgotten.

We had come to the Hut Circle. Massimo was conversing energetically with Angelo. Paolini had walked to the fence line, no doubt checking on the cache pits left by Marc.

The rain had let up, but there was a blustery wind that shook big drops from the trees. Jim shivered.

How my heart yearned to warm him up.

"Many activities took place here, long, long ago, *Dottore* Lewis," said the demi-magician excitedly to Jim as we came up. "I was just telling *Dottore* Cotto."

"I imagine *Dottore* Cotto is aware of that," responded Jim: very drily, considering.

"Of course," murmured Massimo with a rich blush. "It is only that the sense is very strong. I feel that many people came here from many places, at many times of year, for many, many years and then . . ." he faltered, looking around. "Then they stopped coming. Suddenly."

I felt a shiver go up my back. As much as I do believe in second sight, it was still unnerving to have it confirm so exactly what science was showing us on the ground.

As Paolini made his way back towards us, Angelo explained, "Yes, we have evidence that the sacrifice of the Roman soldiers was the beginning of the end of the power of Tarquinia on many levels. In no particular order, there was a famine, a pestilence, the road system passed them by, their port silted up, and their people left for other, more prosperous towns. They thought their gods had forsaken them. Perhaps they had! Even after they became Christians, the Goths came through, then the Arab corsairs. They finally moved the city to Corneto yonder."

"Leaving behind only *gli elementali*," agreed Massimo in all seriousness. "Tages may have controlled them once, but he has moved elsewhere." He turned to me. "I believe you said his cult statue was here until recently. What happened to it, do you know?"

"There were two," Angelo answered for me. "A pair of holy *bambini* kept in a church near here that were sent to visit local people in need of healing."

"When my father was a boy," confirmed Paolini, pocketing his notebook, "he saw them. One was black, one was white. The black one did the most good. The white one was extra, in case there was so much illness that than one was needed. What happened to them I never heard, but no-one around here uses them anymore."

"We think the Nazis took them for their magical value," I

explained. "I have recently tracked down the American soldier who 'liberated' them. His daughter promised to ship them to me, but . . ." I shrugged. "Would the site be safer if they were returned?"

"Perhaps," said Massimo. "Even if we are successful with the Vanth, other forces might rush in to fill the vacuum. Tages could prevent that." Then he shifted his feet uneasily. "I think we should go. Something is happening, further down."

Massimo pocketed a handful of pebbles then led the way forward, hands and *lituus* out. Soon the *hypogeum* shelf at very end of *La Castellina* came in sight. Above it soared a tremendous mass of storm clouds. Another downpour was headed our way.

"Wait here," Massimo commanded as we reached the bare limestone.

Taking the handful of pebbles in his left hand and with the *lituus* outstretched in his right, he proceeded forward, stopping occasionally to mark a spot on the ground with a pebble or two. As he made his slow progress, apparently defining the limits of the astral blast, we four consulted quietly amongst ourselves.

"Now that I see it, I'd like to put a cordon across the narrowest part of the ridge here, with perhaps six officers, perhaps more," frowned Paolini, folding his arms and looking back the way we'd come. "If we could fence it, I would be even happier. I'd like to keep the media well away from what happens here."

"Why?" asked Jim. "They are here to observe the re-enact-ment, surely."

Paolini scratched the back of his head in perplexity. "I honestly couldn't say why, *Dottore,* but I would feel happier if the cameras were set up here and the media were required to watch the event on a large screen at a safe distance."

He sighed.

"Perhaps I am catching the witchery of your friend

Massimo, but I have a great uneasiness about this end of the ridge. Some of it is the thing that attacked Franco Cotto. Can a little fence really hold in such a monster? But some of it is the feel of the ground under my feet. I am tempted to call my brother-in-law the geologist to ask whether this limestone is full of caves. Have you found any, *Dottore* Lewis?"

"The *Pian di Cività* is riddled with waterways and wells, most of them now dry," said the acknowledged expert on archaeo-hydrology. "*La Castellina* has an entirely different drainage system, however, centered on a single well near the Temple of Vanth and Tages. It is possible that the *mundus* is connected to a second well. What do you say, Angelo? What did the robot find while we were off getting married and whatnot?"

La Sapienza had a cool device—a sort of archaeological Roomba to explore crevices.

"There is a very deep, narrow pit off the back of the *mundus,* partly filled with animal bones. There also seems to be a cave system about two meters down, parallel to the surface."

"Do we have many earthquakes in this part of Italy?" I inserted.

"Virtually none," said Paolini.

"*Attenzione,*" called Massimo. "I am ready for those stakes now."

So, with Jim's assistance and as the ringing sound of iron on iron echoed through the trees, I hammered iron stakes around the nearly-ring of pebbles that Massimo had placed around the *hypogeum.* Angelo hovered nearby, making nervous comments about *damaging important features.*

It was "nearly" a ring because it included the root-system of the big walnut tree that hung over the *hypogeum* entrance.

Massimo followed behind with the chain, looping it through each stout iron ring welded onto the side of each stake. Drawing from his bag a big pair of pliers, he pried open the last loop, then crimped it shut, closing the circle of chain.

Stretching to ease my back, I looked high up into the tree. There I glimpsed something white among the upper branches: huge and hulking. It stirred and clicked its beak.

The most extraordinary spurt of panic shot through me. Dropping the hammer, I leapt away from the tree and was halfway back to the Hut Circle before I knew what I was about.

It was an effort to force myself to stop there, my heart pounding fit to burst my ribs.

Jim came jogging down the track and hastened up as he caught sight of me.

"Did you hurt yourself, sweetheart?"

I shook my head. Unable to speak, I pointed back at the thing high in the tree.

He saw it and paled. "Christ Almighty! Is that our Vanth?"

"Must be," I gasped, hoping to God it couldn't escape. "Can we leave now, Pericles?"

"Absolutely," he declared, taking my arm and escorting me briskly to the Fiat. "Enough weirdness for one day!"

Excerpt E from The DIARY of M. G. BURNSEY: "Artist Dies On One-Hundredth Birthday"

[*C**lipping from the* Boston Globe *front page, November 1, 1952.]*

"CAMBRIDGE, MASS: Barnstable native Mary Greenough Burnsey died suddenly in her studio here yesterday at exactly one hundred years of age, in what appears to be an accidental fall. The artist had become a legend during her lifetime for highly imaginative, yet strikingly-lifelike color portraits in oil paints, long before the advent of color photography made such things commonplace. Her deft ability to capture a likeness, the incorporation of dream-like images in the 'Burnsey-style' visual-collages she originated, combined with an uncanny ability to see into her subject's personality, made her works sought-after by collectors and sitters alike, though some likened them to 'Dorian Grey' portraits, revealing secrets the subject would rather keep secret.

"A famous example of this was Richard Loeb, whose wealthy family hired her to paint him in 1923 only to have the young man and a friend kill Loeb's cousin 'for fun' the next year. Forensic experts claimed at the time to 'see the murder in his eyes.' More often, however, beloved subjects were captured at the height of their appeal, with likenesses so perfect that a few experts assumed photography must have been involved, or perhaps even a *camera obscura*. More, however, attribute the faithfulness of her renderings to creative genius and a keen eye, heightened with tireless sketching of the subject from all possible angles . . ."

[More follows, about her birth, family, early life and training, much of the intimate details of which we know better than they, her diary never having been made public.]

"Her continuing health and vitality were as much a part of M.G.B.'s mystique as her art, and yesterday's sad accident only confirms what experts have long noted, namely that her physique was that of a healthy, fit woman of forty or fifty years of age. She had never suffered from any kind of serious illness, her sight was unimpaired to such an extent that she never needed to wear glasses at any point in her life, and her mind and memory remained clear to the end.

"Doctors examining her at her studio yesterday have concluded either that she slipped from the high scaffolding erected around the large sculpture—upon which she has been working for half a decade, to the exclusion of all other work—and broke her neck, killing her instantly, or that her heart simply stopped, and she was dead before she fell, as there was little or no blood around the body. She was found 'as if asleep' by her grand-daughter, Claudia Burnsey Todd, worried when she failed to come in from the studio to lunch.

"The sculpture upon which she was putting final touches was a massive grouping in white marble informally known as 'Erebus,' a departure from her usual two-dimensional work, but something she had long wished to accomplish, according to her grand-daughter. Mrs. Todd, who had been the artist's secretary and companion for many years, staying at 'La Serpentara'—the artist's beautiful property in suburban Cambridge, not far from Longfellow House—also told our reporters that 'Erebus' was inspired by a dream of the artist's, five years earlier, in which the many, many friends and relations who had pre-deceased her in her long life, yet had never been painted by her, appeared to her, wishing to be commemorated.

"She envisioned the sculpture as a banquet of people sitting or standing, dressed in the clothes they wore in life, feasting, talking, and making music together. To make the group more lifelike, and true to the skin-tones of her friends, Burnsey had begun experimenting with flesh-tone and jewel-tone stains, likening the process to that of the ancient Greeks, who are said to have painted their statues. Critics seeing the sculpture for the first time yesterday report being stunned by the artist's masterly handling of stone and color, exaggeration and simplification, and insist that this work will re-write existing understanding of her accomplishments as an artist.

"According to family members, the body will be embalmed and transported to Italy for a private interment at the Non-Catholic Cemetery of Rome, Italy, in the same vault where her brother William and sister-in-law Zeya were laid to rest, some thirty years earlier."

NOT YOUR AVERAGE FUNDRAISER

FINALLY, IT WAS THE FATEFUL EVENING OF 14 MARCH. ALL THE bizarre preparations were complete. The children were safely delivered to the Cotto's house with their overnight bags. I was driving Jim to the Museum in the little Fiat. The tiny space behind our seats was full of his pack in which was his laptop, his most recent notebook, his roll of overnight gear, and a sack supper.

It felt as if I were transporting my heart to the Museum, to be left until called for.

To say that my sleep had been a little disturbed by mildly-upsetting dreams was a vast understatement. I had been having full-on hallucinations, day and night. My Tanny-sense was off-scale. Reading M.G.B.'s diary certainly didn't help. If anything, it taught me to expect the unexpected on a massive scale. Jim, as if to compensate, had been breezily cheerful.

Of course, there had been that brief outburst before breakfast that morning.

"Honestly, Greenough," he'd hissed. "What if the River-bankers saw you like this?"

At which point I'd pulled myself together and smiled through tightly-gritted teeth.

Now here we were at the back-door of the Museum on Piazza Soderini. Three smartly-dressed policemen stood flanking the entrance. Paolini, standing beside them in jeans and jacket, put his hand up in greeting. I pulled up in front of him and we both got out.

"*Signora* Lewis, if you could take me back to *La Castellina*, I would very much appreciate it," he said in elaborately polite Italian. "I had my men bring me back here from the site for a little detail I had overlooked before. I will explain as we go back. *Dottore* Lewis," he smiled in English, taking Jim's hand. "You seem in good spirits."

Jim hefted his pack significantly. "Plenty in here to keep me happy. Plus I will be hanging out with those Attic vases all night. I have to do some drawing, or will pretend I have to."

"My men will be roaming the building all night or at least two at a time will, with one resting. They are armed," Paolini added with a significant look at both of us, taking a long, antique rifle from where it had been leaning, unnoticed, against the Museum wall. He now handed it to Jim with a little bow. "As will you be, *Dottore*."

Jim took the gun with a look of honest delight, hoisting it to his shoulder. Stepping back a pace or two, he sighted along its elaborately-chased barrel at one of the decorative chimney-tops of Palazzo Vitelleschi, then exclaimed, "Dang" —just as Tanny would say—"what balance! And all those silver fittings. How old is it, Pasquale?"

"Two hundred years," said the colonel with pardonable pride, "and the fittings are not the only thing about it that are silver." The policemen looked very wise at this, exchanging glances.

Jim and I frowned at each other.

"Bullets," said Paolini archly, touching his nose with his

index finger. "I melted down my *nonna*'s silverware and had a full set of bullets made for every gun here. *Elementals* like silver even less than they do iron, your friend Massimo tells me. My *nonna* would have agreed."

"And mine," spoke up one of the policemen, patting his own firearm, evidently satisfied with his protection. Jim, frowning at such superstitious twaddle, turned to give me a peck of farewell. I had different ideas and pressed him unabashedly to my heart.

"Use it if you have to, best beloved," I choked out, wiping my eyes. "Just stay safe."

"You, too, sweetheart," he said, producing a clean hankie and tenderly mopping my face before kissing me properly. "See you in the morning."

And so we parted.

We were on the outskirts of town before I heard what Paolini was saying about the sacrifice of his *nonna*'s silver set.

"Sorry, Pasquale," I apologized, shaking myself. "Say that again?"

Most of the media were already waiting outside the gate when we arrived, a mere hour before the ritual was to start. Inside the gate waited two wreathed, barefoot women in white. Drawing closer, I could see they each wore what looked like a Greek *peplos*: a garment made of soft, heavy, white homespun linen, hanging straight from shoulders to ankles, belted with heavy red ribbon and pinned with long, straight bronze pins.

Like any *peplos*, the garment gapped open all along one side, from ankle to bare hip.

Very early that morning I had helped Massimo and Medea, who had arrived the night before with *il dottore*, erect from heaped stones a temporary altar beside the Enclosure, but no-one had said anything about a dress code.

Then I noticed that Medea had a wreath on her wrist, a pair of long pins and a bunch of red ribbon in her hand, and a folded linen cloth over her arm. A sweet, faintly gamy fragrance hung around her: verbena. The wreaths were made with it, bound with more red ribbon.

"They will disguise your 'Christian smell' and so protect you from the Vanth."

She held the clothes out to me. "Take everything off in the camper, and put this on," she said. "And take care: the pins are very sharp."

I took them, joking, "What, no flying oil?"

She didn't laugh.

"It may come to that. If we are unsuccessful, you may have to *go in*."

"For Franco?"

And who was that with her?

"Angelica," I cried, hurrying over and kissing both her cheeks.

"Yes," she said a little shamefacedly, "Angelica. Anna-Maria begged me to come, to 'stand for' Franco in this ritual. What could I say? I still love him, and that *puttana* does not."

"It's good you're here," I smiled.

Medea drew me aside again, whispering, "*Il dottore* is weaker than I have ever seen him. I believe he can perform the banishment ritual, but more than that . . ."

"Do you *have* the oil?"

"Yes, in the case at the altar. Dress," she ordered in a louder voice, "and join us as soon as you can. You, come with me," she added coolly to Angelica. "We must soon take our places."

I ducked into the camper. Beside a folded *peplos* with pins, ribbons and wreath, marked with a card labeled DSSA. Bradley-Arnold were two neatly-folded heaps of women's clothing on the cot, to which, after pulling down the shades, I soon added a third.

The linen felt rough against the more-than-usually-sensitive skin of my breasts and the snugness of the ribbon around my waist was irritating, reminding me that I had still not told Jim I was pregnant. With that thought, the feathered presence alighted, invisible, on my shoulder.

"I'm frightened, Minnie," I whispered aloud.

So am I, she replied.

Irritating though it was, the linen was thick and warm, at least where it covered at all, and my bare feet soon grew numb to the chilly March earth. All the same, every hair on my body stood on end as I padded down the path past the grinning officers and technicians.

I had a strong sense of going to my doom.

What was I here for, anyway?

I had no beloved in a coma, nor did I know a thing about the ritual, other than that there was an altar fire to feed all night and that I must do it. I knew that there was a stack of small-splintered firewood heaped not far off, along with a ladder and a broom that I must burn when I was told to.

Feeding the fire will keep me warm, at any rate.

Sweet incense smoke was already rising from the altar when I reached it at last. Tethered outside the Enclosure were three small, hooved animals standing close together: two kids and a lamb. They were bleating nervously. Who could blame them?

High above, a white shadow moved from branch to branch, staring avidly down.

Lying to one side of the altar fire was the copper blade I had seen Massimo draw across his thumb, no doubt to cut the little creatures' throats. An unglazed bowl full of coarse salt stood on the other. Two golden rings lay beside the salt, reminding me to take off and add to them Jim's old wedding band, which I had that morning slipped onto my thumb. It was our contribution for the Vanth, to be offered as sacrifice sometime in the night.

Beside the altar was a stone water-jar full of dark water,

with a smaller clay pitcher beside it and a fine bronze dipper hooked on its side. For what purpose, who could say?

My godfather was sitting to the left of the altar in a throne-like wooden chair, his silvery hair crowned in verbena, his bony body covered in a red woolen tunic and white woolen toga. He looked very frail indeed. His great hands were skeletal, and his great eyes—glittering uncovered, under dark, beetling brows—were more deeply sunk than ever.

But there was a smile of triumph on his red lips and one hand was firmly in Medea's. She stood so close beside him that one of his lean cheeks pressed against her ample hip in a gesture both intimate and revealing. She glowed with the same glow I had myself. I thought I could see the fluttering of a creature on her shoulder.

Godpapa will have his heir.

Massimo stood behind the *padre-stregone,* ready to assist him in whatever action he must perform. He was similarly attired as his master except he wore no tunic. His broad, hairy breast was bare under its swath of white woolen cloth. A long-handled, two-headed hammer leaned against a small anvil by the altar. On the anvil itself was a long pair of tongs.

At LoCieco's feet poor Franco lay asleep, pale and still on his narrow cot. His dark hair was brushed off his brow and crowned with a verbena wreath, his otherwise-bare body covered from feet to armpits with a heavy red woolen blanket. On the ground beside him Angelica sat cross-legged, holding one of his cold hands, anxiously watching his face.

"Ah," declared Godpapa, glancing past me up the track. "We are all here, at last."

I turned to see Lavinia, hastening up in her *peplos,* flustered and flushed, her short red hair vivid against the green of her herbal crown. A roll of vellum was crushed in one hand.

"Not quite all," she said in the soft, raspy voice that always reminded me of the Rat, "there is someone behind me with some kind of sound equipment."

It was Arturo Bianchi, a popular Tuscan newscaster, tossing his leonine head of salt-and-pepper hair and smiling all over his big-featured face. From the side pocket of his black-velvet blazer peeped a large, baffled microphone. This he mounted onto a black tripod beside a cluster of equipment half-hidden in the trees, including a wide-lensed television camera of the small, portable variety, hooked up to a spiral antenna.

"I just need your names, then we will leave you to your work," he said briskly. "Does anyone have a smartphone hidden on your person?" I raised a hand, having one pinned under my ribbon belt, between skin and *peplos*. There was no way I was not going to be in quick communication with Pericles. Of course, signal was bad and the ringer was off, as usual.

"Good," he smiled, turning to me. "We will keep you informed about the progress of the fund-raiser from the studio. As of five minutes ago, you were already at Euro 1,550. Congratulations," he added, showing me the screen of his phone as it clicked over to Euro 1,600. "Now your names."

He typed them into his phone as we spelled them out.

After a quick glance through the viewfinder of the camera, he made a quick adjustment, checked the big battery-pack on the ground.

Bianchi pressed the *on* button, saying chirpily, "We're live."

Then, with a wave, he was gone, and, except for an unknown number of live audience viewers, we were alone.

Judging by the failing light it was very nearly time to start.

Beside the altar I noticed a curiously-made silver-fitted wooden box about the size of a carpenter's tool-chest. It was provided with many drawers and compartments of various sizes and shapes. Massimo now unlocked its lid with a small, coin-silver key. My godfather opened it, revealing a recessed space lined with green felt from which he drew a very fine basket chronometer, a small silver hand-bell, and apparently, the same *lituus* Massimo had used.

He pulled open other drawers, perhaps to have their contents ready to hand. One had deep compartments filled with what appeared to be grains of incense, both white and golden. Another held a series of wicked-looking copper blades of various shapes and sizes. The last held small blue-glass jars of uniform size and shape, each lid labeled in his graceful, spidery-thin script.

I caught a glimpse of one I knew, Volans, which meant flying.

Godpapa looked sharply up.

"Take it, Tanaquil," he said, handing it to me. "If I fail, use it for Franco Cotto."

I wedged it into the bosom of my *peplos,* opposite my phone.

Godpapa now palmed the chronometer and, with the press of a lever, popped open the golden filigree lid to reveal a clock-face with three dials. All were set to the same time.

He set it on the altar beside the bell.

"Tanaquil. You will watch the time and ring this bell. Begin ringing at the instant you hear the chime of the first dial and do not cease until I have poured the very last drop of blood for the needed sacrifice upon the altar, beginning with our own, and Massimo has butchered the lamb and thrown the first piece to the Vanth. When six hours have passed, the second alarm will chime and you must follow the same procedure with the black goat. At the halfway point you must also check levels of wood and incense for the rest of the night, making smaller portions of each if you need to. With the red goat we will follow a different procedure, as you will hear.

"Lavinia. You must repeat the incantation every hour, beginning on the hour, for all twelve of the hours. You are welcome to sleep between those hours. Tanaquil will wake you."

I blinked.

I would not be getting a moment's rest all night!

Good practice for having me around, Mor laughed a small voice in my ear.

"Medea, you and I will walk the perimeter of the enclosure every hour on the half hour for the first half of the night, performing the secret incantation and spreading salt. After midnight, you and I must sleep, Medea my darling, behind the tree there until a quarter-hour before the last strike of the night. You, Tanaquil, must rouse us.

"Massimo my son, once you have pounded the gold offerings as flat as you may, you must divide them into eleven pinches. Tanaquil will add them to the flame with the incense on the hour, every hour. I have brought a first pinch," he went on, speaking to Lavinia and me, "my personal offering, which Massimo has prepared for me in advance."

Looking at that pinch of yellow gold, I heard the musical chime of *crotales. It seemed that the rest of the pectoral was indeed in the house next to No. 3, Via del Fico.*

"Dr. Bradley-Arnold," he was saying, "did you bring your gold?"

Without hesitation, Lavinia dragged off her own narrow wedding band and set it on the altar. "James gave it to me," she muttered dismissively.

I felt a spurt of anger.

"I brought his from you," said I, pointing to my offering.

"How appropriate." she smiled wryly.

"Massimo, you will make the three animal offerings: one now, one at the halfway point, and one at the morning. They must be given in the following order: white, to Lord Tages, black, to Nefluns, then red, to Begoia. The procedure must be as follows . . ."

He paused a moment, drew in a breath of air, and at me and everyone else—one by one.

"You must cut the throat in one gesture, using the larger knife. Pour the blood onto the sides of the altar, then you must cut up the first two victims into six pieces to feed to the Vanth every hour thereafter—all the while Tanaquil must ring the bell, remember. Before you throw each piece within the Enclosure you must keep and roast one small piece of each sacrifice over the altar fire, then divide it into five. One piece we must each eat, ourselves. Medea and I will make a breakfast of our second six at the time of the last sacrifice."

Angelica made a face. I was reminded she was vegan.

How far is she willing to go, I wondered, *to save her erring fiancé?*

But there was a bit more for Massimo.

"The last victim, the third one, the one for Begoia, Massimo, and listen carefully, everyone, you will *not kill or divide or roast!* It must *be put alive into the Enclosure at my direction!* I will personally call upon the goddess to take up the victim whole, do you understand? Good. Now . . ."

He sighed wearily, pointing to the tall clay jar beside the altar.

"Each of you take a dipper-full of this sacred water from the Pantunaccio stream to this patch of open earth here, and make mud with it: with this mud you must cover your faces, so the Vanth will not recognize you. I will not do so, as I want her to know her adversary. Wash your hands afterwards and prepare to cut your thumbs for the opening incantation—how long will that take, *dottoressa?*"

"Exactly two minutes," replied Lavinia.

"Then at exactly two minutes before each of the three pivotal hours, you will begin the incantation, *Dottoressa*. Now go and smear your faces, quickly: the time has almost come! At three minutes out, I will give you the warning to stand here around the altar. After the incantation we will offer blood from the roots of our thumbs, starting with Tanaquil, who must then ring the bell until Massimo is entirely finished butchering the white lamb. If you once cease to ring, Tanaquil," he added with a darkling look, "the beast will pounce on the altar at once, or try to, perhaps breaking the iron barrier.

"One more warning: *speak not a single word unless I bid you to!*" He looked at each of us in turn. When satisfied we had heard him, he gestured to the dirt. "Go and smear yourselves!"

So, me and the others dipped our water from the stoup and made mud. I had never noticed this patch of greenish dust before, but when done, we each smeared our faces with it. Then we stood around thinking, or at least I know I was, about all that would happen, rehearsing our parts in it.

A faint breeze came up and I looked toward Bolsena, where sunset was gilding the underside of a dark cloud shaped like a snake.

A chime was heard from the basket chronometer.

"Hark," said my godfather sharply. "Three minutes."

From that moment, and for the hours of the ordeal that followed, we left behind the world of everyday. We had stepped through a portal into sacred time. At once I felt a deep humming as though I over my head in water, and it was not the blood, rushing in my ears. It came up from the limestone into my body through the soles of my bare feet as it had before.

Now I knew what it betokened: Nethuns was in the earth under me. Overhead was the fire of Begoia. The trees of Tages flanked me, right and left.

My time and my body were, for the space of twelve hours, no longer my own.

We stood in a circle around the altar. Even my godfather rose resolutely to his feet. Lavinia began her sing-song *shloka* as I held the copper blade over my thumb. The strange *Rasenna* words coruscated and crackled like the altar fire itself. They were nothing like Latin, nothing like Greek, nothing like Hebrew. They were the language of magic.

As a student of *Rasenna,* and having heard the English version, I could recognize some of the words, but moreso I could *feel* their meaning. They struck my flesh like pulses of magnetism or like hammers on piano strings or like waves of power, radiating outward.

On her last phrase, I cut my thumb. The thread of blood followed the knife as I handed it off to Lavinia, taking up the bell with my uncut hand. This I rang, and rang, and rang, unable to staunch the rivulet of blood that continued to drip on the stone until it ran off upon the ground. Still I dripped and sounded the sweet clangor of that little bell, as the others cut theirs in turn. Finally, Massimo, his own cut stanched, pulled up the little muzzle of the white lamb and caused its white throat to split into red halves and its delicate knees to buckle.

Taking the little hooves into his hands, he walked it clockwise around the altar and washed the feet of the stones with the gushes of hot blood until it gushed no more. He took it then to a table I had not noticed, and began to disarticulate and disembowel it. The hot smell of interior animal steamed up in the still, cold, humid air.

All the innards he hurled over the Enclosure as the first one-sixth offering. My godfather gave the sign. I ceased ringing and stanched my bleeding thumb.

At that moment, Angelica broke away from where she had been kneeling by Franco's head and ran, retching, for the bushes beside the limestone surface, then came and washed her mouth out with the dipper.

But as she washed and spit upon the ground, a thing like a

vast ball of white stone dropped from the top of the walnut tree to feast upon the offal and lap the blood the blood that puddled around it.

Such a horror came over me that if my godfather had not nudged me, having completing his first circle of sprinkling salt, I would have ceased feeding the fire, frozen as I was.

Massimo had spitted a small piece of meat and leaned it over the hottest part of the fire, which I now mended and fed. Now he divided the kid into five portions: four quarters of meat and the head, and set them aside, under a red cloth.

Once the meat was cooked, Massimo cut it in five and we each ate our portion, even Angelica. And from that day to this, oddly enough, she has resumed eating meat.

Massimo now took to hammering gold, and put the first pinch on the fire as I added the incense, and so ended the first hour. Keeping my attention fixed upon the fire and keeping the flames clean and bright, I was able to block out sight of the creature inside the chains. Massimo now took to hammering gold, and put the first pinch on the fire as I added the incense, and so ended the first hour. Keeping my attention fixed upon the fire and keeping the flames clean and bright, I was able to block out sight of the creature inside the chains.

In time, I was able to detach myself, to send forth my imagination to the Cotto's house in Lido di Tarquinia, where the Riverbankers were lost in lively competition, playing *Scopa* with Anna-Maria, eating peanuts from a cracked *Raffaelesco* bowl. Or I might send my spirit out to the squat, ancient church where John-Allen lay prostrate in the form of a cross, his face to one side, praying constantly, a golden fume rising from his lips to Heaven. Or I might go to the Museum basement, where my Pericles sat smiling at his desk, running loving fingers over the glossy black surface of the Berlin Painter amphora.

Hours came and went. Lavinia spoke the *shloka*. Gold and

incense were added to the fire. The supply of firewood dwindled. I circulated constantly, pulling every splinter into the
shrinking center of the heap, keeping all trim and in order.

Standing for six hours, I figured, *was no worse than teaching
four sections of lecture.*

The six-hour point approached. I roused everyone I
needed to, and again we offered gold and incense, again we
passed around the copper knife. I rang the bell as the black
goat gave up his little life, not silently like the lamb, but with
a fierce bleat. The world jerked sideways.

An earthquake. Hadn't I feared just this? I thought in terror
as we clung to one another and the altar to keep from falling.

But it was soon over and the creature descended heavily,
to feed again. This time Angelica lay full length beside
Franco, hiding her face in his cheek and covering her ears
with her hands, whimpering. I wished I could do likewise.

Their salting finished, Medea and LoCieco retired to
their spot behind the tree, just outside the Enclosure:
perhaps to sleep, perhaps not. The beast gorged on black
goat as it had gradually gorged on white lamb. It seemed to
me, when I dared to look, that it grew larger and heavier
every, less able to fly.

Lavinia, Massimo and I did our hourly chores, then, at
nine hours out, three hours from the end, a dreadful sleepiness struck me. I could hardly stand upright, let alone mind
the fire. Lavinia, Massimo and I did our hourly chores, then,
at nine hours out, three hours from the end, a dreadful
sleepiness struck me. I could hardly stand upright, let alone
mind the fire.

All was silent, behind the tree. Angelica slept sweetly
beside her Franco, tucked under his blanket. Massimo had
long since made eleven pinches of the gold, of which only
three were left. He lay curled up on the ground, covered with
the white woolen thickness of his toga, stained here and
there with blood, the red goat in his arms. Lavinia had gone

off to the bushes to relieve herself and came back to sleep on the far side of Franco.

I alone was left, fighting sleep, unsure whether I would hear the tiny warning whirr before the chronometer struck the chime of every hour or whether, by my failing, the whole venture would fail. If so . . .

The place would remain cursed by the obscene beast that hulked beyond the chain. Franco would never awaken. His parents would curse me. Angelica would hate me forever. Godpapa would dwindle horribly over the centuries into a thing like a cricket. God help me!

The night opened up and I saw John-Allen again, now pacing the use-polished floor of San Martino, hands raised, reciting the Great Litany. As I joined him on the responses a fresh energy filled me, almost indescribable.

It was like a cold draft of Chimay on a hot Texas summer afternoon, or like a bowl of red risotto after hours of dusty labor in the Temple of Vanth and Tages, or like kissing sleeping Riverbankers after being away, or making love to my Pericles after days of fear and illness.

Pericles. There he was, asleep at his desk, his cheek against the warm metal of his laptop, his arms around that lidded amphora, the scent of its ancient honey reaching me, even here.

Refreshed, I did my work, the remaining hours passed. The firewood, gold and incense dwindled. Then, somewhere in the valley of the Pantunaccio, a rooster crowed.

There came a rustling from behind the walnut, and *il dottore* emerged, leaning heavily on Medea's arm. The thing in the tree had been silent, high in its eyrie, since soon after its last feeding. Now I could sense it moving, greedily waiting.

In the light of the altar-fire, I could see the time. It was ten minutes until 5:00 AM: twelve hours since we had begun. It was the end of the "historical reenactment."

It was time to call down Begoia and send the Vanth to hell.

How? We would know soon enough.

When I told my godfather the time, he limped over to his equipment case, took out the *lituus,* anointed it with his blood and took it firmly in his right hand.

"Massimo, untie the red goat," he whispered. "Once the *dottoressa* finishes the third recitation of the imprecation, I will begin my own invocation of Begoia. When I begin, Tanaquil, you must ring the silver bell and you must keep ringing until I swing my *lituus* towards the sky, and say a great word of power."

He then turned around to face Medea, arms raised.

"Medea, you must then quench the altar flame with the sacred water, holding back enough to wash Franco Cotto, by and by. Understand."

Medea only nodded.

"Massimo," he said. "You must throw the goat into the Enclosure then run. Run, my son. Go as fast and as far up the path as you can, taking the *dottoressa* with you."

Pausing he seemed to take a moment to regroup his thoughts, then glanced at all of us at once.

"I repeat, at that moment, listen carefully, all of you, at the same *instant and moment,* the bell must stop, the flame must go out, the goat must be tossed into the Enclosure, and Massimo and the *dottoressa* must go!"

He rubbed his chin and shifted his weight from one foot to the other.

"Tanaquil must stay near me until all is over. Medea and Angelica will stand by Franco Cotto. The instant he awakens, you two must give him some of the sacred water to drink, wash him with the last of it, then take him back up the path after the others. If he does not awaken, Tanaquil, you must go into his hearth that instant and bring him out, do you understand?"

309

I nodded, wondering wildly why there were no commands for me to *run, run*.

Medea eyed me darkly, her thoughts clearly the same.

"Wake the *dottoressa*," he now told me. "The time is at hand. Tell her."

"I heard," said Lavinia, getting stiffly to her feet.

I went to read the chronometer. It was five minutes until Lavinia must start. My godfather was standing beside me, facing north. Both his arms were raised over his head, and he was already whispering soft words in *Rasenna*—words of conjuring and of flame, and then he repeatedly chanted, "*Begoia. Begoia. Begoia.:*

There was a distant rumble of thunder and a flash in the still-sunless east.

"What's happening?" said Angelica in a faint voice. Medea came to her, the pitcher of the water in her hand, saying quietly, "Stay here, *carina*. It is almost over."

As for me, I could feel through my feet a rumbling that grew closer and closer. The air grew thick around me with a tangible, malleable, ductile sense of ineluctable fate.

Or, as Lavinia put it, muttering under her breath, "Damn' big storm coming."

BANISHING THE VANTH

"It's time, Dr. Lavinia," I whispered back. The blood pounded in my ears as I grasped the slender handle of the silver bell. With a swallow of stoup water, she squared her slim shoulders and began the *shloka* for the last time, in *Rasenna*, of course:

> "*O Vanth the Beautiful,*
> *We unworthy mortals call upon you in humble supplication . . .*"

At which point the first short temblor came, making us all—all but Lavinia, who kept doggedly reading—gasp aloud with the feeling that someone had just tried to jerk the ground out from under our feet.

But Dr. Lavinia persevered right to the final *Rasennese* "Begone" at which point my godfather rose from his wooden chair, raised his *lituus*, and began to declaim, gesturing to me *not to ring the bell.*

Down like a stone swooped the horrid great owl for the third time. But his time, like Rumor, the thing grew and changed with going, putting out arms and booted legs with which it strode the narrow ground within the iron fence, its wings going green, and all of it growing to the size and fell beauty of a white, green-eyed goddess, fluttery blue skirt held up by blue suspenders that criss-crossed between bare, red-tipped breasts, the golden torch in her fist shedding a fierce yellow light, her red mouth slavering, white claws reaching hungrily for red goat.

It was the food she had come to expect at the end of each recital of the imprecation, for which she might possibly obey and leave.

But Lo Cieco was taking no chances.

Raising the *lituus,* he spoke the word of power, *"Begoia."* Upon which we all did our parts: my bell began ringing, the fire was quenched, and the goat was tossed skyward to the Vanth.

But it was taken by Begoia.

Through the sudden, hissing darkness sliced down a white coruscation of light that struck the little animal in mid-fall, reducing it at once to smoke and ash, exploding overhead in a flash that lit the whole scene, freezing it in time. Then down came the a light rain, masking the dawn.

Into the choking blackness that followed came a confusion of sounds.

Massimo, crying to Lavinia to, *"Corri, corri."*

A deep groan from Franco and Angelica's cry of joy as the two of them rose to their feet.

From the corner of my eye, I saw all four of them vanish up the track, faint shapes beyond a soft grey curtain of rain.

My godfather took off his wreath and stood with his face lifted to the downpour, transfigured: youthful, beautiful, tall and strong.

But a strange second dawn began to glow golden through the rain, from under the walnut tree. The Vanth's upraised torch sputtered to life, showing clearly both her murderous hunger and a broad opening in the iron Enclosure, still smoking from the stroke of Begoia.

One booted step forward and she would have been free to harry the world, but in stepped my godfather instead, dropping the *lituus* and raising his hands.

He would be her goat, her Christian. The protective smell of verbena had washed away.

A shriek beside me revealed that Medea had not followed the others to safely. She would have rushed into the enclosure after him, but I caught her as tightly as I had held Lavinia in her desperation. Even in her desperate writhings she could not get loose. I knew as clearly as if I were as fluent in *Rasenna* as Lavinia that my godfather had made some bargain with Begoia and that this act must be allowed to play out to the end.

All the same, it was hideous to see.

One claw in his now-dark hair, the Vanth thrust her fanged face into his beautiful throat, gorging on his blood as it came up, hot from his fading heart, drinking deep, deeper. Finally, she threw down his carcass and stood there covered in his blood, stunned with satiation, the rain pattering gently on the drained husk that had been *Padre* LoCieco.

"*Tito*," howled Medea, tearing at me with her fingernails. "*Titono mio*."

Out from the cavern of LoCieco's ravaged throat sprang a mouse, darting towards the iron fence, was foiled, then found the opening and ran directly towards us.

Dismayed, I turned to escape the fate of *stregheria*. Medea, released, rushed forward with an eager cry, but the Vanth was too quick for her. Reverting to owl-form, she caught it greedily in her beak, tossed it back into her throat, and swallowed, wheeling off on brown wings into the rain but down came Begoia's second bolt with a light like the end of the world.

The startled Vanth shot, back-first, out of the owl and into the heart of the walnut tree's massive trunk, as off fluttered the stunned and much-diminished Antonia.

In the blindness that followed came a third and final temblor, racing off towards Tarquinia like a huge snake making for its prey. The rain came down now in Texas-sized torrents, drenching everything in moments.

Nefluns is not satisfied, I realized with a pang of dread, *and Tuchulcha is loose.*

A small voice in my ear called urgently, '*Mor, Mor. Save Papa.*'

I took off running for the car through torrents of running water, leaving Medea to cradle what was left of LoCieco in her arms, her shrieks swallowed by the rain.

As I struggled blindly along in my sodden skirts, I saw a vision projected on the gray curtain of rain ahead.

Jim, supine on a heap of crumbled plaster in the Museum basement, his eyes staring at nothing, his body spattered all over with blood, a long hunting rifle in his hands. At his feet lay the Berlin Painter amphora, whole, but empty. Beyond that, sheer darkness.

Someone in a regulation policeman's hooded raincoat broke through my vision, slithering towards me down the track. He looked up from under his dripping hood: it was Paolini.

Something in the way he blinked at me made me suddenly aware that, while the right half of my body trailed long folds of muddy linen, my left half entirely bare.

Somewhere back there I had lost a *peplos* pin.

What about my phone, and that jar of flying oil?

Groping in the cloth above my right breast, I found them safe and damp.

"Thank God," I muttered.

The Colonel had meanwhile taken off his raincoat and handed it to me, turning his back. It was a struggle to wrench out the other pin, extract myself from the mess of knotted ribbon, and jettison my *peplos*, then get my phone, flying oil, and self into the raincoat, but nothing could have saved

Paolini a drenching in that rain, no matter how fast I'd worked.

I, on the other hand, was now decent enough, thank God and Paolini, to get past the huddle of media and bedraggled electronics and into the back of his squad car without incident. I figured the Fiat could wait.

Getting into the front, he slewed around in his seat to explain, "Your clothes and backpack are there on the floor, *signora*. Word has come of collapsed buildings in the *Centro*. I am very fearful something has happened to *Dottore* Lewis, and thought you should come. I hope you did not want to stay at the site?"

"Not for worlds, Pasquale. Bless you."

As he started the engine and turned his attention to the potholed, slippery road, a shocking thought occurred to me.

"Did you see what happened to LoCieco on the live feed?" I asked, beginning to wriggle into my dry clothing in the back seat as Paolini kept his eyes strictly ahead.

He shook his head. "The line went dead at the first stroke of lightning."

"Thank God!" I said again and yet more fervently. It was my big phrase, that day.

"We never have earthquakes here," remarked Paolini, making the turn past Mazzola's. "Up in Umbria or down in Campania around Vesuvius, yes, but not here."

"That's because you never have priest-warlocks calling down spirits of fire on you."

He looked at me long and hard in the rear-view mirror. "Where is your godfather?"

"Dead, but he trapped the Vanth in the walnut tree. It is over."

He sighed gustily. "I am very glad we do not have to arrest him."

"So am I," I agreed, then surprised myself by bursting into a storm of tears.

"I saw that Franco Cotto was awake," he said hurriedly. "He seemed well."

"He is," I gulped, fighting for control. "So, will you investigate *Omeopatica Argo*?"

"We are more interested in *Antiquità Colchis*, but yes, I have told my men to detain Benevento, and that witch Medea."

"Massimo is harmless, I'm certain of it. As for her, she never got the *Padre's stregheria*, so she is not technically a witch." I sighed. "But she does know Marc Short."

"You should call *Dottoressa* Ficino," he said suddenly.

"Heck, yes," I gasped, pulling out my phone. I got Anna-Maria instantly. The *animali* were fine, she said. There had only been the tiniest of quakes in Tarquinia Lido, and they were eating custard-filled *cornetti* for breakfast.

I told her that Franco was well, and that there was nothing to fear.

I hung up, grateful to her but ashamed of myself. *What a big, fat liar.*

We drove in silence until Paolini made the turn onto the main road, rain gradually easing. Then I described to the colonel in detail my vision of Jim in the basement, asking what he thought it meant. Naturally I had my own ideas.

"You say he lay *on* the fallen plaster, not *under* it? It happened *after* the earthquake, then, whatever it was," he said decisively. "Had he shot the gun, do you think?"

I described the appearance of the gun as minutely as I could.

"Yes," he nodded, "yes, I would say he had shot the gun. I would also say the spatter of blood was from the thing he shot."

"Not his own?"

"Unlikely, if it is all over his clothes, as you say."

"Just as I thought," I murmured, not adding that I thought Jim had momentarily distracted an enormous snake with a snack of ancient honey before destroying it with a blast of silver bullets, an act that either sent him deep into shock or had killed him outright.

Oh hurry, hurry, hurry.

Siren blaring, Paolini raced along to where SP43 branched left towards Jim's near-fatal roundabout. When he found a police road block in place, he switched off his siren and waved someone over from the gossiping crowd of officers. A young policewoman ran up, threw back her hood and saluted.

"What's the situation in town?" he demanded. "We need to get to the Museum."

"Many retaining walls have collapsed into the streets, Colonel," she said, producing from her raincoat pocket a photocopied map and pointing out various locations, "here, here, here, and there are several here, near the *Municipio*. It was very bad at the Museum, Sir."

Paolini clicked his tongue. "What do you recommend?"

She took back the map to the others, consulted with them a moment, then returned.

"Filippo says they are getting people out around this way, *dottore*, by *Chiesa* San Martino. If you go straight, right across the Corso, don't turn there, the street is very bad, as you can see by these 'X's, and keep going until you have to turn left, you can approach the Museum from Via di Porta Castello, past the Duomo. There was no damage to the Duomo, sir," she added cheerfully. "We are using it as a shelter for people from that part of town. San Martino, too: no damage. It is bad along Corso and Via Cavour. I hear the parking lot is being used for first aid."

"Many thanks, Traffic Officer . . ."

"Leonini, Paola, *dottore*," she provided with a blinding smile and another sharp salute.

"Isn't that the officer who brought in *Giacomo* after his

accident?" I mused as we moved on. "Pretty much saved his life? Her name will be in the hospital record."

"If so, she has earned herself promotion to the regular force," he growled, moving cautiously ahead. "Those other jokers will be hearing from me!"

Piles of rubble had slumped onto the side of the street here and there from un-reinforced garden walls, but most of the houses were made of ashlar masonry from the fine local limestone, much of it good Roman work, robbed from the ancient town, so I hoped for the best.

Passing the end of the street where the church of San Martino was, I peered up it, searching for the familiar form of Prester John, and, *yes, there he was.*

"Oh, Colonel Paolini. There's my friend, Father Prester. He may have news." And my feet were on the ground before the car could halt entirely, running of their own accord.

"Prester John. Prester John. You're all right."

I would have thrown myself into his arms, but he was looking with concern into the face of a *nonna* gesturing down the street towards town, so I stepped aside.

"*Un attimo, signora,*" he said to the lady, explaining rapidly to me that her husband had been buying flowers for his mother at the flower shop in the Corso when the quake hit, and now he wasn't answering his phone.

The woman, who had been squinting anxiously down the street, now gave a cry of relief, kissed Father Allen on the cheek, and hurried off towards a stout man coming our way, waving a big posy of red and yellow flowers wrapped in green crepe-paper.

"Ah," he sighed. "All's well that ends well."

I finally got to hug him. "Any word from Waldo?"

He sighed gustily. "Yes, he and Caterina are both safe. What about Lavinia?"

"Okay, when last I saw her."

"Jim," he slapped his forehead. "Holy cow, is he still at the Museum?"

I nodded, and turned to go as Paolini honked his horn.

"We're headed there now. Did he call you?"

"No! But listen, comrade, I had a vision of your pal Tony an hour or so ago."

"Tony?" I paused, flabbergasted.

"Yes. He says to tell you *he is free of the Vanth and to feel free to move in soon,* whatever that means. Okay, run. I'll join you at the Museum just as soon as I can. Be safe."

A quick cheek-kiss, and I was back in the squad car.

"Just got word," the colonel said bleakly, hanging up his portable phone. "Two of my men are trapped in the Museum."

On we went, passing more rubble and seeing our first people in pajamas, their heads wrapped in blood-stained towels, sitting dazedly on doorsteps. When Paolini asked after them, they all told him help was on the way, and not to worry about them.

Paolini pulled the squad car into the Piazza Soderini, where a cluster of emergency vehicles stood outside the back-door of the Museum, lights flashing.

"Here we are," he said with a forced smile. "Let's find your man."

Almost at once, he had good news. There were his two missing officers, sitting on the tailgate of an open ambulance. Both were drinking Lemon Fanta and one of them had a blood-stained bandage on his forehead. Glimpsing Paolini, the uninjured man leapt to his feet and hurried forward. The other, a man I knew as Ettore Quagli, was Paolini's right-hand man.

"*Dottore* Paolini," cried the officer, whose badge labelled him as MARZI. "A relief to see you safe, Sir. And you, *signora.*" He touched his hat.

"Yes, yes,'" said the colonel testily. "What's the damage like, inside?"

"Mostly fallen plaster, and exhibition cases smashed, sir. We," he began, then halted, glancing at me. "May I speak with you privately, sir?"

They stepped out of hearing as I watched them in an agony of fear.

At that moment and instant, there was a tapping on my shoulder, and I turned with a sharp "*Cosa?*" A young woman in bright red and yellow jumpsuit stood there with a hand-cart. Behind her was a similarly-bright DHL van.

"Forgive me, *signorina,* but I have a delivery for the Museum, and I need a signature. Do you know who could sign for it?"

On the hand-cart were two boxes, each about the size of the proverbial bread-box. Both were labeled in an unknown hand, *Attention: Tanaquil Greenough.*

"I can. I'm Tanaquil Greenough, or was until recently," I said, pulling out my wallet to show her my New Jersey driver's license.

She held out a pen. "Sign here. Say, what's going on? It was hard to get through."

I laughed, handing it back. "Just an earthquake: no big deal."

"Huh. Where do you want these? They're *un po' pesante.*"

"Well, actually, there is a ramp, down to this door here, but it may be hard to . . ."

We walked past the policemen, deep in conversation, and down the ramp to the broad back door to the Museum, now hanging half off its hinges. Heaps of plaster or fallen asbestos ceiling tiles cluttered the dark hallway.

Asbestos. That must be what all the argument was about, up topside: they had been talking for years about replacing those things.

"Here should work," I told her, as we came to an alcove

with a water-fountain, "at least for now." Sliding the boxes neatly off, she went back out into the open air.

I, on the other hand, forgetting about those soon-to-be-misplaced boxes for another three years and leaving Paolini to argue behind me, made my way deeper into the labyrinth of hallways. I headed without hesitation for the vault, alone.

The damage seemed worse the closer I got to Jim. Plaster was everywhere. It rose in such choking clouds that I pulled my wool scarf over my nose and mouth. I found that light-switches didn't work in the dim hallways, so I pulled out my phone and put it on flashlight mode.

There was the door to the basement, at last.

These had been Jim's bachelor quarters for many years, even though access was by keypad and its inhabitant was locked in, every night.

I knew the eight-digit passcode from two years ago, when I'd been running in and out all day with finds and notebooks. I tried that one now, with shaking fingers: 5-2-9-7-3-6-2-3. Lawrence, Ratty's middle name).

No luck.

Then I remembered: the summer before I had covered Jim's classes, Franco had lived down here, and may have changed it to Angelica, maybe? I tried 2-6-4-3-5-4-3-2.

Again, no luck.

Think, Mor, came the voice in my ear, as I heard the pounding of many footsteps in the hallway overhead. *Think how grateful Papa was to you, last fall.*

8-2-6-2-7-8-4-5 .Tanaquil.

Shoving open the door with one shoulder, I looked out over the vaulted chamber. Once the palace chapel, it had been fitted with row upon row of tall steel, cross-braced storage shelves bolted to the floor, in each of which were many tens of labelled boxes of small finds or rows of larger objects such as bronze strainers or pottery vases. In the thickness of the wall was a safe we called "The Vault," where the most precious finds were kept.

Little good that did, when the wolves were minding the sheep.

But never mind that right now. *Where was Jim?*

Morning light came filtering in through oblong, street-level windows, shining down through the still-settling cloud of ceiling plaster upon a strange scene: while most of tall shelves had stood firm, two were *bent* away from one another, though still anchored to the floor, their frames buckled as if by some tremendous outside force.

As best I could make out, between those shelves there lay, in a welter of gore, a small, garden-variety snake, blown in half, poor thing. And there in the open space beside his desk, his feet not two meters from the snake's head, was Jim, still clutching the gun that killed it.

FINDS AND KEEPERS

I CLAMBERED LIKE A MADWOMAN OVER THE HEAPS OF RUBBLE and was kneeling at his side in a moment. I pressed a finger to the skin under the corner of his jaw. It was warm, thank God, with a rapidly-beating pulse. Prying the gun from his grasp, I held both his hands, kissed them, looked into his staring eyes and called all his names, every pet name I could think of, over and over.

Nothing.

"Shock," I muttered aloud, "You're supposed to elevate their feet, but we know better, don't we, Minnie?"

All the same, I dragged his desk chair over to put his feet on, his legs stiff as boards.

Sitting cross-legged beside him, I laid one bared arm of his against one bared arm of mine. Then I got out my jar of *Volans* oil and creamed it onto my throat.

At once, I was at my hearth.

The fire is burning bright, and the One half-rises from his seat to greet me as I climb up onto the settle beside him. At once I begin visualizing the blue diamond, my heart yearning towards my best beloved, and in a flash the portal has swallowed me and I am in Jim's hearth.

No Jim on his tummy on the floor, no dog lying beside the fire. The fire itself is down to bare embers, and Grandpa Jim sits in his rocker, hands clasped, staring at the empty rug.

"Never could abide snakes, that boy," *he remarks sadly.*

"Where is he, Grandpa Jim?"

"Here." *He pats the left breast pocket of his blue-plaid flannel shirt.* "Not dead, not yet anyway. Can't understand it! It's not his time."

"May I?" *I ask, touching the place.*

"Be my guest," *he says, and I am in the blue place.*

Blue, blue, all around.

For a long while I wonder, Why am I here?

Mor, Papa's spirit is 'Deeply Buried' *comes Minnie's voice.*

That instant, I could see the entire page that began De Spiritum Magne Sepultum Trahendo or, in English.

II. HOW TO FIND A DEEPLY-BURIED SPIRIT

A – Enter your hearth, as above. If the One is missing, call upon the One.

B – Rise, face the One, closing your eyes and pressing your hands together in front of your face, and say, "I am seeking (subject's full name). Lord, take me into your heart!"

So far, so good, though we had not used correct verbiage or gestures. I reflect for a moment how much like his grandfather the One looks to Jim.

C – The Heart of the One will become a portal, and you will be within the Oneness. All around you will be solid blueness, but one sphere of blueness will be surrounded with white fire.

D – Cup that sphere between your two hands, then close your eyes and tilt your head back, visualizing your hearth. Your subject should be standing before you in human seeming.

Oh, There it is, *just up and to the right, and a smaller flaming sphere beside it. I take both gently into my hands, lean back, and take them partway back, not all the way to my own hearth, but to his, and there stands my Pericles, in the center of the hearth-rug glaring at me with unfocussed eyes. A blue-feathered creature flies from him to sit on my shoulder.*

"Did he follow?" he asks me wildly, gripping my shoulders. "Is he here?"

"Tuchulcha?" I laugh. "No, you blasted him off the face of the earth!"

Weak with relief, he drops into a chair and runs a hand through his hair, looking around.

"Tanny? Where are we? Are we dead?"

"Nossir. We can go back anytime you like."

His eyes must be working better, because he sees who that is over there in the rocker by the fireplace. "Grandpa Jim," he cries. "Is Grandma Cecy here?"

"No, Jimmy, she's gone on. But you'll see her again, by and by."

Then he makes as if rise stiffly to his feet, but Jim is too quick for him, and rushes over.

"No, don't get up. How," Jim looks around, taking it all in, "how did I get here?"

"You tell me," he smiles, and Jim scratches his head.

I just look on, arms folded.

"Well, I was asleep at my desk when I heard this voice in my ear —a child's voice, a girl's voice, but not Clo's—say very clearly, "Papa, get under the table." So I woke straight up and took the Brauron Vase and my laptop and hunkered down under that steel finds table I like to use, not a minute too soon.

"First, the ground started to go kind of liquid. Then, something like a piledriver hit the basement wall, and all the plaster came off the ceiling of the basement, sad, really, it had some fine frescoes. Once the shaking stopped, I looked over there," he turns to me for verification, "where that drain in the floor is, on the north side of the basement was the biggest damn' snake I'd ever seen in my life.

"Hell, sorry, Grandpa, it was the size of a . . . do you remember that barbecue place you took me to in Trenton, Tanny, with the smoker made of oil drums? It was as big around as an oil drum, and no end to

it at all, and jaws like. Well, it struck me that it would eat me whole, and that would be the end of me. But I got the idea it would like the honey in that amphora, so I took off the lid and set it on the floor. I was as careful as could be, Tanny, I promise, and if it is broken. I will kill myself, and it started lapping it up like nobody's business, giving me time to get Paolini's gun. I aimed high, so as not to break the vase. Gave it both barrels, then I wound up here. What in creation was it, Tanny?"

"Tell you later, Pericles. Grandpa Jim, we should go."

"Yes, go on. Your friends are worried, and Tanny can tell you how to visit me, anytime."

And he kisses us each on the forehead. But before we leave, suddenly Jim sees Minnie perched on my shoulder and puts a hand out to her.

"Who's your little friend?"

"Guess." laughed Minnie, hopping onto his finger and clinging there.

"Easy, you're the voice from my dream. But who are you?"

"My middle name will be Cecilia, Papa. Guess why."

He turns to me sharply. "Is there something you're not telling me, Greenough?"

I awoke to a terrific hammering on the door. An instant later the door swung inward the wrong way, leaving the lock assembly attached to the frame. A man with a chisel in his fist stepped back, calling to someone behind him.

"We've broken through, *padre*, if you'd like to go in."

I was still sitting cross-legged on the heap of plaster, Jim's arm still in my lap. His blue eyes opened, and he picked up the conversation where we'd just left off.

"Tanny, seriously, are you—you know?"

"Yeah," I said shyly, bending to kiss him, "Since the time after you took off my crown."

He took my dusty hand and kissed it. "How long have you

known?"

"Why didn't you answer the door, Tanny-Sue?" yelled John-Allen from the doorway, more upset than I ever remembered seeing him, "Could have saved us a lot of time and worry and chiseling." Then he strode over the rubble to stand angrily over us.

"Are you happy?" I asked my best beloved.

"Happy? Are you kidding?" And he sat right up, not a thing was the matter with him, put both arms around me and sent the world away.

From the corner of one eye, I'd seen Paolini clamber down the stairs behind Prester John and go to the gory welter by the bookshelves to collect his silver bullets.

Now he stood beside John-Allen looking down at us.

"*Per carità*. They were making love."

We got Jim out to the ambulance for an examination. He was pronounced unhurt but covered with a sticky substance that turned out to be snake blood, unaccountably mixed with honey from the Brauron Vase, which was later found empty but unhurt.

Waiting by the ambulance was Françoise Pinard.

"Dear friends. *Mes braves* Keepers," she cried.

Pulling out her phone, she recorded our interview, her photographer Pino clicking away non-stop.

"How good to see you both safe. I understand that your fundraiser has raised in the five digits of Euros, Dr. Lewis, and that more is coming in every minute. What are your future research plans, now that you have the necessary funds?"

"Well, Françoise," Jim answered jauntily, one sticky arm around my shoulder, "we will start by setting up a proper security system in case Mr. Short and his cronies ever visit us again. Then we will get ready for the summer season, or rather I will, since Ms. Greenough-Lewis has to take her preliminary exams by August, before returning to Italy with me, in the fall."

She turned to me. "Can we look forward to seeing you both back at *La Castellina*?"

This time I spoke up, trying to match Jim in jauntiness.

"Jim will be in Rome, Françoise, serving a second term as Director of the Rome Center for Ancient Studies, but I will be here most weekends to supervise work at the Hut Circle, at least until . . ." I glanced into the clearing March sky, doing a quick calculation, "around November twenty-third, after which day I will be busy with other matters that will take me from my work entirely for a couple of weeks at least, then just part-time for a while after that."

A beat of startled silence, then Jim added soberly, "That is certainly true, Greenough, but I will do my part, as agreed, being a past expert at changing cloth diapers, a full set of which are in the attic in Princeton. I am also quite good," he added modestly, "at singing lullabies."

"But how?" gasped Mlle. Pinard, looking from one of us to the other. "How can you be certain, *Professore* Lewis? November twenty-third is more than eight months from now."

"A little bird told me," smiled Pericles.

FINIS

SNEAK PEEK: DEEP SCANSION

BOOK II IN THE FINDS & KEEPERS ARCHAEOLOGICAL ADVENTURE SERIES

Cursed gold resurfaces, engulfing the whole Lewis family in danger.

Caught in a web of deceit, Jim and Tanny draw all those they love into danger, culminating in unforgettable struggle on the erupting brink of Mount Aetna. Can even Tanny's uncanny sixth sense save them this time?

After narrowly surviving the removal of an ancient curse from the Etruscan site they have dug for years, archaeologists Tanny and Jim Lewis must face the consequences of unfinished business. The cursed gold stolen from the site is still at large, as is the man, Tanny's ex, Marc Short, who stole it.

Although profoundly changed by the exorcism, Marc must find a way out of a criminal maze of his own construction and also dispose of the gold. The apocalyptic cult that promises to solve both of his problems only ensnares him in yet-deeper danger as they make the most audacious fake of all time. When a genuine treasure found in the center of Rome launches the appearance of the fake, Tanny's metallurgical expertise is called upon to debunk it, shutting the door on Marc's only chance of escape.

How can she hold fast to the truth when the cultists, assisted by her vengeful ex, threaten her and all those she loves with death if she does? And will her soul-deep union with Jim be shattered in the process? Their perilous adventure culminates in a nail-biting struggle at the edge of an erupting volcano, as the cult demands a human sacrifice in the place of sunken treasure.

1

A LESSON IN SCANSION

JIM SNATCHED UP MY PEN-KNIFE AND SPRINTED ACROSS THE screen. Marc, lit by the glare of fountaining lava, was running flat out for the Hummer. Marc is the younger man, but Jim is a runner, and his heart was filled with bloodlust enough to level a phalanx of Marcs.

"Think you're a long syllable, you pipsqueak?" he yelled. "I'll cut you down to size!"

A single, panicked backward glance showed Marc his peril. I could feel him thinking about the gun he'd left in his camera bag. I wanted to scream to Jim to "Watch out, Pericles!" but my body was lying back there at the rim of the crater.

Marc was reaching into his bag when my best beloved, with a laugh any Viking might envy, raised his knife hand for the downward plunge.

Marc turned, raised the gun and fired it.

I awoke to sit bolt upright in bed, certain I had heard a shot.

I was equally certain this was no ordinary dream. For sure, the "long syllable" part was weird, but something very close to the rest of it would happen or my name was not Tanaquil Susannah Greenough-Lewis, "Tanny" for short.

I am half a witch on my Daddy Bill's side and my Mor's side is uncanny, too, both adding up to something we call my "Tanny-sense," a kind of second sight. My right eye sees things my left eye can't, things like more like visions than dreams.

But how could I "see" Jim and me up Mount Aetna with Marc Short? And wasn't it sheer nonsense to imagine that a peaceable man like my husband would plunge my favorite pencil-sharpener into anyone, even my ex-boyfriend, even after Marc had...what? Killed me?

Okay, well, maybe then.

I sank my hands into my wild, curly, gilded-bronze hair in a gesture of perplexity I'd copied from Jim. It seemed to help.

Hmmm.

Yes, later this semester we would be taking the Arca students to a spot in Sicily not far from Mount Aetna, and yes, Jim might get bent out of shape if somebody stabbed me.

As to why Jim was yelling insults to do with poetic scansion, that was easy. I'd been studying Poetics non-stop for days, readying myself for an online retest this coming Saturday.

The retest would be on September 11, not an auspicious date, but hopefully luckier than July 15, when I hadn't exactly passed that part of my preliminary exams with flying colors.

Okay, I'd flunked it.

Dr. Potts' Poetics class had been taught on warm, spring afternoons two years back, in a droning monotone so soporific that my notes were a shambles. Now it had invaded my dreams.

But I really had heard something. Not a gunshot but a rolling slam! like the door of a big van shutting hard. From somewhere near at hand.

I ran lightly to the barred windows flanking the front door. They looked onto the gravel drive at this upper entrance to Villa Parrasia. No vehicles of any kind. Jim had the car.

Returning to my north-facing bedroom window, I switched off the box fan and set it quietly on the floor. Then I leaned out as far as I dared, staring eastward towards the corresponding gates at the bottom of the Villa park, listening hard.

A police siren tweedled down along the Tiber, but otherwise Rome was as still and cool as it ever gets on a mid-September night. No breeze stirred and no birds sang in the ancient Bosco Parrasio, the woods surrounding the building that housed the Rome Center for Ancient Studies (RCAS, or "Arca," for short), home of a semester-long overseas-studies program for thirty-odd fortunate scholarship-supported undergraduate fellows.

Fragments of eastern sky showing between the heavy leaves showed no trace of dawn.

I glanced in at the clock on the dresser: 2:06 AM. My stomach growled.

Come on, feed me, my unborn daughter was demanding. Only two months to go!

Just a few hours earlier, I'd devoured so much of the *pasticcia* (an insanely-tasty kind of lasagna) I'd ordered in a day or two ago that I thought I'd never want to eat again.

"Again?" I complained aloud, but Minnie just laughed.

So out I went into the pitch-dark common room of the top-floor Director's apartment to rummage in the kitchen by the light of my phone.

With no Faculty or students expected back until next week, the windows out here were shuttered night and day. I didn't want any old friends to know I was back and distract me from cramming. Even with all Rome beckoning, I hadn't gone out all week.

The harder I studied, I reckoned, the more time I would have with my colleague and best beloved, Professor of Classics James Pericles Lewis, gifted archaeologist and that year's Arca Director, and the Riverbankers, aka Mole and Ratty, Jim's children and now mine. They were all now up at our new house in Tarquinia, an hour's drive away, letting me work.

With a sigh, I reached for a carton of shelf-stable milk.

Once I passed this last prelim, there was still my doctoral dissertation to finish and defend before the baby arrived in November. Jim was a past master at baby-care, but even so...

Had we bitten off more than we could chew?

I tore off the corner and took a long pull of milk, considering a more sinister question.

Did my vision mean the stress of this year would either kill us or make us murderers?

It seems to me, looking back on it, that life is a lot like scansion.

Consider the saying, "some are born great, some achieve greatness, and some have greatness thrust upon them." Well, scanning a line of Latin poetry is something like that. We figure out upon which anceps (place where stress goes) the poet put the ictus (stress) to make each word fit the poem's meter (rhythm), to make it beautiful. Scansion helps us work out each word's form and syntax, that is to say, how it works in its sentence and what it all means.

Without knowing an arsis (stressed syllable) from a thesis (unstressed syllable) here's the bottom line: each syllable of a Latin word is naturally either long (worth two shorts) or short (worth half a long). It is simpler than music, where notes can be all sorts of lengths.

But syllables, like people, can change. As can what it all means.

That's because, if a short syllable is followed by two consonants, it becomes long by position. Syllables at the very end of a line of poetry on the other hand, like Jokers in a card game, become whatever the meter requires. Long becomes short or short long, through a process called syllaba anceps. In other words, "some syllables are long by nature, some are short, and some have length thrust upon them."

Looking back on the year that followed that dream, the one person I knew to be long by nature was pushed to the very end of his line, while a cruel and selfish other – short by nature and by name – would change beyond recognition.

As for me, I would be transposed, written over, all but erased. It felt like hell.

Let's call it deep scansion.

2

HALF A CROTALIS

I WAS POLISHING OFF THE MILK WHEN THE FAINT SOUND CAME of a single car-door slamming. Even through the shutters I knew it came from the lower end of the property. And no-one had any business being there, this time of night.

I ran back to my bedroom window to lean out, my Tanny-senses tingling with alarm.

Earlier, the dark bulk of the Studio building had drowsed at the bottom of the park. Now I saw a faint light on the trees behind its ground-floor entrance, quickly extinguished. Then, sweeping slowly around the last bend on their way to the Lower Gates, came a pair of headlights outlining a delivery van – the Arca delivery van: I could just see the faun logo! – to shine a moment later on the tall gates, which parted to allow the van's passage...then closed behind it.

At that instant, the four big skylights in the Studio roof flashed into life with an eerie white glow, so quickly gone as to be almost an illusion.

Thieves were prowling the Studio with their phone-lights!

Piero Buoncompagni, Site Manager of Villa Parrasia and his wife Lydia-the-Chef, lived right across the street from the

Lower Gates. Jim said I could call them, "any time day or night."

I hoped he was right!

Piero's line rang many times before a sleepy male voice answered, "Ciao, Tanina! It is very late! Are you calling from the States?"

He spoke in Italian, so I followed suit.

"No, Piero, we came back early. I'm at the Arca, studying for an exam. Jim is in Tarquinia with the children. I think there's an intruder in the Studio!"

I could feel Piero pull himself together. "What happened?"

I mentioned the light at the studio and the van's loading-and-leaving.

"What if they are stealing equipment...and the van?" I asked anxiously.

After a beat of silence, Piero offered dubiously,

"Serafina did say someone was testing the gas-jets in the Forge this week."

"In the middle of the night?" I cried incredulously. "Can't you come check?"

Two beats of silence, this time.

"Giovanni gave you the keys, vero? Didn't he tell you we are in Sardegna?"

"Sardinia? No," I told him with an audible sigh, "he didn't."

"Listen, cara, go back to bed. In the morning, call Giovanni. Don't go down there alone."

"But Piero, I have a feeling that..."

"In the morning, cara. Promise me you'll wait?" He hung up before I could promise.

Just as well, since there was no way I would.

Serafina said...

Serafina Fidati, Senior Secretary and uncrowned queen of the RCAS, was Lydia-the-Cook's incredibly beautiful and endlessly capable sister. Each year when I exchanged

Christmas cards with Contessa Erminia Egidio-Doria, Acting Director of the RCAS, she sang Ms. Fidati's praises and listed her latest undergraduate conquests (not that she gave in to any of them).

Surely Serafina was to be trusted?

Maybe the gas-jet check was just taking longer than planned?

My Tanny-sense said far otherwise.

I got dressed in the darkest clothes I owned, jammed my phone in a pocket, wrapped a black scarf over my hair and lower face and stuffed my fat bundle of keys and a pair of dark socks into my navy Converse All Stars, keeping them for now in one fist as I ran barefoot down the dimly-lit stairs two at at time. I passed two floors of darkened dorm rooms and came out at the ground floor, where a side door opens out of the cave-like kitchen onto the Terrace.

Carefully disabling the alarm and triple-checking that I had my keys, I slipped out, perched on the balustrade for a moment to brush off my feet, then put on my socks and shoes and tied up my laces, noticing suddenly how good the woods around me smelt.

Instantly I was back at the "Welcome to the RCAS" buffet reception of ten years back, when Jim had first directed the RCAS and I was a green undergraduate.

I'd wandered from the noisy buffet to admire the wrought-iron tendrils of one of the lovely lamps that stand at the four corners of the terrace.

A slim, tall, dark-haired man I'd assumed was a local artist had materialized beside me and started explaining how, more than a hundred years earlier, Gian-Lorenzo Egidio-Doria had envisioned building a center of learning in his family's ancestral woods.

The steep site meant the Villa had its back against the Janiculum Hill, its feet in Trastevere and its head in Monteverde Vecchio. The latest (for then) technology was used, its all-electric lighting provided by a miniature power station that would later become the Studio.

He'd hired every skilled worker in Rome to make it, including these gates and lamps.

"Nicest wrought-iron I've ever seen," I declared. "Pretty sure I couldn't do better!"

"So you are a metallurgist, Ms.," frowning at my nametag, "Ms. Greenough? That's a famous name, in my line of work!" Then he'd really looked at me in my tank-top and jeans.

"Your eyes are gold, like...like the rest of you!" he'd gasped foolishly, his own pale skin flushing up red, his own eyes, magnified by their scholarly glasses, the most gorgeous blue...

I'd almost uttered my usual response ("Really? I hadn't noticed!") but recollected my manners. "My stepfather taught me to work iron," I smiled back, "and yes, I'm what they call a 'woman of color,' and yes, I'm The Great Classicist's great-granddaughter!"

"Hence your being named for an Etruscan queen," he'd laughed. His embarrassed smile could have melted more than iron.

"So," I'd gone on, heart pounding, "you're in Classics?"

"Forgot my name-tag," he confessed cheerfully, shaking my hand. "I'm Jim Lewis, this year's Director. Welcome to Villa Parrasia, Tanaquil! Better reserve a locker in the Studio soon if you want to do metal-working this term."

I'd just about dropped my teeth. Why had no-one warned me that the author of my very dry Practical Archaeology textbook was this young and beautiful?

I'd also taken his advice about the locker and won a prize at the Arca Festival for my hammered "Chapel of the Nine" silver filigree, now sitting on Jim's desk back in Princeton.

After which, by dint of ten years of archaeological field work, a Masters degree, two articles, caring for his kids as a paid babysitter-cum-chef and finally teaching four classes for him without complaint – oh, and some pretty powerful mutual attraction – I'd won the man himself. Last fall he'd divorced his estranged wife and last February we were married amidst dangerous adventures. Which is how I came to be in Rome alone, seven months pregnant, and investigating a robbery.

I got heavily off the balustrade and onto my Converse-clad feet. Why not call Jim himself? I thought as I descended one of the many footpaths that criss-cross the ivy-clad slopes of the park, reflexively supporting my heavy belly with one hand. And wake the Riverbankers? I told myself repressively. Besides, if it takes him an hour to get here, what good would it do?

Call Giovanni, then! Giovanni Egidio-Doria was the Arca's distinguished photography instructor and brother of late Gian-Carlo, the RCAS founder who'd been killed in a riding accident five years earlier. Both were direct descendants of the Villa's builder.

Giovanni, however, was now eighty years old and lived in the Parioli neighborhood on the other side of Rome. I would not be calling him.

If I had to, I promised myself, I would call Col. Paolini of the Tarquinia Metropolitan Police. Especially if, as my senses were screaming that he was, Marc Short was involved.

Quickly leaving the Terrace behind, I soon reached the Studio's upper door. From a window beside it, barely visible through a massive rhododendron, a light shone out.

Someone was in the Studio Office.

To my knowledge the office had nothing of value in it other than a sofa popular with student couples looking for a little illicit sex. According to my tingling instincts, Marc was putting that selfsame sofa to its usual use, celebrating with his partner-in-crime.

I needed to know not only who she (or he, Marc being flexible) was but also to estimate – based on their, er, progress – how long I had to check out the downstairs forge.

For sure, I couldn't run as fast as I used to but at least, judging from Piero's reaction, they should not be expecting me.

I crept through the tangle of branches right up to the window, having entirely covered my face with my scarf. Peeking through its loose weave, I saw that a pale, strikingly-beautiful woman with abundant flaxen hair was pulling a crimson sweater over her head, exposing a pair of perfectly-formed breasts to the darkly-handsome man lying full-length and quite naked on the infamous sofa. He reached up to her.

Holy crap! Marc Short and Serafina Fidati, just getting down to business!

Backing out of the bush, I stumbled away, down the steep little path along the north wall of the Studio down to the forge, stunned to know that the Arca's most trusted employee was hanging out with my ex-boyfriend, a dangerous antiquities-smuggler.

Didn't bode well for the year ahead!

Whether she knew it or not, Serafina was in danger of serious bodily injury. I was pretty sure Marc been infected by the same supernatural blast that had filled me with such a strong desire to eat Jim alive that he'd once had to tie me up with his dress socks.

I'd been cured, but rumor had it Marc was now too dangerous even for his favorite crony, Cecco Casti. If so, I shuddered for Serafina!

But rumor had been wrong before.

From the smell of blended diesel exhaust and cigarette smoke outside the open door to the forge it seemed that Cecco – a heavy smoker who drove Marc everywhere – was still a part of the gang. A white Citroën DS3 was parked in the lot by the Lower Gates: Serafina's?

I stepped boldly – too boldly – into the dusty forge to investigate. The lights were out and jets of the casting table were off. I touched them: still hot! A crucible lay on the table, also still hot and lined with what also spattered the table: bright yellow Arretine gold, Etruscan gold.

Crap! They would be back soon, to clean up! Nobody left gold around for long!

Chances were that if I took a drop for testing, they would miss it.

Then – with a tingle of awareness that raised every hair on my head – I noticed something like a tiny golden cup, gleaming on the floor in the shadow of the table.

It was half an ancient jingle-bell, called a crotalis, one of hundreds bordering the golden pectoral stolen from La Castellina. Last spring, I had found its mate in a pit at the site.

It was too perfect a piece of evidence to leave behind. I took three silent photographs of the gold-spattered forge then, licking my finger-tip, I lifted the crotalis out of the dust. I had only just tucked it into the cup of my bra when quick feet could be heard on the metal stairs above.

Jeepers, they'd been quick about it!

I scuttled out the back door and waited just out of sight, holding my breath.

"So what do we do with this?" Marc's voice was asking in Italian. I imagined him pointing to the single biggest piece of evidence against them: the crucible.

"Bury it in the ivy," said Serafina coolly. "Can't risk any trace of gold in the trash. There's a spade in that closet. I'll sweep off these spatters and we'll bury them, too.

"What are you looking for?" she added sharply.

My heart leapt into my mouth.

"Crotalis," grunted Marc, perhaps dropping to his heels. "Saw it roll over here."

I heard a quick intake of breath.

"Someone's been here!" he hissed. "Look at those prints! Not my shoes, not yours!"

"Cecco?"

"Never came into the building!"

"I told you I heard something! I'll call Piero. Maybe the Lewises..."

But I didn't wait to hear what we Lewises may have done.

I was sprinting up the dirt path to the Terrace, clutching Minnie close, lungs burning with unaccustomed effort, hoping desperately Marc was not right behind me.

At the kitchen door I punched in the security code in hot haste, pulled the door shut behind me and reset the alarm, wiping my feet on the rug before, still shod, I ran for the stairs. The elevator was faster, but so noisy it would give me away if they were truly on my heels.

But I had a gut sense that they were in Serafina's Citroën, driving up the winding Via Garibaldi to the Upper Gates: if so, I had about ten minutes.

As I ran, I wondered wildly,

What would happen if they found the crotalis on me?

An accidental fall, maybe, from the kitchen balcony, three floors to the terrace?

A little girl's voice inside my head cried, "Mor, Mor, get out!"

"Minnie!" I gasped aloud, running to the coffee table, scooping up my laptop and dissertation files and stuffing them into my pack, followed by my pregnancy vitamins, toothbrush, phone-charger and our silver-framed wedding picture.

The site notebooks I hid in the dish-cupboard.

Other notes and reference books were left behind with all the clothes not on my back.

I rushed out the door but got no further than one of the huge planters beside it when car lights shone onto the Upper Gate, casting shadows of its graceful oak and laurel wreaths onto the peaceful facade of Villa Parrasia's upper-most floor.

No time to lock up, Greenough!

As the gate jerked into life I ducked down, waiting until the car lights swept past me to park at the top of the outer stairs, over to my right.

Then I ran left, low and fast, for the narrowing gap before the gate closed again – something we students had been told never to attempt. "Someone lost a foot, doing that!" the staff always said. I could feel the iron edge brush my pack.

No shout came behind me. Crossing to Fontana Paola I glanced back in time to see them make purposefully for the door before I hurried out of sight, down the way they had come.

Then I stopped, and checked my Skagen: 2:55 AM.

Who in the world would take me in at THIS time of day?

"Erminia will!" said Minnie. Her namesake the Contessa lived at the American Academy between semesters and was there now, God willing, just two long blocks away.

I now shamelessly phoned her, praying hard that she would be both in town and not furious. It rang and rang but when her voice came on it was calm and mildly humorous.

"How can I help you, cara?"

I told her as briefly as I could. She cut me off impatiently.

"Yes, yes, hurry over at once and I will buzz you in. I expect you are hungry."

I strode up the silent, lamplit street with a grateful heart, sending as I went the gold spatter photos to Col. Paolini, saying I had evidence on my person and had seen Marc on site, but leaving out with whom.

My mind was in turmoil, but not so much that I couldn't foresee the outcome if the world knew that Serafina was a crook.

In less than a week the faculty would arrive, fully

expecting the peerless Serafina to organize their field trips and do the thousand other things she did with practiced ease.

And I couldn't risk her sister Lydia quitting in protest, leaving Jim to scramble after a new cook, or risk losing Piero, without whom all practical matters to do with the physical plant might collapse, nor would there be Friday pizza or Sunday soccer. Disaster!

I couldn't risk Jim getting the blame for it all – as he would, I had no doubt, the world being the place that it is – when the RCAS Board had taken a chance appointing him, knowing he was still dogged by dangerous elements in the antiquities-smuggling world.

I loved the RCAS and I loved Jim. This would spare them both a scandal, right?

Sure it would, but what about me?

How could I know that the genius Serafina would call my spouse pre-emptively – while Marc ransacked the apartment in search of a tiny piece of gold – and tell him she had seen me at the Studio, melting down the pectoral and making love to Marc Short?

What did she care if she woke the Riverbankers?

GLOSSARY & DRAMATIS PERSONAE

- *acqua gassata* – (Italian) "fizzy water"
- *aiuto!* – (Italian) "Help."
- *al fresco* – (Italian) "in the fresh air"
- *alle sette nel pomeriggio* – 7 PM. Italians usually use the twenty-four-hour clock nowadays, but occasionally slip back into older forms.
- Angelo – See Cotto, Michele-Angelo
- antefixes – decorative stones or tiles placed at the end of a row of roof tiles on ancient temples.
- Arca – see RCAS
- ashlar masonry – stones cut into rectangular blocks, used in building.
- *aspetti un attimo* – (Italian) "wait a moment" (polite)
- *attenti, voi due!* – (Italian) "(be) aware, you two!"
- Attic pottery – black-figure and red-figure vases, a desirable export from Attica, Greece. Read John Boardman's standard text on the subject or a Wikipedia search of "Attic pottery" should put you straight.
- *il babbo, Babbo* – (Italian) "daddy" = Dr. Michele-Angelo Cotto, "distinguished professor of

archaeology in the Department of Historical, Archaeological, and Anthropological Sciences of Antiquity of Sapienza University of Rome, had been lead archaeologist at the ancient city site of Tarquinia – aka *Pian de Cività* – for thirty-odd years, universally beloved at the site."

- *bacio, bacio-bacio* – (Italian) "kiss," "kiss-kiss," standard (for friends) Italian greeting of hand-clasp and air-kisses, right cheeks first.
- Badger, the – a character from the children's book *The Wind in the Willows,* by Kenneth Grahame, who lives deep in the Wild Wood and has a great deal of authority. See Lewis, James.
- Bassi, Luisa – an Italian exchange student to the Tucson, AZ high-school which Jim Lewis attended, his first girlfriend, three years older than he.
- Benevento, Massimo – *Padre* LoCieco's assistant, a trained nurse, and his *son.*
- Benevento, Titono Empedicleo – the original name (so far as we know) for Tanny's godfather, he was born in or around Florence in the year 1826, became a priest in 1851 and a *stregone* in 1857. After 1882 he took to wearing smoked glasses to mask his mesmerizing gaze from others, and so was called *lo cieco,* "the blind man." Became Tanny's godfather under the name *Padre* LoCieco, pretending to be his own descendant.
- Beneventum – Italian city associated with witches / wicca.
- Bess – see Vanderbilt
- *Bestemor* – (Norwegian) "grandmother" See Greenough, Hailey.
- *bistecca fiorentina* – a Florentine steak, traditionally of fine Chianina beef, served rare with fries and spinach, in sizes of a kilo of meat and up.

- Bonifazzi, Caterina Maria – talented miniaturist, a native of Florence and once the department secretary at the Institute of Advanced Study when her parents were on the Art History faculty at Princeton. Lavinia Bradley-Arnold's lover, wants children, so set Lavinia's divorce in motion.
- boss, the – see Lewis, James.
- Bradley-Arnold, Delbert and Alice – parents of Lavinia Bradley-Arnold. Delbert was professor of Legal Studies and Alice was president of the Society for Marriage. Together, they pressured James Lewis to marry their lesbian daughter Lavinia, hoping for grandchildren and normality.
- Bradley-Arnold, Lavinia – Dr. Lewis' wife, distinguished member of the Princeton Institute for Advanced Study and world-renowned expert on *Rasenna,* the Etruscan language.
- Brauron – in Attica, Greece, was a famous ancient sanctuary of the goddess Artemis, served by young girls dressed up as bears, as depicted on some pottery.
- *bunad* – a woman's traditional Norwegian costume, specific to a certain areas, usually a skirt, vest and blouse. Evidently the skirt of the Kåfjord area, where Hailey is from, is navy blue.
- Burnsey, Mary Greenough (M.G. Burnsey) – born in 1852, youngest of twelve children of Samuel Sandhurst Greenough and Eliza-Jane Baker Greenough of Barnstable, MA, became renowned for her striking oil portraits, and the monumental sculpture "Erebus." She was both great-great-grandmother and great-great-aunt of Tanaquil Greenough, as M.G.B.'s daughter Susannah married her first cousin Augustus Zinala "Gus" Greenough, son of W. S. "the Great Classicist"

Greenough and his African wife Zeya, in whose house in Rome she was raised.

- Burnsey, Stephen Hayes – heir to the Burnsey's Better Biscuit fortune, born in Boston in 1858, whose older sister Bess introduced him to her schoolmate Mary Greenough, later his wife.
- Buster – see Sparks, Christopher.
- *cacciucco* – a kind of fish soup, like *cioppino*.
- Ca'Foscari – the University of Venice, Italy, famous for its focus on training in diplomacy and economics, but with an excellent center for Etruscan studies.
- *calcio* – (Italian) "soccer"
- *cara / caro / carina* – (Italian) "dear" used frequently in conversation with friends.
- *carbonara* – rapidly-made dish involving spaghetti, egg, *guanciale, pecorino* and black pepper.
- Carter, Howard – Egyptologist Howard Carter opened the tomb of the pharaoh Tutankhamen on November 26, 1922, saying when he first looked into the tomb's unrobbed outer chamber that he saw "wonderful things."
- *Cartoleria* – a variety store carrying paper goods, school supplies, books and toys.
- *casa* – (Italian) "house."
- *Casalinga* – a store selling household appliances and tools, especially for kitchens.
- Casti, Francesco (Cecco) – henchman of Marc Short, pre-med student at U. of Florence, likes to experiment with knives and anesthetics.
- *cattivi bimbi* – (Italian) "bad babies, bad children"
- *cella* – the central room of an ancient Greek or Etruscan temple.
- *certo!* – (Italian) "sure!"

- *che bella Tessana* – (Italian) "what a gorgeous Texan woman!"
- *ciao* – (Italian)
- *chianina* – from Tuscany's broad Val di Chiana, famous for its beef and dairy products. Also a famous ancient breed of enormous, docile white cattle, still used in pulling festival carts.
- *come il morto* – (Italian) "like a dead thing."
- *come si dice...?* – (Italian) "how does one say...?"
- *come va?* – (Italian) "how's it going?"
- *cornetti* – Italian croissants, brushed with sugar syrup, often with jam or custard fillings.
- Corto, Boetio – Marc Short's Italian name, especially as a professional photographer.
- Cotto, Andrea – youngest son of Angelo Cotto and Anna-Maria Ficino, owner of the Fiat.
- Cotto, Michele-Angelo (*il babbo,* Angelo) – Director of Excavation at La Castellina, professor of archaeology at La Sapienza. Father of Franco and Andrea Cotto, and owner of the Range-Rover.
- Cotto, Francesco (Franco, Franceschino) – eldest son of Anna-Maria Ficino and Angelo Cotto.
- *Crepi!* – see *al bocca al lupo!*
- *da affittare* – (Italian) "for lease"
- *dall'Inghilterra* – (Italian) "from England"
- *dimmi!* – (Italian) "Go ahead, tell me!" or "Tell me what you want!"
- dodecapolis – alliance of 12 Etruscan city-states, not always the same twelve, but always including Caere, Populonia, Tarquinia, Veii, Volsinii, and Vulci.
- *dottore / dottoressa* – (Italian) – "doctor, sir, ma'am," an honorific for any educated person, not just a doctor or academic.
- *drachma* – (Greek) a silver coin of ancient Athens.

- elementals – animistic demons in control of natural forces like earth, air, fire and water.
- Ellingham, Anthony Ardelean (Tony) – art-collecting ex-pat of the United Kingdom who has lived all his adult life in Italy, specifically on Via San Giacomo, Tarquinia.
- *et ruat caelum* – "and may the heavens fall" said when taking a step one knows to be right but possibly disastrous.
- Fanta – favorite soft-drink of the Riverbankers, generally Lemon, but Orange also good. Italian version much better that that in the States due to higher percentage of fruit juice.
- *Farmacia* – a pharmacy with a prescribing druggist and also selling toiletries, always marked with a green neon cross; one in every neighborhood is open 24 hours.
- Ficino, Anna-Maria – professor of jurisprudence at La Sapienza and wife of Angelo Cotto, mother of Franco and Andrea.
- *fidanzata / fidanzato* – (Italian) "fiancée, fiancé"
- Foscolo, Ugo – a poet and very romantic figure.
- François Tomb – In 1857 Alessandro François and Adolphe Noël des Vergers excavated the famous François Tomb near Vulci. Des Vergers describes the opening: *"Per alcuni minuti vedemmo forme, vesti, stoffa, colori: poi, entrata l'aria esterna nella cripta dove le nostre fiaccole tremolanti minacciavano di spegnersi, tutto svanì."* Jim Lewis translated that as: "For some minutes, shapes, garments, cloth, and color were all very clearly distinguished: then, as the outside air came into the underground chamber where our flickering torches were almost blown out, everything disappeared."

- *Frecciarossa* – a kind of intercity-express train in the Italian rail system.
- Fred – nickname for unborn child.
- fulminant hepatitis – see *hepatitis,* below.
- *furfanti* – (Italian) "scoundrels"
- *gabinetto, -i* – (Italian) "toilet, toilets"
- Gesualdo – see Verbicaro
- *Giacomo* – Italian verson of James. See Lewis, James.
- ΓΝΩΘΙ ΣΑΥΤΟΝ – GNOTHI SAUTON ("know thyself"): motto of the Delphic Oracle, tattooed on the inside of Tanny's left arm.
- *Grazie al buon Dio* – (Italian) "Thanks be to (the good) God!"
- Greenough, Tanaquil Susannah (Tanny-Sue) – our heroine, about thirty years old at the time this story begins, she is a doctoral student in archaeology of J. P. Lewis, at Princeton University.
- Greenough, William T. Burnsey (Daddy Bill) – Tanny's father, a pilot and Air Force training officer, died in a plane crash – likely a suicide – when she was fifteen.
- *Hardangersøm* – a kind of drawn-work embroidery, usually white-on-white, from the Hardanger region of Norway.
- *haruspex / haruspices* – Etruscan seer(s) who read the sky, the behavior of birds and the entrails of animals for divine signs.
- hepatitis – a severe disease of the liver, the *fulminant* version of which causes the failure of more organs than just the liver. Can remain dormant in soil or on surfaces for many years.
- Hut Circle – the northwestern part of *La Castellina,* consisting of a cluster of simple wattle-and-daub,

thatched huts around the Ash Altar, where visitors to the Vanth Oracle stayed.

- *hydria* – (Greek) a large, open pitcher, often with three handles, for pouring water. For all other vase forms and information on Greek Attic Pottery, consult the text by John Boardman.
- *hypogeum* – (Latin) a chamber intended to be underground (as contrasted with chambers buried by fire or other destruction that raised the normal street level of an ancient town), often housing offerings to infernal gods.
- Iacomini, Angelica – long-term girlfriend of Franco Cotto, studying viticulture at Florence University.
- *Il Messaggero* – the morning daily paper of Rome.
- *Il Prof* – see Lewis, James
- *in bocca al lupo* – (Italian) "into the mouth of the wolf," said before starting a difficult endeavor, to which the reply is *Crepi!* "may the wolf explode!"
- *incidente* – (Italian) "accident"
- *in coitu* – (Latin) "in a state of coming together," vaginally speaking.
- *in flagrante delicto* – (Latin) "in blazing offense" often in the sense of caught in the act of (illegal) sex, as in a spouse finding another spouse with a lover. Not in this case, of course, though the Pantanos may have found it offensive.
- Koko & Katisha – tenor and contralto characters, respectively, from *The Mikado,* a Gilbert & Sullivan operetta.
- *kyare* – (Norwegian) "dear, sweetie"
- La Castellina – the northerly outcrop of land dug for ten years by Lewis and Cotto, part of Sector C in the whole excavation scheme of *Pian di Città,* the ancient city site of Tarquinia.

- La Sapienza – the University of Rome, one of the largest and oldest universities in existence. Official title: Università degli Studi di Roma "La Sapienza."
- *La Signora degli Anelli* – (Italian) "The Lady of the Rings," Tanny's nickname after her comment about the missing rings. A take-off on the Italian translation of "Lord of the Rings."
- La Stampa – morning newspaper published in Turin, Italy, center-left leaning.
- *La Storta Ammalata* – (Italian) "the sick bit of land" = La Castellina
- Lewis, Cloelia Agnes (Clo, Moley, Aggie) – oldest child of J. P. Lewis and Lavinia B-Arnold, about ten years of age when this story begins. Called "Aggie" by her mother and cousins.
- Lewis, Horatio Lawrence (Ratty, Rat, *il rattuccio*, Larry) – second child of J. P. Lewis and Lavinia B-Arnold, about six years of age when this story begins. Called "Larry" by mother and cousins.
- Lewis, James Pericles (*Il Prof*, the boss, "massa," *Giacomo*, Jim, Pericles) – Tanny's academic advisor and area supervisor at La Castellina, professor of archaeology at Princeton University.
- *lituus* – (Latin) a kind of Roman magic wand, made of a curved piece of wood, generally used by seers to delineate a region of the sky for the observation of divine will in the form of the flights of birds.
- LoCieco, Titono Empedicleo – see "Benevento, Titono Empedicleo"
- *lo sa? l'ho saputo!* – (Italian) "Get it? Got it!"
- *Luisa – see Bassi*
- *Lungomare* or *Lungarno* or *Lungotevere* – a street that goes along the sea or the Arno or the Tiber, respectively.
- *macchinetta / Moka* – (Italian) a standalone, usually

octagonal espresso coffee-makers that can be heated over a small burner.

- *mangiamo!* – (Italian) "Let's eat!"
- Mariarosa, Medea – chief assistant to *Padre* LoCieco and C.E.O. of *Omeopatica Argo.*
- *marito* – (Italian) "husband"
- "massa" – rude name for Lewis, James, to get Tanny's goat, she being a descendant of enslaved persons, on her father's side of the family.
- Massimo – see Benevento, Massimo
- *matrimoniale* – (Italian) "conjugal" an adjective that may refer to a double bed, or a hotel room with a double bed.
- Mazzola, Martino – owner of the farm at the corner where the road to La Castellina branches off. He has several large sons, and is proud to host the end-of-dig luncheon every season.
- Minnie – nickname of Erminia Cecilia Lewis, Jim's third child and Tanny's first.
- Mole, the – a character from the children's book *The Wind in the Willows,* by Kenneth Grahame, Ratty's best friend, loyal, kind and mild-mannered. See also Lewis, Cloelia.
- *moglie* – (Italian) "wife"
- *Mor* – (Norwegian) "Mom"
- Mr. Toad – a character from the children's book *The Wind in the Willows,* by Kenneth Grahame, who is self-centered and impulsive. See also Short, Marc.
- *mundus* – (Latin) "world," in this case (in ancient Roman religion) a deep pit opened on certain unlucky days of the year to act as a link between the upper world and the Underworld.
- *Municipio* – Town Hall, here same as the *Palazzo Communale.*

- Museum, the – refers in this book to the National Etruscan Museum of Tarquinia, located in the historic Palazzo Vitelleschi in the middle of medieval Tarquinia.
- *Nolo contendere* – (Latin) "No contest" literally "I don't want to compete."
- *nonna / nonno* – (Italian) "grandma / grandpa"
- *Palio, il* – The name of two famous horse-races held every summer in Siena in honor of two of the Madonnas of the town, one on July 2 to Madonna di Provenzano, one on August 15 to the chief Madonna of the cathedral or Duomo. It is named for the *"pallium"* or hand-painted banner given to the winning part of town.
- Panificio – a bakery specifically making bread.
- *panino* – sandwich made on a sort of pizza-bread bun, sometimes long like a baguette.
- *Panorama* – weekly Italian news magazine, based in Milan.
- Pantano, Giulia Colonna – the Director of the Tarquinia National Museum, of a famous Roman aristocratic family, but unfortunately dabbling in antiquities theft. Customer of Padre LoCieco.
- Pantano, Riccardo – husband of the Director of the Tarquinia National Museum Giulia Pantano, and member of an obscure local aristocratic family. Owns family retreat in Sardinia.
- Pantunaccio – the small stream that runs from the back of *La Castellina* northwest to the Marta River, known by excavators for its cool swimming hole at the bottom of the slope.
- Paolini, Col. Pasquale – head of Tarquinia Police Force and frequent collaborator with Dr. Ficino in her work on jurisprudence.

- *paparazzi* – (Italian) photographers, particularly of celebrities.
- *Parcheggio* – parking lot
- *Paris Match* – a French-language, weekly magazine featuring large pictures and celebrity lifestyles, along with international news.
- *pasta 'ncasciata* – pasta casserole involving rigatoni, eggplants, and other good things.
- *pausa* – (Italian) a siesta running from 2-4 PM, during which traditional shops are shut.
- *penteconter* – (Greek) a fifty-oared ancient Greek fighting galley.
- *peplos* – A garment worn by Greek women during the late 5th century B.C.E. consisting of a rectangular length of very wide cloth, roughly the size of a sheet, folded, pinned at the shoulders with dagger-like pins, and belted at the waist.
- *per carità* – (Italian) "mercy's sake!"
- Pericles – see Lewis, James. Also the prominent Greek statesman who commissioned the Parthenon of Athens, among other things.
- *pizza rossa* – pizza bread with just marinara sauce, baked in big rectangles, sold by weight.
- Place of Sacrifice – a large mound at the *La Castellina* site, in which traces of hepatitis had been found. Tanny says it is full of plague victims. Jim insists they are sacrificed Roman soldiers.
- *poliziotti* – (Italian) "cops"
- *precisamente* – (Italian) "exactly"
- Prester, John-Allen (Father Allen, Prester John) – best friend of Tanny's since middle school at St. John's Episcopal School, San Antonio, TX. Started out in Family Law but currently Associate Vicar at All Saints, Rome, living in a wonderful apartment on the slopes of the Pincian Hill.

- *prima colazione* –(Italian) "breakfast"
- *pronto soccorso* – (Italian) Emergency Room (literally "fast help")
- *puttana* – (Italian) "slut"
- Pyrgi – an ancient Etruscan port near modern Santa Severa where, in 1957, three golden tablets, a kind of Etrusco-Phoenician Rosetta Stone, in a triple-*cella* temple.
- Raffaelesco – a style of decoration of faience made in Deruta, Umbria, with grotesques, fanciful swirls and yellow bands.
- *ragazzi* – (Italian) "kids, young folks"
- Rat, the – a character from the children's book *The Wind in the Willows,* by Kenneth Grahame, who becomes Mole's best friend, brave, clever, good at boating. See also Lewis, Horatio.
- *rattuccio* – (Italian) "the little rat"
- RCAS – Rome Center for Ancient Studies, located on the Janiculum Hill of Rome, an intercollegiate program for undergraduates studying art, history and ancient languages.
- Riverbankers (*animali*) – what the animals call themselves, who live beside the River. Nickname given by Fred Cole to Clo and Larry during their time at Oxford, and used thereafter.
- River, the – not so much a character from the children's book *The Wind in the Willows,* by Kenneth Grahame as its defining feature. The animals live "by it, and on it, and in it." See also Greenough, Tanaquil.
- *settimana bianca* – (Italian) "white week," a holiday for Italian school-children in the middle of February, when families often go skiing.
- Shaggy Man, the – a character from the Oz Books of Frank L. Baum: a homeless, kindly wanderer

whose only possession is the Love Magnet, which makes everyone he meets fond of him on sight. He was introduced in the 1909 *The Road to Oz,* which also features Polychrome, the Rainbow's Daughter.

- Short, Marcus Boethius (Boetio Corto) – Tanny's former boyfriend, Dr. Lewis' amoral and amorous former doctoral student and photographic genius, born in Rhode Island to a violent father and an over-protective mother, with relatives in very unsavory businesses.
- *signore / signora / signorina* – (Italian) "mister, missus (mistress), miss"
- *sogni d'oro* – (Italian) "sleep tight" literally "dreams of gold"
- *solje* – a typical Norwegian brooch, usually a silver filigree circle set with fluttering gilded "spoons" – dangling concave disks of silver.
- Sozzini, Lelio – Sixteenth-century religious thinker, a founder of Unitarianism.
- Sparks, Christopher "Buster" John (Daddy Buster) – Tanny's step-father, a mechanic at Lackland Air Force Base. Had been good friend of Bill and Hailey Greenough before Bill's crash. Taught Tanny everything he could about casting and smithery.
- Sparks, Hailey Niilasdatter Greenough (Mor, Bestemor) – Tanny's mother, originally "Aile" from Kåfjord, Norway, she earned a B.A. in journalism with a minor in English at the University of Oslo before working as interpreter at the NATO Air Force Base near Tromsø. Met and married pilot W. T. B. Greenough, moved with him to Pordenone, Italy, where Tanny was born.
- *Sposi, gli* – An Etruscan terracotta tomb group dating from the late sixth century B.C.E., on

display in the Museum, showing a couple dining together in egalitarian amity.

- St. John's – an Episcopal day school in San Antonio where Tanny went to high school with Johnny Prester, frequently performing with him in operettas.
- *Sta attento!* – (Italian) "Watch out!" (informal)
- *Stazione Termini* – Rome's main railway station.
- *strega / streghe / stregone* – (Italian) "female witch / witches / warlock, male witch"
- *Sul Leccio* – (Italian) "Under the Ilex," an imaginary Romagnolo folk-song, sung by Piero Pellico.
- *Tabaccheria* – a shop selling cigarettes, salt, and sundries such as umbrellas.
- *talpa* – (Italian) "mole" (the animal, not the beauty mark)
- *tantissimi auguri!* – (Italian) "very best wishes!"
- •*tarocchi* – blood-oranges, their flesh and juice maroon and tasting of berries.
- Tarquinia – ancient town in what is now northern Lazio. Notes from Tanny's publications on this location: Tarquinia was an ancient Etruscan city, member of the Dodecapolis of 12 chief Etruscan city-states located in what are now the provinces Lazio and Toscana, in Italy and is the modern name of a neighboring medieval city 60 miles north of Rome, once known as Corneto. For more about the *La Castellina* archaeological site, see the accompanying maps as well as the following selections from J. P. and T. G. Lewis, *The Sanctuary of Vanth and Tages at La Castellina*, Chapter Four, "Iconographic Clues to Worship of *La Vanta*:"
- Northerly location of the sanctuary in ancient Tarquinia
- La Castellina seems to have served no military

function, not being as high in elevation as the arx, yet it is surrounded by the city wall as being somehow important to the ancient city of Tarquinia. Extending as it does due north from the Pian di Civita, however, another importance to such a mantic city is suggested. For just as it was to the northerly land of the Cimmerians that Odysseus is said to have travelled in order to reach the Underworld for his encounter with the death oracle of Tiresias, it is from the direction of darkness, namely the north, that evil is frequently thought to arise in many traditional cultures. The positioning of the hypogeum at the north end of the Tarquinia city site was the first clue that we might find associated with it an entrance to the underworld in the form of the mundus, which seems itself to have been a death oracle, as well as serving an apotropaic function for the city as a whole.

- Temple of Vanth & Tages – only formal temple in *La Castellina,* a small cella with two columns *in antis* and a deep overhang. It had a pediment with terracotta figures depicting the Discovery of Tages: as a baby in a ploughed field. Interior fresco fragments thought to show his one-day existence teaching the local people about magic before he died of old age at nightfall.
- Tony – see Ellington
- *traforo* – (Italian) "tunnel, underpass"
- *trollkors* – (Norwegian) "troll-cross," little good-luck loop of iron like a crossed omega, recently popularized in Norway.
- Tuchulcha – (Rasenna) an elemental in charge of sudden death, ruled by Neffuns, god of springs and earthquakes, and Tages, god of wisdom and magic.

Known by his donkey ears, snake hair, leering face, green skin, wings and hammer.

- Vanderbilt, Elizabeth Burnsey (Bess) – Mary-Louise Greenough's best friend.
- Vanth / *vanta* – (Rasenna / Italian) an elemental in charge of fever, one of the demons in charge of guiding the dead to the underworld, also amenable to bribery for oracular information. Ruled by Begoia, goddess of lightning and storms and Tages, god of wisdom and magic. Known by her skimpy clothing, white skin, green eyes, tall boots, wings and torch. Selections from J. P. and T. G. Lewis, *The Iconography of the Vanth* as follows: As *Demon of Fevers:* Based on the evidence of many inscriptions at the La Castellina site, the Vanth can bring fever with her, thus corresponding to the Roman spirit of the fever, Februa, starting the sad work that Kairun/Tuchulcha will complete with a blow of his soul-releasing axe. As such, the Vanth will need to be propitiated with offerings in the deadly month associated with fevers, named by the Romans Februarius. It may be demonstrated that the sealing of the mundus must have taken place in the month of February, given the nature of the well-preserved floral offerings found, namely plum sprays and crocuses, which are only to be found throughout the Tuscan countryside in the month of February. Perhaps, as her special month, this would be the ideal time to honor the Vanth, but perhaps as well it was the very month in which the disastrous plague occurred which so decimated the Tarquinian population that it gave up worship of the Vanth for good and all, by way apparently of punishment. As *Deity of Merchants or Travelers.* Third, we have seen that Etruscan deities combine

rather differently with the Greek than Roman deities do, and there seems to have been a female deity of good luck in trade and of the dawn, Tesana, who corresponds to Téramó, the Etruscan Hermes. If the Vanth may be seen as the travel done by night, and Tesana or Téramó the travel done by day, they may be seen to be aspects of the same goddess, which potentially protects the traveller but who may harm him or her if unpropitiated. Certainly, the torch implies dawn as much as it does any other thing, Eos, goddess of the dawn, often being shown with a torch [note]. The rich Etruscan merchant, setting forth at dawn to do business, or sending his grain out on the seas, would do well to propitiate this deity with a blood sacrifice and a ring. As *Oracle*. The torch is a symbol of Demeter or Ceres, who used it to scour the surface of the world in search of her stolen daughter, Persephone or Kore (Persipne of the Etruscans); it may thus be said that the Vanth is a Seeker of lost things. One of the key uses of ancient oracles was the search for lost items, persons, and ships, as well as to discover the proper course to take in one's life, and whether or not – and where – to found a new colony: a chief function of the Delphic Oracle, we are told [note]. It is my contention that La Castellina served as a Death Oracle to the surrounding countryside, due to the presence of the mundus, which acted as a direct conduit to the world of the dead, much as did Avernus at Cumae, or Kastalia at Delphi. In accounting for the presence of the bier in the hypogeum in connection with the oracular nature of the La Castellina site, our primary contention is that it was used to communicate with the dead through incubation, as at the sanctuary of Aesclepius at Epidauros. We suggest that the seeker of counsel at La Castellina (as of healing at Epidauros) would sleep at the site, and be shown the answer to the oracle in a dream. I would say then, that, until its final use to take the body of the final human sacrifice which, along with the child burial in the mundus, would seal the sanctuary for ever, the bier was likely provided with the sort of comfortable mattress and thick pillows which we see on Etruscan ash urns, the seeker, having obtained the right to a night in the hypogeum by payment of the proper animal sacrifice with which the priest of the sanctuary would be feasted in the Hut Circle as the god's portions were burned at the Ash Altar, would sleep – perhaps aided by drugs – in order to receive news from the world beyond.

- Verbicaro, Gesualdo ("Waldo") – acrobat of mixed Rom-Italian ancestry, so rejected by both. Father a strong-man with the circus, mother a fortune-teller, he himself became an acrobat at an early age. An orphan, he was raised at All Saints as part of their service to at-risk gypsy youth. John-Allen Prester's lover, but Caterina is his child's surrogate mother.

- *Volans* oil – Latin: "flying" oil, a combination of fly agaric and black henbane.

- Vino Nobile del Montepulciano – This big red wine from the Val d'Orcia of Tuscany is the favorite wager-award at the site.

- *"zitta, zitta"* – probably was *State zitta*. "Be quiet."

MAPS & PLANS

Map One: N. ITALY REFERENCE MAP—Places important to Keepers & Finds.

Map Two: PIAN DI CIVITÀ—TARQUINIA ANTICA. An overview of all Sectors of the site.

Map Three: TARQUINIA ANTICA northeastern part. Also called Sector C, Dr. Lewis' area.

Map Four: TARQUINIA ANTICA La Castellina Site. Detail of Sector C with *hypogeum*.

ACKNOWLEDGMENTS

R. B., who professed a partiality to ampersands in titles, T. B. and A. LoP., who blithely provided a key reference, R. L., who houses me, keeps me honest and who spoke up for the man of the piece, B. W. H., whose keen eye found the bits needing the most improvement, S. M., who reminded me about Coke and peanuts, and the late Dr. Frances Willmoth, who doggedly revised a very early version of the book.

ABOUT THE AUTHOR

A life of travel, teaching and reading has filled DeLuca with stories that are just now working their way to the surface. She has trained as a classical archaeologist and earned a doctorate in cultural geography. She also has two children, now with children of their own, and has loved the same man for more than forty years. All of that finds its way into her stories, too.

Made in the USA
Las Vegas, NV
12 April 2021

21231299R20210